THE AGREEMENT
THE EPIC STRUGGLE FOR THE TEMPLE MOUNT

Lionel I. Casper

gefen publishing house בית הוצאה לאור

Copyright © Gefen Publishing House
Jerusalem 1996/5756

Typesetting: Marzel A.S. – Jerusalem

Cover Design: Mordechai Bar-Katz

ISBN 965-229-157-9

Edition 9 8 7 6 5 4 3 2 1

Gefen Publishing House Ltd.
POB 6056, Jerusalem
91060 Israel
972-2-5380247

Gefen Books
12 New St., Hewlett
N.Y., U.S.A. 11557
516-295-2805

Printed in Israel

Send for our free catalogue

Contents

Cast of Principal Characters

The Israelis

David Ben Gurion	Prime Minister
Gen Moshe Dayan	Minister of Defense
Yossi Foux	Army Major
Levi Eshkol	Prime Minister
Golda Meir	Prime Minister
Yitzhak Rabin	Prime Minister
Menahem Begin	Prime Minister
Avraham Nissim	War hero and settler
Ketselle	War hero and settler
Dr. Heitner	Pathologist
M. Ben Porat	Judge
Arik Sharon	General
Kobbi (Ya'acov Kreitman)	Shabak Deputy Head
Ehud	Shabak agent
Seffi	Shabak section head
Meir Peled	Civil Servant
Benzi	Night Vision Expert
Sari Butbul	Bank Clerk
Rami Feffer	Jerusalem lawyer
Arturo Be'eri	Businessman
Aboud Mugrabi	Burglar
Inspector Haft	Police Chief
Tali Goldberg	Secretary/War widow

The Iranians

Ayatollah Khomeini	Head of State
Mullah Ali Mashdi	Teheran Komiteh
Mullah Sayeed	Evin Prison
Faizal Bakhtiari	Businessman
Isaac Levy	Accountant
David Levy	Isaac's son
Sayeed Bakr	Safe cracker
Hushang & Nader	Aqaba Komiteh

The Palestinians

Taher Jabari	Finds the Agreement
Amin Jabari	Father of Taher
Mohammed	Leader of fedayeen
Amin el-Husseini	Ex Mufti of Jerusalem
Azziz Shehadeh	Leading lawyer
Hilarion Capucci	Greek Catholic Archbishop
Blind Haji	Mullah in Damascus
Ahmed el-Alamy	Jerusalem Muslim

The Jordanians

King Abdullah	1st King of Jordan
Tallal	2nd King of Jordan
Hussein	3rd King of Jordan
Hassan	Crown Prince
Samir el-Rifai	Prime Minister
Fawzi el-Mulki	Defense Minister
Samir	Manager of Spa
Gen. John Glubb	Chief of Staff
Shukri Ushu	Abdullah's Assassin
Jammal	Abdullah's bodyguard
Nasser & Ziyad	Jammal's grandchildren
Mario	Palace Official
Ismael	Palace Official

The Italians

Monsignor Paolo Angelo	Vatican official
Eduardo Angelo	Banker
Vincente Freiz	Mercenary

Chronology

1830 – Ottoman Rule in Palestine opens up Jerusalem to the Churches and permits Consulates from East and West

1852 – Ottoman firman divides responsibilities for Holy Places amongst religions and introduces concept of status quo

1856 – Treaty of Paris confirms basis of status quo

1878 – Congress of Berlin broadens and reiterates basis of status quo

1916 – The Sykes-Picot Agreement carves up for the British and the French the old Ottoman Empire

1917 – Balfour Declaration, confirms British support for the establishment in Palestine of a National Jewish Homeland

1919 – Faisal-Weizmann Agreement

1920 – San Remo Conference grants Mandate over Palestine to the British

1921 – Churchill gives Abdullah area of Transjordan

1921 – Haji Amin el-Husseini appointed Mufti of Jerusalem

1929 – Massacre of Jews in Hebron

1941 – Deposed Mufti Haji Amin el-Husseini relocates to Berlin

1948 – Establishment of the State of Israel

1950 – Jordan-Israel Agreement initialled and rescinded

1956 – Sinai Campaign. French, British, Israelis attack Egypt following Nasser's occupation of the Suez Canal Zone

1967 – Six Day War

1970 – King Hussein defeats PLO in "Black September"

1973 – Yom Kippur War

1977 – Egyptian President Sadat visits Jerusalem

1982 – Israel invades Lebanon

1993 – Israel signs Peace Treaty with PLO

1994 – Israel signs Peace Treaty with Jordan

Author's Notes

This is a novel, and apart from known historical figures, the characters are fictional. There are, however, some exceptions. Ya'acov Katz, known to everyone as *Ketselle*, fought in the Yom Kippur War, survived a fearful battle as described in the book, and has subsequently devoted his life to building the *yishuv* of Bet-El and its large residential yeshiva. His two close friends, Reuven Sporen and Eli Feig, were both killed, as described, in the line of duty.

Taher Jabari and Avraham Nissim, who play a vital part in this narrative, are fictional composites of descendants of Arabs and Jews, whose families have lived for thousands of years in the Holy Land, or in countries nearby. The stories they tell, through the pages of this novel, are not solely the products of my imagination, but reflect situations, incidents and happenings that occur in this region.

Though the plot is fictional, this novel draws on many real events, places and characters. Meetings did, indeed, take place between King Faisal and Chaim Weizmann nearly 75 years ago, between King Abdullah and Dayan in the years 1949-1951, and between King Hussein and Golda Meir on the eve of the Six Day War. The fedayeen was an unhappy development, administrative detention without trial is an unfortunate and undemocratic part of the local scene. And after thirty years of Israeli government of the Old City, the control of the Temple Mount is quite clearly in the hands of the *wakf* and the Hashemites in Jordan.

My research and sense of purpose in writing this historical novel derive from my late father, of blessed memory. His teachings and example guide me in life; his unlimited love for Jerusalem was the background that gave me the resolve for this work.

The Jewish concept of *hakarat hatov* calls for acknowledgment, as an expression of gratitude. I would like to thank my sister, Batya, for reading my proofs and converting many of my thoughts into readable English, as well as the publisher's nominated team of editors, whose patience, experience and language mastery were put unstintingly at my disposal.

Book I

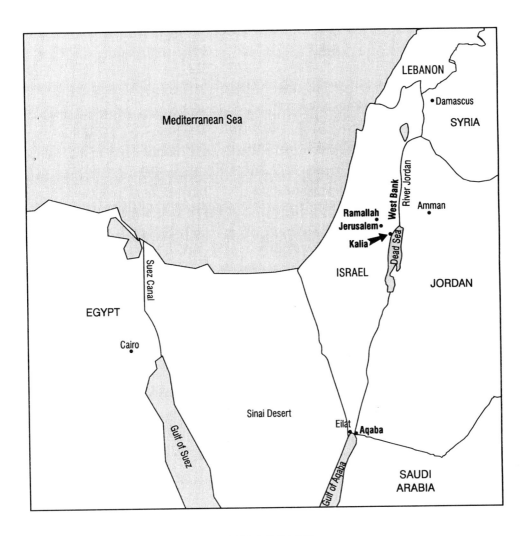

THE LOCALE
Showing the principal places
referred to in the narrative

Chapter 1

The king had insisted it was to be him and no other.

If King Abdullah wanted Ben Gurion's favorite general, the favorite general it had to be.

Summoning General Moshe Dayan home for tonight's meeting with the first ruler of the Kingdom of Jordan was no arbitrary whim on the part of the Israeli Prime Minister. For two years now, since 1948 and the establishment of the State of Israel, these neighboring strategy-builders had been attempting to iron out the differences between their two countries.

That is why on this April evening in 1951, Moshe Dayan crossed the fields of the Ramat Rachel kibbutz followed by his aide, Yossi Foux. They slid into a trench marking the frontier between Israel and Jordan. They waited. There was a quarter moon, the air was cool on the outskirts of Jerusalem.

The painful aroma of dry earth attacked Yossi's nostrils as he leant up against the clay wall beside his commanding officer. Memories, smells – even sounds – of past battles came rushing back at him as he speculated on the nature of the task ahead. Beside him, Yossi felt Dayan adjust the patch over the socket of the eye that he had lost in Syria, ten years earlier, when fighting the soldiers of Vichy France. For their present mission, Dayan had been especially summoned from England, and Yossi sensed that something momentous was about to occur.

At thirty, Major Foux of Southern Command was some six years younger, but he had served alongside Dayan for most of the past thirteen years. Back in 1939, they had both been sentenced by the British to 10 years in jail for participating in an illegal Haganah Commanders' course. In '41, the British had invaded Syria, both were released and sent to fight the Germans. Memories of their joint escapades flooded back to Yossi as he squatted in the trench waiting to cross into Jordan.

Commander of the Southern Region of the Israel Defense Forces, Dayan was attending training courses at the London School for Senior Officers, when Ben

Gurion placed a personal call to Dayan at his lodgings and ordered his immediate return. A car from the Israeli embassy had whisked him off to London Airport. Ben Gurion himself briefed Dayan on his mission. No other party was present; no notes of the meeting were taken.

On a cold February day a year earlier, Moshe Dayan – still a colonel at the time – had crossed the border in the company of one of Ben Gurion's advisors, later to be appointed head of the Israeli Secret Service. Their mission at that time was to sign an agreement which Abdullah believed would:

"slowly change (the Jordanian-Israeli relationship) from a state of war through a period of good neighborliness to a state of peace."

The agreement marked the culmination of talks covering a vast range of topics, the most pressing of which was the cessation of aggression. It was an attempt to define a normalization process, focusing on such issues as the Jordanian access to Mediterranean ports in Israel; access of Jews to the holy places in Jerusalem, then under Jordanian control; Palestinian rights to properties that had been abandoned in '48; and trade between the two nations.

King Abdullah had clearly foreseen the hostility that was to be unleashed by the Arab countries against the Jewish State, and had hoped to stem it by locking the neighboring countries into a five-year contract of trade and non-aggression.

But, as has happened so often over the years, the winds of good fortune did not blow in the direction of the Middle East. Negative, Pan-Arab pressure bent the will of King Abdullah. When Colonel Dayan and Reuven Shiloah arrived at His Majesty's Shunni Palace, the ground rules were already changed. At the last minute Abdullah had tried to force the hands of Samir El-Rifai, his Prime Minister, and Fawzi El-Mulki, his Minister of Defense, into placing their initials on the agreement in place of his own, leaving himself a mere witness to the agreement. They were thrown into a panic by their king's machinations, terrified for their own safety. Within four days of the initialling ceremony, His Majesty King Abdullah backed out of the agreement.

Negotiations had nevertheless continued, albeit in a far more limited form. The King knew that it was simply a question of time before he would have to relinquish his hold on the West Bank of the Jordan, but he was determined to maintain control over the places that were holy to Islam. His dream was to bequeath the stewardship of these holy places to future generations of his Hashemite dynasty. It was to this end that he directed his energies.

And so, a year after the failure of the original agreement, Ben Gurion presented Dayan with a new one and with it his summary of the Israeli position: *"This new document is of limited use to us; in signing it we are merely pandering to the King's hunger for immortality. But it is an agreement which will be signed by the King himself – no underlings this time, no prime ministers that can be replaced tomorrow. It will be his signature, and his alone, that you will secure. When fully completed, this pact will pave the way for others, agreements which will cover all the aspects that should have been ratified last year by our two parliaments."*

While Dayan sat in the trench, his thoughts drifted back to earlier periods of his life, his work with the British forces and the broadcasting network he had set up for the British for the purpose of conducting clandestine operations behind enemy lines should Palestine fall to the Germans.

During the War of Independence Moshe Dayan had commanded the defense of Jewish settlements in the Jordan Valley. Later he had been appointed commander of the Jerusalem front and had negotiated a cease-fire with the local commander of the Arab Legion. He knew the locality intimately, all of the areas through which they would pass on what he knew would be an historic mission. He was also familiar with the peoples of the area, he understood and respected Palestinians and Beduin alike.

Dayan looked at Yossi, his friend of many years, "We are making for Kalia, I'll fill you in when we reach our destination." Kalia was some twenty miles east, on the northern tip of the Dead Sea.

The signal that Dayan was waiting for – a long whistle followed by another two of different lengths – came within less than ten minutes. The two men hoisted themselves up the Jordanian side of the trench and walked into enemy territory. Abu Djemal, their contact, guided them quickly and silently down a grassy hill and onto a dirt track that skirted the village of Sur Baher. He led them around unkempt stone houses and down a slight incline to a forked eucalyptus tree. A Land Rover of the Royal Jordanian Army waited.

The inhabitants of this village were accustomed to rise early each morning and to fold themselves into their homes in the early evenings in preparation for sleep. And so it was that the only person on the streets at this hour was a Christian Arab priest who was passing through from a neighboring village. The stranger saw three men hurry around a corner and, as he was of a suspicious nature, he allowed his mind to dwell for some hours on the question of their identity and the nature of their business.

Safely out of sight, the three bade each other the briefest of sala'ams. Abu Djemal turned and melted into the night. The two Israelis stepped, silent as cats, into the Land Rover and the army driver slid the vehicle away from the sleeping village and into its journey down the mountains and across the desert towards their destination. It was with impressive dexterity that the Beduin driver manipulated the vehicle on its bumpy, hour-long descent from Jerusalem – some two thousand five hundred feet above sea level – to the Dead Sea – thirteen hundred feet below sea level, a total descent of nearly four thousand feet.

The driver turned out to be dexterous, handsome, but uncommunicative. He travelled on rough, seldom used and uncharted roads that ran along dry wadis, connecting Greek Orthodox churches and Catholic monasteries with ruins of ancient castles, remnants from the times of the Crusaders. The higher levels were still green following the winter rains, but the terrain quickly changed to the colorless sand and stone of the desert.

Emerging between the foothills of two mountains, they reached the asphalt road that skirts the northern part of the Dead Sea at Ein Faschkha, a small spa just South of Qumran, where fresh water springs bubble from the mountain and fuse with the salty waters of the lake. The salt in the lake is so concentrated that no fish can live there and swimmers cannot sink.

The driver turned left, pointed the vehicle in the direction of Jericho and proceeded to drive around the northern end of the lake, known as the Dead Sea.

Although the salt and minerals are malodorous and unconducive to growth, there are a number of attractive fertile oases around the lake, rich in palms, lush undergrowth and sub-tropical fruit. Halfway down the western side of the lake towers the craggy mountain of Massada, home to the remains of Herod's ancient winter castle, eternal testimony to ancient Jewish bravery in the face of the tyranny of the Roman Empire.

The drive from Jerusalem was uneventful: not a single other vehicle was encountered throughout the hour-long drive. Dayan seemed wrapped in his own thoughts, unwilling to engage in conversation either with the silent Beduin or with Yossi. Finally, the Land Rover pulled to a halt beside a single-story structure, familiar to the general as a retreat for the more privileged of the Hashemite Kingdom of Jordan.

A deferential, whiteclad waiter welcomed the Israeli guests, bowing low as he opened the door, shuffling annoyingly with his feet. He could have saved himself the trouble. The general with the eye-patch didn't seem to notice him as he strode through the open door and took a seat under a great revolving ceiling fan. The room was spacious and furnished with several deep armchairs, a desk of dark mahogany, a number of large, strategically situated lamps and a central coffee table strewn with newspapers. "Like a British Army clubroom," thought Dayan. Yossi sank into a bamboo armchair near his friend. The Arab army driver was stationed outside with his vehicle. Dayan and Yossi accepted gin and tonics from the attentive waiter and rested in the pervasive hum of the fan.

For ten minutes or so the two men sat in silence. The only sounds were the persistent drone of the overhead fan and the gnawing threat of a single, tenacious mosquito. Dayan popped an olive into his mouth, took the remains of his drink and strode out of the windows onto the terrace which overlooked the lake. He smiled to himself at the thought of calling them *French windows*, aware of how much King Abdullah despised the French ever since 1920 when they had ousted his older brother Faisal from the Syrian throne. But that was all a long time ago he thought, time to return to the present and the purpose of their visit.

"We've come here to meet King Abdullah," he told Yossi. As usual, Dayan came out with the unembellished version. "I have drafts of an Agreement which, if signed, will transform the map of the Middle East, affect the entire region for generations to come."

The general began to pace, seeming to ponder how best to continue. "I don't know how much time we have before His Majesty arrives, but I'll fill you in as much as possible. First let me go over the history."

Yossi, who had guessed that it was for no small matter that Dayan had been summoned from London, was not particularly taken aback. Yossi waited for the general to tell him more, confident that he would benefit from his commander's personal insights.

"During the First World War, the French and British implemented the Sykes-Picot Agreement: They divided the rapidly declining Ottoman Empire in such a way that the Arab world was split into separate French and British zones of influence.

"In the early years of this century, the area immediately to the east of the River Jordan had enjoyed the crudest form of self-rule in the form of tiny, so-called 'independent states.' British soldiers in the area spent most of their time and energy, trying to prevent smoldering rivalries from bursting into open fire. The entire region was some kind of free-for-all. So, for example, at one point, a British Major by the name of Kirkbride established a body called 'The National Government of Moab.' He was elected President, and was supported by a force of fifty policemen.

"Given these conditions, the British attempted to seek a comprehensive solution." Dayan cleared his throat and paced for a while. "In 1921 Winston Churchill offered Abdullah the administration of a Transjordan Emirate, an honor which was to be handed down, in the form of a hereditary title, from generation to generation. The area to be administered by him and his descendents was restricted to the east of the Jordan River. The terms of government were set out in a treaty with the British, the terms of which specifically excluded those clauses of the earlier Balfour Declaration which pertained to the Jewish National Homeland.

"Unfortunately governments and their good intentions change with the times. The ideas of Churchill, so acceptable to Abdullah in the 1920s, provided him with an appetite for expansion some twenty years later." Dayan leaned against the low, ivy-covered stone wall of the balcony and lapsed into silence. For a moment he seemed to forget that he had an audience. Then: "Historians will more than likely judge Abdullah as a dreamer and an opportunist. However, his principle aim is still to establish a dynasty within clearly formed and lasting borders."

"You see," Dayan continued, as though reasoning with some voice within himself, "the King claims that he can trace his Hashemite descent directly from the prophet Muhammad, and indeed it was on the basis of that claim that Abdullah's father, Hussein, was enthroned as the Emir of Mecca. His claims to Jerusalem are influenced by his family ties to the Prophet."

Again Dayan stood up to pace back and forth along the terrace, apparently reflecting his own pronouncements.

"Well," he continued, "Abdullah's opportunity came toward the end of '47 when, under the terms of the proposed but never adopted United Nations Partition Plan for Palestine, large areas of Judea and Samaria on the west bank of the Jordan were allotted to the Arabs. A year earlier, Transjordan had gained its independence from Britain under special treaty. Abdullah's luck peaked when the British, who were looking to relinquish their rule under the U.N. mandate, chose Abdullah over us Jewish newcomers. In Britain, Bevin was eventually to take Churchill's place and, as Foreign and Colonial Secretary, he encouraged Abdullah to grab whatever he could on both sides of the Jordan. So it was, that the small Emirate of Transjordan, with its police force transformed during the years of World War II into an effective Arab Legion, became the much larger Hashemite Kingdom of Jordan, a kingdom that now straddles both sides of the river.

"Of course, Yossi, you know only too well that, during our War of Independence, the Jordanian Arab Legion was the most effective and dangerous of our enemies. Under John Glubb, the general who had refashioned the Legion into such a potent force, the Jordanians proved to be tenacious to the point that when the cease-fire was called, it was they who controlled the Old City of Jerusalem. They held access to the holy places of three religions.

"But political matters never run smoothly," mused the general. "King Abdullah has never been able to consolidate his control over Jerusalem. Never has he considered moving his capital there. He prefers Amman, nestled in the secure Moabite Hills, where the issue of his monarchy goes unquestioned. Jerusalem is controlled by his arch-enemies the Husseinis. His old enemy the former Mufti of Jerusalem, Haji Amin el Husseini who lives in exile in Egypt, wields more clout in Jerusalem than does Abdullah.

"Incidentally the Mufti's great hatred for Abdullah stems from the year 1933, when the King agreed to lease to the Jewish Agency some 20,000 acres of his land in the Jordan valley. The Arabs never forget – remember by Arab standards retribution taken within forty years is considered hasty! And that brings us nearer to today's business...."

The general's voice dropped again. The song of a myriad, invisible crickets pierced the still, evening air. Within a few moments the two Israelis heard the rising purr of an approaching limousine, and Yossi knew that his history lesson was over.

"Abdullah believes in the Arab concept that the enemy of his enemy is his friend," warned Dayan. "It is for good reason that we share a hatred of the Mufti. For his part, Ben Gurion believes that now, after extensive contact with Abdullah, the King is prepared to enter into a treaty with us over Jerusalem."

The Israeli general's voice tightened as he kept his eye trained on the door opening at that moment at the far side of the clubroom. "Listen only," he instructed. "Answer only to a direct question. Leave the negotiations to me – and hopefully we will walk away with a done deal."

Dayan crossed the terrace followed by Yossi, and reentered the room just as His Majesty King Abdullah, followed by Lt.General John Glubb, entered the room through its front door.

With the exception of Yossi, all the parties knew one another. Since the early thirties, King Abdullah had maintained secret contacts with Jewish and Israeli leaders, and had personally had intermittent talks with Ben Gurion, Golda Meir, Moshe Sharett, Yigal Alon and of late also with Dayan. Although he wouldn't have wanted John Glubb to know, he had always preferred Dayan to other Israeli leaders. He liked his local, Israeli, no-frills approach to negotiations. What had initially impressed him about the man was the description he had read of his marriage ceremony in Nahalal, a Jewish settlement that had been founded by Dayan's father. Dayan had invited the entire, neighboring, Arab El Mazarib tribe to the ceremony.

In the privacy of his own mind, Abdullah considered Ben Gurion too clever, Golda Meir too powerful, and Sharett too diplomatic. He had warmer vibes from Alon and Dayan, and it was he who had suggested, at his most recent meeting with the Israeli Prime Minister, that Dayan be brought back from England for the finalization of today's business.

Abdullah wanted to discuss matters privately with the Israeli general; so, after a few brief formalities, he ordered Glubb to go out on to the terrace with the young

Israeli major. With the coolness of a cat on the watch, and without missing a beat in his niceties with His Majesty, Dayan instructed his subordinate not to discuss anything with Glubb. "Talk football," was all he said, as Yossi walked past him. The gleam piercing the center of his single eye said the rest.

Dayan was pleased that no Jordanian cabinet ministers had been brought along. His instructions were specific: it was the King's own signature that was required.

Left alone, Abdullah turned and embraced his Israeli friend.

King Abdullah had driven down from Amman unostentatiously, in an unmarked black Packard saloon preceded by a single jeep. No flags, no fanfare, no publicity. He sat in the rear, protected by bullet-proof windows; in the front sat the driver, an old retainer, and Jammal, his trusted bodyguard of many years. Jammal's brother, the King's scout on this occasion, drove the jeep. With him rode Lt. General John Glubb.

On the way to Kalia, the king mulled over the enormity of the step he was about to undertake. Fate, he believed, had left him little choice. At seventy, Abdullah was not in the best of health. An eye disease had caused him not only many hours of pain but a general deterioration of his physical condition.

His great disappointment in life was that his son Talal was mentally deranged, hospitalized in an expensive Swiss sanatorium, and would never succeed him. His hopes of creating a dynasty now rested on the shoulders of his eldest grandson, Hussein – barely sixteen years of age. Driving down from the mountains, Abdullah allowed his mind to slip back to the days of his youth, to the beginnings of his journey.

Abdullah and his younger brother Faisal are raised and educated in Constantinople, capital of the Ottoman Empire. Five hundred years of Turkish rule are drawing to a close. Behind-door schemes and the law of the *Baksheesh* are now the only tangible symbols left from what was once a mighty empire.

Abdullah's father, Hussein, looms a powerful figure within the ruling classes, his friends holding high positions. He claims direct descent from the prophet Muhammad and accordingly is much honored in this predominantly Muslim society. In 1908 Hussein is appointed Emir of Mecca. Young Abdullah becomes his father's political secretary.

The political map of the region is divided between three powerful forces: the Turks – clearly on the decline; the French, who stake powerful claims in Syria, Lebanon, Egypt, and the Sudan; and the British who, after the Victorian era, remain the unchallenged superpower of the modern world.

Mecca is the hub of the Muslim world. It is here that the young Abdullah, as a lad in his twenties, is involved in secret negotiations with the British. Following the Arab Revolt of 1916, the British and the French recognize Hussein as King of the Hejaz. The Hejaz occupies much of what later becomes known as Saudi Arabia and includes in its territory both Mecca and Medina, the two most holy places of Islam.

Abdullah's negotiations with the British stand him in good stead for many years. In 1920 the British conspire with him to return his brother Faisal to the throne in Syria, which had been wrested from him by the French. The British sponsor a Beduin army which Abdullah marches north to Syria. This campaign fails and Faisal who, two years previously, had begun friendly negotiations with Chaim Weizmann who represented Zionism, is offered the throne in Iraq.

Meanwhile, their father has begun to feel the brunt of Ibn Saud's success in Arabia. Ibn Saud is responsible for the annihilation of the greater part of the Hashemite family.

Abdullah's relationship with the Beduins, as with the British, remains steadfast throughout his lifetime. At all times, he is confident of their loyal support.

World War One is over and General Allenby rides into Jerusalem. The League of Nations grants Britain a Mandate over Palestine.

In 1921, Winston Churchill, as British Colonial Secretary, visits Jerusalem. There, he confers on Abdullah the Emirate of Transjordan. Transjordan is to be an adjunct of Palestine within the terms of the general British Mandate, in an area to be forged on the east bank of the Jordan River. Churchill even bestows upon Abdullah a hereditary monarchy.

A small rock, thrust from its pocket on the side of the road by the force of the Packard, hits the window on the King's side of the car and jolts him from his reflections. Once more he directs his attentions to the implications of the contract he will sign that evening. In the hours that follow, he will reestablish the geopolitical position that had been mandated to him by the British over a quarter of a century earlier. His father had gained and lost control of Islam's two holiest places, and now his own enemies would claim that he was abdicating control of Jerusalem, Islam's third holiest city.

From his own perspective, the purpose of tonight's meeting was to ensure his dynastic control of Islam's holy places in Jerusalem in perpetuity, albeit at the cost of a territorial withdrawal from the West Bank of the Jordan River. The King believed that he was the single most qualified contender for the position of custodian over the Islamic holy places, places which should be entrusted to him by right of his direct dynastic descent from the Prophet Muhammad.

But Abdullah was a realist. He knew that his descendents would have more effective control over the Holy Places of Islam in Jerusalem with the city under Israeli rule, than were they to remain in the custody of the Husseinis. He believed that the Jews could be trusted. A deal with them would be honored. He was ready to wager his kingdom on that trust.

The King's small entourage knew nothing of his immediate plans, nor did they know what to expect when they reached Kalia, their intended destination. It was not that he did not trust Jammal more than any other person, it was simply that he was paying heed to his training. It urged him to keep his own counsel.

King Abdullah carried no notes. In order to come to an agreement, he had to cover five points. An additional point, one of a more personal nature, and which would not be duplicated, would be dealt with under separate cover and would be issued by a Swiss bank. He was satisfied from previous negotiations that Israeli officials would adequately draft out the requirements of both parties. The crux of the negotiations centered on the concept of Jordanian withdrawal from the West Bank and the consequent control of the relinquished territory by the Israelis. One of the issues anticipated Palestinian autonomy in certain areas; another granted Israel sole rule over the whole of Jerusalem, subject to the control of Abdullah and his descendents over the city's Islamic Holy Places. Abdullah had made sure that specific mention would be made in the agreement of the Jordanian guardianship of the Temple Mount with its Dome of the Rock and the el-Aqsa Mosque.

As the small convoy approached its destination the King issued more immediate instructions: "Jammal, the meeting to which I am going, must maintain the lowest profile. An accumulation of vehicles at Kalia might attract interest. When we reach Kalia, you and I will drop off and enter the spa house. I will enter the main room with General Glubb and you will stay in the anteroom to protect me. Youssouf and the driver will take the car and the jeep around the lake and hide themselves near the Qumran caves, where they can see the spa house. After ninety minutes Youssouf can come back on his own and check if we are ready: if we are, we will leave in his jeep and join the car at Qumran; if we are not, he can drive back to Qumran and try again every fifteen minutes. Have you any questions?"

"Yes," replied Jammal, "What if you want to leave earlier?"

"Then we will switch off the lights on the spa terrace three times, in which case the two vehicles will both come back as quickly as possible."

CHAPTER **2**

Three terrorists made their way from a Palestinian refugee camp south of Jericho. They came along the road to Kalia, from where they intended to proceed to Qumran and then commence their climb through the foothills on the western side of the Dead Sea and up to Jerusalem.

The three men were in their early twenties. They travelled light, each armed with two hand grenades, a revolver, a mean looking knife of unrecognizable origin, and a small Kalashnikov semi-automatic machine gun. They arrived at Kalia, which they had expected to be deserted, to find a Land Rover parked nearby. The lights were on in the spa house where, at that very moment, King Abdullah and a guest were sipping drinks.

"Some officer is probably living it up while his poor sod of a driver is left to hold the fort in the darkness," scoffed the eldest of the three, recently returned from a Russian para-military training course in Syria, "typical of corrupt governments."

Silently they approached the Land Rover. It would be a useful vehicle for their plans. Swiftly and silently, with the blunt end of a gun, they rendered the sleeping driver unconscious. They dragged him out to the side of the road and debated what to do with him: It was obviously not in their best interests to keep him alive. Muhammed, the leader of the group, picked up a rock from the side of the dirt road and with it brought a quick and sudden end to the young life of the Jordanian driver. "A shot from a gun would be heard," he muttered, as if apologizing for the unprofessionality of his method.

They slid the Land Rover into neutral and pushed it in silence for the first few hundred yards before igniting the engine and starting on their journey into the night.

The Land Rover passed within just a few yards of His Majesty's two vehicles, parked off the road in total darkness. Its progress was then followed by both Jordanian drivers. Youssouf recognized the moving vehicle as the one he had seen parked at the spa, but he did not know who was driving it, and was ignorant as to the nature of its mission. His only instructions had been to sit and wait – and that was all he intended to do. And so it was that the Land Rover began its ascent to Jerusalem, bumping over the same unpaved and often uncharted roads that it had traversed with different passengers less than an hour earlier.

Before settling down to the specifics of the contracts, Abdullah wanted to hear Dayan's views on the region and its projected development. He knew that Ben Gurion and Dayan were of one mind in these matters. The two men made themselves comfortable in the deep, cushioned chairs: arak, cognac, choice cigars, Dayan's special strong brand of cigarette and even some halva and bakhlava, the sticky sweets of the Middle East, were spread out before them. Now that they had dispensed with the services of their attendants, Abdullah was able to sip his drinks without a qualm for the Islamic prohibition of alcohol.

"We are fewer than two million Jews in Israel," began Dayan, "the areas that you will vacate are vast and populated by many Muslims that reproduce at a far higher rate than we do."

The King was impressed by the direct, no-nonsense attitude of the young Israeli opposite him. As he watched, listened and sipped his arak, Abdullah found himself wondering more and more about Dayan's eye-patch. Where and exactly how had he lost his eye? What lies beneath the patch? Could it be that this man lost his cool under fire?

"As you are aware," Dayan was saying, "our government can't afford the image of the colonialist. We will not govern others: to do that would be to contradict the fundamentally socialist ideals of our homeland."

He paused, carefully filled his own glass and that of his friend. "Ben Gurion favors the concept of limited autonomy for the Arabs in Judea and Samaria," the general continued in slow and measured tones. "Exactly what form that will take I cannot tell you. Indeed, I myself don't know. No doubt our politicians, civil servants, lawyers and constitutional experts will have a great time arguing the merits and demerits of such a system."

The sharp edges, the natural wariness that existed between the two, the strangeness of the room and its clumsy furnishings, were already beginning to fade beneath the smoke of Dayan's cigarettes. The arak Abdullah was drinking was warm, his chair surprisingly comfortable. Slowly Abdullah felt himself being drawn into the spell of the general's speech pattern. He realized that this man's accent was different from those of the European Jews with whom he had had previous contact, while it didn't sound anything like the English spoken by his fellow Arabs. It was strange, but appealing. The handsome young Israeli sitting opposite him, with his stark black eye-patch and his tightly pulled features, spoke as one that was reading a foreign text. His English was fair, even good, but his accent! "Well," thought the King, as he listened and nodded in agreement, "it is refreshingly different."

"However, Jerusalem, as has been agreed upon by yourself and the Prime Minister, will remain under our direct rule. A united city, capital of Israel. There will be one municipality, and the Arabs that stay in Jerusalem will have to accept our sovereignty." Dayan drained his glass, thought carefully for a moment and continued: "I have heard that Ben Gurion favors taking down the walls around the Old City in order to unite the East and West parts of Jerusalem; I would very much hope that his view on this will not carry; I for one would do everything in my power to prevent it."

Abdullah was charmed by Dayan's candid admission that differences of opinion did exist between him and his Prime Minister. It was his turn to let down his guard: "Such differences of strategy," he warned, "would never be revealed in a monarchical system."

"That's one of the hazards," laughed Dayan "of running a social democracy. Don't misunderstand me, however. In most matters, BG gets his way. I only hope that in this matter – one that is more in the nature of esthetics than of political strategy – his friends, myself included, will be able to dissuade him."

The gentle sipping of drinks continued. The overhead fan groaned steadily on, and the smoke silently measured time as it twined its way upward from Dayan's dwindling cigarette and fanned out and back again as it hit the ceiling. The talk – candid and to the point, the thoughts – private and guarded behind the talk, continued undisturbed for several minutes more, as the king and the general relaxed together in this odd political oasis.

Finally the King collected himself, suggesting that Dayan pull out the papers and explain them to him. As anticipated, all the required five points were expertly covered.

Just two copies of the Agreement were placed on the table, both of which had been previously signed by the Prime Minister of Israel. King Abdullah signed the two copies in his turn, and then asked Dayan to countersign them. "I want to keep your autograph," he teased.

Dayan obliged. The King presented him with his own, personal gold fountain pen. The Israeli general had no problem accepting this gesture of friendship. Dayan then handed an envelope to the King, embossed with the emblem of a bank in Geneva. The King placed it in an inside pocket without opening it or examining its contents.

"A hundred years from now," the King said, "people will wonder why we met in secret and signed in secret."

"And your grandson's heirs will bless your name," said the general in his near perfect colloquial Arabic.

"This is no mere agreement," said the King. "It is a partnership which must bring peace to this troubled region."

"I pray," said the general "that our pact will secure the future cooperation of our two countries."

At that, the two statesmen called to their aides who had been pacing on the terrace, and their private encounter ended.

Yossi was a young Sabra with few pretensions. As such, he had little in common with the stiff British Arabophile in whose company he found himself. For the ninety minutes that their principals were busy inside, the two officers exchanged hardly a word. Yossi for his part knew that later he would be told everything. The general knew that he would be told nothing.

The King preceded the three army men out of the room. Jammal opened the outer door just as the jeep – his brother at the wheel – drove up. Dayan and Yossi emerged from the spa in their turn, to find that their Land Rover had disappeared. Within moments Yossi came across the inert body of their Arab driver, propped against the half-hidden trunk of the eucalyptus tree.

Instinctively Dayan took charge. Without a word he reached out for the King and Glubb, and propelled them back into the spa, leaving Yossi and Jammal to reconnoiter. For his part, Glubb came into his own once inside. Arrogant and pompous he might be, but he was also a good soldier and a practical man of action. "It's clear that whoever killed the soldier has absconded with the Land Rover," he observed. "Unless the two outside come up with anything new, Your Majesty might have to change whatever plans you have made."

It rankled Glubb that he hadn't the slightest knowledge of what those plans were. Rather than put his foot in it, or let on to Yossi that he had not been taken into the king's confidence, he awaited His Majesty's response. But the King had his own calculations. "I think," he said, turning to Dayan, "that you and Yossi will have to split up. I suggest that, unless our men outside indicate otherwise, you should return home by different routes. The problem with you, Moshe, is that even in our country your face, and especially your eye-patch, are too well known. Yossi however, travelling alone, should have a better chance of making it back the way you came. Clearly we must disperse immediately and send you on your way. May Allah watch over you."

Dayan was silent for barely a moment. "I agree with Your Majesty. If a driver could take me up north to the border at Tulkarem, I would be able to make my way easily to our coastal town of Netanya which is only a stone's throw away from there. As for Yossi, if we could take him up some of the way, say to a point west of the foothills at Qumran, I think he would make it home without too much difficulty."

"Fine," said His Majesty, "you will travel in the jeep with Jammal. I will travel back to Amman with Youssouf and General Glubb. Take Yossi with you and drop him off as near to Jerusalem as you deem safe. Needless to say, this meeting has never taken place, and if by any chance we discover later that we have been observed, we are all to deny any allegations or reports that are made."

Yossi and Jammal returned empty-handed from their reconnoitering. It was agreed that the robbers had probably killed the driver of the Land Rover. "Possibly fedayeen on their way to Israel," surmised Dayan.

Dayan and Jammal drove Yossi for some thirty minutes into the mountains that stretch toward Jerusalem. All three were familiar with the area and, on the way up, they discussed the best place to let Yossi off. In the rear of the vehicle, behind the back of the Arab driver, Dayan passed the signed copy of the Agreement to Yossi, telling him in Hebrew that he believed Yossi had a better chance of getting home than he had himself.

It was after 10.30 at night when Yossi stepped down from the jeep. The vehicle promptly turned and retraced its journey towards the Dead Sea, but before Yossi slipped into the night, Jammal turned and asked him if he had a gun. Leaning forward, he opened the glove compartment in the dashboard and took out a Beretta with clips of ammunition.

"You shouldn't wander around these hills without a weapon," he warned. "I hope you won't need to use it, but we can't be too sure. Return it to me when you can, I'm sure you will find a way."

Left alone, Yossi felt surprisingly energetic, almost light-hearted. Quickly he adjusted his backpack in preparation for his trek through the mountains, a journey, he calculated, of no more than 15 miles.

There was hardly a path that he hadn't traversed during the period between the World War and the War of Independence. Besides, he knew that the Arabs of this region were early risers and were accustomed to going to bed with the sun. He felt quite confident that he would be able to pass the two villages on his route, A-Tur and Tsur Baher, and reach Jerusalem without mishap.

Of course there was an alternative route, that of entering Jerusalem by way of its northern suburbs, but this didn't appeal to Yossi as it would have brought him too close to the Old City, an area which he knew would be heavily fenced and policed. His friends at Ramat Rahel and the Arab guide at Tsur Baher were waiting for him to return, so although it probably added as much as four miles to his trek, Yossi decided to stay on the open road.

He plunged into the darkness.

Dayan's journey was longer than Yossi's, but uneventful. The hour and more that it took to drive along the Jordan Valley and from there through an opening in the hills and up to Tulkarem, only eight miles from the Israeli Mediterranean coast, became an opportunity for the Israeli general to practice his rusty Arabic with Jammal, and to question him about conditions on the West Bank.

He wished to learn about attitudes among the various ethnic groups: the ties and conflicts that existed between the minority Christians, and the various factions within Islam.

He probed as much as he could and was pleasantly surprised to find that Jammal was refreshingly candid. For his part, the Arab driver was still trying to come to terms with the spectacle of friendship that he had just witnessed, between his King and the famous Israeli now riding so amicably in the back seat of his car.

CHAPTER 3

The three fedayeen terrorists were young, raw and inexperienced. None of them had participated in any previous mission, which was not surprising, as all previous fedayeen expeditions had ended in failure – the terrorists being either killed or captured. For the purpose of extracting information, the Israelis would take pains to capture one member of each team; the others were usually shot, so that none ever returned to their base. All subsequent missions were dispatched with novice terrorists, fighters with no field experience.

War discriminates between the "haves" and the "have-nots." The wealthier Arabs left for Beirut or Amman and quickly reestablished themselves by means of their financial resources and their quick Palestinian wits. The less fortunate were herded into the squalid conditions of refugee camps.

The camp outside Jericho was neither better nor worse than many other camps dotted along the Jordan valley, or further north in Lebanon. The houses, little more than mud huts, were shabbily constructed breeze-blocks that had been sprayed, both inside and out, with a white wash seed. Homes were situated in painfully close proximity to each other, the crude sand pathways dividing them naked of asphalt or paving.

In winter, the pathways were permanently water-logged. In summer, the dry air swarmed with flies and mosquitoes, was clogged, night and day, with uncontrollable whirlwinds of sand that filled the throats, burnt the eyes, and left a constant film on drinking-water. Toilet and washing facilities were primitive, dysentery and other hygiene-related ailments ran rife.

The refugees slouched indolently, stared vacantly into space on every street corner, waiting for food and clothes – handouts from the United Nations Works and Relief Agency, known as the UNWRA organization, which maintained an office in each camp. Few camps provided opportunity for gainful employment, and the general impression made on an outsider was of dirty, fly-infested beggars, devoid of occupation, plan or hope.

Terrorist groups flourished and fed off these conditions, drawing their recruits from the bitter resentment of the poor, the disillusioned and the hopeless; from the youngsters who had nowhere to go and nothing to achieve. The leaders, who organized conscription, promised excitement, action, even glory.

Muhammed had been chosen for advancement. At almost twenty, he was three years older than the average recruit, and a quick learner. One's first impression of him was that of a quiet, even perhaps a surly, youth; he never answered back, was quick to grasp instruction, and was known for his reliability.

In 1950 Muhammed had been singled out for participation in a six month paramilitary course at a camp in Syria. There he had received instruction in martial arts: shooting, survival tactics and leadership. Armed with these qualifications, he was given the leadership of a mission for the liberation of his birthplace.

The leaders of the fedayeen were a mixed bunch. Some had extreme leftist leanings, while others, probably the majority, were Muslims with religious principles. It was a lottery, whether a young recruit became a Marxist or a Muslim fundamentalist.

The methods used to induce the young terrorists into leaving on these suicidal raids were, therefore, varied. The Muslim leaders promised redemption and a Garden of Eden replete with choice foods served, in the next world, by beautiful women. The Communists, on the other hand, promised – and delivered before the onset of each mission – more immediate rewards: a good time in the brothels of Nablus and Jericho. Thus, when the novice terrorists set out on their first and usually last mission, they were both satiated by the immediate satisfaction of their sensual pleasures, and imbibed with the religious fervor of everlasting glory.

Thus it was, with their senses still tingling, and their hopes still high, that Muhammed and his two young unit members left the camp and launched into their mission against the women and children of Israel. None of the fedayeen attacks were ever directed against Israeli military installations; their purpose was strictly to spread terror among the civilian population.

The journey up into the hills above the Dead Sea was bumpy and nerve-racking. None of the three had managed any vehicle for more than a couple of hundred yards, nor had they ever received driving instruction. Muhammed, who had driven various Russian-made lorries during his stay in Syria, had never before been inside a Land

Rover. He understood that this was a complicated vehicle, he even knew that it had a four wheel drive, but he was ignorant as to the purpose or use of such a sophisticated device.

Their troubles began when they began to wind their way up the mountains, at which point changing down the gears, something he had witnessed in the larger vehicles in Syria, became a near impossible chore. Over difficult terrain, Muhammed had to cope with three pedals, gears, a heavy nonpower-steering system and two inexperienced but volatile back-seat drivers.

Despite efforts to hide his shortcomings from his companions, Muhammed's difficulties were rapidly revealing themselves to his men. The more voluble their advice to him, the more nervous and uncertain his driving became. After forty minutes along roads wide enough for only a single car, Muhammed skidded toward a sharp bend and a precipitous drop just as he was endeavoring to down-grade the gear in order to maintain momentum.

One of his companions screamed, "Beware, we will go over the edge."

This rattled Muhammed all the more. "I have it under control," he screamed back. Almost instantly the Land Rover hit the bend and careened around the corner, gaining speed as the incline flattened out to a level suface. Slamming his foot down on the brake pedal, he hit the clutch instead of the brakes. The front left wheel bounced off the asphalt like a frightened colt. In the absence of a shoulder to the road, it bounced off a jagged rock and skidded off the surface.

Again Muhammed slammed the full force of his weight on the pedals, this time hitting the brakes. The Land Rover lurched like a drunken beast to a stop, its undercarriage firmly caught on a rock off the side of the road, its left wheel dangling precariously between two large boulders at a lower level.

For the first time in two hours, Muhammed's two friends were speechless. All three were drenched in sweat. The previous night's frolicking in the brothels of Nablus, the fervor of the farewells at the camp, the unexpected killing of a Jordanian army driver and forty minutes of careening dangerously in a vehicle which they were ill-equipped to handle, had drained them. Painfully, they extricated themselves from the stalled vehicle; silently they walked around the back and surveyed the damage.

By now, the quarter moon had disappeared behind a cloud and visibility was limited. None of the three carried a torch. Muhammed made a mental note to suggest, in the event that he return home alive, that future teams come better prepared for emergencies. The Land Rover was stuck on the asphalt. The free wheel was badly punctured and it was now nearly ten thirty at night. Muhammed decided that they would sleep through the night and reassess the situation in the first light of the morning.

The two younger men fall asleep almost immediately at the side of the road. Muhammed lies with his head propped in the crook of his elbow, considering the implications of their predicament.

Suddenly, the night sounds are punctuated by the steady, dull thud of approaching steps. With the silent subtlety of a snake, Muhammed arches his body over to his young friends. With one hand over their mouths to prevent them from calling out, he wakes them and motions in the direction of the oncoming danger. A second later, Yossi walks round the bend into full view. Muhammed has no idea who the newcomer is, but he does know that it is unlikely to be an Arab in these mountains, at this time of night.

Seeing the stranded Land Rover, Yossi recognizes the familiar stench of trouble. In a split second, before the terrorists have time to stir, he dives off the asphalt, rolls down the short bank, coming to rest about four feet below the level of the road.

Recognizing that, despite the darkness, he is still dangerously exposed, the Israeli soldier searches around him for cover. Pulling Jammal's pistol from his belt, he utters a silent prayer of thanks to the Beduin driver for having thrust it upon him. Dragging his body behind a large thorn bush, Yossi selects a clip from his pocket and prepares his weapon for defense.

Meanwhile, Muhammed and his two terrorist friends are readying themselves for their first real encounter. There is no doubt in their minds: A stranger who dives off the side of the road the instant he sees an overturned Land Rover is the enemy. The three take cover behind the Land Rover and wait. Silence. The call of distant jackals wailing on the mountain top. No sign of the enemy. Muhammed realizes that if he were to approach the side of the road, he would present an easy target for the man waiting for him in the darkness.

Yossi has come to the same conclusion. He feels sure that he saw three men on the ground in the split second before he dropped below the level of the road, and he surmises that they can take cover on the far side of the Land Rover. His army training tells him that he has two choices: either to try and escape down the mountain and away from the road, or to take the initiative and attack.

The former is difficult given the visibility, the friable earth and the loose stones under foot. The chances of his sliding, falling or catching a foot in a rut are high. The slightest sound might bring his enemies closing in on him. Deciding for the alternative, Yossi veers away from the Land Rover and back towards the brow of the hill. He moves slowly, stealthily, yet he is not too worried, his instincts tell him that he is probably better trained than his adversaries.

Muhammed's two associates willingly leave strategy and planning to their leader. After all, he has already taken care of one potential enemy tonight. Their numerical superiority gives them confidence. Each secretly harbors a wish that it will be his bullet that brings down the enemy.

Muhammed decides to stay with his policy of waiting for the enemy to reveal himself. It doesn't occur to him that Yossi might retrace his steps in the direction of the brow of the hill. On the contrary, he keeps his eyes riveted on the area between the spot on which he has seen Yossi disappear, immediately to the rear of the disabled Land Rover.

Within minutes Yossi gains the brow of the hill. Surfacing on the far side, he rolls over the asphalt road until he disappears again over the edge. He then begins working his way down the ditch, on the side of the road opposite to where he had been minutes earlier. Silence is his only alibi, very soon he will be within feet of the three Arabs, with nothing dividing them but the darkness. He worms his way on his belly, keeping his head low until he figures that he is immediately below the vehicle. Slowly, silently, Yossi inches his way up from the ditch to the level of the road.

His eyes are now level with the roadway. In the darkness opposite, he sees two young Arabs, barely out of their teens, it seems to him. "Clearly fedayeen terrorists coming to grief early on their first mission," he thinks. There is no sight of any others, but he calculates, correctly, that a third is probably hidden around the front of the vehicle.

The idea of opening fire on the unsuspecting backs of two young boys is alien both to Yossi's nature and to his training. On the other hand, he realizes how difficult it will be, for him alone to overpower three terrorists without shooting them, especially since he still hasn't located the whereabouts of the third. He has to make a quick decision, he can't risk one of the two turning and seeing him.

Selecting a stone from the side of the road, Yossi hurls it over the heads of the two Arabs so that it comes zooming down on the far side of the vehicle. The effect is dramatic: The pent-up tensions of all three fedayeen snap simultaneously.

One man dives underneath the Land Rover. "He must have been stationed at the front of the vehicle," Yossi thinks. A second runs to the back of the vehicle, opening fire indiscriminately in the direction of the thistles where Yossi originally left the road. The third is unfortunate enough to have keener instincts and a steadier will. It is he that stands his ground. It is he that turns to face his enemy at the very moment that Yossi raises his loaded gun in front of him. Yossi has no choice. With a single shot he kills the stranger.

His element of surprise is spent. Both the terrorist at the front of the Land Rover, and the one at the rear of the vehicle are aware of his position. Yossi hurriedly hurls himself back into the shallow ditch from where he can reassess his position, unexposed.

His line of vision is now level with the ground beneath the vehicle. He can see the rear limbs of Muhammed's prostrate body quite clearly, but he is unable to locate the exact position of the other man due to the lopsided tilt of the Land Rover. Steadying his aim, Yossi shoots directly at what he sees of Muhammed, causing the latter to swivel round with the speed of an adder darting from its hole, and return wild, desperate, blind fire in his direction. Yossi can now see the frantic eyes of his enemy beneath the car. He shoots with the cold, steady fire of total control – and finds his target. "Two down," he sighs, and lowers his gun.

At that precise moment the third fedayeen becomes a hero. Bursting from his cover at the rear of the vehicle, he charges head on at Yossi, firing furiously as he runs. His second bullet finds its target. Yossi is dead. The battle is over.

The terrorist is not jubilant. He stands over the dead body of his victim, shaking with blind terror, cold sweat pouring from every limb. His two comrades lie crumpled, splattered against the side of the Land Rover.

All at once, sounds of the night, unheard or unnoticed until that moment, come crowding in upon his consciousness – the mournful wail of distant jackals, the scream of invisible crickets, and the wind that suddenly, out of nowhere, whips against the higher crags of the black mountain peaks. Loneliness and fear overwhelm him.

Turning his back on his dead comrades, the young fedayeen runs in sheer panic – in the direction of the refugee camp, in the direction of his people, in the direction of his only home.

CHAPTER 4

Taher Jabari was sleeping gently in his one-room shack when he was awakened by the nearby shots. He rose from his bed but did not venture out into the darkness, choosing rather to wait until first light before looking for the source of the trouble.

The twenty year old shepherd was spending one of his regular visits in the region, tending his father's sheep and looking after the family's property. The single room in which he slept and ate during these interludes, was his castle. He cooked and fended for himself. Only on rare occasions did he encounter another soul.

Years earlier, Taher's father had left Hebron where most of his family lived, and had reestablished his own family in the region of Ramallah, fifteen miles north of Jerusalem. He had left Hebron in 1929 in conflict with his neighbors, under a cloud because he had refused to participate in the Hebron massacre of Jewish residents. He had gone so far as to risk his life to save two of his Jewish neighbors and their children; had stood at the door of his home, machete in hand and had prevented his Arab friends and family from harming those who were under his protection.

The Hebron massacre had been well planned. The execution would have been even more effective were it not for Arabs like Taher's father who were not *man enough* to see the job through. As it was, some sixty or so Jews were murdered and about the same number wounded. Torah scrolls were burned and synagogues razed to the ground. The Hebron Jewish community was destroyed. Amin Jabari had told his son about the massacre and why he had left Hebron; Taher was proud of his father; proud of what he had done.

With first light, around five in the morning, Taher rose and left the hut. The chill dawn air was still and there was no indication of any earlier violence. Taher traced his way along the mountain path until he reached the asphalt road. From a distance of some hundred yards or so, he saw the abandoned vehicle. Approaching it cautiously, he was horrified to discover three dead bodies, blood-spattered, crumpled and stiff at the side of the road.

Taher had never seen a dead man before. Muslim law dictated that bodies not be allowed to lie exposed, but be buried without delay. So, retracing his steps back to his shack, he returned with a shovel and, in the ditch at the side of the road where the earth was softer and less stony, he dug three shallow graves.

The first to be buried was Muhammed. The second Arab was placed next in line. Taher saw the various different weapons lying near the bodies and realized immediately that the men had been terrorists, probably on their way to some godless mission. He took the guns and the grenades and covered the bodies with earth.

He then turned his attention to the body of Yossi. This was not the body of an Arab. It had none of the signs of a terrorist, although its frozen fist was still clutching a pistol. As Taher turned the body over, the jacket flipped open and a large, formal-looking envelope fell from the front inner pocket. Taher couldn't read and therefore had no idea what the nature of its contents could be. Nevertheless, he was impressed by the formal stamp embossed on the back of the envelope. "This," he thought, "must be important. Probably the cause of all this carnage."

By 7 am Taher had buried the bodies in the three shallow graves, one adjoining the other in a single line parallel to the road. The Israeli had been placed in the grave nearest to the brow of the hill. Not a soul had come by and Taher was pleased that he had started his day early and had accomplished his unusual chore without being observed.

For a moment he considered marking the graves, but some instinct warned him to keep hidden all traces of the horrors that had been perpetrated that night. Instead, he paced ten steps up the hill and there he made a makeshift mound of stones. Such mounds were common in this uncharted territory, as they usually signified dividing lines between properties. This marker would not attract attention.

Taher was not due to return to his father's house for another two days. He realized, however, that sooner or later the abandoned Land Rover would be discovered and would attract attention. Consequently, he moved his herd of sheep to new pastures some two kilometers to the north-east. This decision had been reached slowly and methodically as he had been taught by his father since leaving school at the age of fourteen. When making decisions of any kind, he would consider what his father would do in similar circumstances.

Although his father had cut off his formal education and closed his mind to the world of books, literature and music, he had compensated by instilling an understanding of right and wrong. Furthermore, the father's love and warmth for his son had injected a primitive but real quality of life.

Taher was by no means simple. He had developed shrewd instincts and a retentive memory. Like so many young boys plucked out of the school system at an early age and sent away from the village to work in the lonely fields and mountains, Taher had received little guidance. He had never been advised to read and broaden his awareness or horizons. On even a mundane level, Taher had little general knowledge. He rarely looked at a newspaper, for his reading abilities were poor and he would see a paper only when visiting a town or village. He had only a superficial knowledge of local current events.

Spending his days watching his father's sheep grazing on lonely mountains, far from modern life, Taher would have little chance of becoming worldly. He had never eaten in restaurants, had no appreciation for good food and, as a Muslim, had never tasted wine or spirits. And yet, despite all of these shortcomings, in fact, probably because of them, the twenty year old Taher had developed a profound sense of decency. Perhaps he had acquired this trait through his genes; perhaps it was an inheritance that came with the land. Yes, uneducated though he was by western standards, Taher Jabari knew how to tell right from wrong.

For some six years he had completed the tasks assigned to him without question. Moving his sheep regularly from one grazing pasture to another as required by tradition and common sense, he lived frugally and by force of circumstances had developed some of the characteristics of an introvert.

Taking his newly acquired cache of arms, he proceeded to bury them in a hiding place in a hollow area near the entrance to a well some two hundred yards from the shack. He threw the shovel in for good measure, on top of the arms. On completing his chores, he began making tracks for home.

Amin Jabari was usually referred to as Abu Taher, for according to local custom menfolk were called by the name of their eldest son. Abu Taher meant simply: the father of Taher. The father of the family was taking an afternoon nap when his son returned home. Although seething inside with excitement, the young Taher waited silently for his father to rouse. The father was a strong and good man and Taher prayed that his own deeds that morning would meet with his approval.

Shortly after 4 pm the father rose, washed and prostrated himself on a carpet in the direction of Mecca, it being his custom, as a devout Muslim, to pray five times each day. Taher joined his father in his prayers and only after they had been completed and fresh black coffee had been served by Taher's sister, did Amin ask the reason for his son's early return.

Taher handed the white envelope with its contents to his father and related what had happened. He told about the shots in the night and of how he buried three bodies. He explained that he had been careful to hide his shovel, together with the men's guns that he had found, in the mouth of a nearby well.

Amin was pleased with his son's account. He trusted that Taher had kept nothing back. "On your return home did you relate any of these events to anyone else?" Amin asked.

"Absolutely not, father," replied the son. "We are now the only two people who know what I have done."

"Was there any evidence that others had, perhaps, participated in the shooting and had left the scene before morning?"

"Yes," replied Taher. "From the way in which the Israeli was lying, it seems unlikely that he was shot by either of the other two. His body was turned away from them facing up the hill, and was probably shot from the direction of the back of the Land Rover. I can only assume that a fourth person left the scene before I got there. Nevertheless, I am convinced that no one saw me. It took nearly two hours to dig the graves, I would have sensed had anyone been watching me."

"And this letter was intact in the Israeli's pocket," mused the father.

Father and son speculated for some time as to what could possibly prompt a fourth man to participate in such an act of carnage, and to leave without either taking any of the guns or other weapons with him, or removing the seemingly important envelope from the Israeli's pocket. There were many possibilities. "Who had been driving the Army Land Rover," Amin wondered aloud, "and who could the fourth person have been?"

They sat, pondering for a few minutes in silence. "Taher, how do you know that the third man was an Israeli?"

Taher told his father about the small metal disc, held on a leather thong, that he had found around the third man's neck. The disc had had a number and two letters engraved on it, probably in Hebrew. He described the disc to his father who asked, "But you said that the third body was wearing civilian clothes?"

"That's correct," replied the son, "perhaps he was returning from a special mission."

"Yes," replied his father, "one day we will know what information is written in this letter, then we will know more about the man that lost his life while carrying it."

"My bet is that it was an Israeli in some kind of skirmish with fedayeen," insisted Taher.

"You may well be right," sighed Amin thoughtfully. "If you are, one day we must help get him a Jewish burial. I remember from my years in Hebron so many years ago, how important it is to the Jews to bury their dead in accordance with their laws."

Taking the letter in his hand, Amin turned to his son. "No one must know what has taken place this night. I will take this letter to my bank. I will hide it in the safe with the deeds of our properties."

Taking complete charge of the matter, Abu Taher, the head of the family, concluded, "We will do nothing in haste."

Chapter 5

General Moshe Dayan was ushered into his meeting with Ben Gurion, at his office at the Ministry of Defense in Tel Aviv.

Five days had passed since the historic signing of the Israel-Jordan Agreement, and no word of Major Yossi Foux. B.G., as Israel's first Prime Minister was affectionately called, was very much perturbed by the possibility that his long and arduous negotiations with King Abdullah might be wasted. On a personal level he was worried for the safety of his young officer. He had insisted that Moshe Dayan should head this delicate mission, and it was for that reason that he had summoned him home from London.

The discussion centered on two possibilities: the first that Foux had been killed; the second that he had been taken prisoner. Dayan was firmly of the opinion that if Yossi had fallen into either the hands of the fedayeen or into those of the Jordanian army, the Israelis would know about it. "After all," argued Dayan, "if he had been taken by the army, he would have been released and returned to us; probably a little worse for wear, but nonetheless in one piece. On the other hand, the fedayeen would have used such a capture for immediate propaganda. They've never had such a victory before. Even from a point of improving their own internal morale they would surely make as big a deal of it as they could."

The two were meeting alone. No secretaries were present and instructions had been given that Ben Gurion was not to be disturbed even by his wife Paula, whose scope and capability for interfering were legendary. Ben Gurion demanded that Dayan give him a second, complete and detailed briefing of his meeting with Abdullah. Dayan left nothing out, concluding with the detail of the missing Land Rover and the subsequent report that this vehicle had been found the following day stuck on a hillside on the way up to Jerusalem.

Dayan reported that he had asked army intelligence to pinpoint the exact area in which the Land Rover had been found, and its distance from the spot where he and Jammal had dropped Yossi off. The situation was delicate and King Abdullah must never be implicated.

B.G. agreed with him that in all probability Yossi had been killed and that the signed Agreement was lost. "For the sake of both parties, our relationship with Abdullah must be suspended," he concluded. "We need a breathing space. Let us just hope that it will not be punctuated by the news that the Agreement has found its way into undesirable hands. We are still officially at war with Jordan, we have no formal relations with them, and we cannot expect them to cooperate with us on any official level. Furthermore, I absolutely forbid any Israeli action of any kind within Jordanian territory. Is that perfectly understood?"

Dayan confirmed that, other than trying to verify information through existing channels, he wouldn't authorize any action. He left the Prime Minister's office intent on a more painful mission: a visit to Yossi's wife and children.

CHAPTER 6

King Abdullah and General Glubb settled into the comfortable leather rear seats of the powerful Packard for their ride up into the Moabite Mountains and back to Amman, capital of the Hashemite Kingdom of Jordan.

For the time being, Abdullah decided not to tell the general the import of his meeting with Dayan. Although he believed in Glubb's absolute loyalty, he was aware of his adviser's anti-Israeli bias, and was uncertain as to his feelings regarding peace overtures towards the Israelis. For the meantime he merely asked the general for an update on the situation in the West Bank. Annexing the West Bank of the Jordan River to his kingdom had been a gamble. Moreover, it had since become clear to many, that, in taking that step, he had bitten off more than he could chew.

Almost thirty years earlier, while apprenticed as political secretary to his father, Abdullah had been trained by experienced British officials stationed in the Middle East. Since that time he had maintained a deep friendship with a senior British civil servant, Sir Alexander Kirkbride who, at the recommendation of the British Colonial Service and Foreign Office, had held various key appointments at the Hashemite Court. Sir Alexander's first loyalties had clearly always been to the British Crown.

Abdullah learnt two political concepts from his British mentors: The first was that of political action versus political verbal policy. "Never the twain shall meet," was the wry way his Scottish mentor had put it, a Scotch in his hand and a twinkle in his piercing blue eyes. The second was the concept of divide and rule. Hence, Abdullah had appointed General John Glubb, a British outsider, as commander-in-chief of the Arab Legion.

In November '47, the United Nations proposed the Partition Resolution by means of which an Arab State would be established side by side with the Jewish State on the West Bank of the Jordan. Abdullah had joined the rest of the Arab world in verbal opposition. Within days Abdullah had arranged for both houses of his Parliament to give their unanimous support to Arab interests in Palestine.

Six months later, and with the support of the British Government, the Arab Legion crossed the Jordan River. In May 1948 Jordan took possession of the Old City of Jerusalem. Despite this aggressive take-over, Abdullah had been careful not to extend his rule beyond those areas outlined in the Partition Plan.

In September, after substantial lobbying on the part of Abdullah and his court, Count Bernadotte (the mediator appointed by the United Nations) proposed that the U.N. accept the status quo and endorse the unification of the West Bank with Transjordan. The rest of the Arab world fought the resolution and had it defeated. Later that month, under the patronage of Egypt, a Palestinian Government in Exile was established in Gaza by Abdullah's arch-enemy Haji Amin el-Husseini, the deposed Mufti of Jerusalem. This was in direct conflict with the interests of Abdullah. In reaction, the Jordanian monarch lobbied aggressively, summoning supporters from around the world to Jericho where he orchestrated a congress of 500 delegates. This assembly, and subsequently the Jordanian Senate in Amman, ratified Abdullah's annexation of the Old City of Jerusalem.

The Kingdom of Jordan, as it was called from that time onward, now ruled the land and peoples on both banks of the Jordan River. On the Western Bank it controlled the towns of Hebron, Nablus, Ramallah and Bethlehem. But – most important of all as far as King Abdullah was concerned – it ruled Jerusalem. Having thus politically consolidated his most significant military achievement, Abdullah appointed a new Mufti of Jerusalem to replace the exiled Amin.

During the following months, with the support of the British Government, the Jordanian king directed his efforts towards bringing the West Bank into mainstream Jordanian parliamentary rule. The old Parliament was dissolved and in its place new elections instituted a new

40 member house, half of its deputies being representatives from the
West Bank.

At His Majesty's request the general began his report.

"First, Your Majesty will be pleased to hear that the elections on the West Bank
went smoothly. Indeed they were welcomed by most sections of the population. Your
Majesty's idea of ensuring that four of the twenty West Bank delegates would
represent the Christian Arabs in the areas will, I hope, pay dividends. Frankly, if it
were in my power to substantially increase the Christian representation, I would."

The King was in agreement with Glubb on this matter. Although a devout
Muslim himself, he was nervous of emerging Muslim fundamentalism creating a
climate of nationalism which might, in the future, prove difficult to curb. Abdullah
was aware that the potential of a Muslim alliance in Parliament, drawn from
members representing both sides of the Jordan, could one day pose a threat to his
own hitherto unquestioned rule. Indeed, from a detailed analysis of all elected
deputies, the King had formed a far less rosy view than Glubb about the reliability
of Parliament, even with regard to the more immediate future.

The general continued: "Our most pressing problems center on our demographic
difficulties. The acquisition of nearly one million Palestinians has just about trebled
the population of the Kingdom of Jordan. The previous Beduin majority has been
totally eclipsed, and in my opinion this has radically undermined the stability of the
kingdom. A number of specific factors cause concern."

Glubb took a small notebook from the inside pocket of his jacket and flipped
the pages. "Approximately half of our new citizens are expatriate Palestinians,
refugees from areas that now form part of the State of Israel. Those in the camps
are frustrated and discontented. Many believe, indeed they are fed constant
propaganda to the effect that Your Majesty did not pursue the war with Israel with
sufficient zeal. They have accepted the notion, fed them by agitators, that your
principal interest was not so much to overcome the enemy state, as to consolidate
an enlarged kingdom on both sides of the Jordan River. In the event of an emergency
they cannot be trusted to be loyal to your Majesty."

As Glubb droned on, reiterating material which was already familiar to the king,
Abdullah reflected on his adviser's tendency to lecture, a habit that irritated him.
"The other inhabitants of the West Bank, the indigenous Palestinian population, feel
politically constricted and deprived of full freedom of expression."

"But surely," interjected King Abdullah, "the balanced parliamentary representation that we have granted them must have some calming effect on their insatiable political discontent."

Glubb, who was becoming uneasy at the king's long silence, welcomed the interruption. "Your Majesty," he urged, eager to appease, "your actions have definitely been a step in the right direction. However, there are two negative factors. The first is that the Palestinians are, on balance, shrewd and well informed, and the second is that there are plenty of rabble-rousers in the pay of your enemies, particularly those working out of Jerusalem. Those people will deride whatever innovations Your Majesty offers, however beneficial.

"Let us take the media for example. Both Arab daily newspapers in Jerusalem have run extensive coverage on *Demography and the Popular Vote*. They have explained, in the clearest, possible terms, that the twenty West Bank parliamentarians represent 900,000 voters, whereas the 20 members in Transjordan represent only 400,000. In short, they insist that they – the Palestinians, that is – have been short changed. However, in the final analysis, politics is of less importance to the rank-and-file than the denial of equal work opportunity. The Palestinians are better educated than those Beduins who live in Transjordan. There are many skilled professional men among them who cannot find employment in what they regard as a primitive economy.

"Consequently, Jordan is experiencing the first signs of a brain drain. Both the American and Canadian consulates have informed me that they are having difficulty coping with visa and work permit applications from doctors, engineers and scientists. Finally, those that want to remain believe that there is prejudice against them at every level where they have to compete against Transjordanians. The friction this causes is clearly escalating."

Glubb looked again at his notes and cleared his throat, "Your Majesty, the detailed investigation that I am conducting inside the refugee camps is not yet completed. However, first reports indicate that the internal organization of the United Nations Relief and Works Agency is far from adequate. A great deal of their aid is finding its way into the pockets of corrupt local officials. The majority of the refugees barely manage to eke out a living. Demonstrations against the Zionists are often coupled with complaints against your own rule. Ironically, it is the demonstrations and the activities of liberation organizations that represent the only growth industries within the camps."

"So," continued the General, "at your request, I have established an office in Jerusalem, staffed by three first-class agents. Our first indications confirm our suspicions, namely that the Husseinis (who are orchestrated by the deposed Mufti now residing in Cairo) are very much in control. There is little evidence of Jerusalem being part of the kingdom. In fact, the general feeling is that Jerusalemites consider themselves independent of the kingdom. I hope to bring you a separate, in-depth report on Jerusalem within two or three weeks. Please, Your Majesty, until then – don't press me on the time frame."

Glubb completed his report just as the car approached the streets of Amman.

Abdullah considered all that he had heard. As a shrewd political observer of many years, he was already aware of most of the findings. Nonetheless, Glubb's bluntness was painful. He knew that, despite his pompous disposition, his British adviser was impartial, careful and thorough, and that, above all, he could be relied on for discretion – a rare commodity in this part of the world.

The purpose of signing an Agreement with the Israelis was to pave the way for radical change. Without such change Abdullah believed his present kingdom might well collapse, and his plans for leaving a dynastic order after him would be doomed to failure. For many years negotiations with Israelis had been conducted behind the scenes. As early as 1918 Chaim Weizmann, who would later be Israel's first president, had crossed the Jordan to negotiate coexistence. In May '48 Golda Meir travelled to Amman, disguised as an Arab woman, to discuss a non-aggression pact with Jordan. Dayan had met various senior Jordanian army officers on a number of occasions.

But, unlike all the previous attempts to negotiate with Israel, the initiative that had led to the present agreement had come, not from the Jewish State, but from the Jordanian king himself. It represented Abdullah's efforts to come to terms with his own problems, problems caused by the growing demographic change within his expanded borders. The information that he now received in the Glubb report merely reinforced his resolve to implement the Agreement at hand.

CHAPTER 7

Samir was a Palestinian from the village of A-Tur which lay just three miles east of Jerusalem. A devout Moslem, he prayed regularly each Friday at the el-Aqsa Mosque on the Temple Mount. This year he planned to make a pilgrimage to Mecca, a trip he had been yearning for most of his life. After this journey he would no longer be referred to merely as Samir the waiter, but as Haji Samir, man of purity and faith who had been on the Haji.

A bus left once each morning from Jerusalem, driving via A-Tur where Samir the waiter lived, and down to Jericho via Qumran and Kalia. Every afternoon it returned to Jerusalem leaving Kalia at 5 pm. As a rule Samir closed the small spa house and returned to his home in A-Tur by the afternoon bus, often in the company of customers who were returning to their homes refreshed by the therapeutic waters of the spa.

Occasionally, the spa was used for special functions in the early evenings. In such events Samir was warned in advance by the office in Amman. In these cases Samir would sleep over at his place of work, for he had no alternative means of getting home.

On the morning of the meeting, the Amman office had telephoned and notified him that some extremely important persons would gather that evening at the spa. Later in the day, two tough-looking Secret Service agents had appeared at the spa to warn him that he would be expected to keep his mouth absolutely shut regarding the participants and any other details of the evening's event. Yet, despite the warning, when the guests had arrived and Samir had seen who they were, he had been thrown completely off his guard.

Samir served drinks to his visitors with as much calm as he could muster, conscious that his knees were shaking and his palms drenched in sweat. As soon as he could, however, he escaped to the safety of his kitchen which had an interconnecting hatch into the main reception room. Surely he was not expected to close his mind off to the presence of such famous people in his own workplace? Succumbing to his curiosity, he eased open the serving hatch just a fraction. From the safety of his hiding place, Samir the waiter, the tedium of whose life had not missed a beat in over 30 years, watched history in the making.

From his kitchen corner he, Samir of A-Tur, observed a rendezvous between his own monarch, King Abdullah, and a top Israeli general, one whose black eye-patch and tight features were known throughout Jordan. Unfortunately, although his English was quite adequate, he was prevented from following what must have been a momentous conversation by the mournful whining of the overhead electric fans, and by the distance of nearly 40 feet which stretched between his perch and the dignitaries in the other room. But he did watch as the dignitaries of the two enemy countries signed two documents: One document, he noticed, was kept by His Majesty, King of Jordan; the other – by the Israeli celebrity, Moshe Dayan.

A while later, the Arab waiter was summoned outside by two strangers and confronted head-on with the dead body of a Jordanian soldier. The murdered man, a soldier of the Legion, was slumped against the stump of a tree. Without so much as one word of explanation, a foreign-sounding Jordanian general informed him that a vehicle would arrive shortly to cart the body away. Until just before midnight he waited – alone and terrified. Eventually a Jordanian army vehicle drove up. Without a word, two men picked up the body and left.

Haji Amin el-Husseini, the deposed ex-Mufti of Jerusalem, lived in modest circumstances in the Giza section of Cairo. Egypt was the latest in a series of exiles that had begun as early as 1920. At that time the British Mandatory Court in Palestine had sentenced him, in absentia, to 10 years in jail for leading anti-Jewish riots in Jerusalem.

Amin spent most of his time reflecting over his past triumphs and failures, and contemplating his own glorious comeback. His political activities were built upon the deep-seated feelings of hostility toward the newly formed State of Israel. He hated the Jews and he hated the British. But more than anyone, he hated King Abdullah. Abdullah was his worst enemy and the worst enemy of the Palestinian people.

In 1921, just one year after his ten-year prison sentence, Sir Herbert Samuel, first British High Commissioner in Palestine, had arbitrarily granted him a reprieve. The paramount concern of the British (and Jewish) Governor was, at all times, to placate the wrath of the Arabs. So, at the same time that the British Mandate granted the Transjordanian Emirate to Abdullah, and underlined its intention of granting the Jews a national homeland in keeping with the Balfour Declaration, Sir Herbert appointed Amin to be Mufti of Jerusalem. Thus in short order, Amin el-Husseini was reprieved from a jail sentence and elevated to one of the highest positions in Islam.

As far as the new Mufti was concerned, territorial authority had been established, irrevocably, by the British authorities: He and his followers were to rule Jerusalem, while Abdullah and his Hashemites were to be restricted to an area east of the Jordan River.

The new Mufti repaid the High Commissioner for his even-handedness: He became the principal source of extremist anti-Jewish and anti-British activities. It was he who organized the major riots of 1929 and 1936. So pronounced was his mark, that the British, who otherwise were the champions of Arab appeasement, had no choice but to remove him from office. Amin was dismissed in 1937 and his various committees were outlawed. By that time, in any case, Haji Amin had become convinced that it was only with the support of the British Government that Zionism was able to survive at all. Therefore, the immediate need of his people was to concentrate attack, not on the Jews, but on their British supporters.

The British never understood the complex character of the Mufti. Endowed with great personal charm, Amin was especially impressive during a first meeting. He seemed most sincere when discussing the issue of Jerusalem and Palestine, both of which belonged, in his view, exclusively to the Arabs. Though small and slight of build, he was quite handsome. He aways dressed in the habit of a Moslem cleric. This gave him a natural, oriental dignity. Over the years he had developed the nack of sitting very still, like a statue; he never raised his voice or gesticulated as did most people in the Middle East, and in fact it was the dignity of this stance that tended to emphasize the vulgarities of others while emphasizing his own qualities. Many saw in him a pillar of virtue and tolerance, and refused to recognize the many manifestations of his bloodthirsty, treacherous personality.

During the period of his second exile in Damascus, Haji Amin ingratiated himself with German and Italian agents. In 1941, while in Iraq, he played an active role in an unsuccessful coup and issued a *"fatwa"* – a summons to Jihad, or holy war – against Britain.

Again on the move, Haji Amin transferred to Germany, where he presented a plan to Hitler to recruit Muslims for the German war machine, offering to cooperate in the extermination of Jews. November '41 the Führer extended him a royal welcome, and sat with him in a two-hour meeting. The two had identical interests: the final solution of the Jewish problem and the war against imperialist Britain and communist Russia.

Haji Amin utilised both the prestige accorded him by the title of *"Mufti"* and his office in Berlin to convey his encouragement of the extermination of Jews to countries under Nazi control. When he heard, for example, that Hungary was prepared to send 900 Jewish children to Palestine, he pleaded that the decision be reversed in order to protect the interests of the Arabs in that region. Consequently, all 900 of those children were deported to concentration camps.

As both the British and the Hashemites of Jordan were enemies of Ibn Saud, Haji Amin worked to secure Ibn Saud to his own cause. Thus he was able to use the cash resources of oil rich Saudi Arabia for the purchase of arms from Germany, arms which he then used in Palestinian uprisings both against the British and against the Hashemites. Toward the end of the war, Haji Amin was taken prisoner by the French. Wily as ever, he managed to escape and make his way back to Beirut and Cairo. There he orchestrated resistance against the establishment of a Jewish State and continued his never-ending battle against King Abdullah.

Haji Amin actually managed, for a brief time in September '48, to establish an Egyptian-supported, Palestine Government in Gaza, for which he received support from several Arab governments. For his part, Abdullah remained true to his own resolve. He ignored the resolutions of the Palestinian Government in Exile, and proceeded, again with British backing, to annex the West Bank.

British support for Abdullah affected the policies of other Arab States, who soon withdrew their backing for the ex-Mufti. The All-Palestine Government in Exile folded its tents.

But all this is history. The holy war must continue and Jerusalem must be redeemed from infidels and traitors.

A classified report is received from a trusted spy in Jerusalem. Haji Amin is informed that a meeting had taken place, two weeks before, between King Abdullah and General Dayan at a spa in Kalia. At that meeting, two copies of a document were signed. Unfortunately, the contents of the documents are unknown. From his reliable contacts in Jerusalem, Haji Amin ascertains that the informant has been unable to provide any information regarding the contents of the agreement, that he was able only to reiterate that one copy had been taken by Abdullah, the other by Moshe Dayan.

Haji Amin probes for more information in Amman. But Amman is Abdullah's territory. Two weeks of inquiries leave him without a single clue. No one knows anything about the meeting or about any agreement signed between Jordan and the Israelis.

The ex-Mufti is only too aware of the difficulties that Abdullah is experiencing, trying to control a population that has been swollen by conquest. He knows that two thirds of Abdullah's kingdom are now Palestinian and therefore hostile to their Hashemite ruler. Shrewdly, he suspects that an agreement with Israel might have been instigated because of this problem. Furthermore, he knows that any solution that sits comfortably with the Hashemites and with Israel is, by definition, detrimental to the Palestinians. Such an agreement, regardless of its contents, must be thwarted.

As far as Haji Amin is concerned, the time is ripe for Abdullah to pay for the plight of the Palestinians. He arranges for his family in Jerusalem to handle the details.

✧   ✧   ✧

CHAPTER 8

On the 20th of July, 1951, His Royal Highness King Abdullah of Jordan, together with his faithful aide, Jammal, and his own appointed Mufti of Jerusalem, Sheikh Hassan al-Din Jarallah, visit the el-Aqsa Mosque in Jerusalem. As he enters the Mosque, Abdullah is accosted by Mustafa Shukri Ushu, a twenty-one year old youth. The young stranger pulls a pistol from beneath the deep folds of his robe and shoots his monarch in the head. His Majesty, the first King of Jordan, has been assassinated by agents of the ex-Mufti.

The King collapses, chaos erupting all around him. Jammal leans over to kiss his dying friend, monarch and mentor. Tears streaming down his face, he remembers to slip his hand through the King's robes and retrieves the signed and blood-stained copy of the fatal document from the shirt pocket within.

The assassination of Abdullah, first monarch of the Hashemite Kingdom of Jordan, took place inside the el-Aqsa Mosque on the Temple Mount, site of the First and Second Temples. It took place in plain view of uniformed army and police officers, secret service agents, clerics, family members....and his people. Mustafa Shukri Ushu, assassin of the king, had acted on the instructions of Haji Amin el-Husseini, the deposed Mufti of Jerusalem. Within seconds of the assassination, the young Ushu was shot by an army officer. Many others present were killed in the ensuing cross fire.

More than thirty arrests were made and ten Palestinians were eventually charged with the assassination. Two of them were sentenced in absentia, having fled to Egypt. Of the eight brought to trial before a military court in Amman, no fewer than five were Husseinis. A promising young Palestinian lawyer from Ramallah, by the name of Azziz Shehadeh, was appointed to represent one of the accused. This lawyer was a rising star with good connections among many of the more prominent families of the Palestinians. He applied himself to the hopeless defense of this client, one who was clearly destined to die, with all the brainpower and energy that he could muster. In subsequent years, while representing other political assassins and terrorists, Shehadeh was to draw on this experience.

From Cairo, Haji Amin published his contention in papers around the world, that the trial was a crime against the Palestinian people, a crime perpetrated by a fascist monarchy acting on orders from British colonialists. There were two absentee defendants on trial. One of them was Colonel Abdullah el-Tel who had served, until shortly before the time of the trial, as Military Commander of Jerusalem. Surprisingly, he received support from two opposing sides: Haji Amin, who claimed that el-Tel had had no connection with either himself or his sympathizers; and General Glubb, certainly no friend of the ex-Mufti, who pronounced the absent colonel a loyal and trusted favorite of the murdered king. "A moderate, a friend of peace with Israel, and a friend of Moshe Dayan. How could he possibly be part of a plot against the king?" he asked in a well-publicized interview.

The military court found six of the defendants guilty, including the two absentees. Of the four defendants that were found not guilty, one – Father Ayyad of Bet Sahour – was a Catholic priest. He came from a small village south of Jerusalem on the outskirts of Bethlehem, not far from Sur Baher, which he had visited only weeks earlier. Father Ayyad was an outspoken advocate of an all-Arab Jerusalem.

> Although East Jerusalem is predominantly Muslim, there has been a considerable Christian Arab presence there since the time of the Crusades. The Christians are divided into many branches, of which the Orthodox Church has three sections: Russian, Greek and Armenian. Then there are the Catholics, the Copts, the Syrians and the Protestants. In the 1830s, and, with the liberalization of Jerusalem by the ruling Turks, the Churches hastened to stake their claims on the city and establish roots there. Initially, the Catholic Church was not as aggressive as the Orthodox Churches, nevertheless, by 1847 it too had appointed a Patriarch in Jerusalem. While the cradle and focal point of their church was still firmly established in Rome, the Catholics formulated a doctrine denying a Jerusalem rebuilt or governed by Jews. The Vatican saw itself as the sole defender of the Holy City against the

Jewish challenge. According to its doctrine, only Christians can possess a new Jerusalem, only they can be the rightful heirs of the Holy City.

In 1904 Herzl, modern visionary and leader of the ancient dream of Zionism, visited the Vatican and Pope Pius X. At that time the Pope maintained that the return of Jews to Jerusalem constituted the demonstration of messianic expectations, deemed invalid by the Catholic Church.

These views conflicted with those of Bible-oriented Christians, who actively encourage Jews to return to Jerusalem, which they regard as a first step in the literal fulfillment of biblical prophecy.

The four condemned Palestinians, held in custody in Amman, were hanged at the beginning of September. On the day of the execution, the following gratuitous observation was made to a British newspaper correspondent by General Glubb: "If not for the Jews who kept us occupied so much of the time, if not for these people without character who cannot be trusted, there would be peace in the Middle East and the area would be free of incidents."

Prior to the assassination, King Abdullah's eldest son Talal had attempted to stab his pregnant wife with a knife in an Amman maternity home. He then compounded this felony by physically attacking his father's British adviser, General Glubb, at which point Abdullah felt he had no choice but to banish his son to the renowned Prangins Clinic for Nervous Disorders in Geneva.

After the assassination of its monarch, the younger son, Naif, was appointed Regent of Jordan. Throughout the period of the trial that followed the assassination, the young Regent and his government were bombarded, on all sides, with pressures and appeals regarding the issue of succession. Palestinians supported the return of Talal, deranged though he undoubtedly was. Support for Talal grew to the extent that, two days after the execution of the condemned murderers of his father, and after visits to Geneva by parliamentarians, doctors and family, Talal

Ibn Abdullah was returned from exile and crowned the Second King of the Hashemite Kingdom of Jordan.

However, Talal was unable to keep a grip either on himself or on his kingdom for very long. Quickly regressing into his earlier, deranged state, he soon lost the confidence of his people. Even his most ardent supporters were forced to recognize their error. The same parliament that had given him the throne, now took it back. The deposed monarch was returned to Switzerland and the Prangins Clinic.

Hussein, Talal's elder son and King Abdullah's favorite grandson, only sixteen years old, was then appointed Regent. Within two years Hussein formally ascended the throne of Jordan. Unlike his father and his two uncles, who had been tutored in the desert by Beduin nomads, Hussein had been educated at Harrow, England's prestigious school where Winston Churchill had studied a half century earlier. After graduating from Harrow, Hussein was sent to Sandhurst, England's finest military academy.

On his return to Amman, Hussein, like his grandfather before him, surrounded himself with English advisers – some inherited, some new. The Arab Legion, with its reliable Beduin soldiers and its English officers, gave him a feeling of security in the midst of what was, in effect, a largely hostile, Palestinian population. Hussein was aware of the fast diminishing nature of the British diplomatic clout. His kingdom was of less strategic importance to the new superpowers than it had been to Britain. The young king embarked on a scheme for the promotion of Jordan as an oasis of reliability in an otherwise threatening environment.

Paying lip-service to his neighboring Arab states, Hussein claimed that, with the establishment of the State of Israel, he was not able to talk as a single voice, but merely as one of five neighboring Arab voices. The one unifying factor, common to all these states, was their hostility toward the State of Israel. In 1953, when Hussein became King of Jordan, his neighbors Egypt, Syria, Lebanon and Iraq, announced to the world that peace in the region could come only after the elimination of the State of Israel. Jordan formed part of that chorus.

The British were about to exit the Middle East. Arab monarchies they had sponsored years earlier were collapsing all over the region. Nationalist socialist parties had wrested control from the kings of Lybia and Iraq, and, more recently, King Farouq of Egypt had been deposed by a military junta. King Hussein did not require the expert advice of foreign counsellors to explain to him the gathering clouds.

After only a short time in harness, the young king decided to shake himself free of a number of the older trusted advisers – remnants of the previous regime. Jammal was one of the first to go. The new king needed to cut the old strings and forge his own associations. Jammal left graciously, aware that the new king needed to flex his muscles in his own way. He packed his belongings, travelled south and settled in Aqaba, Jordan's outlet to the Red Sea. There he joined two of his sons in their growing fishing industry.

In 1956, in line with local political changes, Hussein dispensed with the services of his British Commander-in-Chief, General Glubb. Sir Anthony Eden was the British Foreign Secretary at the time. Appalled at the effrontery of what he regarded as little more than a young puppet king, he demanded that Hussein revoke his decision. However, the twenty-one year old Jordanian monarch stood his ground.

Endowed with a natural penchant for public relations, Hussein consciously promoted the image of himself as a moderate. In the process he found it necessary to thwart numerous political and military plots directed against his regime and against his own person. He was set to play a long innings of Middle Eastern diplomacy.

It was not long before Great Britain played its own swansong in the region. In collaboration with the French and the Israelis, a strike was made against President Nasser in Egypt in an attempt to reopen the Suez Canal for international traffic. The English and French blitzed the area, dropping commandos by parachute to take control of the canal, while Israeli troops stormed their way through the Sinai Desert to the banks of the Suez. With the dexterity of the little guy in a game of giants, King Hussein kept Jordan out of this conflict.

In 1973, just a few days before the outbreak of the Yom Kippur War, King Hussein met face to face, in Israel, with Prime Minister Golda

Meir, and warned her of an imminent Egyptian and Syrian attack. To Golda's deep regret, she disregarded Hussein's warning, just as she and Dayan disregarded the warnings of Israel's own army intelligence.

Six years earlier, Prime Minister Levi Eshkol had, in his turn, delivered a warning to King Hussein. He had advised Hussein that war was impending and warned Jordan not to participate. Unfortunately, Hussein had bigger worries than that of maintaining a balancing act between Israel and its neighbors. The tension between his Palestinian subjects and the pro-Nasser subversion within his own kingdom was a constant threat to the stability of his rule, a threat which escalated to the point that by 1970 Hussein's control was almost completely shattered.

In September 1970 an attempt on Hussein's life rendered him a virtual prisoner within his palace. Armed confrontation became an absolute requirement. A short and bloody civil war ensued in which the army joined forces with the Jordanians loyal to the king and fought against the Palestinian guerillas. The result was a resounding victory for the king, firmly reestablishing him as ruler of his country, a victory which caused the loss of thousands of Palestinian lives and which is still annually commemorated by King Hussein's enemies as Black September.

With the Jordanian forces preoccupied with fighting the Palestinians, Syria decided to look to its own advantage. No fewer than 300 tanks crossed over the border into Jordan. Ostensibly the aim was to come to the aid of the Palestinians. Syria's real intention was to probe a possible takeover of Jordan and thereby to activate an old dream of a Greater Syria.

King Hussein had his back to the wall. In desperation he sought help from the Americans and Israelis. Nimble American diplomacy and the immediate response of Israelis conserved the status quo in the region. The Israelis dispatched tanks and massed troops on its Syrian border. The memory of the Six Day War was still freshly engraved on everyone's mind. Syria and her Russian backers withdrew.

CHAPTER 9

Jerusalem sits in the center of the country. Seven hills surround her. In a mythical sense she is for many the center of the world. On the eastern side of the city, the Judean hills drop into the desert and the Dead Sea – the lowest point on earth; to the west are the coastal plains and the modern towns of Israel; to the north – the Galilee, Lake Kinneret and the ancient cities of Bet She'an, Tiberias and Safed; to the south – Be'er Sheva, the Negev, and the Red Sea. The connection that Jerusalem has with its environs is physical, spiritual and historical. Four thousand years of history have left indelible marks on the fabric of this Holy City.

Throughout the ages conquerors have descended upon Jerusalem, City of Peace, spurred by the burning passion of their separate faiths – to pillage, to vanquish and to occupy. In each generation they destroyed what they found, and built on the ruins their own particular, and often emotional testament to Jerusalem.

One element common to all the conquerors, builders, and lovers of this city was the local stone. The physical city is one of ancient, pale stone gates, walls and arches that glow pink and gold when hit by the piercing sun and crystal-clear light of the Middle East. Naomi Shemer, the poetess who sang to her beloved "Jerusalem of gold, of copper and of light." It is a city built over thousands of years, hewn, layer upon layer, from the local stone, by a multitude of peoples – peoples from different continents, different races, different views, different religions, All have come and been captured by the spirit of Jerusalem, a city unique among the capitals of the world.

For four thousand years, Jerusalem has maintained its status as the central and sustaining focus of the Jewish religion. Thrice daily, religious Jews in all areas of the world face Jerusalem and pray:

"And to Jerusalem Thou shall return with compassion, and dwell within her as Thou has spoken; May Thou rebuild her soon in our days into an everlasting monument."

Our own story begins with King Herod who ruled for over thirty years under the authority of Rome during the period immediately before the Common Era, and who died, a sick and lonely man, in the year 4 B.C.E. Jerusalem is known by seventy names – all expressions of affection. In the Talmud it is written about Herod:

"He who has not seen the Temple rebuilt (by Herod) has never seen a beautiful building in his life."

Herod the Great is the earliest developer whose indelible imprint is still to be felt in and around Jerusalem. The Emperor Hadrian tried later to eradicate Herod's efforts. After decimating the city, he built a new one in its place.

Taher Jabari, who found the historic agreement and deposited it with his father, is cut in a mould very different from the conventional product of western civilization. Born and reared in a village outside the Palestinian town of Ramallah, he graduated from elementary school at the age of fourteen and went to work for his father, minding the family's sheep on the slopes of the Judean Hills.

By western standards he had little culture. He had never read the literature of Shakespeare, Tolstoy or Hemingway and had never heard of the artists Van Gogh, Rubens or Picasso. Taher had never been to a concert in his life and knew nothing of the music of Handel, Beethoven or Bach. He had rarely visited Jerusalem, which was the largest town he had ever seen. He had never been served by a waiter in a restaurant.

Taher was closest to his father. The menfolk worked for the family's survival; they earned the daily bread and took all important family decisions. The women in the family did local shopping, cooked the meals and took care of the house. When their menfolk talked business among themselves or with invited guests, the women would bring coffee and then retire to the kitchen.

Another factor of Beduin life that is difficult for a westerner to grasp is relative timelessness. In the Middle East, Arabs calculate time in terms of decades or even centuries. In trying to understand this facility for inordinate patience, we must come to grips with another Arab characteristic, arguably a virtue, that of limited curiosity. Taher combined all of these symptomatic traits.

Only when we can understand this strange and different temperament can we cope with the perplexing notion that the envelope enclosing the historic agreement was to be placed by the Jabaris in a bank deposit box and left there, unopened and unread, for some seventeen years.

CHAPTER 10

The Jabari family had lived in Palestine for nearly two thousand years. Their ancestors came from Edom, which was conquered by Hyrcanus, who forced their conversion to Judaism, along with all their compatriots. Thereafter, the Edomites became a part of the Jewish nation and their land a southern adjunct of the Hasmonean State.

King Herod's grandfather, Antipas, served as a ruler of Edom on behalf of his Hasmonean masters. Later, when King Herod himself ruled in Jerusalem, he surrounded himself with Edomite advisers and military officers whom he considered to be more loyal than the native Jews. He brought three thousand Edomites from their land in the South and settled them on the west side of the River Jordan.

King Herod ruled Judea from 37 to 4 B.C.E. As a newcomer and descendent of a family forced to convert, he was regarded by many Jews as an impostor to the throne. His mother was still looked upon as a Nabatean princess, and hence, a foreigner.

Herod inherited not only the wealth, the administrative ability, the military prowess and the cunning of his father, but also the belief that power lay with the protection of Rome.

Herod was a tyrant. He consolidated his early rule over Judea by executing forty-five members of the Sanhedrin, the Supreme Jewish Court of Law. In later years he executed his wife Mariamne, her brother, two of his own sons and many others, in his manic efforts to prevent insubordination within his household.

Like many dictators, he was a man of unusual charm, an able administrator and an outstanding developer. He was dubbed, in the ancient world, Herod the Great. His reign, while it undermined the authority of Jewish law and custom within the state, restored to Judea a period of economic stability and security.

To compensate for his inferior birth, Herod married Mariamne, the granddaughter of Hyrcanus, his father's patron, Hasmonean king and High Priest to the Jews.

Herod rebuilt the Second Temple, employing eleven thousand workers for nine long years on the Temple site. The result was acclaimed one of the most beautiful structures of the ancient world. In addition, Herod built many palaces and cities, both within and beyond the borders of the Jewish state.

He was able to outmaneuver political and military enemies for the duration of his reign – only to be vanquished, eventually, by the women and the sons within his own home.

Paranoia and mistrust ran rampant in his family. His mother-in-law, Alexandra, spent her time trying to protect her father and daughter, and wrest the rule from her son-in-law. Ultimately, it was Herod's discovery of Alexandra's machinations that led to his murder of Hyrcanus. Herod was so fearful for his throne that he began to suspect even his much beloved wife, Mariamne. When he left on a state visit to Rhodes, he gave orders that his wife and his mother-in-law be imprisoned and that, should he fail to return, they be executed in order to leave the kingdom to his brother. The task of guarding Mariamne and her mother was entrusted by Herod to his fellow Edomite, Sohemus, ancient ancestor of Amin and Taher Jabari.

Although endeavoring to remain faithful to his absent master, Taher's ancestor, Sohemus, quickly fell prey to the spells and machinations of Mariamne and Alexandra. The ladies realized that the fortress of Herodium, to which they were committed, was designed not for their security, but for their imprisonment. They realized they were not intended to survive the king, should any misfortune befall him.

The loneliness in the secluded palace, ten miles south of Jerusalem, brought the two royal ladies and Sohemus much into each other's company. The females flattered him and spoiled him with gifts. They dined and wined with him and won his affection and admiration.

Mariamne explained to Sohemus Herod's difficult position with Octavian, owing to his previous allegiance to Mark Antony, Octavian's arch-enemy. She reasoned that Herod's days might well be numbered and that if he were to succumb to the evil intentions of his enemies, government would be returned to the Hasmoneans with whom Alexandra and Mariamne wielded much influence. Sohemus responded: He revealed to the royal prisoners the instructions he had received from Herod.

It was clear to Mariamne that her position was unenviable. Proposing an alliance with Sohemus, she offered that in consideration for his new loyalty she would ensure his rapid advancement. If Herod triumphed with his new Roman masters, she would entreat her husband to promote Sohemus. If Herod would not survive she would canvass his successors.

Herod did indeed triumph with his new Roman lords and returned home in the highest of spirits. Mariamne kept her part of the bargain and sang the praises of Sohemus to the king, who made him a minister in his government. However, Mariamne could not forgive her husband his recent behavior in locking her away in Herodium. She refused to come to him when he desired her and she chided him for the many murders that he had orchestrated, particularly those of her brother and of her grandfather, Hyrcanus.

Relishing the deteriorating domestic affairs, Herod's sister conceived a wicked plot involving an alleged love potion that they claimed Mariamne had made for Herod. Looking for corroborating evidence, the king decided to interrogate his wife's eunuch, who could disclose nothing about a potion that Mariamne, in fact, had not known of. However, under torture, the poor eunuch did reveal the close relationship that had developed between the queen, her mother and Sohemus, their guard.

Herod had grown to appreciate the efforts of Sohemus in government and had believed in the man's loyalty. However, treachery in the realm had to be snuffed out. Sohemus, the Edomite and ancestor of Taher, was executed.

One hundred and thirty years after Herod's death the Roman Emperor Hadrian, in an effort to crush renewed Jewish nationalist feeling, fought a long, arduous war against the brave Bar Kochba and his army of zealots. Hadrian defeated the Jewish soldiers and razed Herod's Jerusalem to the ground. On the ruins he built a Roman city which he named after his own family: Aelia Capitolina. On the site of the grandiose Temple so magnificently built by King Herod, he erected a Roman temple to Jupiter. The rubble of what was once the magnificent retaining wall of Herod's Temple Mount was not cleared, but left as a silent witness of Rome's mighty conquest until the end of the Byzantine period (640 C.E.)

Jews were forbidden, on pain of death, to enter Aelia Capitolina, a ban which was to remain in effect for almost two hundred years, when it was only partially lifted. At that time Jews were allowed, once a year only, on the 9th day of Av, the anniversary of its destruction, to return to Jerusalem and to mourn for their Temple.

The national character of the Jewish People changed with the destruction of Jerusalem. The joyous dancing that had symbolized Temple worship ceased. Jews were now characterized by their mournful behavior, once a year, at the remains of the Temple's western wall, known to many as the "Wailing Wall."

The Caliph Omar captured Jerusalem six hundred and fifty years after Herod's death. He came with the zeal and industry of a convert to the new religion of Islam. Many local citizens followed his example and converted to the new religion. The descendants of the poor, lamented Sohemus, one time servant of Herod and minister in his government, were among those that converted to Islam.

As Herod had exploited Sohemus's usefulness some centuries earlier, so too did Omar use the energies and trust of Sohemus's descendants. Living in a city of constant change, this family, ancestors to Taher Jabari, was an unusual fixture of stability. Secure and resourceful, they were quickly advanced in the ranks of the new conquerors of Jerusalem.

The Omayyad Caliphs of the Islamic period, (640-1099 C.E.) restored part of the southern wall and, out of the ruins of Herod's Temple, on an area that extended beyond that of the Temple Mount, they constructed their own complex of religious and administrative buildings.

After the Caliphs came the Crusaders (1099-1291). They completely barricaded the southern access to the ancient Temple Mount, and built a city wall in front of it. What a change! To the detriment of both Muslims and Jews, who suffered from this change, the city returned from Muslim domination to Christianity. Throughout the period, the descendants of Sohemus that had converted to Islam in its earliest days stayed steadfastly loyal to their new religion.

The next great and lasting empire was the Ottoman Empire (1517-1918.) Under this regime, Jews were allowed to return to Jerusalem, but once again the entire area of the Temple Mount was transformed – this time, to meet the needs and the character of Islam.

The 19th century saw a burgeoning of Jewish life and culture in the Holy City – a second renaissance due, in part, to the efforts of the English Jewish stockbroker, statesman and philanthropist, Sir Moses Montefiore.

At the same time, European churches reinvested their interests – and assets – in the Holy Land. A period of rivalry and economic activity was generated by money sent by church members and investors to their dependents in Israel. The Eastern churches – in particular, the Greek

Orthodox Church – staked their claim to the holy sites, and to Jerusalem, the Holy City. In 1845, the Greek Orthodox patriarch moved his official residence from Constantinople to Jerusalem. There he initiated what was to become the consolidation of a property empire throughout the Holy Land, much of which is owned by the Greek Orthodox Church to this day.

Sir Moses Montefiore made many visits to the Holy Land, eager to fund projects that would lead to the economic independence of the Jewish community. He initiated several agricultural communities and started a printing press and a textile company. He was particularly eager to help the Jews of Jerusalem. He strongly believed that they must move beyond the walls of the Old City.

CHAPTER 11

In the last quarter of the nineteenth century, Abed Jabari, a local Muslim Arab, came to assist the French Consul in Jerusalem in his non-consular activities, which included particularly his work in the realm of archeology. Abed's ancestors had welcomed Suleiman the Magnificent and assisted him in his massive undertaking to rebuild Jerusalem's walls in the sixteenth century. Their ancestors in turn had cheered the return of Jerusalem to Islamic rule which Saladin had brought in the twelfth century.

Earlier generations of this family had contributed to the efforts of the sixth century Caliph Omar when he had conquered Jerusalem, and even centuries before that family members had ministered to Herod the Great.

The French Consul, Monsieur Clermont-Ganneau, subscribed to the notion that Jerusalem was the center of the world and acted as a magnet for numerous peoples of different persuasions, religious and ethnic backgrounds from many parts of the globe. The magnet of Jerusalem attracted the widest mixture of visitors. There were emigré Russians and other East Europeans, Moroccans and other North Africans, and immigrant Yemenites from their ancient country on the Red Sea.

Some poor Yemenites complained to the consul about the nefarious activities of a scoundrel who had established himself as a dealer in antiquities. The Yemenites had only recently arrived in Jerusalem and had no other party they could turn to; so they came to sing their sorry tale to the kindly Clermont-Ganneau, who found that he could indeed help these wretched people.

The story had all the ingredients of Ali Baba and the Forty Thieves. Some years earlier a young Hungarian Jew named Shapiro had converted to Christianity and arrived in Jerusalem to study his new religion in a Church seminary in the Old City. He quickly tired of this pursuit. In short order he married a German Lutheran deaconess and established a small shop to deal in antique ceramics and manuscripts. Outside the shop, the sign *ANTIQUARIAN* advertised his new profession.

The scoundrel antiquarian was astute and quick-witted. He set about making his fortune dealing in forgeries, some of which he manufactured or doctored himself. For a period Mr. Shapiro's forgeries were undiscovered. However, the Yemenite newcomers now came to tell that they had encountered Shapiro in their former home town, in Yemen, where Shapiro had stolen from their community one of their oldest and most valuable Torah scrolls.

The consul called Abed Jabari into the room and asked him to check out the story as best he could. M. Clermont-Ganneau was interested in the story for, in addition to his duties as consul, he followed assiduously the callings of his life-long hobby. He was a noted archeologist. Furthermore, the consul detested the errant Shapiro with whom he had crossed paths before.

The consul, an easy-going man of character, and his assistant Abed sat down in the consulate with the short, dark skinned Yemenite guests. The group listened to the tale of the Yemenites' leader.

"More than a year ago, a bearded man, purporting to be a rabbi from Jerusalem, visited our community in Sana'a. He stayed with us for some three months and tried to gain our confidence. We all treated the visitor as an honored guest, for we believed that he was a learned Jew from the Holy City, in the direction of which we prayed thrice each day. During this time we showed him our coveted Torah scrolls, some of which we have guarded since the Jewish dispersion after King Solomon. Nothing in the community was cherished more than these sacred scrolls and it was with enormous pride that we showed them to our learned guest.

"After he had gained our confidence, the rabbi tried to buy one of the finest of the scrolls, but we told him that no sum on earth would entice the Jews of Yemen to part with their heritage. For a while Shapiro persevered, but soon he realized that even his considerable charm, his abundance of cash and his tales of how the scrolls would enhance the City of Jerusalem would not secure their release from our care.

"We Yemenites have gained a reputation for stubbornness. And indeed in this situation our reputation was well earned, for despite the community's poverty, not a single member would consider any possibility of parting with our treasure. Seeing that his personal charms and his money would not secure his objective, Shapiro then decided on other tactics. He bribed Turkish army officers, for even Yemen is part of the Ottoman Empire, and they simply confiscated the scrolls.

"I will never forget the awful scene when a dozen armed soldiers stormed their way into our small synagogue while some two dozen members of the community were preparing for evening prayers. The soldiers had been well tutored and knew exactly where to find the scrolls. They marched through the prayer room and opened up the Ark. In front of their eyes were some eight scrolls, three of which were ancient and the others more recent additions. They didn't even ask which of the scrolls were the old ones. The non-Jewish Turkish officer, who had never before been in the synagogue, immediately plucked out the oldest and most valuable scroll, the one that the Jerusalem rabbi had been trying to buy. Taking it from the Ark, the officer turned on his heels and stalked out of the synagogue. The rape of our Ark had taken less than two minutes. And now, over a year later, we have seen this same man, Shapiro, the so-called rabbi, here in Jerusalem."

Abed Jabari, who had listened with the others to the tale, was instructed by the consul to find and follow Shapiro and try and detect the whereabouts of the scrolls. This was an assignment that he accepted with joy. The French consul, for his part, made attempts to find out whether the scrolls had been placed on the market.

Abed soon set up a schedule to spy on Shapiro's imposing house, built in one of the newer Jewish areas of West Jerusalem, outside the Old City walls. He also set up a watch outside Shapiro's shop on a narrow lane inside the Old City. But Shapiro himself was nowhere to be seen. Within a few days, both Abed and the consul had to report that the whereabouts of the scoundrel antiquarian were unknown.

Further inquiries were then instituted by Abed among the various members of the Shapiro family. Some years earlier, Shapiro's sister and her physician husband had come to Jerusalem in an attempt to save her brother from the ignominy of conversion to another faith. Unsuccessful in their mission, the physician and his wife nevertheless stayed in Jerusalem, where the husband had little difficulty in establishing himself as a family doctor. The wife and her errant brother kept in touch, notwithstanding Shapiro's resolve to stay converted.

Contact with the family was made through the sister's children, to whom Abed had previously been introduced. And thus it was that the young Muslim, working for the French consul furthered his investigations into the immigrant Jews. These investigations eventually revealed an amazing tale which, in due course, he came to reveal to his incredulous master.

"Mr. Shapiro is in London, where he is trying to sell the 'Temanite Scroll' to the British Museum. The antiquarian claims that the scroll dates back not to the

Solomonic period but to Aaron the High Priest and the earlier period in the wilderness."

While the French consul digested this information, Abed remembered another morsel: "And the price that he is asking is – one million dollars!"

Recovering his senses, the French consul said in chilling tones, "I have contacts at the British Museum. I will make inquiries and we will plan our next moves."

M. Clermont-Ganneau had excellent diplomatic contacts, for in that select community he was a man of good standing. Within a short while he had contacted the party at the museum that was dealing with Shapiro and had solicited a promise that negotiations would be delayed until the consul himself could get to London.

In the meantime, other avenues had revealed interesting information. The informer was a disgruntled former employee of Shapiro's. He had from time to time offered archeological finds to the consul. He now revealed that Shapiro had spent the past year "aging" the scrolls and that Shapiro was supremely confident he would be able to fool the experts at the British Museum. Indeed, he had journeyed to London with this goal as a challenge. He was going to wager his reputation on the results.

Shapiro's sacked worker bore a considerable grudge against his former boss. Once he had ascertained that the French consul was the best conduit for revenge, he set about providing the evidence to nail the victim. "I myself worked many hours for many months in the efforts to age the scroll. In addition to being unscrupulous, my old boss is very greedy. He therefore cut the scroll into three parts and has taken the first with him to London; the other two he has kept here in Jerusalem to sell at a later stage.

"Now the second and third parts have not been aged and are in exactly the same state that they were in Yemen, other than the fact that they have been separated. As you must be aware, the scrolls were written on parchment which comes in limited widths. There are usually some three or four sections written on each parchment sheet and the sheets are sewn together. The entire scroll, before being separated, consisted of approximately one hundred sections."

M. Clermont-Ganneau had gained a reputation for being an astute observer of people. While the story of the parchment sections was unfolding, he had kept two steps ahead and could foresee where it was leading. The Arab conspirator was just getting there: "Shapiro has taken the first part consisting of thirty sections. The very next section, in its original state, is in my possession."

The story was now revealed and all that was left was a matter of negotiation between the parties. The consul eventually parted with fifty pounds, and the promise of the same again if a mission to the British Museum was successful.

Armed with the sequential section of parchment and the detailed information gained from Shapiro's vengeful ex-employee, the French consul in Jerusalem travelled to London. There he assisted the museum experts in better understanding the scrolls. Hearing of these developments, the scoundrel Shapiro grew alarmed and fled to Rotterdam, where he committed suicide in a hotel bedroom when he heard that Scotland Yard was on his trail.

Back in Jerusalem there was an interesting side development. Abed Jabari continued to see Shapiro's sister's family, and particularly his Jewish niece Rosa, whom he eventually married at an inter-denominational ceremony attended by some Christian friends, the French consul and the grateful Yemenite Jews who had recovered their scrolls.

Previously Abed had lived in the Moslem quarter of the Old City and Rosa had lived with her parents in the new Jewish suburb of Nahlat Shiva. The mixed marriage of a Muslim and a Jewess was considered undesirable to both their communities, so the young couple left their familiar surroundings and went to live in the village of Silwan just beyond the Old City's Dung Gate.

Soon the Jabaris were to have two children, the firstborn a boy, followed by a girl within less than a year. The children were educated as Muslims, but the little girl grew up much influenced by her mother, who maintained many of her Jewish customs.

CHAPTER 12

The Ottoman Empire sank into decline. Jerusalem was drained of energy, initiative and direction.

In December 1917, toward the end of World War Two, the Turks surrendered to the British. General Allenby followed the example of the seventh century Caliph Omar. Dispensing with pomp and ceremony, he entered the Holy City, modestly, respectfully – on foot.

Allenby enjoyed a special sense of history. He had his soldiers encamp some distance from Jerusalem on the very spot on which King Richard the Lion-hearted, during the period of the Crusaders, had encamped nearly nine hundred years earlier. Richard the Lion-hearted had died without ever entering the Holy City.

Nevertheless Allenby may well have had more on his mind on entering Jerusalem than Caliph Omar and King Richard. Only a few weeks earlier, the British Government had unanimously endorsed the famous Balfour Declaration which, according to Lloyd George, the British Prime Minister at the time, had been granted out of political as well as religious considerations. Lloyd George considered the British to be under considerable debt to Dr. Chaim Weizmann, who invented and supplied the British war effort with wood-alcohol, essential for the production of cordite.

When Lloyd George had asked Dr. Weizmann, whom he considered his valued friend, how he could repay the favor, Weizmann had asked for the opportunity to plead, before the British Government, for a Jewish Homeland. Hence – the Balfour Declaration. Tradition has it that, as Allenby fought his way toward Jerusalem, Lloyd George was filled with a sense of prophecy concerning his commitment to the Jewish State.

The Arabs declared open war on any Jewish claim to Palestine, regardless of British presence in the area, and the Jews resented British control, British-set curfews, British restriction of Jewish immigration, and the so-called British *even-handedness* in their dealings between Arab and Jew. At no time were the British regarded by either camp as *even-handed*, at no time was British rule either "even" or easy.

Beyond the walls of the Old City, West Jerusalem began to prosper. New residential areas were developed, continuing the pattern set many years earlier by Sir Moses Montefiore. They stretched from Romema on the edge of the city, facing Tel Aviv, to Kiryat Moshe, Geula, Mekor Baruch, Rehavia, and on towards Talpyot to the south.

Slowly, inevitably, Jerusalem was transformed from a sleepy Turkish provincial outpost, to a city worthy of the title: Capital. A number of major public buildings were constructed, including the Central Post Office, the National Library, churches, the Vatican Pontifical Library and the adjoining, exquisitely beautiful home of the French Consulate. Meanwhile, inside the Old City, between 1938 and 1942 the Mosque of el-Aqsa was embellished with Italian marble pillars – a gift from Mussolini!

Throughout the years of the Mandate there was a Jewish majority in Israel, but the British appointed only Arab mayors in Jerusalem. Each mayor had a Jewish and a Christian deputy. The first mandatory census in 1922 recorded 34,000 Jews out of a population of 62,500. On the eve of the British withdrawal from Palestine, in 1947, the Jewish population had expanded to 97,000 out of a total Jerusalem population of 157,000.

Towards the end of the Mandate, the fabric of Jerusalem was under permanent strain, her people and buildings alike, blistered and bruised from constant explosions. In March 1948, members of the British Palestine police collaborated with Arab terrorists in blowing up the Palestine Post, the Jewish business center in Ben Yehuda Street, and the main Jewish Agency building.

Two months later, the Hurvah Synagogue which had towered, for more than a century over the Old City as a Jerusalem landmark and as a symbol of Jewish renaissance, was dynamited and completely destroyed. The Jewish underground retaliated by blowing up the south wing of the King David Hotel. The underground gave the British forty-five minutes warning to evacuate the building. Not only did the British refuse to evacuate, they also refused to allow any employees to leave the building.

Next – a Jewish convoy carrying nursing staff to the Hadassah Hospital on Mount Scopus was attacked and destroyed. Seventy eight nurses and doctors were killed within two hundred yards of a British police post – stationed there for the specific purpose of safeguarding the road.

With the end of the British Mandate and the creation of the State of Israel, Jerusalem became a divided city. The Old City remained under the jurisdiction of the Kingdom of Jordan; the western part of the city became the capital of Israel. Jerusalem's City Hall, tucked beside Barclay's Bank at the beginning of Jaffa Road, was the last building on the border of the divided city.

In the Armistice Treaty, drawn up between Jordan and the State of Israel after the Israeli War of Independence, Jordan pledged to respect the Jewish holy places and allow Jews to bury their dead in their traditional cemetery on the Mount of Olives.

The Jordanians reneged on their commitment. They plundered, ransacked and destroyed almost all of the synagogues in the Old City, vandalized the cemetery, removing many thousands of tombstones, some of which they used for the paving of pathways to latrines in a nearby military camp. The luxurious, five star Intercontinental Hotel, with its panoramic view of the eastern approach to the city walls, was placed directly over the Jewish cemetery. The road leading up to the hotel was carved out of the cemetery; graves were cut open; bones were scattered. Tombstones were used as building blocks.

Statehood for the Jews in 1948 meant housekeeping, and housekeeping entailed planning, moving – and an entire new flurry of major construction. The seat of government was transferred to Jerusalem, the new capital, along with government ministries and an ever expanding network of civil service offices.

In 1967, one result of the Six Day War was the reunification of Jerusalem. The most momentous decision, whether or not to tear down the walls that divided the city, was too much even for Mayor Kollek to handle alone. That decision was handed over to General Moshe Dayan as the one most likely to appreciate the historical and cultural significance of such a traumatic act.

For almost as long as history books have been in existence, Jerusalem has been like a powerful magnet to the wandering Jew in the far flung corners of the world, the diaspora. In ancient times the first and second dispersions were each followed by the return of the tired and homesick nation to its cradle. In medieval times Jews flocked to the Holy Land in desperate flight from religious persecution.

With the reunification of Jerusalem in 1967, pilgrims and tourists thronged, as in ancient times, to see the "Old City." They moved, unhampered, from the fast expanding, white-stone high-risers of modern Jerusalem, to the city of antiquity and timeless beauty: to the vaulted alleyways of Crusader times; to the narrow lanes and colorful bustle of the Arab shuk; to the silver and gold domes of the Temple Mount.

Chapter 13

For many years Egyptian President Gamal Abdul Nasser, had schemed the ultimate revenge against Israel for its participation in the 1956 Sinai Campaign. By early 1967 his preparations reached boiling point, his objectives had become obvious to all.

May '67: Nasser's plans escalated dramatically. He dismissed the United Nations Emergency Force that had been stationed (according to an agreement that had earlier been drawn up between the superpowers and Israel) both in the Sinai Desert and at the entrance to the Gulf of Aqaba. In their place he deployed 80,000 soldiers and 900 tanks. On May 22nd he imposed a blockade on the Gulf of Aqaba, cutting off the Red Sea – and with it both trade and oil supplies – from Israel.

Just in case his intentions were still unclear, Nasser made a major policy speech, adding, inter alia: "Taking over Sharm-el-Sheikh (the source of the blockade) means confrontation with Israel. Such action means that we are ready to enter war with Israel. It is not a separate operation. The battle will be a general one and our basic objective will be to destroy Israel.... Today, some eleven years after 1956, I say such things because I am confident." Nasser went on to talk of the help pledged to the Pan-Arab effort by Syria, Algeria and Kuwait. "This is Arab power," he concluded.

Until the last moment, the President of the United States, Lyndon Johnson, cautioned Israel against firing the first shot. Combining naivety and ineptitude, his administration attempted – but failed – to put together an international armada with which to break the sea blockade.

Israel could not hold out indefinitely. At the last moment an indecisive Israeli government and its worried Prime Minister, Levi Eshkol, realized that it could no longer hold its people at ransom. The damage that an Egyptian strike might inflict on the civilian population was too large a threat.

Historians agree that in over forty years of rule, King Hussein has made few serious mistakes. His first large-scale error, however, was made in 1967 when he ignored Israeli warnings. Instead, Hussein opted to believe Nasser's claim that, after only one day of fighting, he had already almost wiped out the Israeli air force. In reality the opposite was true and, in the space of only one hour, Israel destroyed Nasser's runways, downed two thirds of his 240 fighter planes and rendered his air force inoperable. Spurred on by Nasser's baseless boasts, Jordanian guns opened fire along the entire length of its border with Israel.

Moshe Dayan, the recently appointed Israeli minister of defense, was hard-pressed to accept Jordan's decision to enter the war.

Ordering his troops to hold their fire, he sent one last, urgent message via a United Nations envoy, warning Hussein to withdraw. But the king was set on his path of self-destruction.

Israel retaliated. Within the space of just a few days, Hussein suffered more casualties and lost more territory than any other of the Arab states that participated in the Six Day War. But of all, the most severe blow inflicted upon Jordan was its loss of Jerusalem, of the Temple Mount and the guardianship of Islam's third most sacred place – the el-Aqsa Mosque.

Four years before the Six Day War, David Ben-Gurion, Israel's first prime minister, had suddenly resigned the premiership, leaving a vacuum in the country's leadership and political instability within it.

At that time Ben Gurion, the aging statesman, had advised his socialist party to appoint Levi Eshkol prime minister in his place. Yet no sooner had Eshkol been appointed, than Ben Gurion started to criticize and undermine the authority of the new leader. To cap it all, he then completely abandoned his old party and, taking a number of his supporters with him, started a splinter faction.

Moshe Dayan, who had served as army chief of staff and subsequently as minister of agriculture in Ben Gurion's government, went into the political wilderness along with Ben Gurion, his mentor. Thus the eve of the Six Day War found Levi Eshkol in an unenviable position, at the helm of a convoluted coalition government, with Moshe Dayan and his errant friends sitting in off-field with the opposition.

With American pressure warning Israel to hold fire on one side, and with escalating Egyptian aggression on the other, Eshkol found himself in the embarrassing predicament of heading a cabinet riddled with indecision. Eshkol realized – Dayan simply had to be brought back.

In preliminary negotiations, Dayan at first wanted to be put in command of the Southern Front, the unit which would directly face the Egyptians, but General Yitzhak Rabin, who had succeeded him as chief of staff, objected to this arrangement. For his own part Rabin, who had long advocated a preemptive strike, was experiencing the symptoms of a nervous breakdown.

Levi Eshkol was a wise man who foresaw the kind of problems brought on by a complicated chain of command. He also realized that having Dayan back in the army was not going to ease his parliamentary problems. However, ever since the Sinai Campaign of 1956, Dayan's name had been a catchword synonymous with military triumph, and Eshkol wanted him placed where his contribution would be the most significant. Taking the bull by the horns, the incumbent prime minister offered Dayan the coveted position of minister of defense, subject to the condition that he and his political partners return to the government. Thus, only days before the outbreak of war, Dayan took charge.

Eshkol did not have to wait long for proof that he had made a wise decision. On the eve of the war Dayan made a much publicized broadcast in which he said: *"It is either too early or too late to go to war!"*

Hearing this pronouncement, President Nasser and the officers of the Egyptian armed forces relaxed.

July 7th 1967

Moshe Dayan sat in his office at the Ministry of Defense in Tel Aviv where the temperature on this mid-summer morning had reached a record forty degrees centigrade and the humidity had notched new highs. The air conditioning in the office could not combat these conditions and auxiliary fans had been acquired to help out. Yet with the noise, the wind factor and the papers flying spasmodically on and around his desk, it hardly seemed worth the effort.

In two hours time Dayan was expected to give his first detailed report on the unparallelled success of the Six Day War. In the South, the Israelis had captured the Suez Canal, taking the key towns of Sharm-el-Sheikh and Suez and leaving an ensnared Egyptian Third Army captive in the desert.

In the North the Syrian Army had been beaten back, up and over the Golan Heights. Fleeing in panic, they had been forced to run back and defend Damascus, only sixty miles behind the new lines. In the East, the Royal Jordanian Army had vacated the entire West Bank of the Jordan and had retreated to the east side of the Jordan River into the area that had originally constituted Transjordan.

All of these victories had followed the successful strategy of General Hod, Commander of Israel's Air Force, who had planned and executed the almost total ground annihilation of the Arab air forces.

Israeli intelligence was quick to recognize the massive Egyptian air force as a creature of habit. It had been observed to rise early each day and regularly patrol all borders, returning to base at 7 am, at which time the crews would leave their planes for breakfast. Consequently, at the outbreak of war, while the Egyptian crews sat comfortably at breakfast, the Israeli fighters wreaked havoc on the Egyptian runways, terminals and aircraft. The Egyptian air force, pride and joy – and major source of expenditure – of the Egyptian government, played no part in the Six Day War.

A similar fate befell the Russian-dominated Syrian air force and after a short pause the far smaller air force of the Jordanians. Thereafter, bereft of their own air support, the Arab armies quickly succumbed. Within six days the war was over.

The battle clash of greatest significance was the fight for the control of the Old City of Jerusalem. The pinnacle of that battle was the return of the Temple Mount to Jewish hands for the first time in nearly two millennia. General Motta Gur had dreamed for years of reuniting Jerusalem and returning Jewry's holiest places to its people.

On the second day of one of the world's shortest wars, General Narkiss looked down at the Old City from the recently captured vantage point on Mount Scopus. His immediate task was to brief his esteemed visitor, the popular Minister of Defense, General Moshe Dayan, on the deployment of his forces, the position of the supporting tanks and artillery, available vehicles and ammunition, and general logistics. When he completed the briefing, he asked for permission to reclaim for Israel the prize that lay tantalizingly beneath them. Dayan curtly refused with the astonishing reply, "Who needs that Vatican!"

However, Moshe Dayan was out of tune with the general public. Within just a few days it was clear even to the politicians that the people in Israel had a right to expect the capture of the Old City and the Jewish holy places within.

Just three days later, General Motta Gur marshalled two brigades on the hills of Scopus and Olives to the north and east of the Old City. Years earlier, as a young officer with somber eyes set in a round face that often glowed with a promise of friendship, he had entertained a partial vision of the future, a vision that had appeared in the fragment of a moment, in which he would one day lead an attack on the Old City and return the holy places to the Jewish People. For some years he had wrestled with that fugitive vision in an attempt to further comprehend its message. Now destiny had put him in command of troops that could turn the vision into reality. Driving ahead of his troops, he led his men to the Lions' Gate. Covered by supporting fire, he burst into the Old City and on to the Temple Mount.

A crash. A scream. A cry of "Over here!" and Yomtov, the slim dark-skinned Jew of Moroccan origin, rushed to intercept the Arab soldiers who swarmed their way back onto the concourse; twenty of them, forty of them, one hundred men swarming back over the ramparts. The British-trained officer in the Arab Legion never believed that such an attempt would be made. He now reviewed the evidence with dismay. "Protect the Mosque!" he barked to his legionnaires and soldiers converged suddenly from many sides, fighting the powerful Jewish invaders hand to hand; scores of local Arab defenders were slain and the fight for the Temple Mount was on.

The going was fast-paced and hideous. Young, suntanned Israeli attackers appeared in wave after wave at various gates that opened to the sacred Mount, and pushed their way inside. Among the attackers were counted several deeply religious men, some from yeshivot with their beards unshaven and fringes from the corners of their undershirts peeping uncompromisingly from under their uniforms. They were all inspired with their mission, linked in their single objective to regain the Temple Mount. On this day there would be no prisoners taken, for the mood of the attackers was grave with grim determination. The Temple Mount, an object of great awe and one that had always been unattainable, was now within their reach and touch. Destiny had led this bunch of men from many backgrounds to fight together and reclaim their prize. The Temple Mount would today be reclaimed for the Jewish People, to whom it belonged.

It was necessary to consolidate the strung out troops, and the general had picked Yomtov as his point man for good reason. The dour young officer was skilled as a scout and valiant as a fighter in close conditions. He knew Jerusalem, knew the terrain better than most of the attackers. He was also one of the few soldiers blessed with an animal sense of where an enemy might attempt to spring a sudden surprise or trap.

As General Gur whispered, "May G-d give them victory," these brave men launched their attacks against the defenders. Entering from the Lions' Gate at a dogtrot, Yomtov proved his skills, quickly organizing teams that fanned out in different directions. Within a few minutes the initial parts of the operation were achieved, with deft maneuvers and the apparent ability to be at one time with all of the units, Yomtov got his men relocated and well positioned. Reestablishing their dogtrot along the level concourse, the vitalized Jewish attackers pushed forward on all flanks, gaining a momentum which Yomtov believed was unstoppable. Even when the going became brutal, with Arab snipers firing at point blank range, the attackers never flinched. They pursued their objectives relentlessly, without protest. Many of these men had now been running for some hours, lugging with them their basic equipment, including a heavy automatic gun and many rounds of ammunition. Down from Mount Scopus they had run, across the valley in difficult terrain and up through the gates. Now they were running under heavy fire and would see some of their comrades fall by their sides. Gently, Yomtov would coax them forward, the killing must continue, the Mount must be taken.

Before dawn the defenders were vanquished, inexorably beaten back by Jews, whose innermost passions had been aroused to a point of intoxication. They shared a single wish – to reclaim their Mount, in the direction of which, prayers and psalms have been offered for thousands of years. By daybreak there were no more defenders moving forward to reverse the debacle of the night. No new assault would be made by the routed defenders of the sacred Mount, no fresh troops would converge on this unique hill, for the land was littered with the horrors of war, with the bodies that had been slaughtered in the bloody battle.

Towards morning the fighting was over, and the soldiers were conducting mopping up operations. One of the few remaining Arabs who had been left isolated on the roof of the smaller, silver domed mosque on the south side of the Mount drew a fine bead on Captain Yomtov, whose successful exploits he had been watching for some time. He pressed the trigger of his English Sten gun, a short ping could be heard among the relative quiet; Yomtov, a hero among heroes, slumped to the ground, blood gushing from his chest. Dashing to his side, his young soldiers were in time to hear his last words, "*Har Habayit Beyadenu.*"

The Wakf clergymen who had triumphantly maintained control over the Mount for so many years peered down in trepidation from the safety of their surrounding homes in the Old City and moaned, "Why has this tragedy overtaken us?"

To a great number of Israelis, the West Bank of the Jordan became known as the "liberated territories." At the end of the war Palestinians were taken with such surprise that they didn't even try to conceal their delight at the unexpected release from the Jordanian yoke. For years they had been saturated with negative Arab propaganda about Israel and its Jews who, they were assured, were soon to be conquered and thrown into the sea.

So great was the general euphoria, that hotels in East Jerusalem were soon catering to both Israeli Jews and those who were pouring into Jerusalem from other countries, all of whom were rushing to visit the sacred Jewish historical sites in Jerusalem, sites which had been closed to them for twenty years.

The stands in the Arab souk, the market that runs right through the Old City, were brimming with new produce, souvenirs and tourist items – many of which were directed solely toward the Jewish buyer. Arab and Jew set aside their differences, bartering with each other as they had done for centuries. Many years had passed by since these stalls had enjoyed such brisk trade. Euphoric Israelis descended upon them by the bus-load, buying almost anything, and carting it away.

Arabs from the West Bank of the Jordan wandered freely around the newly built up, western Jerusalem. Others drove on Israel's asphalt roads to the seaside towns of Tel Aviv, Netanya and Haifa. Many reunions took place between Jews and Arabs who had been neighbors and friends twenty years earlier. Old friends visited one another, trade between Arabs and Israelis began to mushroom and many of the old wounds were forgotten.

All of these matters would be included in Dayan's report to the cabinet, which would be asked to approve the operations of the civilian government that he had already established. For now the Israelis would rule a changed map and new demographic scene. But first Moshe Dayan waited for a call from the Director of Pathology at Abu Kabir, the Government pathology facility south of Tel Aviv.

Within two weeks of victory Dayan had sent two teams of soldiers into the area between Jerusalem and the point on the road where he and Jammal had left Yossi

Foux sixteen years earlier. Within a couple of days they had discovered the three shallow graves. The bodies had been sent to Abu Kabir to be studied by forensic pathologists. Dayan was waiting for the results.

The phone on Dayan's desk rang. Dayan pounced on the receiver. "Dr. Chaim Heitner on the line," announced his secretary from the outer office. "I'll put him right through."

Heitner had served with Dayan many years earlier and was pleased to be speaking with his old friend, now the celebrated Minister of Defense. "Shalom, Moshe," he began, a ring of anticipation in his voice. "Well, you certainly didn't give me a difficult case this time. Two of the bodies are Arabs and, by the most superficial glance at their clothes, we can safely assume were fedayeen. As for the third, under his shirt he wore his army disc. As you expected, its Yossi Foux, poor chap. No doubt about it."

"Thanks Chaim, I'm sorry that it has taken the death of a mutual friend to get us back together after all these years. But now we can at least ensure a proper burial, and ease the pain of his family. Do you know, to this day Ruth believes that Yossi is still alive and that one day he'll come home. She keeps her husband's clothes in the closet, just as they were the day he left the house."

"Yes," interjected Chaim, "I've kept in touch with his family and have been worried about Ruth for some time."

"Now tell me," asked Dayan "were any documents found?"

"No," replied the doctor, "following your orders, a detailed search at the site was made. The area around and inside the three graves revealed nothing. The bodies were brought to Abu Kabir prior to any search either inside pockets or anywhere else inside the clothes. All of these searches were, according to your explicit instructions, carried out by me, alone." Dr. Heitner, not a man to waste words unnecessarily, concluded with the brief words, "I'm afraid there were no documents."

"Excuse me for running now," said Dayan, "but I have a cabinet meeting in less than two hours and I want to drive around and break the news to Ruth and her children myself. My secretary has already warned them to expect me, I was just waiting for your confirmation."

Dayan replaced the receiver and charged down the stairs from his office to the car waiting for him below. On the drive through the streets of Tel Aviv, Dayan pondered the question that had been on his mind for so many years "What happened to Foux's copy of the Agreement?"

After some deliberation, Dayan decided to reveal to Prime Minister Eshkol the nature of the Ben Gurion mission to Abdullah so many years earlier. Although the document in question was still missing, he felt that it was appropriate, now that the territorial boundaries in the region had changed and the whole of Jerusalem was in Israeli hands, to inform the cabinet of the Agreement and of its implications. The cabinet would have to decide whether Israel should honor its side of the Agreement and refrain from assuming control of the Temple Mount.

The prime minister sat in the high-backed leather chair in his office at the back of the impressive Jewish Agency building in the Rehavia quarter of West Jerusalem. An uncharismatic leader, Eshkol had long mastered the art of compromise. He governed by consensus rather than by decisiveness, and yet, those who were close to him, had learned to respect his wisdom and the measured approach with which he faced issues. His political enemies, on the other hand, claimed that he was incapable of making clear-cut decisions: When offered a choice of tea or coffee, Eshkol would opt for a mixture of the two, ran the anecdote.

The weekly cabinet meeting was due to begin within the half-hour. Various ministers had already arrived and were discussing points to be raised. The principal item on the agenda was the first in-depth survey of the war and the immediate implications, as seen by the Minister of Defense.

The chief of staff and some of his senior officers were expected to attend the meeting, and to bring with them their newly drafted situation maps. The chief of police, whose department would be responsible for patrolling the new areas in Judea, Samaria, the Golan Heights and Gaza, was also expected. The inclusion of these military men in this kind of meeting represented a significant change in policy from that of Ben Gurion's cabinet, for the former prime minister had held that such meetings should only be attended by cabinet ministers. Other unusual invitees, expected to submit a report of their observations in the region, were the head of the Shabak, the secret service, and two of his senior aides, men who were already stationed and operating among the Palestinians in the new areas.

A buzz over the intercom reminded the prime minister of his promise to meet with Dayan before the meeting. The door opened and the minister of defense walked directly across the room towards his boss. Eshkol waved him to a seat and, pushing his own seat back from his desk, he leaned back and crossed his legs.

In a couple of sentences, Dayan related the entire story of his meeting sixteen years earlier with Abdullah, and of the Jordanian king's assassination shortly afterward. He completed the report with the account of the recently discovered body of Yossi Foux.

The prime minister did not interrupt his defense minister during his report but, from time to time, he leaned forward and jotted down some notes on a pad. When Dayan lapsed into silence, he turned to him. "We need some answers: First, what has happened to our copy of the Agreement? Second, how do we know that the Jordanian king has the other copy?"

Then, after the briefest pause: "We must decide on our own policies, both in the event that the Jordanians have a copy and in the event that they don't."

Dayan couldn't fault his PM's methodical approach. However, he had already formulated his own policy, and as events in the Old City of Jerusalem were escalating with a dynamism of their own, he was anxious not to allow a resolution to delay procedure any further. Dayan addressed his PM carefully: "You must be aware that I have been pondering over these questions for some time. Frankly, Jordan's participation in the war came as a surprise, and as a considerable disappointment to me personally. With their first rounds of ammunition, I began to doubt that the Agreement had survived the murder of Abdullah. To the present time I don't know the answer.

"I believe that if we were to formulate a policy, one that we would not publish, one which would guarantee that the Temple Mount be administered by Arab police and the Arab religious administration, we would be keeping our end of the bargain, a bargain which, in the long term, would pay dividends. We have two factors to take into account:

"One: We don't know how long we will maintain control of the West Bank.

"Two: Will we be able to keep a lid on the messianic dreams of our own politically active religious minority if we ourselves are in control of such a sensitive area?"

Eshkol was following his own thoughts: "In the light of Hussein's behavior in this last war, we no longer have to treat him with kid gloves." The prime minister brooded, silently a few minutes more, then: "Hussein has caused us considerable loss of life. Many of our finest young men fell in the Old City and in other areas against Jordanian forces."

Then, as though shaking himself free of some depression, he rose, and paced the room on the far side of his desk. Looking sheepishly at Dayan he said, "I hardly need to tell you that."

Eshkol paused, leaned forward and hunched over his cluttered table: "On the other hand, I have already had the heads of the British and French governments phoning me, complaining about our demolishing sections of the Old City. They are especially upset about our clearing the area in front of the Western Wall."

He chuckled: "In London they are sore at the beating we gave the British-trained Jordanian troops. The French are probably responding to squealing from the Vatican, who can't complain directly to us as they refuse to acknowledge our political existence in the area."

"Indeed," continued the PM, "one of the questions I intended to put to you at this cabinet meeting will be: How much more time do you need to complete your 'cosmetic' refurbishment of the Old City? And while we are on that subject, what can you tell me about the nonsensical rumor I have been hearing that the Old Man (Ben Gurion) wants us to tear down the walls and reunite the Old City with new Jerusalem?"

The two were interrupted by Eshkol's secretary: He had letters to sign, and the cabinet was assembled down the hall, waiting for him to start the meeting. The PM signed the letters, saying that he wouldn't keep his ministers waiting long. He returned to Dayan and the matter under discussion: "I hear what you say. You know that I have a great deal of respect for your judgment. Nevertheless I'd like to think this one over for a week, so please don't bring it up at today's meeting. I want to hear the opinions of our secret service. I suggest that after the meeting you should brief the head of the service, with a view to getting me some professional feedback within a few days."

The prime minister walked down the passage to the cabinet room followed by his minister of defense. There, they were greeted by their colleagues with a tumultuous welcome.

✧ ✧ ✧

After the cabinet meeting, Moshe Dayan asked the head of the secret service, whose surname was never released to the public, to stay behind. He was known simply as "M". After the last of the stragglers had departed, Dayan walked over and closed the large wooden doors. The two men sat alone in the spacious cabinet room. Moshe Dayan, who had a busy day ahead, came quickly to the point: "We found the body of Major Yossi Foux ten kilometers east of Jerusalem. He was probably killed on the evening of the 7th April 1951. Next to his body were found the bodies of two fedayeen whom he presumably killed before he himself was shot. That would suggest that there was a third terrorist, one that got away. I want you to find that man."

"You don't know for sure that there was another participant at the shoot-out?" asked M.

"No, not for certain. However, fedayeen usually travel in threes and the chances of a clean shoot-out where all the participants are killed – are rare; and then buried! My gut feeling is that another member shot Yossi and then ran back to his base – probably in one of the nearby refugee camps. In any case, that's all we have to go on. I need to talk to the missing fedayeen, as there is an important document missing from Yossi's belongings."

Within days of this short meeting, Israel secret service agents swarmed around the camps interrogating inmates and looking for records or clues. Sixteen years had passed and such a period represents a long time in a refugee camp where time stands still.

Eventually some older men sitting in the sand next to their mud huts in a camp near Jericho seemed to remember that three young men had left on a mission at that time. One came back, but stayed only briefly before moving on. Where had he gone? – they had no idea. What was his name? – they couldn't remember.

CHAPTER 14

Taher, now thirty four years old, and his father Amin Jabari, who had recently celebrated his sixtieth birthday, cut a striking pair as they booked their seats at the Ramallah taxi-station for their half-hour journey to Jerusalem. The father, dressed in the traditional Arab garb of his generation, wore a long grey jacket and black highly polished leather shoes. Taher was dressed in the costume of the younger generation: a colored sweater over a clean white shirt, flannels and sneakers.

Six months had elapsed since the Six Day War. Amin's kindly views of the Jews that governed the State of Israel had, in his opinion, been borne out by events. The Arabs of the West Bank enjoyed more freedom of movement now than they had enjoyed prior to the war. They were free to travel and conduct business anywhere in Israel. Israelis were seen regularly in the coffee houses of Arab towns and villages discussing plans, exchanging ideas with local Palestinians, eating humous together and drinking Turkish coffee.

Today the two Jabaris were making their first return trip in many years to the Hebron region, to see the land that had been in their family for generations. Their plan was to discuss the possible sale of some of their land to Jewish settlers, eager to build a community just one hill away from the burial site of their Patriarchs: Abraham, Isaac and Jacob.

Amin did not intend to discuss the possibility of a sale with any Arab other than his son. As he wished to avoid contact with the Hebron members of his family, from whom he had become estranged so many years ago, he had chosen a somewhat circuitous route, the first leg of which was the trip in an Arab taxi to East Jerusalem.

Over and over again, Amin Jabari mulled over the details of their route as they sat in the back of the taxi: They would walk over to West Jerusalem, crossing the old no-man's-land that lay opposite the Old City and immediately beyond the bullet-riddled building of Barclays Bank. From there, they would continue down to the old Palace Hotel, now used to house an Israeli ministry, and up Agron Street to the more recently built Kings Hotel on King George Street. There, at 11 a.m. they were to meet the young Israeli land-broker, Duddi Shimmel, who represented those Israelis that wanted to settle the land around Hebron. Duddi would take them in his car in the direction of Hebron, where they would meet their customers.

Amin marvelled at the reconstruction that had taken place in Jerusalem, at the beautiful Independence Park which they passed on their way up Agron Street, and even at the large, modern-looking supermarket at the top of the road. On an impulse, he tugged at Taher's hand and pulled him into the supermarket. They entered with the excitement and curiosity of tourists in a foreign country.

The glass doors slid away from them as they approached – a minor miracle for Amin. Inside, father and son stood in amazement, staring at the enormous sales-space divided by long banks of floor-to-ceiling shelves. Throngs of people were pushing metal carts, selecting boxed and bottled items at whim from the shelves and dropping them – carelessly – it seemed, into their carts.

Following the stream of customers, Amin selected a metal trolley for himself and pushed his way excitedly between two banks of shelves. His right side was flanked with hundreds of jam jars and different kinds of wine, while on his left there were endless boxes of cookies, breads, then pasta, macaroni and jars of spaghetti sauce. Taher joined in his father's new game, also relishing their new experience. Eventually the two returned their empty trolley to the stack at the entrance and, munching happily on two Israeli chocolate bars, they emerged back on the street through the magical glass doors. Crossing the traffic lights opposite Terra Sancta they met their young Israeli contact.

Conversation in the car was limited. Amin spoke only Arabic. Their Israeli host, Duddi, had been trying, desperately, for some time to learn Arabic but couldn't yet attempt a conversation. He had arranged to meet one of the settlers outside Hebron, a man who had been born in Syria and who spoke Arabic fluently. In the meantime, the three found little to say to each other.

Amin had decided to sell land to the Jewish settlers, despite the threat of the Hashemite Court that anyone caught selling land to the Israelis would be liable to the death sentence. For his part, Taher was extremely nervous about the arrangement, so much so that a day earlier, when he had first digested his father's intentions, he had left his father's house and gone for a long walk in the surrounding fields, to calm himself. He loved his father, he respected his father, but he knew that many Palestinians would simply not tolerate land sales to the Zionist enemy.

Of late, Taher had also been worrying about his father's health. Although Amin still cut a striking figure outwardly, he suffered, particularly at night from stomach pains. Taher's mother had told him that his father had recently felt a hard knot in his stomach, but that he refused to discuss it or visit a doctor. Now, however, sitting next to his father in the rear of the Israeli's car, Taher was conscious of his father's steady breathing and the gentle warmth of his body. He couldn't detect any signs of worry or pain on his father's face; on the contrary, he seemed right now to be at peace with the world, with nothing on his mind but the easy conclusion of the business at hand.

"Sala'am Aleikum," greeted them as they emerged from the car. The speaker was a black-bearded giant of a man standing one meter eighty tall. With one hand cradling a smouldering pipe at his mouth, the giant extended the other, first respectfully to Amin, and then to Taher. For some reason, as he looked into the open, weathered face of this stranger, Taher felt his hesitations melt away.

For Avraham Nissim exhibited no signs of hostility as he greeted Taher. On the contrary, as though reading his thoughts, he joked in Arabic: "And how have you been getting along with Duddi? Duddi's a 'yeke.' His family came here from Germany, so there's no chance that he will ever learn Arabic." A guffaw of good-natured laughter rolled off the man in a series of friendly waves infecting the others, even Duddi – the butt of the joke.

They spent the next hour and a half comparing area maps to the rough terrain over which they traipsed, looking for anything that might indicate the dividing borders between one property and the next. Avraham and the two other settlers who joined them had done their homework. They knew what to look for and understood how to work with these large-scale maps. By means of a rather complicated route, they had previously ascertained that the Jordanian Land-Tax Register had recorded the land under the name of Jabari.

They had also paid the local *mukhtar* quite handsomely. From him they had obtained a certificate testifying to the fact that no other party had ever registered a claim against the properties and that, to his knowledge, the land was owned solely by Amin Jabari. Such a record might have been considered dangerous for Amin and Taher, had it not been that this particular *mukhtar* had made countless such records available to Jewish buyers. The settlers had paid him so much money that they did not consider him a security problem.

One of the settlers was living in a caravan in a temporary compound not far from Amin's land. When they had completed the land-identification process, Avraham drove Amin and Taher in his jeep to the caravan, the others following in Duddi's car.

The settlers had set up camp on the brow of an arid, grassless knoll. A primitive water-tower supplied fifteen caravans that stood in three rows, crude stone slabs forming paths between them. The compound was surrounded by a barbed wire fence. The group approached and made for the single gate, manned by a young, bearded man with a large woollen skullcap on his head and a Talmud lying open on his lap.

"Shalom," the gate-keeper greeted Avraham. "If these men are your guests, they are welcome; Sala'am Aleikum," he concluded in Arabic.

Taher looked at the primitive conditions and was surprised to learn that the average small caravan housed a married couple with at least three children, often more. "Why do these Jews choose to live in such cramped and primitive conditions," he asked his father in Arabic, "when they can live near the nice supermarkets in their cities?"

"They have their own ideals, and time is on their side," answered Amin. "They want to build a mighty country, and they know that they have to start small. These people will grow strong under stark conditions, while others around them grow soft."

Coffee, Arab style, was served inside the caravan by Moshko, the settler who lived in the two tiny rooms with his wife and four small children. The children ranged in age from 1 to 8. The babies hung on to their mother's skirt, while the older ones were introduced to the visitors. Fruit had been sliced and prepared, and Israeli chocolate and home-made cakes were handed around.

Taher found himself relaxing, enjoying the warmth of this cramped home and the undemonstrative company of these strange, bearded men. It seemed curious to him that both the women that were present, though dressed modestly, with their hair, arms and legs well covered, sat down with them, ate with them, and participated quite freely in the conversation. One of them even knew some Arabic. Taher had been surprised, a moment ago, by the answer he had received from his father. Amin was usually tight-lipped and far from philosophical. But a bigger surprise was yet to come.

Amin Jabari recognized that Avraham was the leader and addressed him as such: "As a boy, I grew up in a small village on the side of a mountain south of Hebron."

Everyone in the caravan looked expectantly at Amin. He continued: "There were eight small houses in our part of the village. We and our neighbors tended sheep and goats. We made goat's cheese which we sold at the market in Hebron. Although a man may have several wives according to Muslim law, my father was one of a number of men in our part of the village who had only one."

Amin paused and sipped at his sweet, black coffee. "We lived a good life according to the laws of our Prophet. We were good Muslims. But, for some reason, each Friday night my mother would light two candles and place them near the window. When I stood at the window and looked out at the houses of our neighbors, I saw similar candles gleaming back at me in the windows of another three houses."

Amin took another sip of his drink. There was complete silence in the room. Everyone waited for him to continue. When he did, it seemed to be with a sense of relief: "I have not discussed this with any man since 1927, when we left the village following the earthquake that did much damage to this region. At that time my parents moved our home to Hebron and my father became a grain merchant. In Hebron my mother stopped lighting candles.

"When I asked my mother why she had lit candles in the village, she told me that the lighting of candles on Friday nights had been an old custom in her family, one which had been handed down from mother to daughter for many generations. She said that, as she had only sons, the custom would cease."

Amin had clearly completed his tale. He leaned upright against the hard, wooden back of his chair and finished his coffee. Wiping away the moisture that had accumulated on his forehead, he stuffed his large, white handkerchief back into his pocket. Everyone else, including his own son, who clearly had just heard this story for the first time, reflected on the implications of the story. None of the settlers said what they thought: that, according to Jewish law, Amin was probably Jewish.

In the car, on the way back to Jerusalem, Amin turned to Avraham who had joined the ride. "With the sale of this land to you Jews," he began, "I will be completing a cycle, started in a small village with my mother lighting candles, and continuing through the Hebron massacres which forced me to leave this region. I don't know how long I still have to live, but I feel good about what we are doing here."

And later when they arrived home, Amin told Taher: "After the land is sold, only one more step will remain to be taken. That, my son, I will leave to you. I'm referring to the document that you brought home nearly seventeen years ago. We still don't know what's written on those pages. It will be for you, Taher, to find out. You must do whatever you deem necessary with the information. I don't want to tell you how to deal with this matter; had I known myself, we would have dealt with it a long time ago. I don't want to place my trust in any of our Arab neighbors. For some time I thought of asking Mr. Shehadeh, my lawyer in Ramallah, but he is too much connected with Palestinian politics. You will have to find the way.

"Today, when we met Avraham, the tall Jew with the beard and the good humor, it occurred to me that perhaps we should seek his advice. But I caution you to get to know him better before placing your trust in him. Our suspicious natures have helped us survive for a long time.

"Today you heard more about your family's history. Once, while we were living in Hebron, a fine old Jew with a white beard and a large, black skullcap on his head, told me that, according to Jewish law, I might well be Jewish. I have never pursued the matter further because I am a believing Muslim, but when I am gone, you will have to choose your own way in life. I have every trust in you and your good judgment. May Allah bless you always."

That night, as he prepared for bed, Taher was much preoccupied with what had transpired that day, particularly with the revelations dating from his father's childhood. During the night he dreamed about his own future. The hazy figures of the settlers, and particularly that of Avraham, figured in the dream, in which he had moved to Jerusalem and married a Jewish girl. She dressed modestly and covered her hair. There was something melancholy about the girl, whose face he could not see clearly, had she been crying? – he could not quite make it out – but his impression was that she had come from a background of tears. There were also many candles, long white candles in silver candlesticks standing on a table next to a window.

When Taher awoke with a start in the middle of the night, the dream was freshly imprinted in his mind. Finding it difficult to get back to sleep, he rose from the bed and went to the kitchen for a cold drink. There he then sat for a while and thought about his future.

Although no longer a boy, he had never been tempted to take a wife and settle down. In this respect he was somewhat unusual; most of his boyhood friends had been married for many years, some had even taken more than one wife. He had never quite understood why he had not been interested in starting a family. His was relatively well off and his father would have been pleased to help set him up.

His thoughts centered on strange notions that perhaps he was destined to a process of radical change in direction. Being unadventurous and possibly even a little timid by nature, he was worried by these thoughts. Later, as he lay on his bed trying unsuccessfully to to get back to sleep, Taher reflected on his father's history and the developments in his life. He numbered off the links in the chain. The Friday night candles in the village; the attempt to stop the massacre of Jews so many years ago in Hebron; the finding and custodianship of the as yet unfathomed document from the dead Jew who had died a brutal death; the Six Day War followed by the return of control of Palestine to the Jewish State; and the selling of land to Jewish settlers. And now the dream, and the Jewish lady with a background of tears.

Two weeks after the visit with the Jewish settlers, Amin Jabari was admitted to the hospital in Ramallah, where a malignant growth was removed from his colon. The surgeon detected signs of secondary complications, and the oncologists decided to set him on a strong course of chemotherapy.

Taher chose a Jewish lawyer from Jerusalem to protect his interests in completing the land sale to the settlers. Taher was obliged to Avraham, for it was he who had introduced him to the lawyer. He had a comfortable feeling that the entire transaction was handled with scrupulous honesty.

Taher had been surprised when this lawyer, Rami Feffer, had recommended that he consult with Azziz Shehadeh, the prominent lawyer from Ramallah with offices in Jerusalem. Feffer explained that Shehadeh had been involved in many large land transactions involving Palestinians and that, despite Amin's earlier caution, Shehadeh was entirely trustworthy. Moreover, Shehadeh still maintained close contacts in Jordan and was able to effect changes in land registrations. Taher was a simple man, he was unused to business transactions, and had never dealt previously with either lawyers or Jews. Nevertheless, he felt confident that he was dealing with good and reliable people.

The many meetings that Taher had in Jerusalem at his lawyer's offices brought him, for the first time, into a regular working relationship with Jews. The interplay between the partners and their staff, particularly the female secretaries, opened a vista into a different world. Men and women had equal rights. The secretaries had minds of their own; they would sometimes offer their opinions and even argue their case.

In the suite of offices there was always great activity and bustle, with all the staff helping one another to get through the day's workload. Phones were always ringing, urgent telexes were arriving; registered letters were being delivered from the courts against signatured receipts. Tea and coffee were always on the boil and clients arriving without appointments were being taken care of by reception. The female employees joked with the clients and with the lawyers, and sometimes the lawyers and their clients joked about their secretaries.

At the outset of his relationship, the informality was strange to Taher, as the Arab offices that he had visited were more formal and even forbidding. However, the friendly atmosphere was infectious, and soon Taher was looking for excuses to visit his lawyer. When he came without an appointment, he would have to wait in the reception-cum-general office area where he was always made welcome. He would sit and chat with the secretaries who spoke frankly with him, even though it was clear they knew that he was an Arab.

One day when he was waiting to see Rami, two rather scruffy looking Arabs came into the office and asked in Arabic to see a lawyer. The secretary, a pleasant young lady called Tali, had difficulty understanding them. Taher offered his services as interpreter and Tali accepted with grace.

While translating from one party to the other, Taher had the feeling that both the Arabs and Tali looked at him as belonging to the Jewish side. The Arabs seemed to distance themselves from him as if he had opted out and changed his allegiance. Moreover, Tali related to him with warmth and friendship as if she, for her part, welcomed him to her faction.

Later that day, on his way by bus back to Ramallah, Taher reflected on the encounter; he thought about the Arabs and the barrier that had been formed between him and them. He thought about Tali, whom he had grown to like, and he felt a warm glow of happiness that today he had been on her side.

It was Rami Feffer who phoned through to his Arab colleague, Azziz Shehadeh, and made an appointment for Taher. On the day arranged, Taher went to meet the lawyer in his Ramallah office. One of the leading jurists of the West Bank, Shehadeh sat behind an old, wooden desk piled high with papers, empty coffee cups and overflowing ashtrays. The day was unusually fresh and the window overlooking the street was open, yet the room smelt slightly of mildew. The walls were lined with books and framed certificates, a large crack in the plaster ran the length of the wall between the book-cases, and a water-machine bubbled noisily in the corner of the room. The lawyer waved at Taher to take a seat.

With the dexterity of one who is personally familiar with every paper in his possession, Shehadeh inched his fingers under the papers on his desk, unearthed a wooden humidor from the pile, withdrew from it a fresh cigar, groped around again and found a large packet of matches. A middle-aged stocky man of medium height, the lawyer sat back and started to puff, contriving to look at once both efficient and friendly.

The Arab lawyer had started his career in the service of his father, who ran a political weekly newspaper allied to the Nashashibi Party. The paper represented a moderate faction of Palestinians, who were ideologically opposed to the Mufti Haji Amin el-Husseini and his policies of violence and intrigue.

Years earlier, Shehadeh had given a much publicized demonstration of his own broad political views, with his brilliant defense of one of the Husseinis, tried and convicted for the assassination of King Abdullah. The case had brought him under the public spotlight and, among other advantages, both the political respect and the personal friendship of King Hussein.

Despite that friendship, in 1954 the young lawyer had challenged the Hashemite Court, charging that it had rigged the Jordanian elections. Such a charge, from so prominent a West Bank jurist, could not go unchallenged. General Glubb, whose passion in the defense of anything Jordanian knew no bounds, issued a warrant for Shehadeh's arrest. At the time of the summons, the lawyer was overseas, where he was forced to stay for two years, until the Jordanian Chief of Staff left, sacked, in his turn, by King Hussein. Only then did Shehadeh dare to return to Ramallah.

In the years that had passed since that time, Shehadeh had flirted with politics, supporting a civil rights movement that had been started by his son. He advocated a plebiscite among Palestinians, to decide whether the West Bank should be joined with Jordan or be declared an independent state. He also advocated a moderate policy, which favored direct negotiations between Palestinians and Israelis, negotiations based on the mutual recognition of each other's rights.

Shehadeh's inquiring mind and balanced views had earned him a reputation for moderation in the few months that had passed since the Six Day War. Top Israeli politicians, senior members of the Israeli bar, Israeli journalists, and Israeli citizens whose politics ranked anywhere from left to center of the political spectrum, all came to sound him out. They believed that Shehadeh, a Christian Arab with years of practical political experience in the region and with a deep, intimate knowledge of Arab and Palestinian history, would be able to point a finger in the direction of compromise, an arrangement that might one day be acceptable to many, if not all the parties.

The Palestinian lawyer's clientele included some of the major foreign churches, he himself being an Anglican. Among his Jewish friends were celebrated Israeli politicians such as Teddy Kollek and Moshe Dayan.

Taher was not aware of any of this as he waited for the lawyer to clear his desk and turn his attention to his own issue. Among the many things on the lawyer's desk was a stack of books, six in all, each of which had the word JERUSALEM embossed, in gold letters, on its cover. For some years now, Taher had set himself the arduous task of teaching himself how to read. Of all the words that he had mastered, ones such as *Hebron, Ramallah,* and *Jerusalem* were, at present, the most engraved on his mind, for they were the words that he looked for on road signposts. They were the words that told him where he was going as he travelled from lawyer to lawyer in his seat at the back of the bus. The six books marked *Jerusalem* stood out as the only orderly series on the desk.

"I see that you have several books on Jerusalem; is that a subject particularly dear to you?" asked Taher.

The lawyer was still trying to collect his thoughts after his previous meeting. He took a couple more puffs at his cigar and addressed himself to the young stranger before him. He had had one or two dealings with Taher's father in the past, but had found him taciturn. He hadn't been able to discern whether Amin was wary of him or just plain introverted.

"You know," answered the lawyer in the measured tone that had become his trademark, "if your father were sitting here in your place, he would never have asked that question. And do you know why? Because he would not believe that I would give him an honest answer."

Taher looked at the lawyer, a sheepish smile plastered to his face. "Perhaps I've had an easier life than my father. My father moved to these parts some thirty-seven years ago, yet I don't know that he ever fully adjusted."

"Yes. Now I remember," replied the lawyer. "He came from Hebron; let's see, he must have left after the 1929 riots."

Taher felt a sudden urgency to explain his father to this stranger. "That's possibly the reason he never felt at home in this area," he said with emotion. "You see, there were no riots in Hebron, there was a massacre. And my father found it hard to live with the shame."

Taher had caught the lawyer's interest: This Arab is a shepherd, probably doesn't even know how to read or write more than his name, yet he thinks for himself and is willing to voice his opinions. Shehadeh puffed some more at his cigar, emitting clouds of foul smoke into the room. "I think that I'll enjoy having you as a client. I didn't mean to belittle your father in any way, sorry if my choice of words was unfortunate. Your father's right, of course, it was a shameful massacre – a blot on our history.

"But to return to your question. Yes, I have always been interested in Jerusalem. I have been using these books here to study the past hundred years or so of its political history, since the time that the Turks opened up the Holy City to western influences. I have been asked to talk on the subject at a meeting with one of the leading Israeli politicians."

Chewing on his cigar, he laughed and added, "No doubt he'll remind me that history didn't start with the Turks." The lawyer Shehadeh looked at his watch, he had a busy day ahead, and in the evening he was invited to Jerusalem, to a dinner party with Moshe Dayan.

Despite the many appointments he had had that day, by 8 p.m. Shehadeh had managed to shower and change into fresh clothes which, according to his wife, were free of cigar smells. He drove an American car with Jerusalem number plates, so he had little difficulty on the road and was flagged, smoothly through two checkposts on the route to Jerusalem. He arrived ahead of his hosts, within only forty minutes of leaving his house.

The dinner party was to take place at the Shemesh Restaurant on Ben Yehuda Street, famous for its special Shemesh steaks and warm ambiance. Shehadeh was recognized as he walked through the door. Yeheskel Shemesh, the proprietor, Jerusalem's veteran restaurateur, came running over to him from the open bar at the rear of the room, massaging his hands together and bobbing his head up and down like a pigeon in the mating-season, out of the sheer glee of having an Arab celebrity in his establishment. Taking him by the elbow, he drew him excitedly into the room at the rear, reserved for special guests. There he opened a bottle of cognac without waiting for the others to arrive.

"We have been informed by security," the restaurateur whispered conspiratorially, "that Dayan will arrive within ten minutes. He will enter through that side door over there." Shemesh pointed to a door that opened on to a small side alley, perfectly designed for such mysterious, high security customers.

Shemesh, one of the best informed men in Jerusalem, didn't discriminate between the famous, the wealthy and the pretenders. He entertained them with the same ease and measure of confidentiality, regardless of whether their political bent was to the right or the left, whether they were G-d fearing or secular, Jew, Arab or Christian. He talked to all with the ease and freedom of the perfect host. So it was that Shehadeh and Shemesh sat at their specially set table in the privacy of the back room, sipped their cognac and talked. By the time Dayan and his entourage arrived, Yeheskel Shemesh had added some nice, tradeable tidbits of information to his own collection.

The meal was good, hot and spicy: Silver tureens were borne in with great gusto, laden with Shemesh's famous rare steaks, steaming mounds of rice and shanks of lamb; a mixed grill of beef and veal, salads of eggplant and beans, sweet-and-sour greens and hot peppers, to be washed down with sweet liquors, dates, nuts and sunflower seeds; and – best of all – the sticky, sweet bakhlava, especially ordered in for their party, as the favorite confection of the Arab lawyer.

When the clutter of salad plates and the messy remains of the charred pitta were finally cleared from the table, the Minister of Defense indulged in one last swig of the red Cabernet wine and addressed his Arab friend: "Well Azziz, you have had plenty of time to prepare your brief. We're all looking forward to hearing your legal opinion on the status of Jerusalem."

With them at the table were Dayan's political secretary and a senior civil servant from the prime minister's office, Meir Peled. Peled held a watching brief over Jerusalem and served as the liaison between the prime minister and the newly established Jerusalem Ministerial Committee.

The four guests were interrupted only by the waiters as they cleared away the messy dishes and brought in second rounds of aromatic coffee and sweet liquors. Shemesh had withdrawn to the main dining-room at the very beginning of the meal and was now happily chatting both with his regular customers and with those first time tourists that arrived each evening at his establishment on the recommendation of their hotels.

With one hand Shehadeh groped in his jacket pocket for a fresh cigar, with the other he leaned across the table and shot an ashtray back in his own direction. He took his time snipping off the tip of the cigar and setting it alight, for he enjoyed the process. Then he sat back and spoke: "My brief, Moshe, will be the political position of Jerusalem over the past 140 years. My starting point will be the year 1830, by which time Jerusalem had already been under Ottoman rule for over three hundred years.

"At that time, as you know, the great Turkish Empire was already showing signs of strain, and the demography of Jerusalem was changing. This was the first time in hundreds of years that Jews outnumbered other ethnic groups in the Holy City by a significant number, and, what is more, it took only a couple of decades before the Jewish population in the city became an absolute majority. It was with this in mind, that the Turks issued a number of new firmans, Ottoman laws, which allowed foreigners to return to Jerusalem and reclaim property that had been in their families for generations, and laws which encouraged people of diverse religions to exercise their religious rights in their various holy places."

"Were they trying to prevent the Jews from realizing their democratic rights as a majority?" asked Dayan.

"They might well have been, although there is no written evidence of such intentions."

Shehadeh obviously loved lecturing. By now he was in full swing. "In 1852 the Turkish firman actually itemized specific properties, and specified the particular rights, duties and powers given to each of the various churches. The most significant of these properties was the Church of the Holy Sepulchre, which nearly all the churches claimed as their own."

Shehadeh waited for the waiter to pour him some more coffee. He took a sip, adjusted his seat so that he could stretch his legs out under the table, and continued: "Now, to understand what was happening, you must remember that during the twenty years prior to the introduction of this innovative firman, several churches had established their headquarters in Jerusalem. Prominent among them was the Eastern Orthodox Church, whose patriarchs actually took up residence in the Holy City. These churches then received the backing of their home governments which consolidated the connection even further by establishing consulates in Jerusalem.

"The result of all this activity was that by 1852 Jerusalem had a Jewish majority, an oppressive Muslim minority and – incredibly – a revived and burgeoning

Christian life. In addition, it now had an aggressive diplomatic community meddling in both communal and civil affairs. By means of their respective consulates, countries such as England, the U.S.A., France and Russia were for the first time staking their claims to the Holy City.

Shehadeh took another break. He relit the shaggy butt of his cigar, sipped his wine and continued, his audience hanging on his every word: "Now I know that in Israel politicians talk about 'preserving the status quo' when they are trying to prevent the religious from forcing their dogma on secular life or, more specifically, when there is talk about opening up new bus routes on the Sabbath."

Dayan and Peled exchanged glances; the lawyer continued: "The concept of a religious status quo, used so glibly by today's media, in fact comes from the 1852 firman. The phrase was first used in 1852. The Turks meted out privileges to the various churches and announced that the resulting state of affairs would be considered the 'status quo.'"

"And what about the Jews," asked Dayan, "what allocation did we get?"

"They were not even mentioned," answered the Arab lawyer. "The Jews had to await the British Mandate, over eighty years later, until their claims to the Western Wall and to places such as Rachel's Tomb near Bethlehem were incorporated into the list of the status quo. But we're jumping ahead. Let's return to the mid-19th century."

Shehadeh cleared his throat with a glass of water and puffed thoughtfully at his cigar. Dayan studied his Arab friend. He had always known him to be an innovative and efficient lawyer, but had never been lucky enough to hear him lecture. He was impressed by the lawyer's knowledge, his wit, and the interest that he generated as he talked. Shehadeh was Dayan's "dark horse" on the West Bank. Both were keen to foster a relationship of mutual respect and understanding.

"The other religous group that was short-changed in the status quo were the Catholics whose Church failed to follow the rush of the patriarchs to Jerusalem. They claimed that participation would accord de facto recognition of the Jewish majority and this would violate Roman doctrine. For their pains, they received a mere one-nineteeenth share in the control of the Church of the Holy Sepulchre, far less than had been given to the Armenians, the Greeks, the Syrians and the Copts, each of whose Churches were insignificant in comparison to the mighty Catholic Church."

"A perfect example of 'no allocation without representation'" quipped Dayan wryly.

The men laughed a little and relaxed for a while. A few more puffs, a few more sips. Shehadeh uncrossed his legs and continued.

"The Europeans came into their own and encroached upon the Ottoman fiefdom during the second half of the 19th century. The Treaty of Paris in 1856 and the Congress of Berlin in 1878 both ratified the 1852 Turkish firman – in particular the concept of the status quo.

"Now – and here's the rub. In 1917 the British government, headed by Lloyd George, was indebted to Caim Weizmann for his help during the war effort. Consequently, they agreed to issue the famous (or infamous, depending whose side you're on) Balfour Declaration. As you well know, the Declaration did not refer at all to Jerusalem."

Shehadeh shifted himself again to a more comfortable position, waiting for this piece of information to take affect. It was clear that the men present had never considered it of any consequence that Jerusalem was not mentioned in the Balfour Declaration.

"And now I'll tell you something even more amazing: According to the British Mandate, the bylaws of which stipulate the exact terms and responsibilities of the British in Palestine, there is no mention, whatsoever, of Jerusalem."

"That is not possible," Dayan exploded, "I mean it simply couldn't be."

Shehadeh held his silence.

"Are you absolutely sure?" pressed the defense minister.

"I assure you," replied the lawyer finally, a low chuckle testifying to the success of his story, "that I come fully briefed."

"So how do you explain it?" defied Dayan.

"Quite simply: Most of the churches, together with the mother countries that supported them, were keen to maintain the status quo. The lack of inclusion of Jerusalem in the terms of the Mandate was no mistake. Jerusalem was quite deliberately left out. Thus, from the mid-19th century the Jews of the Holy City were effectively disenfrachised by the international community, despite the fact that they comprised the majority of the population."

"That is – until the establishment of the State of Israel," inserted Meir Peled.

"No sir! I repeat, no sir!" the lawyer barked at the other men. Quite suddenly the lawyer had changed. No longer sipping at his wine, or puffing at his cigar, he faced his audience eye to eye, his chin thrust defiantly into the ball of his hands with his elbows aggressively on the table.

To the relief of everyone, Shemesh appeared, asking how the meal had been and whether they wanted anything more. Two more bottles of red wine were ordered with yet another platter of bakhlava, and a truce was tacitly agreed to by all.

Shehadeh stood up and said that he needed to stretch himself and use the facilities. "I've eaten too much of your Jewish food, drunk too much of your Jewish wine, and talked too much about your Jewish history," he grumbled honestly.

Dayan and his companions sat in silence until Shehadeh returned from the bathroom. He seemed to be feeling better. Without further ado he took his seat and resumed his lecture.

"As I have said, there is no mention of Jerusalem in the Mandate. However, mention is made of the holy places. Stipulation is made that the status quo be maintained with two provisos: the first, that freedom of access and worship be ensured; the second, that the requirements of public order and decorum be guaranteed.

"The Mandate required that Great Britain, in association with the League of Nations, set up a commission in order to study and define the various claims to the holy places. In fact, Great Britain and the League of Nations were never able to agree on the terms of their brief, so the commission was never established.

"Britain was determined not to be outsmarted by the Europeans, whom they saw as the source of the problem. Hence they then passed a law in their own Parliament, which removed the question of the holy places from the courts, and placed it directly into the hands of the British High Commissioner.

"The result of these maneuvers was that within just a couple of years of receiving its Mandate over Palestine (in which Jerusalem was not mentioned), the British took control of the holy places. And, what is more, in order to seal their jurisdiction, they established Jerusalem as the residence of their High Commissioner.

"With a hundred years of imperial rule as their guide, the British then set about putting into practice their nifty little policy of 'Divide and Rule.' In short order, the Hashemites were banished to an area east of the Jordan River. The ten-year jail sentence of Haji Amin el Husseini was reprieved, and he was brought back to be made Mufti of Jerusalem. The Jews were told to be patient. Throughout the period of the British Mandate the Jews had an absolute majority in Jerusalem, yet the

British never appointed a Jewish mayor. Instead they appointed a Muslim mayor with two deputies: one Jew and one Christian.

"In 1947, when the British Mandate was running out, your friends from that cold and wet island prepared a farewell gift: the Partition Plan. Fortunately for you, it was rejected by all your Arab neighbors. In it the British proposed that newly defined Jerusalem remain independent, autonomous, demilitarized and neutral.

"A special international police unit would supervise all the holy places, and a governor, to be appointed by the United Nations, would have total control. Let us take the municipality as an example. The municipal officers were to be elected by the local residents, i.e., by the Jews who were in the majority, yet if the governor did not approve of the laws that they passed, he could simply have them rescinded.

"Oh – and before I forget! The area of Jerusalem was to cover more than you and I would think. According to the Partition Plan, it was to include the Tomb of Rachel and Bethlehem to the south, and Ein Karem to the west. Very simply: Jerusalem was being tailored to take account of Christian interests, just as the Turkish 'status quo' had done one hundred years earlier."

Moshe Dayan sat impassively, pretending not to register his interest in this last point.

"And now come the funnies, as the Yanks would say. In 1949 the Israeli Knesset approved a resolution which decreed that Jerusalem be, for all time, the capital, and an inseparable part of the State of Israel. Within a few months, King Abdullah of Jordan formally annexed both the West Bank and Jerusalem. Not one single state ever approved Israel's resolution. The Jordanian annexation was approved by two countries: Pakistan and Great Britain. But the British went one step further. They refused to accept Jerusalem as part of the kingdom of Jordan, maintaining that the Holy City was international property.

"Apparently, the British view is still upheld by the majority of the member states of the United Nations. During the 19 years of Jordanian rule in East Jerusalem, many countries maintained two consulates, one in the eastern part of the city and one in the western. Neither section would apply to the central government for permission to operate, as each believed that it was functioning in a divided but international city.

"Now, of course, in the wake of the Six Day War and the reunification of Jerusalem, we have a new situation. Immediately following the war, your Prime Minister Eshkol assured all the Church leaders that he would maintain the status quo. To prove that you were serious, he then passed a Preservation of the Holy Places Law, which guarantees protection and freedom of access.

"And yet again – I say: here's the rub. When the *Ne'emanei Har Habayit*, that group of Jews, faithful to their Temple, want to go up and pray on the Temple Mount, they are denied access by the Wakf police. So what do they do? They sue: and your own Israeli Supreme Court reverts back to Mandate times and recognizes the authority of the Wakf police, whose job it is to guard against any breach of law and order.

"Recently, at the United Nations, US Ambassador Goldberg stated that according to the US view, Israel is merely in provisional control of the city, and that the future of the city would be decided by negotiation.

"And that, my friends, brings me to the end of my brief." Azziz Shehadeh leaned well back in his chair, took out a new cigar, refilled his glass and lapsed into silence.

"Interesting," mused the defense minister, "the British released me from jail in order that I be available to fight their wars, and they released Haji Amin so that he could serve them as mufti. They might well have given us the Balfour Declaration in order to prevent the Jews from taking Jerusalem. There is one area that you have not addressed," added Dayan thoughtfully. "From time to time the Jordanians tell us of their historic role in respect to the Holy Places. What exactly is the basis of their claims?"

"I'm not sure that I know the answer to that, but I'll try and answer you, anyway." Shehadeh was obviously feeling much more relaxed. He rummaged for a moment among some papers in his attache case, pulled out a relatively thin file and continued: "As you know, Emir Faisal signed an agreement with Chaim Weizmann in London in January 1919. Article Vl of that agreement states simply: *The Mohammedan holy places shall be under Mohammedan control.* The Hashemites consider themselves to be the direct descendants of Mohammed. In their view, they are the genuine Mohammedans, which should explain Article Vl."

"It seems a reasonable answer to me," said Dayan. "Why your hesitation?"

"Because, at the time of the establishment of the Hashemite kingdom, the British denied the Jordanians any such license. Then, in 1922, when the League of Nations formally ratified the establishment of Jordan under the terms of the British Mandate, they accepted the British proposal – and I quote: *That Transjordan should be exempted from all clauses in the Mandate providing for a special regime in the holy places.*

"Thus, whatever original intentions Faisal might have had in 1919, when representing his family in Hedjaz, the British managed to expunge them just three years later, by means of the Charter for Transjordan. Of course, today's Hashemites might claim that it was the 19th century 'status quo' which accorded their family the custodianship of the holy places of Islam. But you are not likely to find many other Muslims who will agree with them on that."

Following his meeting with Shehadeh, Moshe Dayan returned by car to Tel Aviv, where he had early morning appointments scheduled for the following day. Sitting alone in the rear seat of his large American car, Moshe Dayan pondered the information from his Arab friend.

Shortly, he would have to apply the final touches to his overall plan for greater Jerusalem and then put it into operation. He had talked over the plan with the prime minister, Levi Eshkol, who had agreed to the plan in general but had insisted on overruling him on the question of Rachel's Tomb, which Eshkol wanted included in Greater Jerusalem and which Dayan wanted excluded. At the time, Dayan had wondered at Eshkol's interest and had put it down to his Polish Jewish origins. Now, reflecting on Shehadeh's statement that Rachel's Tomb and even Bethehem had been included in the 1947 British concept of a Greater and International Jerusalem, Dayan wondered if his canny prime minister was basing his insistence on precedent.

At all events, Dayan had made up his mind. He would defy his prime minister and exclude Rachel's Tomb from the Jerusalem equation. After all, this reasoning was consistent with his decision on the Temple Mount, which he would turn over to the Moslem Wakf. The larger picture, Dayan reasoned, was the massive rebuilding of Jerusalem with numerous annexed suburbs around its circumference. These would secure its future as the capital of Israel, not places of worship which would be challenged by other religions. Also, by excluding these places when his own popularity was at its highest, he would defuse arguments in the future by messianic and fanatic religionists. In eventually agreeing to peace with its Arab neighbors, Moshe Dayan couldn't see how Jewish sovereignty over the Temple Mount and Rachel's Tomb would assist the Israelis. Yes, he would follow his instincts and defy his prime minister.

✧   ✧   ✧

CHAPTER 15

Jammal lived in Aqaba with his sons and their families. Life was good for all of them. The fishing business was prospering and the cannery that they had started at Jammal's suggestion had succeeded almost from the first day.

Like many Arab extended families, they lived together in a multi-apartment house. The boys, for that is how Jammal referred to them, were happily married and each year one or two babies were added. Altogether Jammal was glad that King Hussein had dispensed with his services.

"My personal relationship," he would tell his sons, during their regular discussions on Jordan and its king, "was with his grandfather. With the young king, I had a double generation gap. His decision to send me away was good both for him and for me. It may have hurt my pride a little, at the time, but in reality it demonstrated the king's maturity."

Nasser and Ziyad were his favorite grandsons. Jammal sat for hours playing with them and telling them stories of the late King Abdullah, of his palaces, of his fondness for the desert, for the oasis and for the late king's trusted friends, the Beduins.

Jammal's approach to the document that he had removed from the murdered body of the late king, that tragic day in Jerusalem, was in perfect accord with his general rule of conduct. He had never opened the envelope, nor did he have any idea as to its contents. He had taken it simply because he didn't want anything that was clearly important to his mentor to fall into the wrong hands.

As the years went by, Jammal thought less and less about the letter, stored in a cupboard under his shirts. None of the members of his family knew of its existence. With the war between Jordan and Israel, however, Jammal changed. Within a few days of the onset of hostilities, Hussein lost the West Bank of the Jordan, an area which had been captured in 1948 by Abdullah with British approval.

Perhaps as a consequence of this, Jammal started to think again about the envelope, tucked upstairs, beneath his shirts. He began to wonder whether he was not shirking his duty to his late king, by keeping the document hidden.

Moshe Dayan was the only living person, other than himself, who had been present at that fateful meeting, so many years ago. Now that the war was here, the newspapers were filled with articles about the Israeli defense minister, and Jammal found himself thinking more and more of his previous connection with him. Jammal saw how the Israeli's popularity had swelled to that of national war hero. Perhaps the old paper upstairs represented some long-term agreement between his own dead king and this prominent Israeli.

In December 1967 King Hussein, his brother Prince Hassan, and a party of their friends took up residence in Aqaba, at the king's winter palace. Jammal still recalled several of the palace staff from the days of his own employment there. So it was, that after only a short period of hesitation, the retired Arab courtier put a call through to the most senior of his contacts and petitioned for an audience with King Hussein.

On the appointed day, the king rose early and, noting that the sailing conditions were particularly favorable, decided to devote the larger part of his day to his favorite water sport. He quickly ran through the day's meetings with his secretary and delegated appointments to the senior members of his staff. When Jammal arrived at the palace, he was ushered into a room and received, not by the king, but by an officiating senior aide.

Without the slightest exhibition of rancor or peevishness, Jammal apologized for wasting the aide's time. Simply but firmly, he explained that his mission to the king was on behalf of the late King Abdullah and could not be conducted by means of an intermediary. Having said that, he stood up and left the palace.

On the evening of that same day, after Hussein had returned from his day of sailing, had bathed, refreshed himself with a light meal and good company, his aide told him about his unusually brief meeting with Jammal. The aide described Jammal's gentle, dignified manner in a way that made the king nostalgic for his youth, for those rough, clumsy days that had characterized the early days of his rule.

The king advised his aide that he wished to see Jammal, and the following day a messenger was sent to bring Jammal to Hussein. This time it was Jammal's turn to be out at sea, busy on the fishing boats with his sons. Only late in the afternoon, with the vivid sky fading at his back, did he come trudging up from the water in his high rubber boots, his knitted hat pulled tight around his head.

He did not allow the news that Hussein had summoned him to spoil his day, however, for he relished the quiet hours of dusk. Instead, he savored the sensations of the sea – the rough boat, the desperate struggle with the freshly caught fish and the smells of the changing early evening air – to slip gently from him as he bathed and changed. After all, he was a fisherman now, not a courtier. Only when he was completely dressed in fresh, white linen, did he ring the palace.

King Hussein was intrigued to find out about Jammal's new way of life. He remembered having dismissed the old retainer years earlier, but he was unaware that he had relocated to Aqaba. During the day his secretary had done some checking and had reminded him that Jammal had always been considered a loyal, faithful and hard working servant to the late Abdullah. When Jammal phoned, a car was immediately dispatched from the palace to pick him up.

Instead of the usual green license plates, the brown Mercedes had the red markings, the distinctive gold crown and a simple number 3 embossed on the front. Rumbling slowly into Jammal's modest suburb, some two miles north of the king's residence, the royal car caused quite a stir.

Children crowded around the car in wide-eyed wonder, calling to others to come see, and vying with each other as to who got to stroke the smooth, brown sides of the purring limousine. Such magic happens only in fairy tales. Here was magic that on the instant transformed Jammal from a friendly neighbor to a superstar.

King Hussein and his younger brother, Crown Prince Hassan, were waiting for Jammal on the grand terrace overlooking the bay. The terrace was suspended over the magnificent garden: a velvet lawn, studded with subtropical plants. Deep exotic flowers hung heavy-headed – scarlet, orange, purple and white – over a lake of silver stillness and gleaming water-lilies, emitting a delicious, hypnotic aroma into the fast-falling darkness of the night.

Jammal passed between two rows of electrically-lit palm trees, climbed the steps that led up to the terrace and bowed deeply to his king. Hussein extended his hand. The crown prince did the same. Drinks appeared. The three men sank into deeply-cushioned reclining chairs, and Jammal began his tale.

"And to this day Jammal, you have never read the contents of the letter?" queried the king, when Jammal finished speaking.

"No, Your Majesty," answered Jammal, "I have always considered the letter the private property of my late master, your grandfather. If he had wanted me to know its contents he would have told me. My aim in taking the letter was merely to prevent it from falling into the wrong hands. It was no more for me to read than it was for the enemies of my beloved master."

Relieved to detect sympathy in the eyes and demeanor of the royal brothers, he continued: "Since the recent war and the border changes, I have begun to have second thoughts about my secrecy. Hence, I have decided to present you with the envelope. Yours is the inheritance. Yours is the legacy. Yours is the burden of decision."

Jammal put his hand into his inside jacket pocket and withdrew a plain, white, sealed envelope, embossed on the back with a red and gold crest. He handed it to the king. Without another word, Hussein broke the seal.

Motioning to his brother to read over his shoulder, the king and his brother read the Agreement that had been signed by their late grandfather, Ben Gurion and Moshe Dayan. When they had read it through to the end, the king took the letter over to a couch at the farther end of the terrace, where he sat and carefully read it again. Meanwhile, Crown Prince Hassan thanked Jammal for his loyalty, and asked him to recall the trip that he had taken so many years ago to Kalia. He asked him also about his subsequent journey with Yossi Foux and the one that he had taken later with Moshe Dayan. Later that evening, after dinner, Jammal sat with his sons in the living room that was the common sitting area for all the members of their extended family. Until late into the night he talked to them about the warm reception that he had received at the palace, about the beauty of the surroundings, and about the impression that the two royal brothers had made on him. On his knees sat his favorite grandsons, Nasser and Ziyad.

"And what were the contents of the letter?" asked his elder son.

"It is an extremely important document. Of historical significance. And it's extremely lucky that I suddenly remembered to take it out of its mothballs. I don't know what I was thinking of to keep it hidden all these years. The document was an agreement between King Abdullah and the State of Israel, according to which the control of the Islamic holy places was given, for all time, to the Hashemites. My trip to the palace today was history in the making."

Jammal's hardworking fishermen-sons and his two grandsons beamed with pride at the head of their family.

✧ ✧ ✧

The following day, after the royal brothers had reflected well over all five clauses of the Agreement, they met again in private. Both intelligent, honorable men, they had always enjoyed a perfect understanding. Both functioned at their best when working together, free of outside interference.

It was now only six months after the Six Day War, a war in which Jordan had suffered deep humiliation. The kingdom was still in the first stages of its recovery.

More than any other Arab state, Jordan had paid heavily for its participation in the war. Syria had lost the largely uninhabited Golan Heights which overlooked the Sea of Galilee; Egypt had forfeited the uninhabited area of the Sinai Desert; but Jordan had lost the entire West Bank of its river. In the process, it had lost its control over Jerusalem and the holy places of Islam.

To make matters worse, Jordan was still riddled with seditious Palestinians. Over the years, increasing numbers of them had crossed the River Jordan and taken root on the East Bank. It was they who posed a continuous threat to the Hashemite rule. It was just possible that, with the document now in their possession, the two brothers held a solution to their problems.

"Has there ever been any indication that the Israelis are in possession of their copy of this Agreement?" asked Hassan.

"How would we know?" answered Hussein. "Until yesterday we ourselves knew nothing of the Agreement. Jammal has said that he left the Israeli major on the Jerusalem road. He said that grandfather Abdullah later learned that the Israeli had never returned to Israel. According to Jammal, it was grandfather's belief that the Israeli government had never gained possession of their copy."

Hussein sighed and paced up and down their private sitting-room for a few moments, before clearing his throat and giving his summary: "The time is not ripe for us to make overtures to the Israelis, direct or otherwise. Meanwhile, we can only thank Allah that the Israelis have not assumed control of the Temple Mount, and that they have left Islam's holy places in the hands of the Wakf, the Muslim custodians. I don't believe that this is due to an oversight on the part of the Israelis. We can only assume that they have decided to honor the Agreement regardless of whether or not they have it in their possession."

"I read things in the same light," answered Hassan. "For the time being we have no choice but to bide our time."

That meeting had taken place in 1967.

By 1973 the situation had not changed: The control of the Islamic holy places, indeed of the entire Temple Mount, was firmly vested in the hands of the local Muslim Wakf. What is more amazing is that those Jews who wished to gain access to the Mount had to obtain permission from the Muslim guards stationed at the mosque.

This time, when Sadat and Assad joined forces against Israel in preparation for the Yom Kippur War, Hussein was careful to lose his invitation to join them.

Book 2

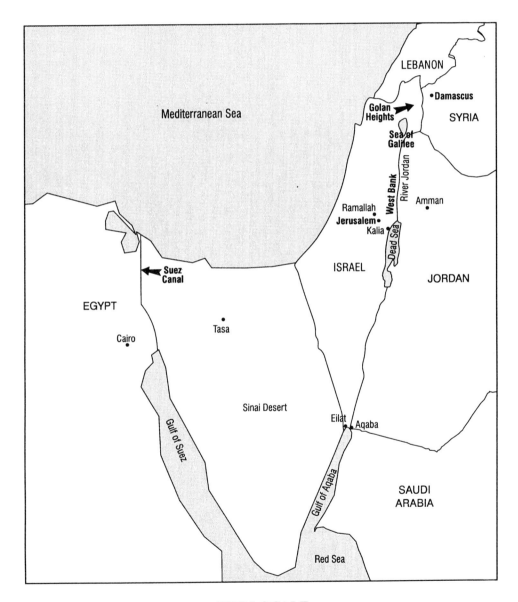

THE LOCALE
Showing the principal places
referred to in the narrative

CHAPTER 16

The Yom Kippur War of '73 was the result of years of failed, multi-lateral negotiations, negotiations in which Egypt had engaged at the same time as it had prepared its army for war.

Nasser made his objective perfectly plain: The complete removal of Israeli forces from his Sinai territory, whether by diplomatic means or by force. Never was a message so obvious.

In an interview in '69, Nasser claimed: "the enemy will not withdraw unless we force him to, by war. Indeed, there can be no hope of any political solution, unless the enemy realizes that we are capable of forcing him to retreat through fighting."

In May '70, however, Nasser did indicate that were Israel to withdraw from the Sinai, Egypt would recognize the State of Israel. Unfortunately, Golda Meir, Prime Minister of Israel at that time, failed to grasp this first opportunity for negotiation. Six months later, Nasser died and Anwar Sadat became President.

Within months, a second opportunity for settlement with Egypt was missed by Golda Meir, when Sadat sent the editor of Newsweek with an offer of peace and recognition. Golda's response was, "That will be the day, I don't believe it will happen."

From that time onward, Israel lived under constant threat.

As part of their war preparedness, Egyptian generals were made answerable for four probabilities: that Israel was superior technically, had higher standards of training, was guaranteed US supplies, and was superior in the air.

In the wake of the September '70 and July '71 operations, in which Jordan had ousted the Palestinians from its borders, Jordan found itself blacklisted by the rest of the Arab world. This situation became harder for Hussein to tolerate when Wasfi Tel, the Jordanian prime minister and his own personal friend, was assassinated by Palestinians in Cairo. Sadat, the new Egyptian president, refused to prosecute the murderers.

Hussein hinted at the possibility of a separate peace pact with Israel with some sort of Federation between the West Bank and Jordan, one which would come into effect after an Israeli evacuation of the West Bank.

If this was bluster on the part of Hussein, it was successful. Egypt and Syria, together with some Arab states that did not directly border on Israel, decided to break their deadlock with Jordan. The possibility of separate talks with Israel simply could not be tolerated, as it would break the united Arab front. Jordan was brought in from the cold.

In the light of these inter-Arab politics, Israeli politicians and military experts concluded that it would be a while before the Arab world was ready to launch a war of any sophistication.

In Washington, Israel's Foreign Minister, Abba Eban, met with US Secretary of State Henry Kissinger on the eve of the war. Each assured the other that the possibility of war ran counter to their intelligence sources. The Israeli establishment believed that Sadat would bluster, that he would advance to the brink of war and withdraw.

What the Israelis failed to recognize was that Sadat had adopted a fatalistic attitude. More disturbing, he had initiated an ingenious system of disinformation which, as 1973 progressed, was managing to confound the traditionally smug Israeli military minds more and more. General Elazar, Israel's Chief of Staff, recognized signs of war on the part of Egypt and Syria. At his insistence in May, Defense Minister Dayan issued a directive ordering the General Staff to prepare for hostilities.

September 25th.

King Hussein makes a brief secret visit to Golda Meir in Israel. Though he claims ignorance as to the exact date, he warns her that an attack by both Syria and Egypt is imminent. The head of the Jordanian desk at the Israeli Ministry of Defense duly passes the information on to the respective heads of the Egyptian and Syrian departments. To no avail: He is reprimanded for his pains and accused, by his superiors, of spreading panic.

By the beginning of October, numerous intelligence reports are being processed, all of which indicate the heavy build-up of both troops and armor in Syria and along the Suez Canal.

October 3rd.

These reports are detailed at a two hour meeting of Golda's famous "kitchen cabinet." When challenged directly, the chief of intelligence responds with an affirmative "Yes!" The Arabs are capable of launching an attack from their present positions.

Once again Golda Meir, this time together with her minister of defense, misreads the situation. What is more, they fail to react appropriately to the messages that are coming, loud and clear from their own generals.

Yom Kippur, the most sacred day in the Jewish calendar.

Yom Kippur morning. 4 am.

Israeli chief of intelligence receives a call: Israel will be attacked at 6 pm. The chief of staff is informed. Within the hour he demands full mobilization and a preemptive air strike against Syria.

In the light of everything that had gone before, the chief of staff is reluctant to entrust his brief into the hands of his minister of defense. He therefore insists on a meeting with both the prime minister and General Dayan. Yet in Golda's office at 8 am that morning, the prime minister again heeds Dayan, rather than him.

In deference to her chief of staff, she agrees to the limited mobilization of 100,000 men, but she absolutely refuses to hear about a preemptive air strike. At her own initiative, Golda Meir then calls in the American ambassador and offers him her personal assurance that there will be no preemptive strike. Her magnanimity proves to be very costly.

2.05 pm.

Israel is attacked simultaneously by the separate armies of Egypt and Syria. The hour chosen for attack is a compromise. The Egyptians had wanted to launch their attack in the evening, with the setting sun blinding the eyes of their enemy along the Suez Canal. For their part, the Syrians wanted to commence hostilities in the morning, when the sun, rising in the east, would be directly in the eyes of the Israelis, defending from the west. The compromise works to the disadvantage of both aggressors.

The majority of the Israeli population spends Yom Kippur fasting and praying in the synagogues, trusting that *The Guardian of Israel* will protect them. The dual attack by the Syrian and the Egyptian armies is devastating. Within two days the advancing enemies both to the north and to the south penetrate deeply into territory that had been taken by Israel in '67.

The first three stars – indicating that the day of rest had given way to a week of secular concerns – came on suddenly and silently in a cloud-free sky. Fifteen men, their sons at their sides, muttered their way comfortably through the evening prayers, bringing the Sabbath to its conclusion. The outer world had passed from the shy paleness of early dusk to full blush, as the sun fell behind the mountains, to the deep acceptance of night. During the period of twilight, between day and night, these men had learned, eaten, prayed and sung together in the makeshift synagogue in their settlement. Still humming gently to himself, Avraham Nissim tucked his prayer shawl back into its embroidered bag, his wife's wedding gift, and walked home to his family.

Avraham Nissim adhered to the admonition *Ein hachana mikodesh lechol* – one must make no preparations on a Sabbath for the secular week ahead. Yet now that the Sabbath had come to an end, he had to make many arrangements before leaving for reserve duty on the Golan Heights.

"*Shavua Tov Ayelet, Shavua Tov,*" – May you have a good week, called Avraham, as he walked from the front door into their modest living room. Ayelet was feeding the children in the kitchen. Aware that he was under pressure that evening, she called back, "the candle, wine and spices are on the dining table, I'll be in for *havdala* in two minutes."

Avraham Nissim approached the table. Carefully, he filled the wine cup until it spilled over into its small silver saucer, silent expression of his prayer that the week brim over with good tidings. "May it be for a blessing for all of Israel." he whispered under his breath.

Ayelet came in from the kitchen, the baby perched high on her protruding stomach, egg still caked to his chin. Michael, their three year-old, made a dash toward his father, jumped into his arms and hung around his neck in anticipation of their little ceremony. They lit the colorful, braided candle, cupping the baby's hands so that he should see the transition from light to shadow, from sacred to profane. They passed the ornate silver spice-box from one to the other, allowing little Michael to open it and dip his nose deep inside. Laughing as the baby emptied its contents, they scrambled to pick up the pieces of clove, bay leaves and cinnamon from the floor. Together they sang the beautiful melody and extinguished the flame in the saucer of wine.

Only after they had eaten and put the two children to bed did Avraham take down his army clothes and boots from storage. Ayelet looked over the shirts and army pants, took down her sewing kit and rapidly added a few stitches to the beginning of a tear on one of the pockets. She examined the heavy-duty army socks and looked around for warm underwear and gloves.

"There's no need to make such a fuss about it," objected Avraham, "I'm not going to the Arctic. It's still summer."

"The Golan is colder than Jerusalem and the weather can change – *keheref ayin* – like in the blink of an eye."

"Nonsense," protested Avraham good-naturedly, "where I'm going, the weather is just like in Jerusalem. I'll boil like a chicken in the Sabbath soup, in those clothes."

It was no use. Avraham might be the one to take the clothes out of storage, but Ayelet was definitely in charge of what he took with him when he walked out through the door.

Avraham turned his attentions to the issues that were really preoccupying him. First he had to call three substitute teachers, to make sure that his students didn't suffer as a result of his reserve duties. He dialled the first number. No answer. Yossi had probably gone to his in-laws for the Sabbath, he thought.

The second number was answered by Shlomo's wife. "No, Shlomo has not yet returned from synagogue," she said, "but rest assured he knows the schedule and will take your classes as promised."

The third call was answered on the third ring by his friend Yisrael Averbach. "I have a problem myself," said Yisrael. "On Friday I received surprise call-up papers from my unit. Tomorrow I'll phone the liaison office and find out what it's all about. I had hoped that it was a mistake as I've already served thirty days this year, but several friends in synagogue today told me that they too had been served with call-up papers."

Avraham was nervous. He had also heard rumors of a large scale call-up. What was more, although he hadn't told Ayelet for fear of causing alarm, he already knew of at least three of their close friends who had received phone calls from their units.

"Yisrael, you must help me out," said Avraham. "I know that you are also under pressure, but I have to report in Tiberias by 4 pm tomorrow and I have the tightest morning imaginable. Ayelet is in her sixth month and I have to take her to the doctor – and I don't want to leave Jerusalem without getting a *Bracha* – a blessing – from the Kadosh. Can I leave it to you either to take the class or to find a replacement?"

"How can I refuse you when you put it like that?" answered his friend easily. "Under the circumstances, I also wouldn't leave without a blessing."

Later that evening he managed to make contact with the third colleague. Yes, he had spent the Sabbath with his in-laws. "No," he laughed, "I haven't received call-up papers. I'll be happy to take the classes as promised. Have a good rest in the Golan and come back safe. Oh – and if Ayelet needs anything while you are gone she just has to phone us. Orit and I will lend a hand."

Avraham was able to sleep easy, happy that his classes would continue undisturbed and that Ayelet would be taken care of by his many good friends.

The next day Avraham rose, as always, before dawn. He didn't switch on the light, for he enjoyed watching as the sky paled beyond the window, moving slowly into their tiny kitchen. In the still dim light he washed, made himself a cup of coffee, and laid his books open on the kitchen table. His day had begun: First an hour of learning on his own; then a learning session with his friends; and then morning prayers. Only today he would be leaving the comfort of his family for the Spartan barrenness of army life.

Six hours later, he had taken care of his banking arrangements, had sat in on an important meeting with his lawyer, and had taken his wife to see the gynecologist at the Hadassah Hospital clinic in Ein Kerem, some thirty minutes south west of Jerusalem.

As he didn't think it safe for Ayelet to drive alone through the West Bank, Avraham had arranged for their next-door neighbors, Menahem and Shoshana, to meet them in Jerusalem. From there the three of them would drive home together in his car.

Sure enough, Menahem and Shoshana met them on time, Menahem looking somewhat bored and utterly out of his element, and Shoshana, thrilled to pieces, chattering away a mile a minute about the crowded streets and the terrible drivers, and how she had almost been knocked over by a bus. She was loaded down with bulging shopping bags – bargains from the big city. Her youngest child, though ignored, was whining at her skirts. With considerable relief, Menahem opened the door of the car. His wife rolled inside, tucked herself, her child and her shopping into the back seat, and dropped out of Avraham's consciousness. Avraham then hugged his wife and kissed the baby and, taking his kitbag, strode off in the direction of the Mahanei Yehudah Market for his meeting with the Kadosh.

Although he did not have that much time, he took the longer, more circuitous route to his Rebbe. He needed the time to clear his mind of clutter, to reach a state, if not of spirituality, then at least of calm, before reaching his mentor.

There is a concept in Jewish thought of *halacha le ma'ase* – of putting theoretical concepts into practice. Avraham, whose Jewish life was rich and heartfelt, tried to adhere to this notion wherever possible. Accordingly, when he had learned, years earlier, in *Sayings of the Fathers* that one must appoint for oneself a mentor, he had diligently set about looking for a worthy rabbi to fulfill this role.

The Kadosh – the Holy Man – the only name by which Avraham's rabbi was known, quickly became the answer to all of his spiritual needs. His most perfect role model. Avraham had experienced no difficulties in becoming his disciple.

In one of the poor areas of Jerusalem, the Kadosh lived in a two-room basement apartment. It was squeezed beneath a small synagogue and a talmudic seminary, situated behind the vegetable market. As Avraham approached the narrow, stall-lined alley leading to his destination, he thought with pride of the differences that exist between the life-style of the Kadosh and that of the Hassidic Rabbis. It was this difference that made his own mentor so special and so appealing.

The Hassidic leader – known as the Rebbe – is the patriarch of his dynasty. He usually epitomizes a combination of mysticism, charisma and supreme religious authority. The *hassid* – the Rebbe's supplicant – believes in him, admires him and follows his directives without question.

The hassid recognizes an all-pervasive radiance in the demeanor of his Rebbe. It is a spiritual illumination, a richness of soul, granted him by means of his mystical union with G-D. For the hassid, the Rebbe functions as confessor, practical adviser and moral instructor; in times of stress he is also miracle-worker and healer.

Most hassidic Rebbes are links in a dynastic chain, and much of their spiritual power is attributed to *zchut avot*, the merits of their ancestors. Many of the hassidim (plural of hassid) are also linked to the dynasty by means of family allegiance. A Sassover hassid, for example, will normally be one whose grandfather came from the town of Sassov, and who adheres to the dynasty that emanated from there.

When a hassid participates at a wedding, visits his Rebbe at the time of the High Holy Days, or attends any other great event, he is in fact making a pilgrimage. He is returning to the court of his dynasty. He is undergoing an act of unification with his brotherhood. In those gatherings, all the hassidim unite around their sage and draw from his spiritual well. For according to hassidism, the Rebbe is considered a link between heaven and earth.

The Rebbe's mysticism links him to heaven, while his concern for his flock ties him to earth. The Rebbe is the vessel through which flows the grace of G-D. At one and the same time, he draws his hassidim closer to the Divine, and showers them with G-D's blessings. Such is the nature of the Rebbe's absolute authority.

Hassidism began in Eastern Europe at the turn of the 18th century. It functioned, at that time, as the Jewish answer to poverty, ignorance and hardship. Through the medium of song, dance, and mystical communication with the Almighty, the downtrodden were able to experience joy; to find relief from their suffering and to learn about their faith.

Since that time, however, the world has seen many changes. First and foremost the hassidim have themselves changed. They have graduated from being largely uneducated people living in the squalid villages of Eastern Europe, to becoming prosperous and worldly members of the modern secular world. Their lives have become largely institutionalized. Consequently, in many cases, they have in turn institutionalized the Rebbes and their courts. Thus an air of comfort, often even opulence, has replaced the humble origins of hassidic happenings; for the hassid who is comfortable in his own home wishes to be comfortable when he visits his Rebbe.

But this form of hassidism held no lure for Avraham. His Rebbe was cut in an entirely different mold. His life was ascetic in the extreme, bare of the most minor material distractions. He rose with the sun each morning to pray. He spent the day closeted in his tiny home and never ventured into the outer world during daylight. Only late at night, actually often not until the small hours of the morning, would he spirit himself wordlessly around his neighborhood, depositing money to people in need. He would place unmarked envelopes of cash into postboxes or push money under the old wooden doors in the neighborhood. The money that he dispensed had been left that same day by some of the many supplicants that had come to ask his guidance and his blessing. Rarely would any of these monies stay with him overnight; as it was credited, so it would be debited; his books would always balance before G-d.

Approaching the poor dilapidated synagogue, Avraham felt light-hearted as a boy coming home to his father. During the past six or seven years his bond with the Kadosh had developed into an unusual relationship which others envied. Avraham entered the synagogue and walked over to the gabbai – the administrator – whose duty it was to screen the supplicants and take their written pleas (known as *kvitlach*) to the Kadosh. There were times when there might be thirty such people queuing and it would be the gabbai's duty to keep order. Without looking up from the volume of Talmud that he was learning, the gabbai said, "The Kadosh is not receiving. He has asked not to be disturbed."

Uncharacteristically, Avraham persisted, "Please tell him that I am here; I am leaving for three weeks army service and would like to have his blessing."

The gabbai envied Avraham's special relationship with the Kadosh who, in his old age, sometimes grew querulous. Closing the volume with signs of annoyance, he lifted himself slowly from the chair behind the table and walked heavily towards the door and down the steps at the side of the building that led to the basement. Avraham waited in the synagogue, praying that he had not been impertinent. Within minutes, the gabbai reappeared and, without any signs of enthusiasm, told him that he should go down the steps and knock at the door.

In the tiny and sparsely furnished room, the Kadosh indicated that Avraham should sit down opposite him at the small table. The Kadosh had aged and looked tired. Avraham felt pangs of guilt at having disturbed him. Reading his thoughts, the Kadosh welcomed him, "I hear that you are going to do your duty and am pleased that you came to see me."

Considerable pain seemed to pass over the countenance of the Kadosh before he continued: "There will be war and much blood will be spilt. But you, Avraham, will come back home to prepare for a big *simcha* (a joyful occasion) in your family."

Avraham had intended to tell the Kadosh of his wife's pregnancy, but it was clear to him that the Kadosh knew and had just referred to it. Avraham prepared to talk to his mentor. Out of respect, he would address him only in the third person.

"I thank the Kadosh for his blessing. It will now be easier for me to leave my family and go to my unit in the Golan. I would like to discuss another matter with the Kadosh."

Receiving no response, Avraham continued: "Recently, together with other settlers, I bought some land from an Arab. His father had fled from Hebron after saving Jews from the massacre in 1929, (known in Hebrew by its acronym, Tarpat). It appears that the father's mother used to light candles on Friday nights. The son wishes to become Jewish and I am counselling him. He will probably meet a Jewish girl and the burden of responsibility is too great for me to carry. I respectfully ask the Kadosh for guidance."

The Kadosh seemed to withdraw in a trance. In a few moments, however, a beautiful smile covered his aging face. "Avraham," he said, *"tachzir attarah leyoshna* – you will restore a crown to its glory. The son is Jewish himself. When you return from the war, you will reveal the full story. We will talk again."

The Kadosh sat back in his chair. The smile had evaporated and he again seemed tired, as if he had completed a physically exhausting effort. "Avraham, *tze beshalom ve chazor beshalom* – Go in peace and return in peace. *Hashem yatzliach darkecha* – G-d will make you successful."

Avraham rose and withdrew respectfully. As he reached the door, the Kadosh raised his hand, a troubled look on his face: "Wherever you are, do not forget to wash your hands before eating bread. Remember, Avraham! Do not forget!"

Avraham did not remember walking to the bus station some fifteen minutes away, nor did he remember getting his ticket or taking his seat on the Egged bus to Tiberias. For he was wrapped in thought – wondering at the revelations of the Kadosh. The Kadosh had known about his wife's pregnancy, had revealed insight into Taher's past that Taher did not know, and, above all else, had revealed that there would be war! These three subjects occupied Avraham's mind until he reached Tiberias two hours later.

On arrival, he phoned home and reached his wife, who was always happy to hear from him. "The Kadosh has given us a *beracha*. He talks about a big *simcha*; that usually indicates a boy! Furthermore, he talks of much strife (Avraham was not keen to talk of war) but says that I will come home safely. I wanted you to know – but please do not talk of what I have told you. All of it must remain secret between us."

Since the completion of his national service some years earlier, Corporal Avraham Nissim spent his annual reserve duty on the Golan Heights with his tank corps. This was now the fourth week.

Initially, he had only been called up for three weeks but, just as his discharge was imminent, he was advised that his reserve duty would be extended by at least two weeks. His wife, in an advanced stage of pregnancy with their third child, was having a hard time coping with the older two. Yet here he was, stuck far from home on the eve of Yom Kippur.

The small camp comprised only ten tanks, their crews, and some minimal support and maintenance facilities. It was situated outside Sindiana as auxiliary to the larger Nafekh camp. The latter was strategically positioned some twenty miles north west of the Bnot Ya'acov Bridge. It straddled the crossroads leading first to Kuneitra, and then on to Damascus.

General Hofi, Commander Northern Command, had minute-by-minute information about the military build-up on the northern border. Not so General Raful Eitan, who commanded the Golan Front, nor the various brigade and battalion commanders. Least of all Corporal Nissim and the men who formed the dozens of small tank and infantry defensive groupings that were spread around the Golan Heights. Theirs was the most limited perspective. Their knowledge of military developments was often restricted to the immediate surroundings in which they operated.

Most of the soldiers were old friends who had graduated, years earlier, from a combined five year, army and yeshiva studies program. The men, all of whom had since married and settled down in various towns and villages around the country, were called up as a group. They had been trained as a close team. Reserve duty gave the men a chance to get together once a year, to renew old friendships and, when free from their army duties, to form small groups and pursue their Talmudic studies.

The Eve of Yom Kippur.

Tremors of war in the air. Tanks lined up. Equipment at the ready. The men are far from their families and their synagogues, yet morale is high.

Order received from Colonel Avigdor, Commander of the 2nd Battalion: Be on full alert. The 40 men in the group are organized into smaller groups, in order to facilitate both maximum, round the clock alert and prayer arrangements for the Yom Kippur fast.

By early afternoon all soldiers had showered and changed into clean clothes. Leather footwear was discarded in exchange for the simple rubber thongs or canvas slippers dictated for that day by Jewish law. Boots were kept ready nearby for emergency. Prior arrangements had been made for the men to take their *seudah mafseket* – the final meal before the fast – in turns. The men of this tank corps were prepared for their Day of Judgment.

As the sun set, Avraham and nine fellow soldiers set down their weapons. They opened their prayer books at the familiar verses. Together they began. Slowly, hesitantly – almost silently at first – they intoned the ancient Kol Nidre service, a litany which dates, it is believed, from the dark days of the Spanish Inquisition:

> *"By the authority of the Court On High, and by the authority of this Court on earth, With the Knowledge of the Almighty and with the knowledge of this congregation, we give leave to pray with those that have transgressed.*
>
> *"From this Day of Atonement unto the next Day of Atonement, may it come unto us for good...."*

Later that night, Avraham lay on his bunk trying to catch some sleep before resuming a late night shift. But his mind was riveted on the possibility of war, a war in which he would be required to fire live shells against the Syrians that had once, years earlier, been his compatriots.

Memories of Damascus, where he was born, flooded back to him: his mother, of blessed memory, who had died when he was a child; his father, trained as a pharmacist, who had made his money trading in gold coins in the Jewish ghetto.

He recalled the privations and pogroms: being herded by his parents together with other children into the basement or the attic, waiting for the Syrians' anti-Jewish madness to subside. He remembered the anguish of families, visited in the dead of night by the secret police, the head of the family, the breadwinner, invariably hauled away, imprisoned or tortured, in most cases never to be seen again.

Often, so often, Avraham had been woken by his nightmares: Jews running along streets, looking for refuge. Himself running madly with them, running from the Arab policemen who were beating them with their batons and cornering them as they huddled together in their synagogues. In his dreams he would see again the mad religious craze in the policemen's eyes, he would hear them shouting, egged on by their hysterical religious fervor. Hatred in the name of Allah and Holy Jihad.

The numerous cases of bribery, the ransom paid by Jews to Syrian officials and policemen to stay their evil decree, were well known even to the children in the ghetto: The knock on the door at night; the herding of the children into the back room; himself shaking with fear, peering through the keyhole, forbidden to sneeze or call out in any way, even though he was too frightened to stay quiet. But of all, by far the most awful: his father approaching the door, the few gold coins shaking in his outstretched hand.

Eventually his father had decided that that life must end – and fortunately he had the means. It must have taken courage, but he managed to bribe a Syrian official. Arrangements were made for the family to leave illegally, and make their way via Turkey to Israel. Jews caught attempting to emigrate were hanged in the public square. Such hangings provided the occasion for public holidays in Damascus and the surrounding areas.

On the appointed day, Avraham, his two brothers and three sisters were led, silently, by their father from their house. Avraham can't recall why or how his father had managed it, but he did remember that they were driven in a large American car toward the Turkish border. They carried a minimum of possessions, among them a small and sacred Torah scroll that had been hand-written by his father's great-grandfather, a scribe, nearly a century earlier. Avraham's ancestor had donated it to a synagogue in Damascus with a proviso that it accompany any of his descendants if and when they left Damascus to live in the Holy Land. In his will he had expressed the wish that the Torah's final resting place be in Jerusalem.

In Damascus it is said that the walls of the Jewish ghetto have ears as well as eyes. The departure of the Jews in the dead of night was invariably reported immediately, the informer rewarded for his troubles.

Despite the courageous way in which Avraham's father had brought his family out of Syria, he was a simple man, in most matters cautious and not very brave. His marriage had not been a happy one. He had, for many years, yearned to emigrate to Israel, less than sixty miles away, but he relinquished his will to that of his wife who had refused to leave Syria. Only after her death, caused by complications that had followed some quite minor surgical procedure, had he begun to plan this momentous and dangerous step.

Luckily for him and his family, the Syrian whom he had approached for help was far more clever than he and had no intention of placing either himself or the generous remuneration he was to receive from the transaction, into jeopardy. So, instead of driving the family directly to the border, the Syrian first took them to their cousin, who lived just a few blocks away. Parking the car discreetly, he doubled back on foot and took up a position above a shaggy knoll overlooking the Nissim home. There he sat and waited.

Things transpired as he had expected: Within a short time, a car drove up and disgorged a group of five or six dark-clad secret policemen who forced their way into the house. After just a few minutes, they reemerged and stuck a large cardboard sign on the front door. In large, black letters the sign announced that the house had been impounded due to the treachery of the Jewish inhabitants. The police then got silently back into their car and drove away. The Syrian guide, watching from his perch on the knoll, knew that the borders would now be sealed off, the police put on the alert to apprehend the family.

The Nissims stayed with their cousins for the night, but in the morning they returned to their own home. It was then that the usually timid Mr. Nissim did something not far short of heroic: He marched to the local police station and lodged a complaint, claiming that his house had been broken into by the Secret Police while he and his family were spending the night with his cousins. On their return, he said, they had found a placard on the front door – a slur to his reputation.

By a stroke of good fortune the officer on duty suffered from heartburn and was a regular customer at Nissim's pharmacy. Like most Jews in Damascus, Nissim had suspected that he might one day need the services of the police, so he had always filled the officer's prescriptions free of charge.

This particular policeman was a young man called Anwar, with problems of his own. His wife was a semi-invalid, and one of his sons was retarded. He would often share his troubles with Nissim as he waited for his medicine. When he had heard of Nissim's own bereavement, he had even come to the shop to express his sympathy with him that he would have to raise six young children on his own. Anwar put a call through to his colleagues at the Secret Police urging them to vent their grievances on the informer, rather than the Jew. The informer was duly taken care of.

Three nights later Nissim and his six children left the house separately. They carried no bags, but walked two blocks to a previously determined rendezvous, got into the same American car that had dropped them off three nights previously, and embarked on their trip towards the Turkish border.

For a number of years Mr. Nissim had been hoarding gold coins, the profit from his trading activities. He had kept them in three small leather pouches. After lengthy negotiations it had been agreed that he would pay Ali Sabry, his Syrian contact, with one of the pouches when the family was safely across the Turkish border.

Nissim considered that, as Syrians go, Ali Sabry was a fair-minded man. For his part, Sabry had every intention of carrying out his end of the bargain, yet he had no intention of undergoing this dangerous transaction for only one pouch of gold coins. As they neared the Turkish border, he began to bargain with his Jewish friend for another bag. "As we approach the border, I will have to go ahead of you and pay the guards on the Syrian side. In view of the scare only three days ago when these borders were closed off, the guards will be nervous and will demand much gold. What's more, I will also have to settle with the guards on the Turkish side. They too will know that the border was sealed. You wouldn't risk the Turks' refusing to let you into their country now would you?" he asked.

Nissim was not in a position to bargain. For several nights he had not slept, but had paced up and down until dawn out of sheer worry for what lay ahead. The obstacles that he foresaw and the responsibility that he felt for his children as a single parent, terrified him. Their lives lay in the hands of this wily Syrian. He could not possibly outsmart him now. By the time they approached the border, the second bag of gold had been ceded to Sabry.

The guide did not tell Nissim how much he had paid the Syrian border police to get them across. Whatever it was, it worked. Sabry was permitted to cross with his charges and leave them in the narrow strip of no-man's land, while he negotiated a satisfactory deal with the Turkish guards.

As Avraham lay on his bunker thinking back on all of this, he vividly remembered the sound of the wind as it had whistled over the crest of the mountain, the way his father's hand had sweated as he had clutched his children to him. He remembered how he had bidden them all to hold on to the Torah scroll, hidden beneath his coat. He remembered how silent they had been as they waited for Sabry to return. He remembered the muffled whimperings of his baby sister as her father held her head against the peculiarly bulging side of his coat.

Their guide returned. The Messiah would never be more welcome! He escorted the family over the border into the friendly territory of Turkey, into a taxicab that was waiting for them, a driver smiling at the wheel. Mr. Nissim marvelled at the brazen efficiency, the sheer ingeniousness of their guide.

Unfortunately, the relief that they felt as they crossed the border was short-lived. The taxi was stopped at a military road-block just ten minutes down the road. A policeman in a neatly pressed uniform beckoned Mr. Nissim to leave the car. Taking him beyond hearing distance of his children, he launched into a lengthy explanation of the difficulties he would encounter in Turkey if he were not to produce the appropriate documents. Papers were essential for their safe passage through the country, for them to be able to leave the Turkish port, and for them to board a ship bound for their final destination.

The policeman was able to supply Nissim with the required documents at a cost of no more and no less than Nissim's third bag of gold coins. The official seemed confident that the money was there, waiting for him. Payment would mean that Nissim would reach Israel without a penny. He was not perturbed by the idea of baksheesh per se, nor did he take the matter personally: For generations Jews had been held for ransom. But he was now fighting for his future, and the future of his children.

There was a degree of stoic pragmaticsm to his reasoning. It wasn't the principle but the amount that he was negotiating. Fifteen minutes later the haggling came to an end. Approximately sixty percent of the remaining gold coins were handed over to the Turk, in return for which the appropriate Turkish papers were made out to the family.

The taxi and the ship that carried them to Israel used up the rest of the gold coins. Mr. Nissim arrived in the Promised Land bearing a small, exquisite, white-and-gold bound Torah scroll beneath his overcoat. He had no wife, six small children, and a handful of Turkish change in his pocket.

With infinite care Mr. Nissim led his family off the ship. At the foot of the gangplank he stopped, gently placed the Torah scroll into the arms of his eldest son and, turning in the direction of Jerusalem, the direction in which his fathers had prayed since time immemorial, he prostrated himself on the ground and kissed the earth of the Holy Land. The entire family, from Avraham down to his youngest baby sister, followed their father's example, each kissed the dry earth and gave thanks to G-d. As Avraham lay on his bunker on the eve of the Yom Kippur War, that first taste of Israel came rushing back to him: the sweet, dusty smell of Israel's earth.

To the north-east, 1400 Syrian tanks were preparing to storm their way into the Golan Heights and down towards the Sea of Galilee. The Syrians had three highly trained divisions ready to invade Israel. The headquarters of the Third Syrian Armored division was less than twenty miles south-west of Damascus. The First Syrian Armored division, situated some 15 miles east of it, was directly south of Damascus. The Fifth Syrian Division was situated some 40 miles south, not far from the Syrian and Jordanian borders, and only 15 miles east of the Sea of Galilee.

The combined force of these three divisions was preparing for penetration into Israel. Their massive tank and infantry corps were preparing a coordinated thrust of such concentration, that the Israeli army was expected to disappear under their sheer momentum. Each division was to split into extending spurs and to pulverize Israeli defenses wherever they were situated.

One objective common to spurs of the First and Third Divisions, was the Nafekh Camp and the crossroads that it controlled. To achieve this objective, it was necessary to eliminate the defensive positions in the areas surrounding Nafekh, including Sindiana.

As the soldiers of Avraham's small tank force prepared for the fast day, they knew nothing of the Syrian plan, or of the timetable that had been approved by the Syrian High Command.

But during the night Israeli intelligence received details as to the intensity and purpose of the attack. Just a couple of hours later, reservists and tanks of the 2nd Battalion were moved up the Golan Heights. They encamped in groups around Sindiana.

By morning, battalion commanders were being briefed on what to expect. At noon Major Efrati arrived at the small tank corps. He approached the compound deep in concentration, preoccupied with the machinations of war: timetables; orders; details of mobilization; supplies. Yet, as he drove through the gate, his meditations were suddenly disrupted, his senses surprisingly bombarded with the collective chanting of men at prayer. As he rounded the bend in the path that led to the drill-yard, he was again assailed by the full force of the irrational.

Memories of his childhood came to him. Fifteen men draped in prayer shawls swayed gently in the open yard. Their bodies moved with their prayers; their voices rose and fell as one. The melody filled the air, wafted out and upward toward the mountains of Syria and Lebanon. Efrati was not an observant Jew, but the sight of these men on the eve of battle, the sound of the prayers that he still recalled from his grandfather's house, pulled him from his jeep.

Somewhat sheepishly he covered his head with his army cap and stood to the rear of this makeshift, open-air synagogue, vulnerable to the power of prayer. Avraham's voice was leading the soldiers in their litany:

> *"On the Day of Atonement it is sealed: How many will pass from the earth and how many will be created; who will live and who will die; who will die at his predestined time, and who before his time; who by water and who by fire; who by sword, who by beast...."*

"..as though the world were standing still," thought Efrati. He waited until the fervor of this particular prayer came to an end. Then he set about the purpose of his visit: preparation for battle. First he told the men to break their fast, as he couldn't foretell when they would be able to eat again once the hostilities had started. The order was not well taken.

Yom Kippur, 13 hours.
The first barrage of Syrian artillery persists for an hour. Then Syrian tanks begin to roll. Planes take to the air to strafe Israeli military targets. The third strike is directed against the area of Nafekh.

14 hours.
Syrian tanks roll into action, covering almost 20 miles in the first hour. Spurs of the First and Third Syrian Divisions have arranged to meet at El Hara, just 15 miles east of Nafekh. But, due to the circuitous courses they have followed, progress is slower than anticipated.

16 hours.
Tanks of the First Syrian Division reach their rendezvous.

16.30 hours.
Tanks of the Third Divison roll into view. From here, both divisions are to split into three new spurs: The first, to break to the north-west, attacking Israeli positions around Kuneitra.

The second, to push straight to the west, running slightly north of Sindiana, and making for the Nafekh crossroads.

The third spur is to push southward to Kudne and from there to turn sharply north-west and drive in a straight line directly through Sindiana toward Nafekh.

Major Efrati had accurately predicted that during the Yom Kippur fast the Syrian tanks would make contact with those of Avraham's unit: The first real battle has begun. Forty tanks thunder down towards Sindiana from Kudne, hopelessly outnumbering Avraham's unit. The Israelis have only two advantages. The first is a detailed knowledge of the area – the result of having served in the same encampment for several years. The second is that, whereas the Syrians have been storming through the terrain in the cramped overheated confines of their tanks for nearly three hours, the Israelis are still fresh.

Avraham's unit punishes the Syrians severely. For several days enemy tanks lie smoldering on the mountainsides. But Avraham's corps suffer, in the process. Half his men lie dead, many his best friends.

At Brigade Headquarters to the north of them, a more overall picture was forming. Losses on both sides were reported, but so were the encroaching waves of heavy Syrian, Iraqi and Moroccan tanks and artillery, replacements for those that had been destroyed. Orders were issued by Headquarters for the tighter reformation of the Barak Brigade, which was splayed over a twenty mile line from Ramat Magshimim in the south to a point south of Kuneitra in the north. Sindiana and Nafekh were to lie behind this line, playing a supportive role.

By the time Avraham and his men had brought the original 40 Syrian tanks to a halt, reports arrived of a new Syrian, 100 tank formation being assembled at Kudne. Its course was not yet established, but Israeli intelligence was assuming that it would be directed southward toward Sindiana along the tapline which ran between Nafekh and Juhader. In response, the Commander of the Barak Brigade left Nafekh and moved to regroup in Juhader.

Avraham puts a call through to his Brigade Commander at Juhader. With the impertinence of an Israeli corporal making operational proposals to his Brigadier General, he offers assistance. Barking over the static of the army telephone to a commander he has never seen, he reports that, as his own unit is now reduced to five tanks, it should cease to function as a group,

"*Hamefaked*, (Commander)," he says, "we have a *balagan* (chaos) here; We must dig ourselves out of this rut, *ein breira* (we have no choice!)."

Avraham proposes that two of his tanks make for the tapline and provide cover for the new command. His suggestion is accepted. He then recommends that he take his own tank, supported by the other two, and work as an ad hoc guerrilla unit against the superior power of the Syrians. "We lost our officers and our best men. I have to report that I am the most senior of the survivors. As a unit, our five tanks will not pose any threat to the Syrians. But I believe that as a small guerrilla force we might cause considerable damage. My friends and I are familiar with every hill, every ridge and every boulder; we know the paths we can use and those we must avoid. We are able to use the local topography to our advantage, particularly in the darkness. We will be effective."

General Ben Shoham is fascinated by the initiative, not to mention the sheer pluck of this corporal. What's more, he appreciates the enormity of his proposal. Here is a soldier who has changed in the past few hours from praying and fasting, to participation in a military debacle, a battle in which he has already lost many of his closest friends. This stranger, no more than a voice down a telephone, has come up with a sound proposition involving personal risk and daring.

As commander, it is the general's turn to address the corporal. Accepting the proposal, he says: "Send me your two spare tanks, *mefaked* and may you and your guerrillas be successful."

Two tanks pull away from Avraham's unit and roll towards the tapline. From this moment on, the members of his tiny unit nickname their leader: *mefaked*.

It is dark. Visibility is limited. Avraham's tanks have insufficient equipment for night vision. As a result, the men are obliged to rely on the more limited second-generation SLS sight-finders, attached to their handguns. Avraham knows the area like the back of his hand and feels confident that the large boulders along the edge of the slopes will afford the three buccaneers sufficient protection.

Edging away from the tapline in the direction of Tel Kudne, Avraham observes a platoon of Syrian tanks proceeding in a majestic line along the ridge of a hill, looking for all the world as if they are on parade. These tanks are equipped with infra-red night vision, their systems giving off a red, tell-tale light. 'Lucky,' thinks the new Israeli *mefaked*, 'we don't have that problem.'

Proceeding along a parallel ridge, one which converges toward that of the enemy, Avraham waits until he has reduced the firing range to 30 meters. None of the enemy tanks is facing in his direction as he skirts the boulders; consequently, Avraham's three tanks are undetected. The three work together in total synchronization.

Avraham gives the signal and his three tanks open fire, picking off three tanks on the opposite ridge. The three targets burst into flames. Within seconds Avraham and his other tanks reposition their turrets; again Avraham gives the signal, again three Syrian tanks are ignited. The thirty remaining Syrian tanks, turn tail and flee. The confidence gained with this first strike is considerable. Three novice fighters sans officer manage to make an entire platoon of enemy tanks turn tail. It helps to ease the pain that still lingers from the afternoon's debacle. Bolstered by success, the three go looking for more prey.

Good judgment, a dark night, detailed knowledge of the immediate locality, and a large endowment of guts kept the three tanks going until the small hours of the morning. By that time they had played havoc with the enemy. As for the Syrian tanks: They had grown weary of the strange cat-and-mouse game, a game played in the darkness, on hostile terrain, to unpredictable, changing rules, with an opponent they could neither see nor gauge.

Sometime after 4 pm, before there was any sign of light, the three tanks ran out of steam and came to a stop in a clearing protected by large boulders. As far as Avraham could see, there was no further sign of Syrian tanks. With the supply of both ammunition and fuel almost completely depleted, *mefaked* Avraham decided to call a break. The weary warriors lifted themselves out of the tanks and prepared for some rest in an abandoned bunker.

Sitting there, they took out some sandwiches and drinks from their kitbags and passed them around. The boys were just about to dig their teeth into the sandwiches when Avraham remembered the admonition of the Kadosh.

"Stop," said Avraham, holding up his hand to give emphasis. "We must wash our hands and say grace properly."

"You must be kidding," answered one of the soldiers, "in our position I am sure we can be lenient. To wander around looking for water would be dangerous."

"We have water bottles in our tank, so we won't have too far to walk," answered Avraham. "I am the *mefaked*, and I order you to come with me – I am assured that it is an important *mitzvah*."

All of the men respect Avraham, both for his religious ideals and for his recent military leadership. Taking the sandwiches with them, they follow him out of the bunker.

As they make their way to the side of the tank, there is a sudden reawakening of Syrian artillery. A shell whines past their heads and erupts on impact behind them.

Just as suddenly as it started it stops – as if the Syrians had run out of shells. The men follow Avraham's lead, they wash their hands and recite grace before meals: "Blessed art Thou, O Lord, Who gives us bread from the earth."

In the dark they retrace their steps to the bunker, or what was left of it. Had they been munching their sandwiches in the bunker, they would have been dead.

600 Syrian tanks still active within the area of the Barak Brigade. Operative Israeli tank force estimated at a tenth of the enemy's strength. Battles rage throughout the night. Many Israeli tanks are left to fight entire formations single-handed. Several are reported darting back and forth among the boulders, picking off enemy tanks like ducks on a shooting range.

But – come morning, and the reckoning has to be made. Among the thousands of casualties is the Commander of the Barak Brigade, the same general that had earlier sanctioned Avraham's proposition. His two most senior officers die with him. 24 hours of fighting has left the Israeli army in desperate straits.

Monday. Day 3.
Israel mounts a massive counterattack. By sundown huge areas have become graveyards for the Syrian army. Over nine hundred smouldering tanks, equipment, supply vehicles, personnel carriers, missile carriers, plus tons of ammunition lie scattered over the hills and down the sides of the slopes. *Mefaked* Avraham and his men have made a significant contribution to the carnage.

Wednesday. Day 5.
The Israel Air Force makes forays deep into Syrian territory, knocking out anti-aircraft missile sites, petrol dumps, and power stations. Several returning Syrian planes are unable to find undamaged airfields and are forced to land on roads. Of more significance: The massive Russian airlift of military parts, spares and ammunition find it difficult to land deliveries to their Syrian allies.

Friday. Day 7.
All Syrian efforts are concentrated on the defense of Damascus, as the Syrians are unaware of Israel's decision not to capture their capital.

In the face of increasing pressure from his Arab neighbors, King Hussein sends an armored brigade into Syria, to join with Syrian and Iraqi forces against the now attacking Israelis. But as the Jordanians advance, the Israelis open fire, knocking out a number of their tanks. In the absence of Iraqi supporting fire, the Jordanians withdraw.

There is a marked lack of coordination on the Syrian front. Only when the Jordanians withdraw their tanks do the Iraqis advance theirs, alone and without support. But things deteriorate even further when Iraqi artillery shells fall on the retreating Jordanians, and Syrian planes attack and down Iraqi planes.

CHAPTER 17

The Southern Front

Saturday. October 6. Day 1.

The Egyptian Army, one of the world's largest, with 800,000 troops, 500 aircraft and 2000 tanks, attacks along the entire 100-mile length of the Suez Canal. Massive amphibious crossings of tanks and armament are their immediate objective. What the Egyptians had not taken into account was the extent to which the Israelis were unprepared. Despite years of almost continuous, overt warmongering on every political level, and despite the easily observed massing of Egyptian troops on the banks of the Canal, no Israeli counter-measures had been taken. Opposing the Egyptians, Israel has fewer than 500 soldiers stationed in small groups along the canal. They are situated in small groups seven miles apart from each other. Only three tanks are at the waterway and another 300 tanks at forward positions inside the Sinai Desert.

The meager Israeli force left to defend the Canal, this fateful Yom Kippur, was better versed in fasting and in prayer.

Eight years before the Yom Kippur War, three teenagers enrolled for studies at the Kfar Haroeh Yeshivah High School. Situated in the center of the country, the school was the forerunner of an educational system built on both Talmudic and nationalistic ideologies. The yeshiva offered a long study day, the first half of which was designated for religious studies, and the second for a secular curriculum. On graduating, most of the students would proceed to a five year program combining army training with Talmudic learning.

Reuven Sporen, Eli Feig and Ya'acov Katz were above average. They were close friends and each wanted to be admitted to the army's most elite commando corps, known in Hebrew as the *Sayeret*.

Upon graduating, the three friends parted company for a while. Sporen was admitted to the prestigious commando unit attached to the Southern Command, known as *Sayeret Shaked*. The unit was comprised of crack soldiers and had been founded by a famous Beduin war hero, Abdul Magid, who later changed his name to Amos Yarkoni.

Sporen's two friends delayed their army training. Out of deference to their parents and teachers, they continued their yeshiva training for a year before they too were accepted into the same *Sayeret*.

Eli Feig, later known as Eli Sagi (like Magid, he also Hebraicized his family name) studied at Yeshivat Hakotel, a seminary built inside the Old City of Jerusalem, facing the Temple Mount. His friend Ya'acov Katz, known since early school days as *Ketselle*, or little Katz (in deference to his older brother), attended the famous Merkaz Harav. This seminary took its name from the late and greatly revered Rabbi Kook, Chief Rabbi and ideological mentor of the religious nationalist movement.

The incorporation of these young men marked the first time that *Sayeret Shaked* had recruited bearded, skullcapped soldiers. The dangerous nature of commando activities calls for small, tightly knit groups of men, usually no more than ten or twelve strong. Our three friends were assigned to different groups, but they remained, throughout, the closest of friends.

One year before the Yom Kippur War, Sergeant Reuven Sporen was killed in action while fighting terrorists in the Gaza strip. From that time on, Sagi and Ketselle were like a three-legged stool trying to manage on just two legs.

The eve of the Yom Kippur War found Captain Eli Sagi sitting on the banks of the Suez Canal. He had served four years in the army and had signed on for a fifth.

Ketselle was home on leave for the holidays. He had also served four years, but had decided to quit the army for civilian life. On Friday afternoon, twenty-four hours before the outbreak of war, Lt. Ya'acov Katz was contacted and recalled to his unit. He arrived at battalion headquarters, at Mishmar Hanegev, at 6 pm that evening, the eve of Yom Kippur.

Prior to the war, the Shaked Commandos had numbered some three hundred highly-trained fighters. Now the unit was split into five platoons: Three were located at different points in the Sinai desert; one was to function as back-up and was held at command headquarters in Mishmar Hanegev; basic training units were dispatched to Khan Yunis and Ba'ad near the town of Shechem, a long way north in Samaria.

On October 2, Major Spector, newly appointed commander of Shaked, was ordered to redeploy. He brought all platoons nearer the Canal and moved the center of control and operations to Tasa, south of Refidim, a central crossroads in the Sinai Desert. The Shaked force as a whole came under the control of the Sinai Battalion of the army's Southern Command.

Shaked Commandos had been trained to act as ad hoc guerrilla forces. Their objective: to prevent the enemy from crossing the Canal and to frustrate all efforts to consolidate enemy positions. The unit's trainee commandos were ordered to guard the airport at Refidim as well as other sensitive facilities.

At the outbreak of war, Shaked was augmented by an additional platoon. This platoon, known as *Koach Pazzi* – the Pazzi force – was initiated by General Arik Sharon and formed, overnight, from some of the finest fighting men in the country. Many of these men were senior Shaked officers who had since either left the army, or had moved to training positions outside of Shaked.

The force was headed by Major Amatzia Chen, commonly referred to as "Pazzi." Just days before the war, Pazzi had attended an officers' course, during which General Arieh Shilo had assured the men that war was not imminent. At that time Pazzi had told his friends that "The general should be locked up for talking such rubbish. War will break out within days."

CHAPTER 18

Feelings that war was imminent were not restricted to some of the officers in the Israel Defense Forces. They were shared by many Palestinian Arabs who lived in what they termed the *occupied territories*. Many of these local Arabs looked forward to renewed hostilities between Israel and its neighbors. Golda Meir did not believe that war was imminent. She refused to accept the notion that Palestine was a nation and Palestinians a nationality. Her attitude to the *occupied territories* was ambiguous.

Just two days before the war, four young Arabs met in a modern Arab house on the slopes of El-Bireh, the twin city of Ramallah. Two of the participants, the host and his brother-in-law, were locals. A third was a young man from East Jerusalem. He was a business associate, engaged in profitable moneychanging activities that he carried on quite openly inside the souk within the Old City walls. The fourth participant was the guest that had come across the Jordan River at the Allenby Bridge just that very morning. It was this fourth guest, Sadam Al-Din, that the other three had come to hear.

Now in his middle thirties, Sadam was a survivor. Three years earlier, he had survived Jordanian battles against his people, the Palestinians. While many of his friends lost their lives in that terrible September blood bath, Sadam escaped an ambush by what he could only term a miracle. Having been forewarned, he managed to distance himself from the heart of the massacre and hide in an adjoining field behind some rocks. Keeping completely quiet until the blood bath was over, he waited until the Jordanian soldiers had left. He then fled down the mountains into the plains on the east side of the Jordan. Subsequently, he made his way north to Irbid, where friends hid and protected him, until that awful month had passed.

Several months later, Sadam returned to Amman where, unostentatiously, he resumed his activities and strengthened his links with the residual Palestinian leadership. Black September had tightened his resolve that the Palestinian people were entitled to their own homeland. In Amman, Sadam became a moneychanger, a profession that enabled him to keep in touch with Palestine.

It is said that emigres from one country to another continue to count in their original language even after many years. In Israel there are many small grocers that count in German or Hungarian, even though they have lived and worked in the Levant for decades. Similarly, Palestinians think in terms of dinars, the currency of Jordan. Throughout the Israeli occupied West Bank, trade continues between Palestinians in dinars, even though Israel and Jordan were officially enemies. Trade between Palestinians and Israelis is transacted in Israeli currency. In the markets – the souks – the currency for trade with tourists is usually the US dollar, although no trader would refuse to trade in sterling, marks or francs. The consolidation of all these trades is in dinars, the position of the moneychanger is paramount.

Moneychangers, pursuing an honorable trade in the markets of the Middle East for many centuries, were grudgingly tolerated by the Israeli authorities. The latter wrongly believed that they could control their activities and keep an eye on large illegal currency transactions. While the Old City traders appeared to play along with the Israeli authorities, the principals in the back rooms cemented meaningful political alliances with moneychangers in Damascus, Amman, Beirut and Egypt. As every Palestinian had dinars, the moneychangers had ready access to the masses. Theirs was the ideal channel to spread political foment.

Hassan, the host for the evening, received his friends graciously into his beautiful family home. He himself was a fourth generation moneychanger and worked with his father in their East Jerusalem office. The father sat in the back office and ran the wholesale department of the business, dealing daily with tens of smaller moneychangers scattered throughout the West Bank and the Gaza strip. Hassan ran the cash business in the front shop, changing large and small denominations from one currency to another. He prided himself on always quoting a good price. Invariably his bid and offer prices were more competitive than the prices quoted by the banks.

Hassan's younger brother lived in Nablus and managed one of the family's branch offices. Another brother had recently established an office in the Hebron market. Hassan's uncle and a cousin ran an affiliated business in Ramallah, which, until the Israeli takeover of Jerusalem in 1967, had been the family's nerve center. Sadam Al-Din, his friend and business associate from Jordan, ran an office in

Amman which acted as the West Bank firm's important correspondent in the Hashemite Kingdom, the ultimate capital market for the dinar.

Patiently, slowly and with great conviction, Sadam spelled out his vision that war was imminent, that the combined might of the well-equipped Arab armies would this time conclusively defeat Israel. "Palestine belongs to the Palestinians by right of history, geography, occupation. The olive trees were planted by our forefathers, and water wells dug by their forefathers. The fields have been tilled by our families for generations. All of the land, for as far as we can see in any direction, belongs to our people."

The four young men sipped the black coffee in small white porcelain cups. Hassan cleared his throat. Looking directly at his guest speaker he interjected: "Our people have never been short on rhetoric, but today we are meeting to be practical. Seven years ago Palestine exchanged one ruler for another. The Jews merely changed roles with the Hashemites. In many ways the Palestinians have prospered under Israeli rule; many have grown soft and contented. If war breaks out as you forecast, what role must we play? This is what we are here to discuss."

"I know only too well how soft our people have grown," answered Sadam. "Before we discuss the role we must play, we must understand our alliances."

Sadam drank from his cup slowly, as if planning his thoughts. "Notwithstanding the atrocities meted out to us from time to time by our Arab neighbors, we must recognize that our primary alliance is with our Arab brothers. We are linked for thousands of years. Coming as I do from Amman, where only three years ago I myself witnessed the Hashemite atrocities, I say this with constraint. However, we must learn to ignore relative trivialities, trials and tribulations. They are but ripples in a vast pond, sent to test our resolve. For Hashemites will come and go in the annals of history, but the Palestinians belong to their land; to the land of Palestine."

Sadam held up his hand in an effort to prevent Hassan from reminding him again about rhetoric. "As you will see, alliances and associations are not rhetoric. We Palestinians are poor and unprepared. We are unarmed and unskilled in warfare. We must never make our move prematurely; we must bide our time with patience. On the other hand, we must encourage our Arab brothers, with their large armies and geopolitical alliances, to wage war on the Jews and help rid them from our land.

"Let them fight in the skies, let them wreak havoc on the battlefield, let them bomb Jewish cities. Our task will then be to return our land to its people. I discuss these plans only with Palestinians whom I trust. If our plans were known to surrounding Arab states, they might prevent the realization of our dreams. Local Arab conditions, our own aspirations, will determine when the time is ripe for us to show our hand and make our claims known. Hundreds of years have not been too long to wait for this propitious moment. If my information is correct, and it comes from an impeccable source, then perhaps our time has come."

The three listeners sat quietly waiting to see what practical ideas their friend had brought. But Sadam was not yet ready, his political forecast not yet complete. "The war, which I believe will commence within days, will shake the Israeli resolve. Win or lose the war, we Palestinians will be a burden on them. Give them their due, they are not colonialists. Israel is a democracy. Democracies grow weary. They lose momentum and direction. They are sidestepped by their own internal opposition; they waste time on examining their principles. Their raison d'etre becomes fudged and subjected to squabbles.

"I can foresee the time when many Israelis, perhaps the majority, will want to rid themselves of Gaza and the West Bank just as Hussein did in his time and Abdullah before him. For they, in their days, were but usurpers themselves, visited upon us by the tyrannical British colonialists. Their takeover of our lands in 1948 was corrupt and had no legal validity. Their loss of our lands in the Six Day War had no validity either. Our people have been defrauded time and again of their rights, the rights of a people to its land, the land of its forefathers. Neither the British in their time, nor the Jordanians in theirs, and certainly not the Jews of today have the right to engage in the disposition of our territories.

"Paradoxically, I do believe that a badly punished Israel emerging the winner, will be better for us Palestinians than victorious Arab forces. But we Palestinians must be ready to show our resolve once hostilities break out. We must increase our efforts irrespective of who will ultimately triumph

"And now I can talk of practicalities. All four of us are engaged in moneychanging. Our offices handle the cash of thousands of Palestinians. Moreover, through our wholesale activities, we have ready access to the offices of many other moneychangers and they, in turn, have direct contact with many thousands of Palestinians."

Sadam sat back in his chair and looked at the faces of his three associates. They all lived by their wits, making many instant calculations each day. They all understood what he was driving at.

"We must spread the word that war is imminent. When the Israelis are under pressure, preoccupied with the defense of their borders, the time will be ripe for civil disobedience. The Israelis must feel our pain. It is time for us to give expression to our frustrations."

"Exactly what will we advise our brothers to do?" asked Hassan

"We are only moneychangers," answered Sadam immediately. "We are not generals and are not equipped to run guerilla forces. We must use our contacts to spread the word – there will be war. Palestinians must use the period of war to advance our just claims."

But Sadam's plans were soon to be frustrated. The meeting at Hassan's house took place on a Thursday evening. The following day, Friday, the offices of moneychangers were closed. On Saturday war broke out and all Arabs kept to their homes, holed up in their villages. On Sunday, amidst radio claims from Sadat in Cairo that the Israelis were being annihilated, Palestinians remained in or near their homes. On Monday the Israeli authorities shut down all moneychanging outlets for an unspecified period. Sadam Al-Din's practical suggestions were never put into effect.

In Amman two weeks earlier, Sadam had been given information from a reliable source that hostilities would soon break out. Syria and Egypt, he had been told, were coordinating attacks on Israel. He was also given to understand, that this time, Jordan would try not to become embroiled.

The source, a young Palestinian attached to the Jordanian secret service, could be trusted; he had proved himself on more than one occasion. Moreover, he was in Sadam's debt. Years earlier, in 1965, the source had come to Sadam's office to change some dinars into French francs. He had precious few to change. He complained that he would not be able to enjoy himself as much as he would have liked to during his free time on his forthcoming first trip to France.

Youssouf, the would-be traveller, had recently been seconded to a security detail at the royal palace and would accompany King Hussein on a trip to Paris. As the two Palestinians sat and talked over coffee, Sadam realized that the young man in his office might develop into an interesting contact. He offered to lend him some French francs. The friendship between the two was to blossom.

On his return to Amman, Youssouf came to see his new friend and tell him of the wonders of France. Slowly, and after gentle prompting, he had told of his duties in safeguarding the king. Youssouf had been puzzled about certain aspects of the trip and felt the need to confer with an older man and trusted friend. It appeared that the monarch's meeting was a tete-a-tete with none other than Golda Meir. This confidential meeting had taken place in one of the finest areas of Paris in the private home of a Jewish personality, a Madame Weill, who had been approached by Israeli Ambassador Walter Eytan. Eytan had been told to arrange a secret rendezvous.

The young guard had been watching the house from a strategic position, when a plain black Citroen pulled up in front of the gate and disgorged the easily recognizable Golda Meir, her assistant Simcha Dinitz, and the Israeli ambassador. Minutes later, a second, nondescript car pulled up, bringing the even more familiar King Hussein. Youssouf was watching the house together with two other Jordanian guards. He was aware that they were not alone and that there were at least three Israeli guards covering the house. There was no contact between the two sets of security men whose jobs were simply to ensure that the meeting and the subsequent return of the VIPs would be conducted smoothly, secretly and without interruptions.

What Youssouf was unprepared for and unable to cope with was the notion that his monarch was sitting talking to the enemy, be it in Paris or anywhere else. His emotions were confused, and he sought guidance from his older Palestinian friend. Sadam had heard rumors of clandestine meetings of this sort. When Youssouf had told him his story, Sadam had not been surprised.

Sadam still had nightmares concerning his early fedayeen training and his shortlived participation in the ranks of Palestinian freedom fighters. Many years earlier, as a young boy growing up in a refugee camp near Jericho, he had been trained for a mission to spread terror in Israel amongst its civilian population.

The group of three ill-trained terrorists had never made it to the Israeli border. After a series of bad calculations and ill-conceived actions, the group had been surprised by a single Israeli appearing from nowhere on a lonely road on the hills leading to Jerusalem. In a quick engagement two of his colleagues had been killed, and more by luck than by judgment he had cut down the Israeli. Although he could not remember all the details, he had apparently left the scene and run all the way back to his camp, to tell his commanders what had happened.

The camp officers had been divided about how to treat the returned warrior. Some wanted to make him a hero, for after all he had uncharacteristically survived a skirmish with the enemy and killed an Israeli. However, others pointed out that the group had not even managed to reach the Israeli border before two of the three had been cut down. Furthermore, there was the unfortunate business of the Land

Rover and the Jordanian soldier who had been murdered. As they pointed out, the Jordanian authorities might well turn ruthless. The upshot was that, after hiding a few days inside the camp, Sadam was spirited up into the mountains and to Amman. As far as he was concerned, it was the best thing that had ever happened to him.

From that time onwards, Sadam had developed his own political theories. First of all, he abhorred futile gestures such as sending ill-prepared youngsters on military skirmishes destined to fail. On a more theoretical level, he believed that a line must be drawn between declarations and action. No political meetings surprised him, and as for political declarations – he believed only very few of them.

Sadam nurtured the friendship with Youssouf, and in September 1970 Youssouf warned about the action planned against the Palestinians. This information had saved Sadam's life, for when he saw the first confrontation forming in front of him, he had quickly fled the scene.

Three years later, Youssouf had come to tell him of another meeting between King Hussein and Golda Meir. This time the meeting had taken place over the border inside Israel where, acording to Youssouf, Hussein had gone to warn Golda of the impending war which Egypt and Syria would launch.

Sadam had no interest in playing a political role. He yearned for a Palestinian homeland and longed to see Palestinian lands returned to their rightful owners. He saw no political role for himself that would speed the realization of such dreams. He was convinced that Palestinian maturity could not be induced by glib politicians in the way of doctors inducing the birth of a baby.

The time for Palestinian action, he believed, would never be ripe unless the world, and particularly the Arab world, saw great changes. He was convinced that, from time to time, such changes did occur, but the Palestinians had simply missed their chances. Looking around at the present crop of Palestinian politicians, he was scared that his long-suffering people would miss further chances.

Sadam did not believe that the Israelis would willingly surrender the Palestinian territories. The combination of war, hard labor, and good fortune that had enabled them to wrest control from the Jordanians was altogether too fortuitous. "The Israelis will relinquish nothing unless they have to," mused Sadam in despair.

At the meeting with the moneychangers in El-Bireh, Sadam had voiced all these thoughts. However, on this occasion he had summed up things differently. "The Israelis won't voluntarily surrender the territories. Conditions in the territories and world opinion will dictate their actions, and the Israelis will be powerless to resist.

It is our duty to set the scene for changing these conditions. A major war between Syria, Egypt and Israel will assist us immeasurably. We mustn't lose this chance, we mustn't miss in this opportunity."

✧ ✧ ✧

Chapter 19

In Israel's army, some officers are strict disciplinarians, sticklers for details. Others are known to be fearless and stubborn, and can be relied on in times of emergency. Most fight by the book, take commands literally, and have little difficulty in answering for their actions. All are versed in warfare. General Ariel Sharon, known affectionately as Arik, is cut in a mould all of his own. A man who truly thinks for himself. Overweight, swashbuckling, a decision maker, his troops believe him to be absolutely fearless. Most of his men adore him.

General Dayan's major concentration during the first week of the war was defense and counter-attack in the face of Syrian aggression. Israel, Dayan believed, did not possess the resources to push the Egyptians back across the Canal. But Sharon had other ideas. He was vehemently opposed to Dayan's concentratoin of military efforts against the Syrians at the expense of the Egyptian front.

During the first few days of the war, the activities of the newly redeployed Shaked Commandos met with a rapid succession of victory, frustration and anguish.

Yom Kippur. Day 1. 10 hours.
Shaked Commandos advised that Egyptian attack on Israel will commence at 18 hours.

13 hours (four hours earlier than expected):
Egyptian Migs and Sochoi jets bomb the Tasa headquarters.
The Shaked Commandos lose their first two men.

16 hours:
12 large M8 helicopters are observed flying low. Two Israeli Phantoms close on the enemy, downing 8. Four Egyptian M8s escape.

Later that night the Egyptian air force planes make their reprisal: Egyptian artillery strafe the Tasa base with 81mm shells.

Shaked's 5th platoon is dispatched down to Ras Sudar, once a holiday village south of Suez. Its orders are to await an Egyptian division approaching from the north. The Sayeret finds Ras Sudar in a state of near chaos. Atmosphere of imminent disaster.

The defense of Ras Sudar is now made top priority. Commandos, tanks and artillery are diverted to it with orders to dig in. An ill-equipped force begins to prepare the abandoned rooftops for guerrilla attacks against the superior forces of the Egyptians.

The Shaked commandos are ordered to move out into the desert, await the Egyptians, and at all costs to stop the first tank. Their orders are then to sabotage and destroy the remaining tanks. Their mission is successful. The Egyptians are stopped.

Ras Sudar. Orders are received to destroy all records and operational equipment compiled by army and navy intelligence. Yitzhak Mordechai takes his men into the desert and stops the Egyptian advance. He pleads against destroying the records. Moshe Dayan flies in, insisting that the cover-up be put into effect. The remaining forces are then evacuated.

Tasa Headquarters. The new Pazzi Force is formed, comprising twelve officers, two jeeps and one half-track. They are directly answerable to General Arik Sharon.

October 8. Day 3. Early a.m.
The Pazzi Force is operational.

The function of the Pazzi Force is to scout out advancing Egyptian commandos and general troop movements. Once formed, the unit prepares itself to cause havoc and destruction amongst any enemy force that it encounters.

October 14. Evening.
Nine Egyptian helicopters land along the Akavish Road leading from Tasa to the Canal, south of the Chinese Farm in Pazzi Force territory. Desert landscape. High dunes and shifting sands. Visibility poor, despite the full moon. The Israeli commandos join with a small, three tank unit and proceed in search of enemy forces.

October 15. Early a.m.
Commandos reach the top of a dune and draw enemy fire. Pazzi orders tanks to approach the top of the dune prepared for fire. Each in turn reaches the summit, fires

and withdraws. The unit then continues to advance. One of the commandos sees footprints in the sand. Pazzi advances to reconnoiter but walks directly into an ambush. Firing from the hip with automatic weapons, the commandos withdraw.

Again Pazzi solicits the assistance of the tanks. Together they advance. This time they come upon a significant stronghold. Three tanks, two jeeps and the half-track advance into the stronghold.

All at once the world explodes. Shots are coming at them from all directions. The tanks and the jeeps persevere, managing to traverse the entire battlefield without incident. But the half-track stalls and gets stuck half way across. The Egyptians fire an RPG shell and gain a direct hit on the half-track. The air is choked with smoke. The noise of fire, of tanks and of men is deafening. Two of the men in the half-track are killed outright; the driver, Eitan Nir, falls across the steering wheel, blasting the horn with his body. The RPG has cut him in half.

Two other soldiers suffer leg wounds but manage to extricate themselves from the half track. A third, Ketselle, is less fortunate, for he is seriously wounded. With excruciating difficulty, he manages to haul his body from the still screaming vehicle and drag himself along the sand before collapsing. Pazzi runs to his friend and draws him to relative safety behind the half-track. Convinced that Ketselle will not survive, Pazzi, the secularist, tries desperately to comfort him: "With G-d's help you'll be OK," he whispers, and he covers the bleeding body with his army jacket.

Unable to stand the noise, Danny Sadeh reaches into the half track and dislodges the jammed horn. Returning to the rear of the vehicle, he grabs hold of the automatic gun lying only a few feet from Ketselle's inert body and continues to fire. Furiously, desperately, he pounds round after round at the Egyptians.

The war around them rages at fever pitch. Pazzi and his driver circle the battlefield wildly, shooting at the enemy with the mad frenzy of dervishes. The air is thick with smoke and dust. Hand grenades zoom through the greyness and tanks belch forth their fodder like thunder. Sadeh remains at his post to the rear of the half-track. He shoots with deadly effectiveness. More RPGs are aimed at the half-track, but it suffers little further damage.

Eventually the battle eases, the surviving Egyptians taking to their heels. Exhausted, relieved, anxious about his friend, Danny Sadeh lays down his arms and goes back to attend to Ketselle. His condition is awful: A fountain of blood gushes from a gaping hole in his side. His limbs seem disconnected from his body. One of the soldiers tries to stop the bleeding by plugging the wound with his shirt. Sadeh is convinced that Ketselle is dead.

Pazzi comes back from the battlefield and stares down at the still bleeding body of his comrade-in-arms. Instantly he places a call through to Arik Sharon. In the steel-low voice of a man with his back to the wall, of a man with an iron will desperate to win, he demands a helicopter. "Immediately," he warns. "Within minutes I will have another dead officer on my hands."

A helicopter arrives and Ketselle is flown to Refidim for a transfusion. No one really expects him to survive.

The following day the Pazzi Force is disbanded. Its surviving soldiers are called upon to take part in Arik Sharon's campaign for the Suez Canal. On that day the Egyptians organize their deadly Tartur Ambush on the central road to the Canal. Sharon needs this road for the transportation of his heavy materiel.

Eli Sagi receives word that Ketselle has been severely wounded. Immediately he writes home informing his parents, asking them to find out where his friend is hospitalized and requesting that they visit him. But, for today, he has to go back into battle.

Preceding a convoy of tanks, Sagi leads the Shaked commandos to a narrow area between the sand dunes and the swamps. The Egyptians surround them on three sides, opening fire on them from the north, from the south and from the east. Sagi and nine colleagues are killed immediately.

Two legs of the three-legged stool are now gone. The one surviving limb – Ketselle – is fighting for his life. After a series of operations and skin-grafts, followed by a lengthy course of rehabilitation, Ketselle is returned to the living. He emerges with a shortened left leg, a fighting spirit, a full heart – and a wife. Ketselle has married Tamar, his nurse.

October 12. Day 6.

Arik Sharon prepares to lead a brigade of paratroopers and tanks. Objective: To force a path through enemy lines and cross the Suez Canal.

Operational plans: To move mobile pontoons, to tow pre-constructed bridges, and to destroy surface-to-air missile batteries.

✧   ✧   ✧

The war over, the army released a number of reserve soldiers. Corporal Avraham Nissim, who had not seen his wife and children for five weeks, was now allowed to go home.

Looking dishevelled, his beard and hair unkempt and unusually long, Avraham made his way first on an army truck from the Golan Heights to Tiberias, and then by bus to Jerusalem. Before proceeding on the last lap to the settlement, he made his way, with thanks in his heart, to the home of the Kadosh.

The gabbai received the returning soldier with warmth. The Kadosh had only that morning told him to expect this visit. Avraham followed the gabbai down the stairs and into the basement where the Kadosh welcomed him: *"Baruch boacha beshalom –* Blessed is your arrival in peace. You must sit down and make a blessing over a piece of fruit," said the Kadosh. The saintly rabbi took an apple and cut it in half, slicing through the circumference. "But you must not stay long, as your wife and children will be waiting for you."

Avraham made the appropriate blessing on the apple. *"Boreh peri haetz –* the creator of the fruit of the trees. The war was terrible. My oldest and dearest friends were killed, several before my eyes. The admonition of the Kadosh to wash my hands before eating bread was adhered to and, indeed, it saved my life."

Quickly Avraham told the Kadosh exactly what had happened in the bunker. Looking at the Kadosh, he had the feeling, however, that the story was not new to him. "There is another matter that I wish to raise with the Kadosh," said Avraham. "Recently some settlers bought a tract of land from an Arab. He had an interesting history. When he was a boy in the Hebron hills, his mother used to light candles on Friday nights. Subsequently his family moved to Hebron. There, during the 1929 massacre, he saved his Jewish neighbors from being killed. Following these events he moved to live near Ramallah.

"I have become friendly with the Arab's son, Taher. He wishes to convert to Judaism and I have been teaching him about our religion. The responsibility is a great one and I seek guidance."

Avraham settled back in the chair. He had told the story concisely. He would now await the decision of the Sage.

"After you have settled down with your family and regained your normal life, you must make further enquiries. You will find that Taher's mother is also Jewish, although she does not know it. You must speak with Taher's father and also with his uncle in Hebron. Take with you a representative of the Chief Rabbinate. I myself will talk to the Chief Rabbi about this matter, and he will assist you. But first you have a pressing duty to your wife and children. Go in peace."

Avraham rose from his chair and backed away from the Kadosh in the direction of the door behind him.

Chapter **20**

The period of the war had been particularly trying to Taher. For some time he had participated in a demanding program that would prepare him for assuming the religious obligations of Judaism. The decision to convert had been his own. He had not rushed into it. He had decided to take the far-reaching step after long and careful consideration. His father had given his tacit approval; his mother, sister and friends knew nothing of his intentions.

"The Jewish nation dwells alone," Taher had been taught. The individual Jew must adjust to separation. Accordingly, as part of the conversion process, Taher had been encouraged to move away from his family home. He had found a small, two-roomed apartment in Neve Ya'acov, a northern suburb of Jerusalem on the road to Ramallah. From this new base he could visit his family with ease. He could also commute to Jerusalem, to attend religious instruction courses. The surburb of Neve Ya'acov was inhabited largely by new immigrants, simple working families. A number of them hailed from Arab countries from which they had been ejected. Surrounding the suburb were Arab villages, some of which were sympathetic to Arab terrorism.

Most of the inhabitants of Neve Ya'acov worked in Jerusalem; they commuted by bus. The route regularly featured on the news programs as a target for Arab stones and Molotov cocktails. Against this background Arabs were not popular in Neve Ya'acov. They were barely tolerated.

Taher was well aware of this, and seeking to emphasize his status as a candidate for conversion, he donned a colored knitted skullcap, a *kippah*. Although this did not bring him any friends, it kept potential animosity in check. When leaving the suburb and turning left towards Jerusalem, he kept the kippah on his head; when turning right towards his family in Ramallah, he removed it.

When the Yom Kippur War broke out, his position was tenuous. The local Arabs, subjected to Jordanian, Egyptian and Syrian propaganda were convinced that all the

Jewish wrongs of 1967 would be redressed. Palestinian lands would be speedily liberated by victorious Arab armies. Under these circumstances, Taher felt little inclination to visit his family.

In Israel, on the other hand, all his male friends and associates were in the army. Young men were rarely seen in the streets.

Taher did not feel comfortable walking around Jerusalem. All his courses had been cancelled. Teachers and students were away fighting for Israel's survival.

Taher learned quickly. He went to the supermarket and stocked up on provisions for a prolonged siege.

The aftermath of the Yom Kippur War

Owing to the October war, from which Israel emerged a badly bruised victor, the general elections to Israel's parliament – the Knesset – were postponed until December 1973. The price of the victory was very high, and tiny Israel, with a war casualty in almost every family, demanded an accounting.

The Agranat Commission was established to investigate the conduct of the military and the government on the eve of and during the war. Israel is home to Jews from all over the world, all languages are spoken. Immigrants from Italian-speaking backgrounds recalled that *granate* in Italian is the motion of a broom used to sweep everything under the carpet.

The commission's findings pinned the responsibility for misreading the situation and lack of mobilization before the war exclusively on the Chief of Staff and some of his generals; the politicians were declared blameless. In the eyes of many Israelis, these findings are a travesty.

Golda Meir, who had recently selected her new cabinet following the elections, was herself distressed by the commission's findings. Within one month she resigned.

General Moshe Dayan, her erstwhile minister of defense, with a combination of prophetic vision and analytical clarity had once pronounced, "the key to war in the Middle East is in the hands of the Soviets, while the key to peace is held by the United States."

At Camp David years later, Dayan was to play a dramatic role in bringing peace with Egypt. But for now Golda's infant government fell.

In Jordan, the royal brothers noted with satisfaction that, despite the token Jordanian participation in the war on the side of Syria, no changes had been made in respect of the Temple Mount. Israel had taken no action to exercize control over the Muslim holy places, which were still controlled by the Muslim Wakf. Jews were still denied free access to the Temple Mount.

The war had done nothing to settle the national aspirations of many Palestinians, a term that Golda Meir still steadfastly refused to recognize. The discontent in the occupied territories, on the West Bank and Gaza strip was escalating. Jews now thought twice before shopping in Arab village markets or drinking coffee off the beaten track. In the Old City of Jerusalem and elsewhere, there were stories of stabbings and unrest.

Golda's successor as prime minister was Yitzhak Rabin, a soldier by training, who had served as chief of staff during the triumphant Six Day War. He had since served as ambassador to Washington, where much of his energies were spent in defending Israel's unwillingness to trade peace with the Egyptians against substantial withdrawal in Sinai. The Yom Kippur War was the ultimate justification of this policy, for had it been commenced by the Syrians and Egyptians starting from the pre-1967 borders, Israel might well have been erased from the map.

For now, Prime Minister Rabin had to deal with rebuilding Israel's badly bruised armed forces and its ailing economy. He also had to deal with ceasefire breaches, exchanges of prisoners, and the thorny problem of the still entrapped Egyptian Third Army in the Sinai Desert.

In the United States, Henry Kissinger, Richard Nixon's secretary of state, developed a theory that Israel had to allow Egypt to come out of the war with its self-esteem, to facilitate an atmosphere that might lead to a negotiated settlement. As Israel's instance of last resort, the United States regarded itself morally justified to lean on its Middle East dependent and felt strong enough politically to arrange for the Soviets to play a similar role with their Arab clients. Prime Minister Yitzhak Rabin had to ensure that an imposed settlement would not be detrimental to Israel's interests. Indeed, he was opposed to any form of settlement imposed by third parties and continued to expound Israel's old demand for direct negotiations.

Chapter 21

Sadam Al-Din spent the weeks of the Yom Kippur War holed up in a small hotel inside the Old City. Moneychanging activities had been stopped by the authorities. His friends and business associates all maintained low profiles. Local Arabs clearly wanted to sit the war out, to take no chances. Any effort to change their mood was doomed to failure.

A full month passed from the outbreak of hostilities until the Allenby Bridge was reopened. A semblance of normalcy returned to the region. Both Jordan, which had played only a minor role in the war, and the victorious Israelis were keen to keep at least one bridge open between the two countries. Nevertheless, Sadam, a prudent man trained to limit his risks, waited for a further week before crossing back into Jordan. The crossing, when he made it, was not uneventful.

Sadam travelled by shared taxi to the Allenby Bridge on a Sunday morning. He chose Sunday, as it was always the busiest day at the bridge, after being closed for two Sabbaths, the Jewish and the Muslim. The larger the crush, the greater the chaos. These were the conditions that might make his crossing barely noticed.

He stood in line at the bridge for over an hour before presenting his papers to the Israeli authorities. A new young military clerk was sitting at a desk behind the window; next to him was a more experienced man teaching him the ropes. Behind them hovered an officer, the single star on whose shoulder indicated he was a major. The clerk took the Jordanian travel documents and flicked the pages without even looking up at Sadam, who stood patiently at the window. As the more senior clerk held out his hand for the documents, the officer, Major Yaron Yadid, took the couple of steps that separated him from the clerks and peered at the papers. Major Yadid looked up at the window and saw before him a young Palestinian who might well have been between eighteen and twenty-two years old in 1951. For this was the period that interested the major. Without a word, the major reached over the shoulders of the clerk, took the documents, turned on his heels and walked towards his small private office at the rear of the prefabricated building. As he approached his office, Major Yadid had a distinct feeling of deja vu.

Six years earlier, while still a junior officer, Yadid had spent an uncomfortable month at a miserable refugee camp outside Jericho. The heat, even in October, the incessant flies and mosquitoes, the squalor, the dirt and the dryness had all contributed to a feeling of despondency. Worse still, he had failed to obtain the answers for which he had been sent to that awful rathole.

His orders at the time were specific and simple. He was given an exact date and told to ascertain the identities of three young fedayeen terrorists that had, on that day, left the camp on a mission. He was then to probe whether one had returned. If the answer was positive he was to find him. As simple as that! Find him and bring him in for questioning.

After a whole month, during which he had questioned every living being at the camp, he had ascertained that three young terrorists had indeed left on a mission on the specified date. Furthermore, it was confirmed to him by different and unconnected sources that one youth had in fact returned. Within days, the youth had left the camp for an unknown destination. There were, however, no documents that could substantiate the reports, none that could provide him with actual names.

On orders from very high up in the Defense Forces, he and a number of more senior officers in intelligence had spent much time and effort considering his findings and juggling with hypotheses as to what might have happened to the surviving Arab terrorist. The final decision of this small think tank was that he had probably been moved to a town like Irbid, maybe Amman.

Major Yadid had retired from the regular army three years later and now served thirty days each year in the reserves, usually at the Allenby Bridge. Bored by the futility of monitoring Palestinians and Arabs crossing backwards and forwards over the bridge, the major had devised his own little plan to keep interested in his work. He would continue to search for the terrorist.

Palestinians are designated as such in Jordanian papers; so too would be recorded their place and date of birth. As the date of the mission had been 1951 and as operating terrorists almost invariably were in the age bracket of 18 to 22, the major paid particular attention to Palestinians born between 1929 and 1933.

Sitting down at his small metal desk, he flipped through the Jordanian documents belonging to Sadam Al-Din. The judgment of his quick glance had been correct. The papers confirmed that Sadam was in the right age bracket. Place of birth – Ramallah. Residence – Amman.

Major Yadin turned the pages, looking for more clues. He found none. There was no reference indicating that Sadam Al-Din had ever been in the Jericho refugee camp. There was, however, one other avenue of inquiry to be pursued, but it would take time.

The United Nations Work and Relief Authority, known as UNWRA, had kept records of all refugee camp inmates. The records were inaccurate and often misleading, as few deaths or transfers were ever registered. Once registered, everyone remained registered! There were always many friends and relatives willing to continue drawing benefits. If an Al-Din family had ever moved from Ramallah to the Jericho camp, it might just have been recorded by UNWRA. And copies of these records were held by the IDF. Major Yadid lifted the receiver and dialed a number in Tel Aviv.

An hour later, when the major sent an underling to bring Sadam to his office, he knew without any doubt that Sadam had once lived in the refugee camp. He had a feeling that he was on to a home run; the question remained – would he be able to prove his gut feeling.

The reserve major waived Sadam courteously to a seat. "I have the impression," began the major, "that your papers are incomplete. Where were you living between the time you left Ramallah in 1948 and your present town of residence, Amman?"

During his many crossings into Israel, Sadam had often worried about just such a question. That he had never been asked it in the past might have softened him a little, but the potentiality for such a question was always taken into account. Sadam had seen the major take the papers and watched him walk with a sense of purpose to his own room. With many references to his watch, he noted that an hour had passed before he had been summoned. Just enough time for the major to make inquiries by phone, he surmised. Suffering from a justifiable measure of paranoia – given that he had indeed shot an Israeli, albeit many years ago – he could always see in his mind's eye the measured searching of UNWRA records which would show the years that he had spent in the refugee camp.

Turning to his inquisitor with a smile, he said in measured tones: "I left Ramallah as a refugee and spent a couple of years in a refugee camp before continuing to Amman."

"And which camp was that?" asked the cunning major. But it was now clear to Sadam that the Israeli knew the answer.

"I had the privilege," joked Sadam, "to live in the Jericho Camp."

"And when did you leave the camp and move on to Amman?"

"In 1950," lied Sadam without turning a hair.

"Have you any documentation to prove that date?" asked the major.

"Isn't it recorded in my Jordanian papers?" asked Sadam slyly.

"I think that we both know that it is not," replied the major, with dark overtones.

Silence. Sadam refused to address the major's previous question. The major found himself wondering how to proceed. He lifted the papers off the desk and walked out of the room. Moving to another room, the major made a second telephone call, this time to Colonel Eran at Intelligence Headquarters. "You remember the inquiries that I made at the Jericho Camp after the Six Day War?" asked Major Yadid. "Well there might be a development."

He proceeded to tell his colonel all that he knew about Sadam Al-Din. "How many boys in that age bracket were there at that camp?" asked the colonel, "and why do you think that this is your man?"

"Firstly, I concede that there were thousands in the age group. As for your second question: Its a mixture of the experiences of one month of questions at that mosquito infested camp and my gut feeling. I do believe the suspect is lying to me."

There was one item of information that the colonel had in his possession that had been denied the more junior officer. The colonel knew that General Moshe Dayan had personally instituted the inquiries. It took the colonel only two minutes to reach a decision. "Wait near the phone, and I'll come back to you – and have someone keep an eye on the suspect."

The colonel placed a call to the Ministry of Defense only a few blocks away from his own office. Within minutes he was retelling the major's story to General Dayan himself.

Two hours later, Sadam Al-Din was back in Jerusalem, where he was delivered to the hands of the Shabak at their Katamon office. For the next two hours he cooled his heels in a basement conference room, all alone except for a feeling that he was being spied on through some undetected device. Sitting on a wooden seat at a small conference table, Sadam had been provided with tea, biscuits and a packet of Israeli cigarettes.

The door opened. An older man in civilian clothes entered and sat down looking intently at Sadam. "I have not come to question you but merely to accompany you upstairs to a larger and more comfortable room. There you will be interviewed by one of Israel's celebrities. He is personally concerned to know details of what happened many years ago on a lonely stretch of road in the hills leading from Kalia to Jerusalem. If you can help him, your assistance would be greatly appreciated. If on the other hand we find that you are not telling the truth, or are keeping back the truth, we will be sorely disappointed."

Some seven hours had now passed since Sadam had approached the window at the Allenby Bridge and handed over his papers. The myths surrounding the Israeli Secret Service had increased their powers and successes, way beyond reality. After seven hours of reflection, Sadam was conditioned to accept the Shabak's paramount superiority. Ushered into the larger room upstairs, Sadam found himself, quite extraordinarily, face to face with General Moshe Dayan. Involuntarily, he turned for support towards the older man who had brought him upstairs. However, that gentleman was just at the point of leaving the room and closing the door.

"Come in, sit down," said Dayan with a crooked smile extending from his eye-patch to his ear.

"Twenty-two years ago, when you were about nineteen years old, a short battle left two young Arabs and one Jew killed on a lonely stretch of road some ten miles or so east of here in the direction of Kalia. The Jew was an old and dear friend of mine, and I am very keen to know exactly what transpired at the time of his death."

Sadam sat terrified. He knew Dayan's reputation for brilliant deduction and ruthlessness. Was he deducing or did he know when he continued, "I understand that you will be able to provide me with the details that I have sought for so long."

Sadam addressed the general in the same measured tones used hours earlier with the major. "I am a Palestinian travelling legitimately on Jordanian papers. I have been improperly detained at the Allenby Bridge border post. In these circumstances, I wish to consult a lawyer."

Dayan sat back in his comfortable chair behind the desk which separated them. "Clever little bugger," he thought, "I'm posing questions about 1951 and he is demanding free travel rights. Or is he cleverer than that? Perhaps he wants to cut a deal and needs to know his legal rights."

"Have you any particular lawyer in mind?" asked Dayan.

After only a moment's delay, Sadam replied, "Azziz Shehadeh. We can probably find him in Ramallah."

Without making any comment or indicating that he might know Shehadeh, Dayan lifted the receiver and asked the girl on the switchboard to find the lawyer. Within minutes the phone rang.

Dayan lifted the receiver for a second time, listened for a few seconds and silently passed the phone to the Palestinian. As if in deference to the Palestinian's rights of privacy, Dayan rose from his chair. Indicating that Sadam could talk freely, Dayan walked to the door and left the room.

Sadam had long followed the career of the Ramallah lawyer. He knew that he was reputed to have several leading Israelis as his friends. However, he was also impressed by the lawyer's record defending the civil rights of Palestinians against the powerful Israelis. In his present circumstances he felt that he had to entrust a lawyer to advise him on his legal rights, and possibly even save his neck. He couldn't guess how Dayan would behave were he to learn that it had been a bullet from his gun that had killed Dayan's friend. He speculated on whether, in similar circumstances, the Jordanians would have so graciously granted him access to a lawyer.

Azziz Shehadeh was in Jerusalem and was found quickly by the Shabak switchboard. After a brief chat on the phone, he told Sadam Al-Din, that he would come straight over to Katamon. After two sessions with him and a ten-minute session with Moshe Dayan, the practiced lawyer was in a quandary.

Sadam was not stupid. He had been very careful about the manner in which he had consulted the lawyer. Although Sadam had not confirmed that he had taken part in the ill-fated mission so many years earlier, Azziz formed the definite impression that such was the case. Now came the problem of what to counsel his client. Had any other personality been involved, Azziz would have recommended to the client simply to deny the whole story. After all, the chance of the Israelis getting direct corroborating evidence, that would stand up in court after all these years, was negligible. Then again, Sadam could make a plea of self-defense. Finally there was the question of jurisdiction. The affair had taken place inside Jordanian territory where the Israeli had been illicitly!

"What a smart chap General Dayan is," thought Azziz, "perhaps there was good reason for allowing the Palestinian access to me."

"What exactly do you want to achieve?" Azziz Shehadeh asked Dayan when he returned to the latter's room. "Do you want me to defend the Palestinian, advise him of his rights, talk to him about jurisdiction – or do you want to do a deal?"

"I need to know about some papers that our major was carrying – they were not found on his body. Everything else is subject to negotiation."

As the lawyer had not heard about missing papers before, he rose from his chair and said that he would have to consult his client yet again. As he was walking towards the door, he turned and said: "You know, this young man is engaged in moneychanging in Amman. His office acts as the ultimate clearing-house for Palestinian moneychangers throughout the West Bank. That makes him a well connected person. A reasonable relationship with such a contact might pay dividends in the longer term."

Downstairs, Azziz confronted his client. "Firstly, let me tell you without modesty that I think Dayan was happy you asked for me. Secondly, Dayan is not interested in pressing any charges – he genuinely wants to know what happened that night on the mountain road. In particular he wants to know about documents that the Israeli was carrying, which were not on his body when it was discovered many years later."

Abandoning caution, and talking for the first time directly to the point, Sadam replied: "I don't know anything about any papers. You – and more to the point Dayan – must believe me! I simply don't know what he is talking about."

Back upstairs with the minister of defense, Azziz began his brief: "I am addressing you as a friend. For the time being, what I am about to say, is privileged and off the record. Many years ago, in his youth, my new Palestinian client was a simple, badly trained, young member of a hopeless mission of terror that never even reached its first goal, the border with Israel. He was sleeping at the side of the road when, over the brow of a hill, your Israeli officer appeared. Shooting broke out in all directions. Your Israeli friend picked off two Palestinians and then turned towards Sadam. As luck would have it, he pulled the trigger of his gun first. In a condition of blind terror, the inexperienced Palestinian dropped his gun, abandoned his friends and fled the scene. He didn't stop running until he reached the shelter of his refugee camp."

"And what about the missing documents?" asked Dayan.

"He knows nothing about them. And by the way, he did not bury the dead, nor did he touch anything at all."

A clearly disappointed Dayan turned to the Arab lawyer whom he considered his friend. "Should I believe this Palestinian? The documents are important."

"Perhaps we should get a full statement," replied the lawyer,

"You and your officers here should then question him freely. Afterwards, perhaps, you should have his testimony tested on a polygraph machine. If it all checks out, I want your word that he will be released and allowed to return home."

"You have my word," said the minister of defense.

CHAPTER 22

A couple of months after the Yom Kippur War, Taher and Avraham travelled by car to Hebron. At the Area Command station they met a Rabbi Meltzer from the Jerusalem Chief Rabbinate and his brother Ephraim who worked for the Shabak. Ephraim had coordinated arrangements with his colleagues in Hebron. They had arranged to bring Samir Jabari, Taher's uncle, in for questioning.

Waiting for the uncle to arrive, Ephraim explained: "It's better for your uncle that we bring him in. The alternative that we visit him at his home might make problems for him among his own neighbors."

Taher had mixed feelings about meeting an uncle that he could not remember ever having seen before. He knew that his father had left Hebron in anger, that there was no love lost between the brothers. He questioned Avraham about the necessity for this visit; surely his own father could be an alternative source of information? Avraham was definite. At a recent meeting, the Kadosh had set the terms of reference; first the uncle, only then, Taher's father.

"You may tell your uncle who you are if you want to. It is up to you. Bearing in mind the subject of our inquiries and the resemblance between you and your father, I would think that he will probably guess who you are."

The uncle was admitted into the small conference room and looked at the assembled inquisitors; he was puzzled. On seeing the family resemblance, Taher made an instant decision: "I am Taher, the son of your brother Amin. We have come to ask you some questions."

Samir looked at his nephew in bewilderment. He knew that his brother had gone to live near Ramallah but knew nothing of his offspring. He continued to appear puzzled at the interruption of his normal way of life. Taciturn by nature, he merely sat and awaited to hear more.

Speaking fluent Arabic, Avraham told the uncle that inquiries were being made into Taher's background. The authorities required Samir's help. No reaction from

Samir. "We are interested to know about Samir's mother. Do you remember her, and what can you tell us about her family?"

Samir seemed to be lost in thought as he cast his mind back to affairs long since forgotten. The four questioners waited patiently. After a few minutes he replied, "The family were not happy when Amin took his wife, for she was his cousin." He lapsed back into silence. "Explain how she was his cousin," said Ephraim in very poor Arabic.

Again silence. Clearly the taciturn Arab was not one to react quickly. "Our mother and the mother of Amin's wife were sisters," came the reply. "That makes them first cousins!"

Ephraim and Avraham exchanged glances. If the grandmother was Jewish, then so, too, was her sister and her sister's daughter. Taking it one step further through the maternal line, Taher was also Jewish. "That is all we require to know," said Avraham as he rose from his seat. "If you want a ride back home I'm sure it can be arranged."

Samir Jabari rose from his seat, looking just as mystified as he had been when he had entered the room. However, he gathered his wits quickly enough and refused the ride. "I'll walk home, it is only down the road." With that, Samir Jabari of Hebron turned his back on the Israelis and on his nephew and walked to the door.

On the return trip to Jerusalem, Avraham had an oportunity to reflect on the wisdom of the Kadosh. Taher's father might well not be forthcoming about his marrying a first cousin. He questioned Taher who confirmed that he had never known this family detail.

"Now we will proceed to your father who will merely confirm what we have been told by his brother," said Rabbi Meltzer.

CHAPTER 23

One year after the Yom Kippur War, Hilarion Capucci, the Greek Catholic Archbishop of Jerusalem, was arrested for smuggling armaments from Lebanon into Israel. He was caught red-handed crossing the northern border in his Mercedes limousine with a cache of arms that included automatic submachine guns, revolvers, TNT explosives, hand grenades, many rounds of ammunition and more.

With the support of his superiors, Capucci loudly proclaimed his innocence, pleaded diplomatic immunity, and brought to bear as much pressure from churches, diplomats and foreign governments as he could muster. He appointed Azziz Shehadeh, the celebrated Ramallah attorney, as his defense counsel, and this experienced lawyer in turn used every ploy to extert as much pressure as possible on the Israeli government.

The Israeli government was in a bind. Had this been an isolated case, there were those who felt that Israel should have deported the errant priest in order to prevent the embarrassment of a trial and the attendant publicity. However, only five years earlier, the Reverend Elia Khoury, of the Anglican Church in Ramallah, had been arrested and deported to Jordan. He had been caught aiding terrorists to plant explosives in Supersol, the busy supermarket on Jerusalem's Agron Street.

The authorities believed that in pursuing his activities, Capucci was sure that if caught, he would be deported as a hero, as had been the case with Khoury. Yitzhak Rabin's government decided that no more cases of terrorist priests would be tolerated.

Although Azziz Shahadeh had built a considerable reputation as a leading attorney, the case of Archbishop Capucci was in fact the first case where Shehadeh actually appeared in an Israeli court. The case was heard in the District Court before Justice Miriam Ben Porat, who was at an early stage of an illustrious career.

Shehadeh's first ploy was to claim diplomatic immunity. The judge, however, ruled that a Vatican passport as such does not secure such immunity. She pointed out that, as no diplomatic relations existed between Israel and the Vatican, there can be no question of reciprocal diplomatic status for prelates in either of those two countries.

In his defense, Capucci maintained that he wasn't actually in the car when it was searched, did not know of and/or was not responsible for the arms that were found, and/or that they were planted by the Israelis in order to compromise him and his church. Eyewitnesses were called by the prosecution, to give their testimony and Archbishop Capucci was found guilty as charged. He was sentenced to twelve years in jail.

With claims that Capucci's health was fast deteriorating, representations were made from the Vatican requesting that the matter of Capucci to be dealt with "properly" by the Israeli authorities. The government of Yitzhak Rabin stood firm to all external pressures in respect of the errant cleric. However, after the May 1977 elections, a new government was formed under Menahem Begin. Beguiled by the Catholic Church, he quickly fell prey to the pleadings of the Vatican emissaries on behalf of the evildoer.

In late 1977 an exchange of letters between the Pope and the President of Israel secured the cleric's release. He had spent only three years of his sentence in prison. The Vatican undertook that Capucci would be posted to a South American monastery, would desist from further contact with the Palestine Liberation Organization, and would not return to the Middle East.

Flown to Rome in his cleric's clothes, the 55 year old priest was given a hero's welcome by PLO representatives who hailed him, "a hero, a symbol of resistance and a man who really loves his people and his land."

Fourteen months later Capucci flew to Damascus to attend a PLO executive meeting, thus breaking the Vatican's promise. Soon afterwards, Hilarion Capucci flew to Iran, where he sang the praises of the recently returned Ayatollah Khomeini and his work for the Palestinians. The following month, after an audience with the Pope, he was given a European appointment.

The polarization of ethnic, religious and nationalistic groups continued with renewed emphasis after Capucci's arrest.

Israel's Rabin government offered nothing to its Arab neighbors that had not been suggested previously; the political deadlock continued. With renewed Russian support, the Arabs began to rearm themselves. However, it looked unlikely that Egypt and Syria would wage war on Israel in the near future.

In 1977 the government resigned and Rabin called for new elections, against a background of charges of personal improper financial dealings.

The Israeli public wanted a change, After thirty years of rule by left-wing parties, the right-wing Likud won the election. Menahem Begin was elected prime minister.

Time magazine deplored the change brought at the polls. Dwelling on Begin's past as a terrorist leader against British rule in Palestine, it bemoaned the certainty that no concessions would be given to the Arabs by the likes of Begin whose name, they advised their readers, rhymed with Feigin.

The first surprise of the Begin administration was the appointment of General Moshe Dayan as foreign minister, straight from the ranks of the new opposition. This coup indicated major diplomatic changes in the offing.

Nobody, however, would have ventured the possibility that Begin the arch hawk, would cede the Suez Canal to the Egyptians; withdraw Israel's forces from the entire Sinai peninsula, and sign a daring peace treaty with President Sadat.

President Carter, himself newly elected, wanted to push through changes where previous administrations had failed. Egypt, in the meantime, had burnt its bridges with its Russian sponsors and was in a better position to be influenced by the Americans than previously. Begin and Sadat were ready to make history and gain world-wide recognition.

Within months of Begin's taking over as prime minister, Anwar Sadat announced that he would come to Jerusalem to make peace. Received by Israel with open arms, he addressed a packed Israeli Knesset where his central theme revolved around his catch phrase "No More War." He won the hearts of Israel's citizens and politicians alike. In short order a peace treaty was structured, based on a complete withdrawal of Israel's troops from the Sinai peninsula, normalization of bilateral relations and full exchange of diplomats.

King Hussein was dismayed at Begin's victory at the polls. He had been slowly cultivating relationships with the hierarchy of the old government, with Abba Eban, Shimon Peres and Yitzhak Rabin. Like so many others, he saw in Begin an intransigent hawk who would take Israel away from regional peace.

The election of a Likud government introduced a potential change in Israel's attitude to the Temple Mount. After all, Begin's government rested on coalition support from the parties to the extreme right of Israel's political spectrum.

As the years passed by, King Hussein realized that Menahem Begin had made no changes of any kind to the smooth running of affairs on the Temple Mount.

The Palestinians could see no improvement in their situation. Foreign Jordanian rule had merely been replaced by foreign Israeli rule. Polarization of extremist groups continued with new urgency.

Israel's security forces had been working among the Palestinians for some years. In every Arab village there was at least one Arab informer who kept the Israelis posted on the extremist elements. These informers were indelicately called "stinkers," pronounced by Israelis as "shtinkers."

As time passed, many arrests were made by the Israelis of dangerous elements amongst the Palestinians. Amnesty International and local citizens rights movements deplored the detention without trial of thousands of so called extremists.

Israel, for its part, claimed that it was at war with the PLO and with all the diverse Arabs whose common link was the explicit determination to see Israel pushed into the sea. It doubled its efforts to identify subversives. As the numbers of detainees increased, the expressions of nationalist anguish came more to the fore.

Arab informers caught in the villages by PLO sympathizers were dealt with without mercy. Groups of execution squads were formed and Arab justice was meted out without trial or explanation.

✧   ✧   ✧

CHAPTER **24**

In 1981, while Taher was at his apartment in Neve Ya'acov, an execution squad visited his father's home. Abdul Rahman, the leader of a PLO squad based in Ramallah, had been informed that Amin had sold land to the Jews and was on special terms with the Israeli security forces.

Whereas the first part of the information was true, there was no truth in the second part, which was based on a simple mistake. During a hospital visit for chemotherapy treatment, Amin had met Avraham, who offered the old and sick man a lift home. That day Avraham's car was in the garage for repairs and he had rented a white Ford Escort similar to the cars driven by numerous Israeli security men. Amin had been seen entering the Ford. This had sealed his death sentence. Abdul Rahman and his two associates had that same evening carried out two similar missions, executing death sentences with brutal efficiency. As they approached Amin's home they felt intoxicated with their own supreme power, for they held life and death in their hands. The name Rahman means *the merciful*. However, Abdul had never allowed this to prevent him from carrying out his duties.

Amin, now in his seventies, was in the final stages of his illness. He had been kept alive by chemotherapy and painkillers for some years and knew that his days were numbered. When the three masked Arab thugs burst into his home late that night he made a prayer of thanks that Taher, his beloved son, was not present.

Taher's grief knew no bounds. He loved and respected his father, his ultimate guide and benefactor. He despised the murderers who had carried out this cruel and needless sentence on a dying man. He could not feel any common links with thugs that dispensed executions in the name of Allah, the Revolution, or Palestinian Liberation. He knew the thugs for what they were, callous murderers.

It was this dramatic turning point in his life that pressed Taher to reveal the contents of the document, still in its original envelope, and stored at the bank in Ramallah in the family safe. He decided that his Jerusalem lawyer should be trusted to decipher the contents.

After taking the letter from the bank in Ramallah, he travelled to Jerusalem. Walking from east to west of the city, he made for the Bank Hapoalim in King George Street, where he had an account, and had recently taken a safe-deposit box. At a print shop over the road from the bank he made two photocopies of the document, having carefully studied the actions of the person before him in line for the machine. He didn't want to entrust the document or the copies to any other eyes, even for an instant. Inserting the original in the envelope, he then crossed the road to the bank and placed it in his safe-deposit box, retaining the copies in his inside pocket.

Arriving by appointment, Taher was shown in to Rami Feffer's office on the third floor of a tatty building on a small side street in downtown Jerusalem. As he remembered from his previous visits, the office was badly lit, gloomy and full of papers and files. They littered the desk and the floor, lying in piles around Feffer's creaky and torn chair, which looked as if it had been in the office since the building had been erected some seventy years earlier.

Rami was talking on the phone. Without looking up from some papers he was looking through at the same time, he contrived to wave Taher to the only chair in the office not occupied by boxes or files. A few minutes passed and his secretary, Tali, rushed in and informed the attorney that a client was on another line from America. Muttering excuses, Feffer rested the receiver on a pile of papers and rushed from the room to take the other call elsewhere. On arrival, Taher had seen no sign of Tali in the general office and had wondered if she still worked for the lawyers. As he now waited for Rami to return, Taher realized how much he had been hoping to see her again.

Guarding the copy of the document, which had lain undeciphered for so many years, Taher had grown to assume that it was of immeasurable importance. Some thirty years had passed before he had built up the courage required to take steps to reveal its secrets. In the hustle and bustle of this law office, he wondered again whether this was the way for him to proceed.

Advocate Feffer spent nearly ten minutes on the outside phone and then returned to resume the thread of the conversation on the phone in his office. When Tali returned a second time to advise that two other callers were holding, Taher rose from his seat with a look of exasperation on his face. It was at this stage that Feffer, seeing his client's patience sorely tried, decided to make amends. He requested his secretary not to accept any more calls and replaced the receiver still in his hands. Turning to Taher, he apologized for not attending to him properly.

Taher rose again and, crossing to the door, closed it firmly behind the receding secretary. Feffer was impressed; he had never before seen indications of determination in this client. It would appear that Taher, who had phoned and asked for an appointment, had some serious matter on his mind.

"How can I help you?" asked the lawyer having come to the conclusion that another land deal was in the making.

"I have come to seek advice in respect of a secret document that I have guarded for nearly thirty years," replied Taher. Choosing his words with utmost care, he concluded, "But first I must ask you some questions."

Feffer looked at Taher with interest and Taher continued: "I have papers in my possession, the contents of which I require to be deciphered, and I would like your help. However, I must ask you how you would treat knowledge of the contents."

Feffer, who had been dealing with routine small court matters in cases involving debts, claims and property transfers, found it difficult to guess what Taher wanted from him. Furthermore, although Taher was choosing his thoughts carefully, his translation into limited Hebrew was a little hard to follow. "Maybe you should tell me the origin of the document and we'll take it from there," said the lawyer.

Taher pondered the suggestion and replied: "In my youth, I was a shepherd, tending my father's sheep. Many years ago, in the mountains leading down from Jerusalem to the Dead Sea, at dead of night, I heard shooting. Early the following morning I hastened to the scene and found three bodies. Two were Arab fedayeen and the third was, in my opinion, a Jew. I buried the three men and left no traces. From the Jew I took an envelope, the contents of which looked important and official. It is written in English, which I can't read."

While Feffer digested these facts, Taher was considering how to proceed. "I am not very well versed in dealing with lawyers. However, I have heard of privileged information. Does that concept apply to the contents of this letter?"

Feffer admired Taher. He was amazed at the time that had elapsed since the letter had been taken and impressed at Taher's inordinate patience. Not knowing that Taher had recently completed his conversion to Judaism, he admired the latter's courage and savvy in coming to him and not taking advice from an Arab lawyer. He was aware of the details of Taher's recent dreadful bereavement.

"I understand what you are asking me," replied Feffer, "but frankly, I don't know how to answer you. You are asking me a question of theory or possibly of legal philosophy, and I don't believe that I'm qualified in these areas. My days are full enough with the practical matters brought to my desk by my clients, who buy and sell properties, fight with each other or don't pay bills. These are the areas in which I feel confident."

Feffer thought for a few moments, then continued: "Let me give you an example of a possible problem. If you brought me a letter which stated that your brother was going to kill his wife tomorrow, it would be my duty as an officer of the court to take action to see that such a crime will be prevented. You could't claim privilege or tell me to disregard the information. I wouldn't know exactly what to do, but I would insist on seeking advice."

"What if this letter tells me that there is gold at the bottom of my garden?" asked Taher with a smile.

"The gold would be yours, and I might buy you a shovel," answered the lawyer in good humor.

"What if the information was political and found us on opposite sides of a fence?" asked Taher.

"I would be guided by my conscience," replied the lawyer without hesitation. "I think that you know me to be an honorable man. That is why you came to me."

Taher handed the letter over to his attorney. Opening it, Feffer nearly jumped out of his skin when he saw the three famous signatures. Without reading the Agreement, he turned excitedly to Taher, "Do you know who the signatures to this document are?"

"I have no idea," answered Taher honestly.

"Good gracious," declared the lawyer, "Well, I can tell you that for thirty years you have had in your possession a document signed by the late King Abdullah, David Ben Gurion and Moshe Dayan."

Advocate Rami Feffer, in a fair, but heavily accented English, proceeded to read the document slowly for the benefit of his client. In a few instances, he translated a word or two from English into simple Hebrew, so that Taher could better understand the Agreement. When he completed the translation, Feffer reread the document slowly for his own further understanding.

Setting aside the document, Feffer pushed forward on the desk and faced his client. "I feel that I must make my own position clear," he began. "My political leanings are to the right of the present right-wing government. For example, I opposed the peace agreement with Egypt for two separate reasons. The nationalistic consideration – I believe we should not return land that was given to our fathers by holy decree. Moreover, the return of land to our enemies will, in my humble opinion, hasten another war, from which we will be attacked from positions much nearer to our densely populated areas, and this will be to our distinct disadvantage."

While disclosing his right-wing views, Feffer eyed his client to see his reactions. Taher, who was still digesting the meaning of the Agreement, showed no signs that he was disturbed by Feffer's convictions.

Feffer continued to talk, "I myself am not active in politics, nor am I a member of one of the various right-wing groups that are registering their disappointment or disgust with the government's policies. However, my sympathies are with them, and in some cases I offer them legal representation."

After a short pause he looked Taher right in the eye and continued: "I can tell you that a number of my friends are upset by our government's lack of jurisdiction over the Temple Mount, something which we never understood. After all, the whole of Jerusalem has now been within our hands for thirteen years. Now that I have read your document, it looks possible to me that government policy is, in fact, dictated by this Agreement."

Feffer took the document in his hand and said, "But this is a copy, what has happened to the original?"

"The original is in my possession and has been deposited in a safe place; I myself made the copy."

The two sat opposite each other each deep in thought. It was Taher who spoke first: "My first reaction is similar to your own; I see no reason why Abdullah's descendants should have control of the holy Temple Mount."

Taher rose from his chair and, moving about the room deep in thought, came face to face with a large picture on the wall. The picture showed the el-Aqsa Mosque on the Temple Mount. Surrounding the mosque on the ground were tens of thousands of Muslims prostrated in prayer. Taher looked at the picture in amazement and, turning to Feffer, asked: "Why on earth would you want to hang this picture?

"Look carefully at the picture," replied Feffer.

Taher looked at the picture again and suddenly it dawned on him. "I see," he replied with a smile on his face. "It's the direction of their prayers; away from the mosque and away from the Temple Mount. They are praying on the Temple Mount, but they face Mecca."

Feffer and his client both felt restricted in the small and cramped office. "How about joining me for a sandwich?" asked the lawyer. "A little walk outside in the fresh air will do us both good."

Chapter 25

Several months earlier, Rami Feffer's partner had represented a young American religious seminary student. The American national had arrived in Israel with the backing of an extreme right-wing political group. Considered by most Israelis to be a lunatic fringe, the movement was in fact subsequently outlawed.

The Israeli internal secret police, known as the Shin Bet, or Shabak, both Hebrew acronyms that mean General Security Services, had recently undergone a restructuring process both organizational and ideological.

This followed the disclosure of a Jewish underground movement of right-wing idealists who believed in making physical reprisals against the Arab population in Israel, particularly in the Judea and Samaria strongholds of Arab extremism. Their motto was simply "terror should repay terror." The distorted idealists were rounded up by the Shabak, tried, and given stiff jail sentences.

Israel's occupied territories on the West Bank and Gaza housed over one million politically deprived Palestinians. The Shabak was entrusted with the task of seeking out subversive elements.

Intellectual Arabs reduced their frustrations by writing letters, attending local meetings and international forums. The rabble resorted to throwing stones. The Palestinians, in between these two groups, were the subversives that the Shabak sought to identify.

In his memoirs, published in 1979, Rabin describes a Gush Emunim (Jewish settlers) demonstration against a visit by Henry Kissinger as *"storming through the streets of the capital like common rabble and laying siege to the Knesset."* In his uncompromising attitude, he continues, *"there can be no excuse for Jews anywhere to stoop to such obscene behavior."* He concluded his account with the ominous stamp of his hard-fisted power: *"The next day I called in the inspector-general of the police and ordered him to put a stop to it – by force, if necessary."*

These sentiments set the tone for future Rabin administration dealings with any views dissenting from those of his own.

The Talmud discusses the requirements for *dayanim*, religious judges. One of the interesting conclusions is that judges should not serve after reaching the age of seventy, for it is explained that at that age one becomes short-tempered, inflexible and unable to be understanding of the views of others.

Unfortunately, Israeli politicians do not share these views and prime ministers since the establishment of the state have usually remained in office past their youthfulness.

Taking a leaf out of British Mandatory law, successive governments used administrative detention without trial as an expedient way to control the Arabs. Over the years, thousands of Arabs considered to be subversive elements, were rounded up. Administrative detention orders were signed by the prime minister or by local military governors, and the unfortunate Arabs were summarily incarcerated. To give some measure of judicial legitimacy to this undemocratic procedure, each Arab had to be brought before a judge who would be given a confidential file of charges prepared by the Shabak officer in charge of the arrest.

The defendant and his appointed lawyer would have no access to the charges *in the interests of state security*. They would not be informed as to evidence collected and used against them. They would not be told who were the witnesses.

Usually, prior to the so-called trial, the judge would review the case in chambers with the prosecution, who would have little difficulty in explaining why the defendant would be better off behind bars. In 1981, Menahem Begin, himself a peculiar mixture of ex-terrorist leader and stickler for due judicial process, decided to extend the system of administrative detention. He applied the system against two Jews from the extreme right wing, who were politically opposed to his views. This course of action had never before been used against Jews in Israel. His actions were to be a precedent for future arrests of numerous Jewish dissidents by subsequent administrations.

Following the arrest of the Jewish underground leaders, the Shabak in Jerusalem decided to pursue a policy of implanting listening devices in the homes and offices of suspected Jewish subversives and some of their associates. Although such actions would require the approval of a judge, the law was bent in many cases – all in the name of law enforcement.

When Rami Feffer's partner unsuccessfully tried to secure the release of one of Begin's political detainees, a listening device was inserted by Shabak agents into a small hole, drilled under the desk in his office. Gaining access and connecting the device at the time, had been easy. By coincidence, within two weeks of this action, Rami and his partner changed their rooms.

It was in this way that Advocate Rami Feffer undeservedly inherited a bug.

At midday on Friday, Rami and his client Taher stepped out to lunch. Less than two miles away, in the district of Katamon, an agent sat back on his chair with a puzzled look on his face. He disconnected the tape. Taking a small recorder with him, he climbed two floors of steps to ask his section controller what he should do.

Within two hours, three agents in the hierarchy had listened to the tapes. A meeting was scheduled for Sunday morning in Tel Aviv with Ya'acov Kreitman. Known to everyone as Kobbi, the deputy commander of the Shabak was the ultimate person in charge of the agency's activities amongst Jews. Having heard from the tape that the subject matter of the document was at least thirty years old, the view in the Jerusalem office was that the matter could wait over the weekend.

Unaware of these developments, Taher and his lawyer enjoyed a sandwich and cold drink and walked to a local park where, sitting on a park bench, far from electronic eavesdroppers, they had an illuminating discussion.

"I don't know if Avraham Nissim ever told you of the first time my father and I went to see him in the Hebron Hills," began Taher, "but at that meeting I had a feeling of belonging, of being amongst my people." Rami had not heard of this meeting and had no idea what Taher was talking about. However, being a patient man, especially on a full stomach, he was happy to listen to the rest of the story.

"I had never before felt really comfortable among Arabs, particularly among Muslims," he continued. "My father was a rare exception; I adored him and had great respect for him, – but he was an unusual man."

"Halachically, under Jewish law, I was told that my father was probably Jewish through his mother's family. In any case, some years back I enrolled in a yeshiva as I myself wished to convert to Judaism. Subsequently, as a result of a meeting between Avraham Nissim and the Kadosh, further inquiries were made and we found that my mother was a niece of my paternal grandmother. This would mean that she was Jewish herself, and that would in turn hold good for me as well. However, the rabbis and I agreed that, in the circumstances, I should continue with the conversion process, which would give me a full grounding in Jewish background and practice. This lengthy process of conversion was completed some months back when the rabbis considered that I was suitably conversant with Jewish laws and customs."

He turned to face his lawyer sitting a few feet from him on the park bench: "I moved out of my father's house and into a flat in a Jerusalem suburb several years ago. When my father was murdered, my last links were severed."

"Well," thought Rami to himself, "he has certainly surprised me again."

CHAPTER 26

Taher lay on the cot in the tiny room at the Shabak's Jerusalem headquarters. For over thirty years the contents of the Agreement had been unknown to him, even though the document had been in his possession during that entire time. During the few days, since gaining knowledge of its contents, the bank at which he had deposited the original document had been burglarized. Now he had been detained by the authorities.

A possibility floated briefly through his mind that Rami Feffer might be responsible for these latest events. However, he discarded it without hesitation. Avraham, his friend, and more recently his respected teacher, had recommended the lawyer, and Taher had a childlike faith in his mentor. Recently Avraham had spoken to him of the Jewish Kabbalistic concept of *Hashgaha Pratit*, Divine guidance. "There are no coincidences," Avraham had explained. "All matters are ordained and are carried out in a vast plan that we mortals are unable to comprehend."

Taher pondered long on this spiritualistic concept of the universe and mankind's position within an incomprehensible system controlled from on High. His mother, lighting Friday night candles far away in the Hebron Hills, his father saving Jews from a wild Arab pogrom, his own involvement in finding and keeping an important agreement, the burglary at the bank and now his detention. All these he saw clearly as milestones in his destiny, minute details in a gigantic scheme directed by the Master of Mankind.

Just a few hours earlier he had taken leave of some new friends. He had met them at a twice weekly lesson that he was attending, given by Avraham Nissim at a community center in the beautiful leafy suburb of Bet Hakerem. The lesson was on the subject of the Ethics of the Fathers, one of the smaller books of the Mishnah. It was compiled by sixty sages over a period of five hundred years. During that same period, Christianity had emerged.

Called in Hebrew *Pirkei Avot*, this Mishnah was introduced in the form of a general statement, "that all of Israel has a share in the world to come." It then proceeds to deal with practical teachings, melding ethics with morality, ritual and civil law into a general code of behavior for the Jews. Avraham had explained in the first lesson of the series: *A Jew who wishes to lead a life of piety and be devout in his daily practices, must fulfill the dicta of Pirkei Avot which cover the full range of human behavior.*

Taher remembered the first lesson, the first in which he had ever participated with other Jewish students. These were a mixed bunch. There were two Russians, both with academic backgrounds. Then there was a delightful young couple that had left their kibbutz to come to Jerusalem and search for their Jewish roots. Another young married couple had been helped by their poor immigrant community in the south of Israel to study for a while and improve their knowledge of Jewish sources.

The others were single men and women of different ages, some with university degrees, some fresh from completing the three-year compulsory army service, and one or two tourists from Western countries. They had all come to benefit from Avraham's great gift of teaching Jewish studies. Taher, the only one from an Arab background, felt privileged to learn with these people.

The excitement of the first lesson and its subject matter remained fresh in his memory, although the class had progressed a long way since.

Moses received the Torah on Sinai, the first chapter had begun, *he passed it to Joshua who in turn passed it to to the Elders. They passed down the Torah to the Prophets who passed it to the Men of the Great Assembly.... Simon the Righteous was one of the Great Assembly, and he used to say 'The World rests on three pillars, On Torah study, on the service of G-D and on the performance of kind deeds.'*

Avraham had discussed the saintly Simon, explained the background of the times in which he lived. He described Simon's motivation in trying to reduce the whole Torah to just these three principles. His explanations and subsequent discussion had continued, long in excess of the sixty minutes allotted.

Another topic that occupied Taher's mind before he fell asleep was the meeting in a local coffee shop, where he had gone with two fellow students after the lesson that evening. Their invitation had been casual enough, and he had been naively flattered that they had singled him out for their attentions. Walking together two or three blocks – for none of them owned a car – they had arrived at the small and cozy shop. There, they decided to brave the cool Jerusalem evening and sit at one of the small tables on the pavement outside.

The two men were both in their early twenties and had recently gained their release from the army. They had left-wing political views and saw in Taher an object of possible Jewish-Arab association. Their political views coincided with the views of extremist Arabs that Taher had known. They offered a conceptual solution to Arab-Israeli difference based on equal rights and opportunities, a shared nationalism that would lead to a new Palestinian state for Arabs and Jews. Israel, the Jewish state, would disappear.

"Why are you here? Why are you coming to Avraham's lesson if these are your views?" Taher had asked them.

"We are open-minded and wish to learn more of our Jewish roots," they replied. "We are not interested in Avraham's right-wing views, we wish to benefit from his talents in teaching Jewish studies."

"Have you ever inquired about the teachings of Islam?" asked Taher. "Are you aware that in their eyes Jews are infidels against whom Jihad, holy war, must be waged? Are you both so naive as to believe that you would be able to live in peace with Arabs who, in reality, would like to see you pushed into the sea?"

Taher had sighed at their naivete, "Believe me, I come from the other side, I know my Arab brothers, what makes them tick and how they think. They think of short-term compromise, long term revenge." The argument between them had continued for some hours, without any indication that they might one day agree. Afterwards, Taher had walked alone for thirty minutes to the central bus station, from where he caught a late night bus home to Neve Ya'acov.

Turning the key in the lock, he wondered why the light was on in the room inside. Then he saw the two agents sitting and waiting for him. In the hands of one of the agents was his copy of the Agreement. They were waiting for Taher to return home, so that they could deliver him to Katamon for questioning.

Setting aside his present circumstances and comforted by the memories of the wonderful lessons and the new Jewish friends that he had made, Taher drifted into sleep, secure in the belief that he would come through whatever tribulations might lie ahead.

The headquarters of the Shabak had been situated in Tel Aviv since its inception many years earlier. Recently, thought had been given in political circles to moving the Shabak to Jerusalem. A consideration was the extra duties that had been added to the considerable work load following the Six Day War. The Arabs were scattered over large areas, but the main concentrations were in the towns of Gaza, Jerusalem, Hebron, Bethlehem, Ramallah, Nablus and Jericho. As most of these towns were either surrounding or more accessible to Jerusalem, its section had grown considerably.

Most senior officers came from the coastal plains. They wanted to continue to live and work in or around Tel Aviv, the cosmopolitan town that boasted it never slept. As the majority of the nation's politicians also tended to live in the Tel Aviv area, the Shabak's leaders had contrived to let things be. Ideas raised from time to time, to move the headquarters to Jerusalem, were killed.

Owing to the Chief's absence abroad, Kobbi had been extending his working time beyond his usually flexible hours. He had arrived after midnight at his small cottage in a farming settlement near the Ben Shemen forest. Now he was on the road back to Jerusalem at a little before 6 am. He wanted to beat the morning traffic into the capital.

By seven in the morning he had gulped down a cup of strong coffee and had been fully briefed by the agents that had picked up Taher. He proceeded to the interview room, where Taher had been brought to meet him. Kobbi entered the room and taking a seat at the single table, motioned Taher, who had risen, to resume his seat opposite. "Good morning," began Kobbi, waving the Agreement in his hand. "I want to discuss what you know about this document, but first allow me a few minutes to read it."

Kobbi invested his efforts in reading the document and understanding its contents. He saw that it conformed to the translation he had heard on the tape. Putting it down on the table, he turned to his detainee. "I am interested to know how and in what circumstances you obtained this document!" said the Shabak inspector.

During the night in his cell, Taher had thought that this would be the first question. He had come to the conclusion that frankness would be appropriate. Accordingly, Taher related the entire account of the shooting in the lonely countryside over thirty years earlier and of how he had buried the three participants of the shootout. He related that he had then taken the document to his father, who had deposited it, unread, in a Ramallah bank. It had remained there for many years until very recently, when he had removed it in order to have it deciphered.

His account, although much more detailed, was, in general, verified by the tapes of the meeting with his lawyer – tapes that Taher did not know existed. "I would like you to take me to the place where these events happened," stated Kobbi.

"I shall be happy to," answered Taher "but you will not find any remains. I myself returned there some months after the Six Day War, and the three graves had recently been emptied."

Kobbi made some notes on his pad and was about to continue with his questions, when there was a sharp knock. The door opened and the Jerusalem section head entered and asked Kobbi to come outside for a minute.

Rising, Kobbi asked Taher, "Have you had anything to drink, would you like tea or coffee?"

"I have had a drink," answered Taher. "But I'd welcome a strong black coffee."

"I'll have one sent in," said Kobbi as he left the room.

Sitting in an adjoining room, the two senior agents faced each other.

"We have assembled some information on Taher that you might wish to know," began the section chief. He consulted his notebook and continued: "First of all, he is undergoing conversion to Judaism. Secondly, his father was recently executed by a PLO death squad as he lay dying of cancer. Thirdly, his late father left Hebron in 1929 after saving Jewish neighbors from a pogrom. Fourthly, he is very friendly with a Jewish settler-cum-teacher, who received Israel's highest reward for bravery for his efforts in the Golan Heights during the Yom Kippur War." He looked through the list of points on the pad to make sure that he hadn't missed anything.

"Thanks," Kobbi replied. "It just remains to be seen if he will hand over the original Agreement; the points that you recited might indicate positive or possibly, negative."

Kobbi returned to the room next door and sat down wearily. Before he could open his mouth, Taher, anticipating the next question, said: "In answer to the question, is there an original of the Agreement...?"

Kobbi sat up very straight. "This is indeed a strange detainee," he thought.

"Well, there was one, and the one you have is a copy that I made only three days ago at InstiPrint on King George Street." He paused and looked carefully at Kobbi, who he guessed was a very senior officer. "The original," he concluded, "was deposited just across the road at Bank Hapoalim. Yes," he said, seeing the look of dismay on Kobbi's face, "it was stolen along with all my other valuables and all the other safe-deposit boxes."

Kobbi sat and stared incredulously at Taher who was, he felt sure, telling the truth.

"Well," said Kobbi after a few minutes thought, "we will have to check out your story. While that is being done, I'll drive out with you and see where the story started."

"The story started in the Hebron Hills with my grandmother lighting Sabbath candles," said Taher with a smile. "But I think you are in fact referring to where I buried the bodies. I guess we can get there in less than thirty minutes or so. When we get there, I'll show you where I stored the guns and ammunition; who knows, maybe we will find them."

On the way down from Jerusalem into the Judean Hills, Kobbi realized how important it was to solve the much publicized Bank Hapoalim burglary.

CHAPTER **27**

In Rome, at the Da Vinci Airport, the arrival of Archbishop Capucci had assumed the proportions of that of minor royalty. A delegation of senior officials from the Vatican were on hand jostling for position in the VIP lounge, with an even larger delegation of representatives from the PLO. Whisked away in a large limo in the company of two monsignors, Capucci headed for an immediate church ceremony, where he would give thanks for his deliverance from the hands of his Israeli tormentors. This ceremony would, of course, receive maximum media coverage.

Monsignor Paulo Angelo was one of two senior officials accompanying Capucci. He had been studying his case and conditions in the Holy Land for some years, since receiving the Israel and Lebanese desks at the Vatican. He couldn't wait to question Capucci, who had been out of reach for over three years. He wanted to learn what Capucci knew of those charged with the assassination of the late King Abdullah so many years earlier. At the time of the trial, there had been talk among the prisoners of a secret Agreement between Abdullah and Israel. The Monsignor wanted to know what Capucci knew about it.

In the back of the car, stuck in Rome's midday traffic, they had plenty of time to talk. Capucci was aware that the ex-Mufti, Amin el-Husseini, had ordered the assassination following information he had received, that an agreement had been signed between Abdullah and Moshe Dayan at a spa house at Kalia. He knew nothing of the whereabouts of the agreement, and a disappointed Monsignor Angelo realized that his own information was more up-to-date.

After the Six Day War a report had been received at the Vatican's Israel desk. It disclosed that a lonely monk, wandering among the Judean Hills, had seen an Israeli search party look for, find and dig up three bodies in shallow graves at the side of a road which led to his monastery some eight miles away. At the time, the report had been filed without raising any interest.

Years later, when the Monsignor was handed the Israel desk, he visited the Holy Land. He first read the Vatican's file with his own inimitable thoroughness. Visiting the lonely monastery, he drove back with the monk who had filed the report, and looked for the graves. The empty graves, filled over without attempt at camouflage, revealed nothing.

Later in Jerusalem, during a scheduled visit at the Israeli Foreign Office, he was accorded all the ceremony usually awarded to a foreign diplomat of standing; this amused the Monsignor. The intelligent Israeli civil servant spoke several languages, including Italian. This impressed the visitor. The Monsignor had a long list of matters to take up with his hosts, quite usual for such visits. One of the points concerned the shallow graves.

Producing a detailed map of the area, which clearly indicated the graves, the Monsignor informed the Israeli civil servant that his monastery in the region understood that three graves had recently been emptied by the military and the bodies had been taken away. The Monsignor informed his host that the priests at the Monastery believed that some or all of the bodies had been Catholics, and in these circumstances he demanded to know what had become of them. The Israeli Foreign Office official dutifully added the question of the bodies to the list of other queries. The Monsignor quickly and astutely continued with his next query, concerned with the provision of electricity to a remote monastery in the Carmel mountain range.

The Israeli official was efficient. Within a month, a report was sent to the Monsignor in Rome to the effect that three bodies, two of them Muslims and one a Jew, had been recovered from the graves where they had been buried temporarily in 1951.

"Assuming that the Jew had been returning from Kalia," mused the Monsignor, "what had happened to the Agreement?" The Monsignor returned to the Holy Land.

Dressed in a simple grey suit not reflecting any vestige of his vocation, he visited the offices of a leading detective agency in Tel Aviv. In simple terms, he outlined what he wanted. The agency were required to find out who the Jew was that had been in an unmarked grave for thirty years, and who were his friends. He gave them the date that the body had been taken by the military.

The agency was as good as its reputation. Within less than two weeks, they sent a two-page dossier on Major Yossi Foux together with an old press photo, taken but never published, of his reinterment in the military section of the large Tel Aviv cemetery. The minister of defense at that time, General Moshe Dayan, was seen standing near the grave of his friend.

By the time that this information had been received, Monsignor Paulo Angelo had other and more pressing concerns. He had been informed about the break-in at Bank Hapoalim, where the Catholic Church had stored a number of valuable, and in some cases very secret, documents.

Monsignor Angelo came from a small village outside of Naples. His poor parents struggled to feed six children. When young Angelo left at a tender age to join the church in a nearby monastery, his family were able to distribute the available food with a little less difficulty. The situation improved again only weeks later, when Eduardo, his brother, older by only one year, jumped on a small ship bound for Sicily, where he soon found work in the personal employment of a local Mafia boss.

During the intervening years, both brothers had applied themselves diligently to their chosen vocations, both were rewarded and both were appropriately advanced. By the time Angelo became Monsignor, with a position of importance at the Vatican, brother Eduardo had become head of a mafia-controlled bank, based in Rome. The brothers kept in close contact with each other.

At a discreet restaurant in Rome, where Eduardo had the best of connections, the two brothers spent an evening together over dinner, cigars and wine. Paulo told his brother about his visits to the Holy Land which Eduardo, a deeply religious man after his own fashion, found fascinating. "On your next visit let me join you," he entreated.

"Eduardo, I have a problem, and possibly you may be able to serve your Church," said Paulo. "For over a hundred years the Vatican has been pursuing a policy towards the Holy Land which has left us far behind the other Churches and, of course, way behind Islam in respect to duties and responsibilities in the Holy City of Jerusalem. The reasons for these policies are theological. Whereas the Orthodox Church and other lesser Churches ventured forth and staked their claims with abandon, our own Mother Church was preoccupied with its doctrine of preventing a rebuilding of the city by the Jews.

"For a time, under Pope Benedict XV, the Vatican flirted with a somewhat pro-Zionist stand, but later, under Pope Pius XI, the Holy See returned to its position of severe disapproval and voiced widespread feelings of suspicion."

Delving back into history, he continued to dwell on matters that clearly caused him pain. "Cardinal Gasquet, in a lecture to the British Ambassador to the Vatican in 1922, suggested that Zionism meant converting the Holy Land into a happy hunting ground for·financiers and concessionaires. Little wonder that with the realization of Zionist yearnings, the influence of our Holy Church waned. But I have faith that in the long term, we will undoubtedly be rewarded. In the meantime, an objectionable situation has evolved. Our own Mother Church, supremely powerful all over the world, suffers in Jerusalem, where we rank a poor sixth in the pecking order behind such nonentities as the Syrian, the Coptic, the Abyssinian and the Orthodox Churches.

"Our frustrations are compounded on the Holy Temple Mount. For nearly two millennia our churches have been built, destroyed and rebuilt there. It was to the Temple Mount that we sent crusades and pilgrimages. Today this sacred place is entrusted solely to the Muslims, whose clerics and police force exercise total control."

Paulo rested back on the soft chair in the private booth in which they were sitting, taking a long drink of the fine dark red wine that brother Eduardo had ordered.

Brother Eduardo was used to being a speaker, rather than a listener. Using the opportunity of a pause, he remarked, "Well, from your report so far, you have my sincere sympathies. However, I can't see how I can possibly help, honored as I would be to do so."

"I don't know. I'm still trawling. But hear me out. At least I can discuss things openly with you, which I can't do at the office in the Vatican," replied Paulo.

He then proceeded to tell his brother about the meeting between Abdullah and Dayan in 1951 with a certain Major Yossi Foux in attendance, who was later killed on his way back to Jerusalem. "King Abdullah was killed within weeks of this meeting," he continued. He told his brother of his detective work and the results so far. He concluded that the whereabouts of the Agreement were still unknown. "If, in fact, the Agreement is not in the hands of the Israeli authorities, but is elsewhere," said Paulo, "we must find it. It might well be of huge benefit to the Church."

This final point, although said with conviction, was based on no more than a gut feeling at the time. However, his gut feelings had served Monsignor Paolo Angelo well over the years.

CHAPTER 28

Sari Butbul, a senior bank clerk, was of Moroccan origin. She and her family arrived in Israel when she was just three years old. The family first lived in appalling conditions in a wooden shack in an absorption camp near Haifa. After twelve years, her father, who worked for the Israeli Post Office, gained a transfer to Jerusalem. There, for the first time, the family, with five children and an old grandfather, had moved to a small three-room apartment in the Katamon area with its own bathroom, toilet and kitchen.

Working hard at school to prove herself and gain advancement, Sari yearned for the good life, for luxuries, fast cars and fun. Finishing school with good marks, she gained an administrative job in the army during the two years she, like other young women, had to serve. Soon she learned that being good to her officers gained her perks and advancement; she also enjoyed the fun that they demanded. She contrived to be sent on a course and, when she left the army, graduated with a diploma in accounting. From the army she went to a good job at the bank.

By her thirtieth birthday, Sari had been married and divorced. She had no children and had gained a number of promotions at the bank, where she was considered to be a great asset. She was popular with staff and customers alike.

After a series of affairs, Sari had settled down to a manageable routine involving a steady arrangement with two married men, neither of whom knew of the existence of the other. Ehud, the younger man, had embarked on a promising career with the Shabak, and Arturo, an older man who had lived in South America, was a high living businessman, involved in importing food products. Between the two of them, Sari had what she wanted, a good time with plenty of action, good food, excitement and varied stimulation.

When Ehud entered the bank on Monday morning, Sari looked up in annoyance. A rule between them was that dates were arranged on the phone; surprise visits during working hours were not to be encouraged. Ehud, however, after a curt nod and a wink, disappeared into the manager's office, and the quick-witted Sari then realized that the Shabak must be interested in the robbery.

"I guess that with all the churches and diplomats having safe-deposit boxes with us, the Shabak has been called in to help," she guessed correctly.

Within a few minutes, however, she was called in to the manager's office, where Ehud, pretending not to know her, asked: "Has a certain Taher Jabari recently opened an account and or a safe-deposit box at the bank?"

The name sounded familiar, and when Ehud showed her a photograph of Taher, she remembered his visit just days earlier. "Yes, of course," she replied, "he was here last Friday and deposited some papers in his box. An Arab, I believe, he recently changed his address to Neve Ya'acov."

"That's the man," said Ehud, "I need a copy of all papers that you have on his account."

"Well," butted in the manager, "you will have to bring me the appropriate authorizations."

"You'll have them by the end of the day; in the meantime please authorize your assistant" – he looked at Sari and winked "to get the papers ready, so that I can collect them from her later on. On second thought, maybe I can cut some corners." Ehud lifted a phone, spoke quietly and then returned the phone to its cradle.

"I think that within a short while you will receive your authorization from your head office. Meanwhile, may Sari please begin to collect the papers."

The manager realized that Ehud, whom he had not seen before in the bank, had known Sari's name. He nodded to her and she left the room.

Soon afterwards, armed with all the papers that the bank could give him on Taher's account, Ehud crossed the road and verified with InstiPrint that Taher, the rather striking looking Arab, had indeed copied a document on the previous Friday.

Taher's alibi and account were intact, just as Kobbi had expected.

That evening Ehud drove Sari down to Abu Ghosh, parking the Shabak white Ford Escort right outside the main Arab restaurant where, as regular customers, they were both well known. They ate a full meal of humous with tehina, zatar and olive oil sprinkled in the middle of the dish where the humous was thinnest, then rising high around the edges of the plate.

This was followed by kebab on long skewers, cooked on a charcoal grill and garnished with fried onions and tomato. They rarely drank wines on their dinner dates, for fear that it would ruin the fun planned for later on. However, before taking the rich black Arab coffee, served sweet in little white porcelain cups, they each had a small glass of arak, to remind themselves where they were dining.

Sari and Ehud lingered over the meal; the restaurant was only half full. They recognized two other male faces in the restaurant, both entertaining partners to whom they were not married. Ehud and a number of his colleagues from work were well known in Abu Ghosh, particularly in this restaurant. The Arabs of Abu Ghosh had generally lived in a state of peace and cooperation with the Israeli authorities since the establishment of the State of Israel in 1948. Over the years Shabak agents became regular visitors.

Tradesmen in the village felt comfortable with them and offered them goods at bargain prices. The tab for the meal, for example, came to less than half of what the same meal would have cost anywhere in Jerusalem. Moreover, for Ehud and Sari and many other couples, the atmosphere was enchanting and safe.

During the meal the two of them had laughed at the scene in the bank. Ehud had immediately realized his mistake in referring to Sari by name. But as he had said charmingly to Sari, "we all make mistakes."

Indeed his mistakes continued and were to become more serious. Pressed by Sari to tell him about the Shabak's interest in Taher, and influenced by the arak and by thoughts of what lay ahead, when they would return to Sari's flat with its large king-sized bed, Ehud threw discretion to the winds and made revelations that were unforgivable. "My first visit to you today was to ascertain that information given by the Arab Taher was in fact correct. It was," said Ehud. "Tomorrow I'll be back to begin an investigation into an important agreement that was in Taher's stolen security box."

"Tell me about the agreement," begged Sari. But Ehud realized that he'd said too much and wouldn't say more.

Back home at her apartment the two eagerly groped for each other and made love. Sari was mildly stimulated from the wine and the food. Tonight there was an additional element, as she rose to the challenge she had set herself to prise the information out of her lover. There was one particular fantasy that Ehud had continually demanded and in which Sari had constantly refused to participate. Tonight, if pressed, she might have to make an exception. By 2 am, while Ehud's wife slept peacefully, believing her husband was far away from home on Shabak business, Ehud satisfied his fantasies and Sari secured her information.

In the morning both rose early, showered, breakfasted and went their separate ways, in their separate cars, just like any married couple. They both had a busy day ahead of them. They would see each other at the bank, where Ehud would be spending a lot of his time until he could get the results that his boss demanded.

Arturo Be'eri had arranged a date with Sari for Friday night. Unlike Ehud, Arturo was not currently married, although he did keep a woman in a flat who might well have claimed to be considered his common law wife. However, as both engaged in affairs elsewhere, it suited neither to make an issue of it.

In the meantime, relationships were such as to permit Arturo to go out on Friday nights, which in most marriages in Israel would not have worked. This was of particular appeal to Sari who, otherwise, might have been hard-pressed to be suitably occupied and have fun at the weekend.

Going to Tel Aviv on a Friday night was considered a must. Jerusalem fell asleep, and Tel Aviv exploded with fun, good food and discotheques. Arturo and Sari left for Tel Aviv at 9 pm with no firm plans to return. They drove in Arturo's Mercedes convertible, one of only three such models in Israel.

Although Arturo was at least ten years older than Ehud, he had a zest for fun and good living and a large pocket. Moreover, he was a man of the world, with more and varied experience. In Sari's opinion, he was the better lover.

For some time Sari had entertained doubts about the nature of Arturo's business activities; she felt that these extended beyond the import of food – what kind of food, she had never been able to identify. Tonight, over dinner, she intended to explore a little. Yes, she thought, it will be another challenge. By the time they both fell asleep in a Tel Aviv hotel many hours later, Sari had formed a definite impression that her boyfriend was involved in importing drugs from Lebanon and had contacts with the mafia.

A few days later, Arturo received a phone call from Eduardo Angelo, his banker in Rome, asking if he could come and see him on a matter of possible interest to both of them. "Frankly, I'd love to come to Jerusalem," said Eduardo. "However, I just can't get away. If you come over, I promise you a good time."

Arturo planned his trip to include the weekend and phoned Sari to persuade her to accompany him. Sari loved the thrill of going overseas; the plane ride – especially with Arturo, for he only travelled Business Class – and getting around in foreign countries, all stimulated her. A journey into fantasy land, far away from the drag of bank routine.

The flight to Rome was uneventful, but the taxi drive from the airport to the Forum Hotel near the Colosseum was dangerous and quite frightening even to the excitement-loving Sari. Arturo, who spoke Italian reasonably well, felt at home in Rome. After a quick shower and a change of clothes, he took Sari for a snack in a nearby restaurant that spilled out onto the street. Afterwards, he left her to do her shopping, while he ran off to his appointment with his banker. The couple arranged to meet back at the hotel later that afternoon. Arturo was welcomed into the splendid executive suite on the third floor of the imposing bank building, ushered in by a black-suited official along the wood-panelled corridor, and into the private office suite of Eduardo Angelo, the bank's president. Eduardo rose from behind his magnificent carved desk and came to greet his friend, pulling him over to a settee and two armchairs set in an alcove on the other side of the very large room. "Good to see you, my friend," began the banker, "what will you drink?" He beckoned to the flunky and sent him on his way to get two mineral waters.

"How was the flight and what delightful young creature have you brought with you?"

Arturo had never doubted that Eduardo was always well informed. "Yes," answered Arturo, "a young and charming girl accompanied me. At dinner I will introduce you."

The drinks came within minutes. The two men then began to discuss the matter that preoccupied the banker's brother.

"I am told that in 1951 Moshe Dayan visited King Abdullah in Jordan and signed an agreement with him. I and my associates would like to take a peek at that document. We have no idea at all where it might be."

That was in essence the whole of the brief. Arturo could never have guessed that this would be the subject of a trip to Rome.

Eduardo then filled his Israeli guest in on the details that had been given to him by his brother, the Monsignor at the Vatican. "We do a lot of things together," he said, "and if they want the Agreement, I'm going to give it my best shot; after all what are family relationships for? But now you must be tired, and I'm told you have a beautiful young lady waiting for you at the Forum. I hope you got the best suite and that you are comfortable."

"Thanks for all your kindnesses, the suite is first class and I'm sure we will both be very comfortable," replied Arturo. "I will stroll back to the hotel and think about your problem. At this moment in time, I cannot imagine how I will be able to help."

"But you will, you will. Had I any doubts about your abilities, I wouldn't have asked for your help. Now run along, and I'll pick you up at 8 pm for an early dinner. Please be sure to bring your charming friend."

"Hi, darling," called Sari from the bathroom, when she heard Arturo enter the suite, "come in and tell me what lucrative deals you cooked up at your meeting."

Arturo took off his jacket and tie, which he always wore in Rome, especially when visiting the banker who always dressed impeccably. He entered the bathroom to find Sari covered by mounds of soap suds, lying provocatively in the huge marble double bath.

"Have you ever wondered why the carpets cover the walls and ceiling in this hotel?" asked Sari, "I've never seen anything like it anywhere else in the world."

"What would you like me to talk about first, the business transactions or the carpets?" asked Arturo good naturedly. "If there is room in there for me, I might answer both your questions."

"Sure there's room, my darling," answered Sari. "Bring a bottle of cold wine from the fridge and I'll make you comfortable."

Minutes later, lying next to each other in the huge bath, sipping wine from two long-stemmed glasses, Arturo began to tell of the meeting at the bank.

"My relations with my banker go back a long time, but only today I learned that his brother, of whom he is very fond, is a senior official at the Vatican." He sipped his wine thoughtfully and relaxed a little more in the hot soapy water. "How can I tell you?" he continued. "This has been the biggest non-business meeting ever; I've come all the way to Rome to hear that Signor Angelo wanted to discuss a historical document signed years ago by King Abdullah and Moshe Dayan."

Sari turned so abruptly in the bath that half the contents of her glass splashed over the balding head of her lover. "I think you should repeat everything that Angelo told you," she said involuntarily.

Acutely aware that he had hit a raw nerve, Arturo suddenly wanted out of the bath. He forgot the playful ideas that had entered his mind when he had found Sari in the tub looking so delicious. All he wanted now was to investigate this particular topic with Sari. The old Agreement suddenly looked as if it had come alive and might have possibilities. The two dried themselves and, dressed in hotel towelling robes, went into the lounge and sat down.

"Trust me," said Sari "I might be able to help, but first tell me what you know."

Arturo repeated all that he knew about the missing Agreement and the steps taken so far by the banker's brother at the Vatican.

"So what they really want, is to know the contents of the Agreement," said Sari.

"I guess that's right, at least for the time being. Of course, they might ultimately want the document itself, depending, of course, on the contents."

Sari had always kept her eyes open for the big opportunity; perhaps, she thought to herself, it had now arrived. "I might be able to help you, and if I do, what's in it for me?" asked Sari.

Taken aback, Arturo acted hurt. "Now wait a minute my darling," he began, "you are here in Rome having a ball, all expenses paid by me. And when you have an opportunity to give me a helping hand, you start defending your private interests. I have already explained that what we are talking about isn't even business; I'm merely being asked to help an old business friend do a favor for his dear brother."

Sari took his point but had no intention of giving up such a windfall opportunity. She chose her words carefully: "The Agreement that your friend wants was stolen from a safe-deposit box at the bank last Saturday. I happen to know roughly what the Agreement was about. Under certain circumstances, I might be able to obtain the full details. But for that, I would have to negotiate with a third party."

She smiled to herself at the thought of the payment in kind she might have to make in order to get more details from Ehud. "One thing I must ask you as a friend, please don't ask me how I get my information. If I ever reveal my sources, I'd lose my job."

Arturo understood her point perfectly. "Don't worry, I'll protect you," answered Arturo. "But let us see how we can placate the banker. What exactly was the Agreement about?"

"I'll tell you and your associate over dinner," Sari replied. "In the meantime, let's get into bed, have a nap, then some fun. I've been missing you."

The dinner was a huge success. Sitting in an alcove at the banker's favorite restaurant, their host wined and dined them royally. Sari was an instant hit with the banker, who couldn't keep his eyes off her. He knew plenty of lovely Italian girls, but he found himself captivated by this mixture of brains, beauty and aggression. Arturo, he thought to himself, was indeed a fortunate man.

Only after the crêpes suzettes had been fried in Grand Marnier in the copper pots in front of their table and handed to them one by one did Arturo refer to the lost Agreement: "As you will quickly see, Sari is not just a pretty face; she is intelligent and very useful."

The banker still had no idea what Arturo was driving at.

"My stroll back to the hotel didn't yield any useful ideas at all," confessed Arturo. "On arrival at our suite, I took the liberty of telling Sari about your problem, and she came up with a startling observation. Perhaps she will repeat it to you."

The two gentlemen looked at Sari with rapt attention.

"The Agreement that your brother seeks was signed in 1951 by King Abdullah, David Ben Gurion and Moshe Dayan. The Agreement, if I remember rightly, has five articles. Although I cannot remember them all, they dealt with the future control of Jerusalem, the West Bank of the Jordan, and most particularly the Temple Mount."

"And how, for the love of Mary and all the Saints, can you possibly know all this?" blurted out their host.

Sari smiled. She felt full of confidence that everything would work out well for all parties. "I work at a bank in Jerusalem which had a robbery last week. All the customer security boxes and bank safes were cleaned out. The Agreement was in one of the stolen boxes."

Sari leaned back and studiously cut her crêpes into delicate little pieces. These she then ate with great purpose, to the rapt admiration of both men.

"You haven't told me how you know all the details of the Agreement," noted Eduardo shrewdly.

Telling a white lie, she replied, "The information I gave you came to me through my job. I believe, however, that I know the source from which I might be able to obtain further details and perhaps even a copy of the Agreement. But that's a long shot which I can only pursue when I return."

The banker's currency was money and he wasted no time. "How much would the details cost? How much for an authentic copy?" he asked.

"I think that $25,000 and $50,000 would cover it," Sari replied without blinking an eyelid.

"Let me report back to my brother and get instructions. In any case, you will be well rewarded for the information that you have already given me," promised the banker. "In addition, I want to thank you personally; for this matter of helping my brother is very important to me; he is the pride of my family."

Two days later, Sari and Arturo returned to Israel. In Sari's bag was an envelope with $5000 in cash. She also wore a small diamond brooch, a personal gift from Eduardo. Furthermore, the Vatican had agreed to her terms; the information had whetted their appetite. They were desperate to know all they could about the Agreement.

When they arrived at Ben Gurion Airport, Arturo apologized to Sari and explained that he needed to spend two or three days in Haifa. "Would you be very understanding and agree to return home to Jerusalem in a taxi?" he asked.

This in fact suited Sari well, as she would need to spend some time with Ehud.

The days passed, with Ehud brooding unhappily. He was tormented with memories of his last fling in bed with Sari. He realized that rather than satisfy his earlier fantasies, the experience had merely whetted his appetite for more.

It was in this frame of mind that he ran over to Sari, minutes after receiving her call.

"I'm tired," said Sari, "rather than go out, I thought we'd eat some tuna sandwiches and go to bed early."

Ehud concurred wholeheartedly. In his frame of mind, Sari had no difficulty in playing him along expertly.

By noon the next day, when Ehud was still walking on clouds of fresh memories, Sari had received into her possession a copy of the Shabak's copy of the Agreement. She was planning to move up in the world. By the time Arturo returned to Jerusalem, Sari had begun to think that she had asked too little from the banker in Rome.

"I have the details you need," she began, referring to notes that she had made neatly in a little notebook. "As I remembered, there were, in fact, five paragraphs." She then gave a short precis of the five paragraphs, enough information to earn the first $25,000.

"So much for the good news. As for an authentic copy, well that is going to be more difficult and more costly. I'm still negotiating, but I think that its going to cost much more than I thought."

"How much?" asked her lover.

"$100,000 is what they want," she replied.

"I'll talk to Rome immediately, can I use your phone?"

Moving into the bedroom, he carefully closed the door. Crossing to the bed, he picked up the receiver and direct-dialed the number in Rome, avoiding the international operator.

Sari did't bother to lift the extension, she waited only a couple of minutes until Arturo came back into the room.

"Fine," he said, sitting down heavily on the couch beside her and groping for her hand. "Go get the Agreement, and you'll get the hundred grand. In the meantime, the first twenty five will be deposited according to your detailed instructions first thing tomorrow morning."

"Arturo," Sari reminded, "we are talking about a copy of a copy, not the original!"

"Yes, yes, I know," replied Arturo looking weary.

"I wonder what he has been up to in Haifa," thought Sari.

In Rome later that week, the brothers Angelo read and reread the copy of the Agreement. The clauses that they read spelled bad news for the Church of Rome.

"De facto," said Monsignor Paulo, "the situation on the Temple Mount is in accord with the terms of this Agreement. What bothers me is that no bilateral agreement of this nature has ever been disclosed. I know that Jordan and Israel are technically still in a state of no peace and no war. However, during such an extended time span, we here in Rome would have expected to receive some hints of such an Agreement, especially as it directly affects the interests of the Holy See.

"The signature that counts for the Israelis is Ben-Gurion's. An arrogant man and an original thinker, I am told, although when he was in control we were but children. I am going to talk with the highest authority. My opinion is that we must try and get the original. We must pray that it is floating around somewhere after the burglary, and not sitting in an Israeli government safe, where it should be. I pray that I will get authority to offer your contacts a great deal of money to bring us the Agreement. I was thinking of a figure of one million dollars; do you agree that such a sum is appropriate, dear brother?"

"Indeed," answered Eduardo smoothly, "its just the figure that I had in mind. I will string along my Israeli contact until we receive your instructions."

Over dinner that night, the banker, fully confident that the Apostolic decision would be positive, advised Arturo of his line of reasoning, why he felt sure the Vatican would authorize an eight hundred thousand dollar fee to secure the original.

When Arturo Be'eri returned to Israel, Sari was in the unique position of having two lovers, each unknown to the other, and each trying desperately to find the original Agreement signed over thirty years earlier.

CHAPTER 29

Taher was released by the Shabak on his return from taking Kobbi to the sight of the battle. The two had searched in the old well and to Taher's surprise had found the long-lost cache of arms. Even the pistol that Yossi Foux had received from Jammal, the late king's bodyguard, was found. Kobbi had expressed a particular interest in this item.

By eleven in the morning, squinting in the bright sunlight, Taher emerged from the well-known building on Kovshei Katamon Street. As he exited the green metal gate, he bumped into Feffer's secretary, Tali, who lived just two doors away. In all her many years in the area, Tali had never seen anyone she knew emerge from that forbidding building. Realizing that Tali might jump to all kind of conclusions, Taher cursed his bad luck, acknowledged her hello and asked if she was going to the office.

"Don't ask," she said. "I am running late with a child sick at home, visits to the doctor's clinic, and then on to a pharmacy; Rami will shoot me."

They had reached her small car and she stooped to unlock her driver's door. "If you want a ride, hop in on the other side."

Taher felt that, perhaps, he should take the opportunity to inform his lawyer of what had transpired. He wondered if, in the meantime, he should give an explanation to Tali of his visit to Katamon but thought it inappropriate.

On the drive into town, Tali realized that she had never before driven a car with an Arab passenger. She had always refused to take a ride in a taxi driven by an Arab, not out of prejudice but out of considerations of security. And yet she had a feeling that Taher was different. She knew that her boss liked him. Moreover, she had heard at the office that he had sold family land to Jewish settlers and had recently converted to Judaism.

During the ten minute drive into town, Tali wondered what Taher had been doing in the Shabak building. Casting furtive glances at him as he sat silently, she admired his complacency. He sat easily without any signs of restiveness. "Altogether an attractive fellow," she thought to herself.

Tali Goldberg was a war widow. She lived in a three-roomed apartment with her twelve year old son. He had been a small boy when her husband Eitan was killed on the banks of the Suez Canal on the first day of the Yom Kippur War. During her own army service, she had met and fallen in love with Eitan, who came from Jerusalem. When he had served his time, one year longer than hers, they had married and set up home in his home town. Eitan studied law at the Hebrew University, Tali took a job as a legal secretary. They planned that one day they would work together.

To accommodate Eitan's study and work schedule, the army agreed that he would do his annual reserve duty late in the summer vacation and during the Jewish High Holy Days. Thus Eitan found himself sharing a bunker with six other young soldiers on Yom Kippur when an overwhelming Egyptian army crossed the Canal. He and his unprepared friends were flushed out and killed by the superior, well-prepared enemy.

The dead Israelis had been buried in a mass grave. Despite the efforts of the Red Cross and a joint Israel-Egypt Commission, it took three years before the bodies were found, identified and returned for burial in Israel. It had been the dental records that finally established Eitan's identity, as the army name tags had been stolen from the bodies of the soldiers.

"Doesn't your husband help with the doctor when your son is ill?" Taher suddenly asked out of the blue.

"My husband was killed in the Yom Kippur War," Tali answered without signs of emotion. "My son and I live by ourselves."

"Oh, I am so sorry," said Taher quietly, "I had no idea. It is so stupid of me to ask questions and upset people. Please forgive me."

Tali looked sideways at Taher and smiled, "Eight years have passed and the pain has eased. You had no reason to suspect that I was a widow." Flashing a smile, she concluded, "You are forgiven."

Taher, who had always been shy and uncommunicative, felt encouraged to continue. For no apparent reason, he felt a warmth from the renewed relationship with this Jewish girl. "I, too, have suffered a great loss," he said with a hint of bitterness. "My loss was caused by Arabs, as was yours. My father, whom I loved very much, was brutally murdered by PLO assassins." Tali recalled that there had been talk in the office linking Taher with an Arab death squad. She felt great sympathy for him. Turning to him as they waited at a traffic light, she reached out her hand and placed it on his as it lay on his lap. Squeezing it gently, she told him how sorry she was. The lights turned to green and Tali moved her hands to engage the gears.

Tali parked the car in a side street, and they walked together to the office. Before reaching it, Taher summed up courage. Turning to Tali, he asked in a low voice, "Tali, please don't think me pushy, but would you be prepared to come out with me one evening for a coffee?"

Tali stopped walking and looked carefully at Taher. "I do believe that you haven't dated many young ladies," she said. "Am I right in that assumption?"

Without rancor and without hesitation, Taher answered honestly.

"You are absolutely right."

"I would be happy to spend an evening with you. I could be free tonight, subject to my son's feeling better. I'll give you my home number, and you can phone me at around 7 pm."

Taher felt as if he were walking on air as they completed the short distance to the office. There he found Rami waging his usual war against incoming telephone calls, while battling with unmanageable paperwork, scattered in small mounds all over his office. Peeking around the half opened door, Taher looked in and saw that not one of the three chairs was free of files. He shrugged and, seeing that Rami was really not very interested in him at all, felt guilty that, even for a fleeting second, he had harbored suspicions about the trustworthiness of his Jewish lawyer.

Eventually Rami banged down the receiver. Looking up, he asked in colloquial Hebrew, *"Ma hadash"* – what's new? It was quite clear that he had no idea of any of the developments that had crowded Taher's diary.

"I've just spent a night with the Shabak. They picked me up late last night from my apartment, when I returned home."

"Why on earth would they do that?" said Rami in genuine horror. Tali came into the office and asked her boss if he needed anything. She then turned to Taher and asked if he would like a drink, "Hot or cold?"

"I'd love a sweet black coffee, if its not too much trouble," answered Taher.

"No trouble at all," said Tali with a smile and left the room. "That must be the first time that she has ever volunteered a drink to a client," said Rami. "I wonder what has come over her."

Taher related all that had happened at the Shabak. He explained that the original Abdullah Agreement had been lodged at the Bank Hapoalim, the branch that had been burglarized. Rami Feffer was a shrewd man. He also had quick reactions. Putting a finger to his lips, he walked around the desk and motioned Taher to follow him. The two proceeded to the office of his partner. Again using sign language, he motioned to his partner to follow. All three left the office and walked down the stairs and into the street.

When they were standing in front of their office building, Rami gave his partner a short account of his meeting on Friday with Taher. Taher then completed the tale.

"Now tell us exactly, where have you been, and whom did you talk to about the Agreement since leaving Rami's office on Friday," said the partner.

"Absolutely no one," Taher assured them both.

He then recounted his Sunday activities: how he had heard on the bus radio of the burglary, his subsequent visit to the bank, his lesson in *Pirkei Avot* that evening, followed by his meeting with two young leftwingers. He completed his story with the scene at his apartment in which he found two agents, one of whom was holding his copy of the Agreement.

"First thing to do is to have a good search in Rami's office. It could well be that there is a bug installed by our friends at the Shabak," he said with a smile. "Second in priority," he continued, "I think that you and Rami should commit to paper as much of the Agreement as you remember, while its still fresh in your memory. When you have done that, I'd like to look it over and then we'll talk again. In the meantime let's get to work."

Taher was impressed with the partner's efficiency and wondered if he was a reserve officer in the army. Without heeding Rami's pleas to treat his papers and files carefully, the searchers gathered everything easily movable into three large piles. They then stacked them on the floor outside the door to the office. Next they tackled the furniture, turning chairs upside down, taking pictures off the wall, stripping a closet and taking all the drawers out of the desk. Without more ado, and with dust filling the air, the desk was turned on its head.

Underneath one of the corners they found the bug. Without any fuss, the partner lifted it from its socket and put it in his pocket. "Let's help you tidy up," he said, looking at his watch. "I must run to an appointment. How about meeting again in two hours, by which time you can have the papers ready."

Minutes later, the agent in charge of recording tapes left his basement office and climbed two floors to the office of the Jerusalem section chief. After clearing with the secretary outside, he entered the room and reported simply, "It would appear that the bug at the lawyer's office has been found and silenced." He then proceeded to play the last section of tape and Taher's description of being picked up by the agents.

"What a nuisance!" said the chief, "I had intended sending you to take out the bug, as it was obvious that sooner or later Taher would tell tales to his lawyer. Had I been faster off the mark, we might have spared a possible confrontation with an angry lawyer; something we should generally try to avoid."

He dismissed the agent and returned to other matters on his desk. A thought struck him and he looked at his watch. Pressing a button on his intercom, he asked the agent that answered, "What time did Taher leave this building?"

The reply came within a moment: "At 10.57 am."

The chief looked at his watch, it showed 12.05pm. "Taher certainly didn't waste any time, it's almost as if he had a taxi waiting for him," he thought.

Minutes later the phone buzzed on the section chief's desk, and the agent then reported, "Taher was seen getting into a car with a young woman, she was waiting outside."

"Did anyone write down the number?" asked the Chief.

"I'm afraid not," came the reply.

"Send Haim to ask Taher about the ride," said the Chief. "He should go easy on him, as it's probably just a coincidence." He switched off the intercom and reminded himself that good agents don't believe in coincidences.

Two hours later, Rami Feffer, his partner Baruch Struk, and Taher reconvened in Baruch's office. Baruch read through the reconstituted Agreement, or at least what the other two could remember, which wasn't such a bad effort.

Laying the papers on his desk in front of him, he leaned back in his chair: "Have you discussed this Agreement with Avraham or anyone else?" he asked.

"No," replied Taher, "as far as I know, Rami is the only person other than the Shabak who knows about the document."

Baruch's office was scrupulously tidy, with all files and papers in neat piles on one side-table next to his equally tidy desk, his phones set conveniently on another side-table. While Baruch had been away, his assistant and secretary had searched the room thoroughly. They were reasonably sure that there were no other bugs. Baruch planned to search the corridors and secretary's outside office later in the day.

Baruch continued to address Taher: "I'd like your permission to show these pages to Avraham; they belong to you, and without your consent we would not break confidentiality. Frankly speaking, they might be of significant interest to the right wing. You are probably aware that my political views are far to the right."

"I have no problem with that; you have my permission, but perhaps we should speak to Avraham together," replied Taher without hesitation.

Advocate Baruch Struk opened his top drawer and withdrew an old and much-used pipe with a large stem, a plastic pouch of a locally packed tobacco, and a box of matches. He bent in studied concentration over his labors and only straightened up when the pipe was smoking merrily in his mouth. After a few puffs, he removed the pipe. Carefully choosing his words, he addressed both Taher and Rami: "My first reaction is that this Agreement should never fall into the hands of our present administration and certainly not into the hands of any Labor government, if Heaven forbid, they ever return to office." He paused and puffed on his pipe, mindful of his obligation to keep it alight. "The effect of the Agreement is to give away our birthright on the Temple Mount to the Arabs – this would not be short of a national calamity. I would want Avraham's ideas on this. Perhaps plans should be made to retrieve the original at all costs."

Chapter **30**

The idea of burglarizing the Bank Hapoalim branch had originated in Ramle prison, where three inmates, all with different backgrounds, regularly played cards together.

Henri Sharon was born in France of a mixed marriage between a Moroccan mother and a Polish Ashkenazi father. He had lived in Israel for twenty years, since fleeing France with some urgency, leaving behind a great number of dud checks circulating around the clubs, stores and restaurants of Paris. He was now serving a five year prison sentence for the white collar crime of fraudulent misrepresentation. In simple language, he had taken some local banks for a ride with false documents.

Morris Benaroush, known to all as "Little Mo," was a Tunisian-born metal worker who had become addicted to gambling. In this activity he regularly lost money. In order to pay his gambling debts, he had developed skills as a locksmith. These new talents he used to break into apartments in the greater Tel Aviv area, where he stole cash lying around in drawers or safes. He boasted that he could break into any safe.

The third card player was Aboud Mugrabi, a Jerusalemite from the Arab village of Silwan. He, too, was born of mixed parentage. His mother was a Jewess who had run away from home at an early age and married an Arab. Aboud, his wife and their five children lived in the village of Silwan, which, until 1967, had been under Jordanian control. The whole family was raised as Assyrian Christian Arabs.

Aboud had been involved in a family feud and, taking the side of his brother who had been maligned, had tried to even scores. Unfortunately, when he was apprehended by the police, he was found with a loaded gun in his hands. This gun had been stolen. Police ballistics confirmed that the gun had once been used in a hold-up at the Jerusalem Electric Company, where a man had been shot.

Aboud Mugrabi was guilty of nothing more than participating in the ancient tradition of upholding family honor, but he was sent to jail for five years. He spent most of his time behind bars planning his revenge; for he intended getting even with the system.

The three friends were due for release within months of each other during 1981. During the year before their release, they planned the burglary. The idea of robbing a bank and making use of Little Mo's skills was obvious to all, and none claimed to be the father of the idea. The particular bank branch was proposed by Aboud Mugrabi.

Mugrabi had worked for years at the Armenian church within the Old City walls. His jobs were menial, included driving the Patriarch, looking after the vehicles, running errands including to and from the banks. He was aware that most of the churches in the Old City had accounts and, more importantly, bulging safe-deposit boxes at Bank Hapoalim in West Jerusalem.

During the years he had befriended the drivers of other churches and had come to realize the extent to which the churches used these boxes for deposits of cash, especially foreign currency, icons, gold, silver and diamonds. The word amongst the drivers in the employment of the various churches was that this particular branch had many millions of dollars worth of valuables in its strongboxes.

The cooperation between these three prisoners was like a marriage made in heaven. All three could play roles in the planned burglary, and yet each required the services of the others. Henri was the chairman of the operation, which they termed "Operation George" after the street in Jerusalem in which the bank was situated.

Henri was first to be released. Before his time was up, the card players had spent months planning Operation George in the greatest detail. Henri was particularly pleased that the burglary would be far away from Tel Aviv, in which town he had sworn not to carry out any activities for some time. The same reasoning was good for Little Mo, who had never before operated outside the Tel Aviv area.

The planning had taken account of the division of the spoils and the care that must be taken afterwards to leave no clues that would lead them back to prison. It was agreed that all cash would be split and that none of the three would spend any large amounts on anything traceable back to them, like a new house or car.

Other valuables, such as financial bonds, stocks and shares, jewellery, icons, gold, diamonds and the like would be sold through fences organized by Henri. Cash proceeds would be distributed. Property deeds and other papers would be handled exclusively by Aboud Mugrabi, who claimed access to church officials and crooked lawyers with whom he could carry out cash transactions.

On gaining his release, Henri travelled to Jerusalem and rented a house for six months. He paid cash in advance for the period. The house, situated on French Hill, a mixed Jewish and Arab area near Mount Scopus, would be used to plan operations. There, they would divide the spoils among the partners. The burglary was executed with such awesome precision that the partners were delighted. The police, the bank, its safe-deposit box and account holders, and the general population of Jerusalem were nonplussed.

Later, the police were at pains to deny it, but on the night of the burglary, a burglar alarm connected from the bank had gone off in the central police station. The duty officer had looked up from his newspaper at the box that housed a number of bank-connected alarms. Remembering previous false alarms, he merely observed to his colleague, "there's that faulty alarm at the Poalim branch again." It ceased after a few minutes, by which time the officer was again reading the weekend gossip.

After dividing the spoils, and when in the opinion of the partners the coast was clear, Aboud Mugrabi took back three large cardboard boxes of papers to his home in Silwan. Buried amongst them was the Abdullah – Ben Gurion Agreement. While the police and the Shabak ran around chasing air, Aboud slowly began sifting through the papers with a view to becoming very rich.

Aboud had a reasonable command of English and after a short while began to understand the meaning of the Agreement. He was convinced, from the moment he saw the signatures, that a great deal of money would come his way if he handled the sale cleverly. First, he had to decide which prospective buyer would pay the highest price.

Through a process of elimination he discarded the Greeks and Armenians who were too tight-fisted, the Jews too difficult and arrogant, and the Catholics too poor. He then began to evaluate the Muslim world. He was aware of the age-old enmity between the Palestinians and the Hashemites, and between moderate Islam and Muslim fundamentalists.

Using this simple evaluation, he realized that the ex-Mufti and his fundamentalists would lose most by this Agreement being enforced. He therefore assumed they would pay the highest price for the original. In the meantime he resolved not to do anything in haste; after all, half the world might well be trying to reclaim this valuable document.

✧ ✧ ✧

The meeting called at the Central Police Station two weeks after the robbery didn't sound particularly promising. Inspector Haft, the policeman in charge of the investigation, explained the view of the police. "The robbery could only have been planned and executed by parties with intimate knowledge of the bank, its interior lay-out, the positioning and workings of the safe-deposit box department.

"There are only two classes of such people that come to mind," said Inspector Haft to the group of men assembled in his office. They included detectives, Shabak operatives and a civil servant from the Prime Minister's Office. "I refer to bank staff, to past employees and to customers who use the safe-deposit box facilities. Accordingly, we have concentrated our efforts on these groups. We have compiled detailed lists of individual names and are laboriously checking by a process of elimination. To do this we have sub-lists; for example, we have sub-listed politicians, churches, well known public and business figures and overseas clients who are rarely here. We have also cross-checked with names known to the police or the Shabak. So far, we have no real leads, although we are following through on some ideas. To tell you that the investigation looks promising would be misleading at this stage."

Most of the agents and detectives present made comments and offered suggestions; these were discussed, and where appropriate, notes were made. Nothing of great import eventuated at the meeting, and within ninety minutes the parties dispersed. Inspector Haft rose from behind his desk and asked the Shabak agent to remain.

When the others had left, Inspector Haft looked the agent in the eye and said, "There is one matter that I didn't want to bring up at the meeting." He cleared his throat and continued: "It appears that a senior bank employee is dating one of your operatives. Whether that has a bearing on this case I don't know, but I do have other information which we are still probing. We are told that the lady employee has a busy social life and has two steady men friends. One of these is your agent, and the other is a questionable businessman whom we have been looking into for some time. We understand that the young lady, Sari Butbul is her name, accompanied her businessman friend on a four day trip to Rome. We are told she returned in great spirits and looking very prosperous."

Looking in the top drawer of his desk, the inspector withdrew a photograph which he passed to his colleague, "This was taken on her return. The brooch on her jacket is new, we understand. We are told that it is valuable. The stones are real diamonds."

Inspector Haft looked at his two hands as if wondering whether to order a manicure. His friend from the Shabak kept his peace.

"The thing is," continued the policeman, "we don't know if this is a lead or not. It might well be that she has a very rich boyfriend who indulges her and there's nothing more to read into that situation. However, in the circumstances, we will have to keep a close eye on this young lady."

While the Shabak agent looked as if he were preparing to say something, the Inspector continued: "I'm not finished. Sari returned from Rome on Monday evening; she hurried home and Ehud, your agent, came round very quickly and spent the night. The next day they drove to their respective jobs, and Ehud later went to the bank to work on our case. One of my men distinctly saw him approach Sari and give her a white envelope. We do not know what was in the envelope, but my policeman felt that it was passed – 'furtively' was the word he used."

"And you want to leave it to me to come back on the envelope," said the Shabak section chief.

"That's quite right. I also think that perhaps you should leave Ehud on the job – and we should both keep an eye on him."

"Now wait a minute, that's a different matter; now you are talking politics. Let me get some advice. I'll come back to you."

"Oh, and one other point," said the inspector as he rose to say goodby, "I would like to ask the Mossad to look into the Rome connections of our dubious businessman. As you work closely with them, perhaps you'd take care of it."

Taking an envelope from the drawer and passing it to his colleague he concluded, "I've prepared a one page summary on what we know of Arturo Be'eri, including telephone numbers in Rome that he regularly dials."

In Tel Aviv, Kobbi approved the policeman's proposal. In a telephone conversation he expressed some reservations; but he did approve.

Meir Peled walked away from the Russian Compound towards the car that he'd parked on a side road not far away. A civil servant for over twenty years, since graduating from the Hebrew University with a degree in political science, he had been asked by the director-general of the Prime Minister's Office to sit in on the investigations into the recent bank robbery. This was the first meeting he had ever had with policemen in any capacity, and he was impressed.

He had been informed of the Agreement that had been stolen and had read the copy of a draft, kept in the classified files. Coming from a left-wing background, he had always been surprised that he had been retained by the new right-wing administration. More surprising was the fact that he had benefited from regular promotions within the office. Conversely, some of his close left-wing friends had been disappointed that Peled had chosen to stay and work under this new administration which they glibly dubbed, fascist.

Recently, Peled had been seconded to assist the prime minister's advisor on terror. He was handed the delicate task of keeping an eye on potential right-wing subversives. In this capacity he had met the PM for briefing sessions on a number of occasions. He had never ceased to be surprised at the ex-terrorist's attitude towards a section of the population that had always regarded Begin as their nominee for the top job. For, in Peled's judgment, Begin was much harder on his own right than had been all the previous left-wing administrations.

Meir Peled had read the recent reports on Taher, compiled by the Shabak. He thought that there was probably no connection between the robbery and the missing Agreement. Nonetheless, it looked as if he would have to continue listening for some time to police and Shabak agents discussing their investigations. After all, the inspector had clearly stated that he had no real ideas how to solve the crime.

Meir Peled's real concerns lay elsewhere. At first he had opposed the recent administrative detention of Meir Kahane and his associates from the extreme right-wing Kach political party. He remembered how incredulous he had been when first informed of Begin's action. Begin was, he thought, one of the most complex men he had ever encountered.

As head of the Irgun Zvai Leumi before the establishment of the State of Israel, Menahem Begin had been held responsible by the British for many acts of terror. These included the hanging of a British sergeant and the blowing up of the King David Hotel, both as reprisals for British atrocities. On his election as prime minister in 1977, Her Majesty's Government had let it be known that the ex-terrorist would not be welcome in the United Kingdom.

Begin's election was considered a blow to democracy and the chances of peace in the region. Yet within months he had hosted Egyptian President Sadat in Jerusalem and quickly sat down to negotiate a peace treaty with Egypt. For this peace, he made large territorial concessions, concessions refused by former governments.

Born and educated in pre-war Poland, Begin had graduated to a Soviet work camp in Siberia, which he had survived by sheer determination. He was one of nature's gentlemen, with highly-tuned Polish manners. He always stood up when introduced to a visitor and enjoyed bowing to a lady and kissing her hand. Another side to his character came into play in debates, where he proved a mean adversary. During his many years in opposition, he had cut the government to pieces with his fiery rhetoric. A neat little man, Begin always dressed with immaculate care, adhering to the notions of *hadar* – majesty, as dictated by Jabotinsky, his role model Revisionist leader. He took his own legal background seriously, priding himself on upholding the law.

And yet, this same man was prepared to reintroduce administrative detention in defiance of human rights, flying in the face of democratic concepts of legality and decent political behavior.

Peled thought back to the days in May 1977 when Yitzhak Rabin lost the election and Begin came to power. Many social democrats believed that, with the passing from power of the socialists, democracy in Israel had come to an end. Many even considered leaving Israel to live elsewhere. On the other hand, many Jews had wept with joy, because on hearing the election results, Begin, the prime minister-elect, had taken a small black skullcap from his pocket. Placing it on his head, he recited a Hebrew prayer in thanksgiving; – *"that He gave us life, that He sustained us, and that He brought us to this day."*

Begin's administration was Peled's conundrum. On a daily basis, Peled had to toil under a right-wing administration that behaved undemocratically to its own fringe elements. And it was within this specific area of administration that his responsibilities lay. To complicate matters further, his left-wing intellectual friends were in the forefront of the many objectors. They wouldn't countenance the government's behavior to its own right-wing backers.

As Peled watched the increasing frustrations of the right wing, he foresaw a growing state of conflict which, in his opinion, would one day erupt into violence. It was only a matter of time.

Peled's views of the Shabak were mixed. He had no doubt that some of the agents, particularly the senior officers, were good men. He had met and been impressed by Kobbi, a frequent visitor for briefings with the prime minister. He had his doubts about the men in the field, some of whom, he felt, operated on the basis that the ends justified the means. This was an unacceptable concept. But it was clearly daily practice in real life.

But all this paled against the behavior in the courts of law. Meir Peled had been brought up to believe that courts were inviolate and unimpeachable. He now had his doubts.

The code provided that detainees under administrative detention had to have their cases reviewed in camera by the president of the district court. He would receive a closed file – closed, that is, to the eyes of the detainee and his lawyer. The file was compiled by the Shabak, whose findings were invariably accepted by the judge at face value. The so-called defense attorney could not refute the charges, because he didn't know what they were. The detainee and his lawyer were denied the most elementary legal tools of defense.

As Meir Peled delved further into the political system, he became alarmed at the undemocratic line of command that emanated from the Prime Minister's Office. It extended through the Shabak, the armed forces, the Ministry of Justice, the office of the state prosecutor and even encompassed the president of the district court. All were linked in this chain of inequity that must, in his opinion, lead to the perpetration of injustice. When the Shabak reported that a certain person was a subversive, that individual would end up in jail. He would not be able to exercise any basic civil or legal rights. All the parties on the chain would play their role. Nothing would be able to stand in their way. No lawyer could prevent the injustice.

Against this background, there was evidence that subversive groups were multiplying. Demonstrations based on political frustration would undoubtedly increase.

"No," he replied to the query from the PM's secretary, "there is nothing of note to report from the meeting at the police; no breakthrough as yet."

Aboud Mugrabi waited for over a month before he made his first practical move to sell the Agreement. As a Christian Arab living in the Old City, he was far removed from the powerful forces operating within Islam and had difficulty in making a preliminary contact.

However, as time marched on, he felt obliged to initiate some action. Contriving an introduction to a certain Muslim fundamentalist, he positioned himself near the

Lions' Gate exit from the Temple Mount in the expectation of catching him when he completed his Friday prayers at the el-Aqsa Mosque. In this way he managed to arrange a coincidental meeting with Ahmed el-Alamy. Taking the Muslim aside, he suggested that they go to a quiet place where they could talk confidentially. The Muslim obliged and the two proceeded to a quiet coffee house where Aboud entertained him.

Aboud's story was simplicity itself. When in prison, he told Ahmed, he had met a Jew who claimed that he could obtain a copy of an Agreement signed in 1951 between King Abdullah and the Israeli government. Under the terms of the Agreement, the Jews guaranteed Hashemite control of the Temple Mount in perpetuity. The Jew, he claimed, wanted $100,000 for his copy. His new Muslim friend, showing no surprise at the story, said that he would make some inquiries and would come back to him if he found anyone interested.

In the nineteen eighties, the Muslim world was in a state of flux. The ex-Mufti had died a decade earlier in exile in Egypt, an old and dispirited man of little influence. In his last years he was rarely heard from. And yet his passing had left a vacuum on a large stage, with no real leader emerging to replace him. Fundamentalist Islam was centered in Iran, whose political regime was based on the religious teachings of the Koran. However, its influence outside Iran was restricted to Lebanon, Algeria and, to a lesser extent, Egypt. It had certainly not penetrated Jerusalem. Nor did it have any influence among Islamic Jerusalemites.

Islamic Egypt, where the ex-Mufti had lived for many years in exile was in turmoil. Opposing the Sadat peace treaty with Israel, the fundamentalists turned violent, going undergound, wreaking havoc and chaos wherever they could, and causing much loss of life.

In Jerusalem, the descendants and political followers of the ex-Mufti had softened their attitudes. They were aiming for political independence from the Jews and had decided to throw their weight behind the PLO. The Temple Mount was in the hands of Muslim clerics. They wanted to maintain the status quo. Against this background, Mr. el-Alamy could find no one interested in paying many thousands of dollars for a copy of a very old Agreement.

In the meantime, Aboud had heard that Jewish extremists were buying properties in the Muslim Quarter of the Old City. Perhaps they would be interested in buying the Agreement.

CHAPTER 31

After leaving his lawyers, Taher hurried home by bus. He bathed, shaved carefully and changed his clothes, choosing his newly-acquired grey English slacks and a smart blue jacket. At 7 pm he phoned the number that he had been given and prayed that Tali would be able to come out with him. Tali answered on the third ring and confirmed that there were no problems. They decided on supper instead of coffee and agreed to meet ninety minutes later at a quiet restaurant near the Mahanei Yehudah market on Agrippas Street.

The bus journey into town had never been so exciting. Taher couldn't remember being so happy. Arriving at the Central Bus Station with forty minutes still in hand, Taher decided to walk to the restaurant. With long steps, the tall good-looking man approaching middle age strode proudly along the pavements towards his first date in two decades.

Tali had dressed suitably for the restaurant, She wore blue pants, a white blouse and a well-fitting tweed jacket. To Taher, who waited for her at the front door, she looked a goddess of beauty.

Waiting for the first course of assorted eastern style salads, Tali took charge of the situation: "Taher, I think that this evening's outing is adventurous for both of us. Seeing you come and go at the office during the past years has led me to like you. Had that not been so, I wouldn't have agreed to come out with you. I lead a sheltered life, making a living and looking after my son."

The salads arrived and Taher ordered soft drinks. They began to pick from the various plates.

"Why don't you tell me about yourself," asked Tali. "I hear all kinds of gossip, but the real information is discussed by you and Rami behind locked doors."

Once again that day, Taher began telling his story. Talking about himself was becoming a habit, one that he had never indulged in previously. He related his father's history in the Hebron area. He then told about the Agreement that he had found on the lonely road and kept hidden for so many years. Taher told of his conversion to Judaism and his special relationship with Avraham Nissim. He told of the murder of his father and of how he had brought the Agreement to Jerusalem for safe keeping.

Tali listened to his unusual tale and prepared in turn to relate her own family history. "My tale begins in Poland where my parents come from," she began. "My father was born in the Polish textile town of Lodz. Before the Second World War, nearly a quarter of a million Jews lived there; they accounted for one third of the population of Lodz. When the Germans marched into Lodz, the Jews were herded into the ghetto. They were plundered, bullied and exploited. Those who could work were spared, to toil for the Germans in nearly one hundred factories established to oil the German war machine. Uniforms, hats, leather shoes and belts were manufactured for the Germans by the Jewish slave labor force. They worked and starved. Many, many died. Those that could not work were sent to their deaths at the extermination camp of Chelmno and elsewhere.

"In August 1944 the surviving 70,000 Jews were sent en masse to the Auschwitz gas chambers. By the time the Soviet army liberated the city in January 1945, there were only 850 Jews still living in Lodz. My father was one of the few that survived. As the noise of the approaching guns of the Soviets grew louder, my father hid under the wooden floor boards in a deserted house in the ghetto. He lay there, perfectly still. Three days later he made his escape. Taking with him a small Torah scroll that had been in the family for generations, he set out for Palestine."

Taher had read of the war, about the deaths of six million Jews at the hands of the Nazis. He had visited Yad VaShem on Mount Herzl, seen the awful photographs and model replicas that depicted so vividly the horrors of the concentration camps. These haunted him and made him wonder at the Jewish spirit. The rebuilding of Israel, rising like a phoenix from the ashes of such devastation, could only be understood in the context of the realization of messianic dreams.

They ate the starter salads. Before the waiter cleared the dishes and brought the next course, Tali continued: "My father and mother met at a deportation camp that had been set up in Yugoslavia to care for displaced persons – meaning refugees. Conditions in the camp were better than either had known for some time. They were, however, still prisoners, for they were not free to leave. My mother came from Warsaw. Her parents had placed her in a Catholic convent before they were sent to their deaths. She, too, had escaped at the end of the war and, together with some friends, had made her way towards the Mediterranean clandestinely with the intention of getting to Palestine.

"After several months they were clandestinely removed from the camp by an officer in the Jewish Brigade. Bundled into the back of a British army lorry, they were smuggled over the border into Italy and driven to Rome. There they joined thousands of Jewish refugees on an illicit ride on a commandeered train, down to Italy's southern port of Brindisi.

"The ship that took them to Palestine was termed by the British *illegal*. The Jews on board did not have proper papers. British policy limited Jewish immigration. On arrival in Haifa, my parents and the other wretched passengers were arrested and deported, this time to Cyprus. And that is where I was born, in a huge Cyprus detention camp, where over 50,000 deportees, would-be immigrants to Palestine, were camped in tin-roofed huts. Some two thousand Jewish babies were born in Cyprus to these miserable refugees. I was one of them. A year later my sister was born.

"In Lodz, my father had gained a reputation amongst the German soldiers as an expert tailor. He soon gained a similar reputation among the British soldiers. Within a short time father was making civilian suits for the British officers and the occasional dress for their girlfriends. One of these officers was posted to Nyasaland in Africa. He wrote to my father and invited him to come and set up trade as a tailor. 'The market will be entirely yours,' he said, 'as there are simply no tailors here at all.'

"It was now 1947 and Ernest Bevin, the British Foreign Secretary, determined that, in respect of the 50,000 Jews in Cyprus, a quota of only 750 per month would be allowed to go to Palestine. Father realized that, under such conditions, he and his family might stay in Cyprus for years. In these circumstances, he accepted the invitation, and our small family went to live in East Africa.

"We stayed there for nearly three years and then emigrated to the new Jewish State of Israel. Unlike the poor Europeans who arrived penniless from Cyprus, my parents came with sufficient funds to establish themselves in Ramat Gan, where they live and work."

"They were idealists, with a good measure of common sense," said Taher. "And here in Israel they can concentrate on their idealism."

"What idealism?" laughed Tali, "All that is long forgotten. Now they are interested in their car and their TV. They enjoy their vacations and the better foods which they can now afford to buy. Believe me, their idealism died a long time ago."

"How can you talk like that about your parents after all that they went through in the war. Surely, after all their suffering, they are entitled to some happiness?"

"Maybe I'm hard on them, but our paths rarely cross, and I find it difficult to accept their materialistic view of life," countered Tali in measured tones. "Let me see if you will change your mind," she continued teasingly. "If my mother could only see me here eating dinner with you, she would be truly horrified. Nothing would persuade her to agree to a relationship between us. So what do you say to that?"

Taher thought for a few moments before replying in somber tones, "I'm sure that everyone in the village outside Ramallah where I lived would agree with your mother."

"Yes," Tali said bitterly, "I suppose you are right. More's the pity, but I guess there are many bigots on both sides. However, until you have met Polish bigots, believe me you've seen nothing."

A truce was called as the main course was brought to the table by their waiter. Both had ordered lamb chops and chips. The chops were quite tasty but not very large. To make the most of them, you had to take them in your hands and chew. So until they finished the course, there was no more conversation.

While he ate his chops, Taher thought about Tali's remark about her own mother. Was this a hint that he would have no chance of having a relationship with Tali? Was this going to be the first and last date? Tali seemed to read his thoughts, for it was she who again took the initiative: "Don't dwell too much on my mother. I can tell you that I wouldn't let her influence my future. She has created enough mischief in my sister's marriage, believe me."

"May I learn from that remark that our relationship might have a future?" asked Taher in hopeful expectation.

"I can't know what the future holds for us. We must both be aware that, unfortunately, the society in which we live is not very kind. It's not just my Polish mother; its the neighbors, the children in the schools, the students and lecturers in the universities, the strangers in offices and at doctors' clinics, and even the rabbis in their synagogues. In fact, possibly the more intellectual people are, the more bigoted they become."

Stretching across the table, Taher reached for Tali's hand. "Tali, I haven't dated for over twenty years and today I am not looking for a casual relationship. As you can see, I am shy and possibly burdensome. Flirting or courting has never been my strong point. I pray that our friendship will grow and make us both happy."

Tali had the feeling that Taher was echoing her own innermost thoughts. For four years after her husband's death, she had not gone out with any man and had dated only rarely since then. Nearly all of her boyfriends had looked for a casual relationship. Many men thought that widows were easy game. A couple of years back there had been one serious young man, but he had been a crashing bore and she soon tired of him. And now this man, a converted Arab, definitely attracted her, notwithstanding all the problems that such a relationship must pose in a tight and unsympathetic society!

Leaving her hand easily in his, Tali replied, "We will let things take their stride. Slowly we will get to know each other. Neither of us is young and we mustn't act foolishly."

Later, after drinking mint tea, and after talking for a long time, Tali drove Taher to the bus station. She wanted to drive him home but was a little afraid of the route to Neve Ya'acov where, according to the newspapers, stones were thrown every day at passing vehicles. In any case, Taher wouldn't hear of her driving out there.

As Taher prepared to leave her car, Tali leaned over and kissed his cheek, "Thank you for a lovely evening, *lehitraot* – see you again."

During the following weeks they dated regularly. They went to films at the local cinemas, ate at various restaurants, visited exhibits at the Israel Museum. They even drove down to Tel Aviv one evening. There they ate a fish meal at the wharf in Jaffa and, hand in hand, walked around the reconstructed Old City of Jaffa like two young tourists in love. After two weeks of dating, Taher was as convinced as he ever would be, that he wanted to marry Tali. But, whenever he tried to raise the subject, Tali, in her charming way, suggested that they be patient. At dinner one evening she reopened the subject of her mother, as if to explain some of the difficulties that lay ahead.

"My younger sister is a wonderful girl. As a teenager she became religious all on her own, without any parental support. She went to Scouts, a local Zionist youth group. It was non-religious but very nationalistic. Shosh, that's my sister, wanted to understand the source of Zionist ideology. 'Why are we entitled to this land?' she would ask. The only answer that would satisfy her was that it was given by G-D to our forefathers, to Abraham, Isaac and Jacob. The two ideologies were intertwined, one without the other was unacceptable to Shosh. As a result she became a religious Zionist.

"Before the army, she enrolled in a seminary in Jerusalem, called Beit Meir. There she learned of her roots, of the Torah, the Mishnah, the Sages, the more recent Bible commentators, the Rambam and the Ramban. She met a wonderful student and decided that he would be her husband. He was studying to be a dayan, a religious judge. His knowledge of Judaism was immense, and they would talk and talk for hours on what Jews call – *dvarim she berumo shel olam* – spiritual matters that transcend all worldly matters. When my mother met this talented and idealistic young man, she threw a fit. He was the son of Moroccan immigrants, and no Polish Jewess would allow her daughter to marry a Moroccan.

"They got married in spite of my mother. Shosh and her husband, David, went to live in a new settlement. For four years they lived in a caravan where they had three children. Later she moved to a small house, and today she has six kids and she's only been married for nine years.

"My mother never forgave her. She still can't stand the sight of David, and as for her half Moroccan grandchildren...."

That night Taher slept fitfully. In the morning Taher decided to go and consult his friend Avraham Nissim, who was now living in a modest stone house built on the land that Taher's father had sold to the settlers. "Why don't you come back with me on one of the days that I come to Jerusalem. You will stay the night, and we'll get you a ride back to Jerusalem the following day," suggested Avraham. Taher accepted the offer and agreed to a date the following week.

Avraham had been teaching Taher for some years. He also acted as his mentor in most matters. When Taher told him of his feelings for Tali, he was, on the one hand, pleased for the young couple and, on the other, well aware of the problems that their love would bring.

As a young Sephardi born in Syria, he had felt the bigotry in Ashkenazi-dominated Israeli society. His wit and deep learning, plus his charisma and physical good looks, had held him in good standing. However, he was well aware of the difficulties within a prejudiced Israeli society which prevented job advancement in so many fields to Jews of eastern or African birth.

His advice to Taher was that he should bring his girlfriend to spend a weekend with Avraham's family. "Perhaps life on a settlement will appeal to you both. If you wish to join a settlement such as ours, I assure you that you will rank as full members and will suffer no indignities. We live in a close-knit community, where we are friends and neighbors in the fullest sense. All are joined by a common ideology and sense of purpose. From what I know of you, I would be pleased to propose you as a candidate for membership."

On their next date, Taher reported to Tali on his discussions with his friend and mentor. Although Tali had not met him, she had heard glowing reports on Avraham Nissim from more than one source. Her son was due to go away for a weekend with his scout troop and she would be happy to spend a couple of days with Taher's mentor and his family. She was also interested to see how these small, cohesive communities functioned.

Tali herself was traditionally observant, but not religious. She kept the Sabbath in a general way, but not down to the smaller details. She kept a kosher kitchen, with separation of meat and milk. However, she did not go to synagogue regularly, nor did she cover her hair. When in Jerusalem she dressed modestly, but she didn't mind mixed bathing. For the visit to the Nissims, she made no pretense. She dressed modestly and behaved naturally. The Nissims and their children welcomed the unmarried couple to their home. Neighbors came to visit and Taher was made welcome at the communal prayers. These were held in one of the larger homes, until such time as money would be found to build a synagogue.

Avraham had been told by Taher about Tali's mother. He decided to avoid the subject of bigotry. He was more interested to test the depth of the couple's love and Taher's and Tali's commitment to each other. As always, Tali was open and candid.

When the children had gone to bed on Friday night, the four adults sat around the table splitting pistachio nuts, drinking cola and talking. While exhibiting candidly her affection for Taher, Tali explained her hesitations. She expressed a very special responsibility to her son for whom she was both mother and father. This situation would continue at least until he left for the army or left to study away from home.

As a war widow, she received a monthly check from the Ministry of Defense. This would cease, were she to get married. There were war widowed friends that had lived for years with a companion without getting married, just in order to safeguard those monthly payments. Tali felt, however, that such an arrangement with Taher would undermine any real sense of commitment.

Taher had never heard her talk about this matter before. She had not asked him about his financial position and, being naturally reserved, he had not offered any information. The truth was that, after various land sales, he was financially well-placed and could afford to support a wife in comfort. He decided that he would discuss this aspect with Tali another time.

On their return to Jerusalem on Saturday night, their car was stopped at a road block outside Bethlehem. At first, Taher couldn't find his identity papers which were in his bag in the trunk. The soldier, who had already paid attention to his accented Hebrew, looked at him carefully as he eased out of the car. Earlier that evening, at another road block, there had been a shootout with Arab terrorists and the soldiers were nervous.

The soldier ordered Taher to stand facing the car with his hands on the roof. Tali was furious and shouted abuse at the soldier. Nevertheless, Taher was frisked carefully before he was allowed to open the trunk and search for his papers. At all times he was watched carefully by a soldier whose gun was held at the ready. Eventually the suspicious soldier was satisfied, although puzzled by Taher, whose Israeli ID had recently been updated to record that he was Jewish, with an address in Neve Ya'acov. His place of birth and parents' names clearly indicated his Arab background.

Taher climbed back into the small car, and Tali shot away from the checkpost feeling embarrassed. She had been humiliated on Taher's account and wanted to erase the affair from their memories. "My son will not return until tomorrow," she told Taher. "Why don't you come back to my apartment, and we will try and forget what we have just been through."

Chapter 32

Among the varied business activities of Arturo Be'eri, his favorite was the illicit trading in icons of doubtful authenticity. In recent years, with the first signs of *glasnost*, the doors of Russia, Rumania, East Germany and Czechoslovakia had opened. Icons were regularly smuggled out and traded in the markets of the west.

For centuries, trading in icons had been delicately balanced by rival Orthodox and Catholic Churches. Whereas the former overwhelmingly controlled the original sources of supply, the latter had been buying up such quantities for so many years that it had emerged a worthy rival supplier to world markets. Jerusalem, with its diverse collection of churches, holy places, seminaries and patriarchs was a magnet to pilgrims from around the world. The Churches and the patriarchs represented formidable economic entities of their own and, during the past decades, Jerusalem graduated to the premier league in the icon trade.

As the demand grew, a parallel secondary market in fakes or touched up icons also developed. It was particularly in this area of commerce that Arturo played a growing role. Icons from many sources were arriving in Jerusalem to be offered to the patriarchs or their subordinates. They would either buy them or decline them. They could also pronounce them genuine or denounce them as fakes. A stamp of approval from one of the patriarchs was a valuable commodity.

Arturo learned many years earlier that patriarchs and subordinates could be bought. Based on this premise and the background of increasing trade in icons, Arturo built a profitable business. As his business contacts were influential in the Old City of Jerusalem, Arturo decided to put them to work to find the old Agreement.

Not that Arturo had abandoned seeking more information from Sari. He had merely decided not to rely on her exclusively. After all, should she deliver, Sari would be handsomely paid, and he would still be able to earn the lion's share of any reward. On the other hand, he had come to believe that Sari had played the full extent of her hand. It would be prudent to look elsewhere for results.

At the same time, Arturo intended to keep an eye on Sari, try and detect the source of her information. Having recently seen Sari jack up the price of the copy of the Agreement, he was sure that, should she procure the original, she would renegotiate her terms. He also reasoned that, whereas Sari might not be able to extract more information from her original source, he and some of his rougher friends might get better results. Accordingly, Arturo set in motion two lines of inquiry.

One of his associates was a young man who had previously worked for the Shabak as a low level agent. Yaron, Hebrew for joy, couldn't have been less aptly named. He was a miserable looking fellow who rarely smiled, never appeared to be enjoying life. He was also not entirely reliable and had once given a report to his bosses at the Shabak that was later described as *optimistic*. For that particular incident he was fired. Not knowing any other trade, he had then opened a small private detective agency in Jerusalem. His principal occupation was spying on husbands and wives to prove infidelity as grounds for divorce.

After leaving a message on Yaron's answering machine, Arturo had finally managed to pin him down, arranging to meet him for morning coffee in Ben Yehuda Street. Yaron considered Arturo to be self-made, rich, powerful and therefore dishonest. In his book, you couldn't be the first two in a sleepy town like Jerusalem, unless you were the third; that, he considered, was a sine qua non.

Arturo had prepared an appropriate tale: "Yaron, I would like you to keep an eye on a young girlfriend of mine, who works at the Bank Hapoalim on King George Street. Her name is Sari Butbul." The coffee arrived and Yaron asked about cakes.

"I want to know if she has other regular friends. But that's not all I need to know," Arturo continued after Yaron's appetite for cakes had been temporarily assuaged. "Sari recently obtained a document. It was a copy of an old agreement which I believe to be of historic interest, as it was signed by Moshe Dayan and King Abdullah in 1951. First of all, I'd like to know where she got it from; she claims she got to know about it in the bank."

Arturo took a leisurely sip of his coffee and looked carefully at Yaron, weighing up in his mind whether to continue with the second leg of the operation. At that moment, Yaron bit off too large a piece of cake and was having difficulty controlling the mound of chocolate and cream. With one hand holding the cake to his mouth, he used the other to search around desperately for a paper napkin as a second line of defense. The gooey mixture split, and part of the cake fell on his shirt. Arturo decided that he had told Yaron enough for the time being.

That afternoon Arturo drove into the Old City through the Jaffa Gate. He took the second left and drove along the cobble-stoned alley called the Road of the Greek Catholic Patriarch. The road, which was wide enough for only one car, changed its name half-way along to Road of the Greek Orthodox Patriarch, whose patriarchate, offices and church dominated the rest of the road.

The Catholic patriarchate had a large gateway opening on to an area in which three large cars could be parked. One of the spaces was reserved for very important visitors, and Arturo, who was well known and who tipped generously, was always made to feel most welcome.

"Shalom, ma shlomcha?" (Hello, how are you?) asked the gatekeeper jovially in Hebrew. Keeping to their ritual of many years standing, Arturo answered with the same in Arabic, *"Sala'am Aleikum, Kif Halak."* Giving the keys of the car to the gatekeeper, Arturo ran up the short flight of stairs and went to find his friend.

While still a young lad of fourteen, Bishop Dimitri Vassilius had come to Jerusalem as a seminary student from the Greek island of Mykonos. Now in his seventies, he was an integral part of the fabric of the Old City. On the rare occasions that he had returned to mainland Greece or the islands, he had felt ill at ease. In his adopted home in Jerusalem, he had confidence, authority and prestige.

Vassilius was considered an authority on the position of the Churches, the juxtaposition of the other religions, and their breakdown into various sects. He understood the theological differences between the Orthodox and the Catholic churches and was thought to know more of the many subordinate groups within the Catholic Church than many of the Vatican's own learned authorities.

During the many years that he had spent in Jerusalem, Vassilius had also studied the mysteries of Islam. He could trace the claims of the branches of that religion back to Muhammad, the ultimate source, arguing with the most paramount personalities in the Wakf, the ultimate Islamic religious authority in the Old City.

In his later life, the worthy bishop had added another expertise, that of icons. Very profitably, he had developed a flawless approach to the trading of icons of dubious vintage. Although the Greek Catholic priest and his Jewish associate, Arturo Be'eri, could not be considered partners as such, there were few transactions that either concluded without the knowledge and participation of the other.

On this particular visit, Arturo had come to discuss various icons that he had recently agreed to acquire from a Rumanian source. He had also come to tap his friend's considerable knowledge and connections concerning the Agreement.

After the two had received their first cups of strong black coffee in small patterned porcelain cups, the bishop walked to a cabinet and took out a box of French imported marrons glacés, his favorite chestnuts. These he offered to his Jewish friend. Looking at his watch, he asked whether it was too early for a brandy. Arturo, who had a busy day ahead of him, assured him that it was.

Arturo had brought with him a leather case that had been specially made for up to ten icons of different sizes and shapes. At the time the bishop had been so excited by it, that Arturo had generously commissioned a second leather case for his friend.

Today Arturo was carrying only five icons in his case. These he took out one by one and discussed them with the bishop, who pronounced each and every one of them to be flawed or repaired. Although not a single one received a clean bill of health, the bishop was quite excited about the commercial possibilities for three of the five. Two of them he could sell as perfect originals, and agreed on a base price with Arturo. Another was a long shot, but he might be able to place it. As for the remaining two, he suggested that Arturo try and sell them in Haifa to one of two dealers who, the bishop assured him, had proven of late not to be very particular.

Arturo replaced the two icons in his leather case and turned to face his friend: "Dimitri, you have been in Jerusalem for a long time, and I want you to cast your mind back to the 1951 assassination of King Abdullah."

"I will never forget it for as long as I live," replied the priest with feeling. "I was standing among the large crowd that had come to see the king on the Temple Mount. The king turned to wave to us before entering the mosque. I remember His Majesty catching my eye in the crowd and nodding to me graciously in recognition. I must tell you that since that terrible day, I have remained a confirmed royalist."

"So you didn't actually see the shooting?" Arturo asked.

"No, I remained outside. As a Catholic, and a cleric to boot, I would never enter a mosque. However, a good Muslim friend of mine stood inside, only yards away from the king when he was assassinated. He was very lucky not to get hurt in the crossfire that followed."

The bishop sat back in his chair and ate a sugar-coated chestnut with obvious relish. Remembering back over thirty years to that sad day, he said: "He was a wise old king who deserved better. I remember reading after the assassination that only weeks earlier he had said that his preferred way of dying was by way of a bullet in his head inside the el-Aqsa Mosque. This would assure him of a worthy place in the next world. Well, he got exactly what he asked for, but he left his kingdom far poorer by his death."

"I'll tell you more," he continued with some evidence of pain at recalling these sad events from so long ago, "my own friend inside the mosque stood petrified during the crossfire that ensued until the assassin himself was shot and killed. A number of guards and clerics were also shot, some killed and some wounded; and then the security men started making arrests of suspected associates of the killer.

"While this was happening, my friend watched the sadness on the face of Jammal, the late king's trusted bodyguard. He bent down over the king's body, straightened his clothes, tried to smooth away the agony of the bullet marks and kissed his old master goodby. And while he was doing this, my friend saw the tearful Jammal remove a white envelope from the King's clothes and secrete it into a pocket inside his own jacket. My close friend, who himself died soon afterwards, claimed to have told no one of this, other than me, of course."

"And what has happened to Jammal?" asked Arturo.

"No idea at all; I've never heard of him since."

"Dimitri, my friend, please use your wonderful contacts and get me some information on Jammal. I need to know everything about him."

Two days later, private detective Yaron gave his first report to Arturo. In it, Ehud figured as Sari's boyfriend. It had not been difficult for Yaron to ascertain that Ehud's position at the Shabak was under review and his relationship with Sari being monitored. In the meantime, however, Ehud was working closely with the Jerusalem police, trying to solve the burglary at the bank. Exactly what Shabak's particular interest was, Yaron had not yet found out. On this point, Arturo felt he knew the answer. Sari had gotten Ehud to reproduce the Agreement from the Shabak's copy of it. He told Yaron what he suspected and instructed him to find out.

"Fine, I'll check it out," said Yaron.

The next day Yaron phoned and agreed to meet with Arturo at the same coffee house on Ben Yehuda Street. Inwardly, Arturo groaned at the prospect of seeing Yaron devouring more chocolate cream cakes.

Back at the coffee house, Yaron was keen to tell his news: "Well, I now know the score on Ehud. A friend of mine, with whom I worked at the Shabak, owed me one – so I collected," said Yaron smugly.

"It appears that the operations room recently took a copy of the Agreement from an Arab who was brought in for questioning. The original was stolen from the bank, and hence the Shabak's interest in the case.

"But there's more. A few days ago the section chief returned to the office looking very annoyed. He phoned down to the operations room and insisted that their copy be brought up and lodged in the safe in his own room. Yossi Levi, my friend, took it up to him.

"The section chief then asked him if he was aware of any other copies, and had he seen anyone actually make a copy. Yossi told him that he thought he'd seen Ehud make one on the copying machine. The chief then told Yossi that he musn't say a word to anyone, particularly Ehud, whom as it happens, Yossi can't stand. Yossi says that Ehud is still on the job at the bank, but Yossi believes that the section chief is keeping a close eye on him."

Meanwhile, not far away in Jerusalem, a meeting was taking place, attended by Kobbi, the Jerusalem section chief, and Inspector Haft of the police. The meeting was not a happy one. Haft advised that they had no real leads and wanted to know if the Shabak or the police should bring Sari in for questioning about what she had done with the copy.

The section chief explained that he was keeping an eye on Ehud, and he therefore thought it appropriate for Sari to be grilled by the police. It was decided that Ehud should be sent by the Shabak to Haifa for two or three days, where he had an unfinished file to attend to. During that time, Sari should be taken in for questioning by the police.

Kobbi explained that the prime minister had demanded that the case be wrapped up as soon as possible. He was authorized from the top to demand that the police put out the word offering a state evidence deal for information that would lead to a conviction. The policeman didn't like it, but as he himself had nothing to offer, he realized that he couldn't object.

"For the record," said the inspector, "please arrange for the formal agreement of the state prosecutor's office."

"You have my word, you'll have it in the morning," replied Kobbi.

Two days later, after a not very rewarding day at the bank, Sari returned home in the late afternoon. On the way she stopped at the local supermarket and bought a week's supply of food and household supplies, working through a list that she had prepared at her desk during the day.

Drawing up to her car space in the parking lot behind the apartment block in which she lived, she stepped out of the car and locked the door with her key. As she turned towards the trunk to take her purchases out, she saw two uniformed policemen walking towards her from a police van parked nearby.

"Are you Sari Butbul?" asked the older-looking policeman. Without waiting for a reply, he continued, "We must ask you to accompany us to the station, as we wish to ask you some questions."

Sari was not feeling her best. She was tired and feeling low. Facing them, she felt shattered. Quickly pulling herself together, she asked if she could bring her own car.

"Yes, if my colleague drives with you," said the more senior man.

At the station, she was taken to a small interview room with a table and four wooden chairs. There, she was interviewed by Inspector Haft himself. She had no idea who he was, or how far up the totem pole he sat. The inspector offered her tea, which she accepted gladly. He indicated that she should sit on one side of the table.

Pacing up and down, the inspector advised her that a policeman at the bank had seen Ehud hand her an envelope two weeks earlier; would she please tell him what was in it. As Sari started to deny any memory of such an envelope, the inspector cut her short: "I must tell you that we have reason to believe the envelope contained a copy of an Agreement, an historical and important Agreement, the original of which was stolen from the bank. Very simply, I want you to tell me why Ehud gave the copy to you and what you did with it."

Sari had tried to contact Ehud that day and had been told that he had gone up north for a couple of days. Odd that he hadn't phoned to let her know, she had thought at the time. They had planned to go out tonight.

Facing the police officer, drinking her tea, and wondering how on earth to answer the question, she suddenly speculated whether Ehud was really up north or perhaps under lock and key. Playing for time, she tried furiously to clear her head and come up with an answer that would satisfy the police and not implicate others. After some minutes that seemed to her like an hour, she couldn't find such a formula.

Inspector Haft, now nearing retirement, thought about his daughter who was about Sari's age. Feeling sorry for her and fearing that she might well crack up altogether, he searched for a formula that would get him valuable information and yet not punish Sari with undue harshness.

"Now listen carefully," he began, speaking softly and without rancor, "we know who gave you the Agreement, and we know where he got it from. We need to know whom you gave it to, and why they want it. We don't want to compromise you particularly. We just want the information that will help us with our inquiries."

There was nothing slow about Sari, she saw an opening: "Do I understand that you are offering me a deal?"

"No, that was not my intention; in any case I am not assuming that you have done anything illegal, I just require answers to my questions."

Sari reconsidered her position and replied, "May I have some time to think? I don't want to get friends into trouble. On the other hand, I'd like to help you with your investigations."

The inspector walked to the door: "You have ten minutes."

When they resumed, Sari had made up her mind that this inspector looked a kindly man. She would try and conclude business with him, rather than risk younger and more difficult officers taking over, if he failed to be satisfied. While he was out, Inspector Haft, for his part, was, in fact, considering handing the interrogation over to younger men, as he felt past this sort of thing.

"I'm sure you know that Ehud and I are having an affair. When he came to the bank to participate in the investigation, it raised my female curiosity and I asked him what he was looking for. At first he refused to reveal anything, but later that night, after drinks and a good time, I persuaded him to tell me. It was entirely my fault – I put intolerable pressure on poor Ehud."

She paused for thought and looked at the inspector for encouragement. His deadpan face indicated that perhaps she had told him nothing that he did not already know.

"The following weekend I travelled with another man friend to Rome for a few days' break. By coincidence, and I swear that this is true, we met a friend of his that referred to this same Agreement. He was most eager to see it, and I promised that I would try and get him a copy."

Sari looked down at her empty glass as if counting tea leaves: "Again I put my female charms to work on poor Ehud. Again he relented, and brought me a copy."

"And who was the man in Rome? What was his interest?"

"I can't tell you what his interest was, I understand it was political," replied Sari, choosing every word carefully. "I'll tell you who he was if you release me and promise not to prosecute me."

"Well, now I'm going to call a break, I want to refer to my superiors," said the inspector. "Make yourself comfortable, and I'll send you in some more tea."

During the next hour, Sari was convinced that the police wouldn't agree to her offer, and that she would be spending the night in a cell. By the time the inspector returned she was wilting.

"We know about Arturo and your relationship with him." Inspector Haft took his seat and continued: "We want to know details of his role and the names of the guys in Rome. If they all check out, you will be free to return home. Unless we receive information about a specific crime, we will not press charges against you. We demand, however, that neither of your men friends are told of our talk."

Sari sighed with relief. She had a feeling that her earlier decision to play ball with this officer had been correct, "Arturo took me to Rome and introduced me to his business associate, a Signor Eduardo Angelo. I think I might even have his card in my bag."

She looked, found the card, and handed it to the inspector, "Over dinner he explained that his brother, a senior official at the Vatican called Monsignor Paulo Angelo, had heard of the Agreement and wanted to see it. On our return to Jerusalem, I obtained the copy from Ehud and passed it to Arturo. He, in turn, sent it or took it back to Rome."

The inspector cleared his throat. "You may go home. We will check out your story and we will keep to our part of the deal. We will also be keeping tabs on both your men friends. If you let on to either of them, we will take you back into custody and our deal will be off; is that perfectly understood?"

Sari heard the hardness come back into the inspector's voice in the last sentence and decided that she would do nothing that might bring her back for another session.

CHAPTER **33**

The night of the ordeal at the checkpost was a night that Taher would always remember, not with anger but with love and great happiness. At Tali's apartment, Taher was quickly made to feel at ease. Pleasant music played on a tape. Taher relaxed with an iced coffee, while Tali prepared a light snack of salads, cheeses, and fruit.

Afterwards, the two sat side by side on the couch. Tali took the somewhat shy Taher's hands in hers, drew him to her and kissed him, at first tenderly and later with great passion. Their lovemaking was the long gentle, considerate and sincere love of a couple deeply committed to each other. They complimented one another to perfection. Previous denial had been predicated on each partner's understanding for the other's reservations. This patience and restraint increased the mutual respect for each other without dimming their expectations. Taher had never known such sublime fulfillment.

Early in the morning they were awakened from their deep sleep by the incessant ringing of the phone in the next room. Rubbing her eyes with one hand and looking at the watch on the other, Tali jumped out of bed to take the call. "I hope that nothing has happened to David," she said to Taher.

The call was from her mother in Ramat Gan. She sounded distressed: "Tali, I am so glad that I caught you. I couldn't remember if you were supposed to be away this weekend."

"I was away, but I'm back," answered Tali. "You sound worried, what's wrong?"

"Your father is very upset and he's behaving strangely." She paused to get her daughter's full attention. Tali, who knew her mother's histrionic bent, waited to hear more.

"You remember that when we came to Israel way back in 1950.... well, of course you don't remember as you were only a child.... but you must have heard that Dad brought with him a Torah scroll that had been in his family for generations."

"Yes, I remember," replied Tali, who couldn't imagine why this subject should be used to wake her from her sleep.

"Well, I wouldn't keep it in the house, so I made Dad give it away to a local synagogue. There it has been for thirty years, and believe me, your father had all but forgotten it. As you know, apart from three visits on the High Holy Days, he doesn't go near a synagogue."

Tali looked again at her watch and saw that it was barely 7 am. What on earth was her mother driving at, she thought. How could this old story justify getting her out of her bed.

"Mum, please get to the point," she said somewhat curtly.

"Did you not see the news last night?" asked her mother.

"No, I didn't – so please get to the point."

"Well, the synagogue burnt down, and your dad's Torah scroll was burned to ashes. And that's not all," added her mother, getting up some steam, "the remains were specially interred last night by the rabbi, the congregation and, of course, your father – who is behaving as though he lost a child, G-d forbid."

"I am so sorry to hear this news," said Tali quietly, "Perhaps I should talk to dad and tell him how sorry I am."

"Well, you had better come over, as he has decided to sit shiva, he has gone into formal mourning – he is sitting on the floor and mumbling under his breath. And he informs me that he will not get up until the full seven days of mourning are completed."

Tali tried to digest this information. However, she experienced some difficulty. Her father and mother were secularists, and her father's behavior was incomprehensible.

"Mum, I'll try and come after work. Have you spoken with Shosh?"

"Yes, and she and her husband will be coming later today; they have to be in Tel Aviv at lunchtime and will see us after that."

Not knowing what the phone call was about, Taher was sitting up in bed with a slightly worried look on his face. Tali explained the somewhat bizarre circumstances that had led to the call and asked if Taher would like to drive down with her meet her parents, "If we go in the afternoon, we will probably meet Shosh and her husband, and that might lessen the impact."

Tali had to report to the office and put in a day's work. She retold the story of her father's loss to the two lawyers, and they agreed that she could leave at 3 pm, an hour earlier than usual.

Arriving with Taher at her parents' home in the late afternoon, she was pleased to find that her sister and brother-in-law were already there. They were sitting on the couch. Their father, unshaven and scruffy, was sitting on a low wooden stool at their feet, mumbling over and over again:

"Hacol Talui BeMazal, afilu Sefer Torah asher beHechal" – everything
depends on Mazal, even a Torah scroll that sits in its Ark.

The word *"Mazal"* would translate as fate or fortune or luck.

Tali's mother was fussing around, offering her children tea and cake, looking, thought Tali, as if she might even be pleased to have a Moroccan son-in-law in her home.

Tali, who was closer to her father than were the others, sat next to him. Her sister Shosh made room for her on the couch. Taher, who had not yet been introduced, but who had previously met Shosh and her husband, sat down in a chair and assumed the role of an observer.

Tali took her father's hand; gently, she asked him to explain the phrase that he was repeating.

"Two hundred and thirty thousand Jews were killed in Lodz by the Nazi swine, may their name be forever blotted out. Along with them, an entire communal structure, including synagogues and Torah scrolls was decimated. I had the privilege of surviving the massacre and escaping the terrible destiny of the rest of the community. Throughout four awful years, I hid our family's holy Torah scroll; it escaped destruction.

"After the war, I was fortunate to escape together with our scroll and find my way to Palestine. That journey was tortuous and terrible. It lasted five years and took me and the scroll to Yugoslavia, Italy, Cyprus, and even Nyasaland. The scroll never left my side. Wherever fate took me, the scroll went with me. Only when I finally arrived in the Holy Land did I relinquish the sacred custody. I placed the scroll in the Ark of a new synagogue that had been built here in our Ramat Gan community. Yesterday there was a fire. The special *Hashgaha Pratit* – Divine protection – that had kept this scroll safe throughout such dreadful times, was withdrawn. The scroll that had been in our family for so many decades was burned to ashes. Woe is me for I have sinned...!"

Her father dropped his head in his hands and wailed *"Hacol Talui beMazal, afilu Sefer Tora asher beHechal."*

Mourning pervaded the room. His wife stopped fussing and sat down quietly. The daughters and their menfolk sat still, keeping their eyes on the floor around the stool on which the father sat and sobbed.

The father lifted his head and turned his bloodshot eyes towards his son-in-law: "You are well aware that I am not a religious man. Frankly, I left my religion behind in the Lodz ghetto, surrounded by the death and horrors meted out to so many righteous men. Good men, saintly rabbis, scholars, kindly doctors, housewives – all were dealt with viciously by the Nazi scum. The only possession which left that dreadful place with me, apart from memories, was the Torah scroll.

"Before the war, when I was still a young boy, I studied in a cheder, a primitive Jewish school, where I was taught the wisdom of our sacred rabbis. One passage in the Talmud I could never understand – *Hacol Talui beMazal, afilu Sefer Torah asher beHechal.* Neither the teacher nor any other person could explain to me the meaning of this phrase. It remained an inexplicable philosophical concept.

"How could a Torah scroll sitting quietly in its Ark be subject to fate, to fortune or to luck. Last night, after nearly half a century of wondering, I learned the explanation. The mystery of this phrase taken from the Talmud has now been explained, and oh, how cruelly."

On the return trip to Jerusalem, Taher brooded silently. He reflected on the passage and the subject of fortune and fate. It was Divine intervention that had saved Tali's father from the ravages of the Holocaust in Europe – of this he was sure. Similarly, it had been *Hashgaha Pratit* that had guided his own father and himself. Meeting Tali was also no accident, and he resolved to ensure that they would live up to expectations. He would assume and shoulder responsibilities and would not discard obligations as Tali's father had done for such a long time.

He looked forward eagerly to discussing with his friend and mentor Avraham the philosophical concept of *Hacol Talui beMazal....*

CHAPTER **34**

Taher Jabari, Avraham Nissim, Rami Feffer and Baruch Struk left their car in the parking lot. They had come to participate in an ideological discussion on the details of the Agreement, as reconstructed by Taher and Rami. The venue, far from eavesdroppers, was the beautiful Aqua Bella park at the foot of the western side of the Castel Mountain, just off the highway from Jerusalem to Tel Aviv.

The four entered the deserted park, found a rough wooden table with two benches and sat down, two on each side. The setting was serene and rustic with the leaves of early winter falling around them and the trickle of water in the brook, swollen slightly by the first rains of the season.

Avraham opened the discussion on a novel topic. He first asked Taher, would he mind if they all discussed Taher's proposed change of name. Taher said that he would not mind one bit, now that he had become Jewish; he felt that a Jewish name would be appropriate.

"I must tell you that I have another reason. Recently I was stopped at a road block and given a hard time. A change of name might make me less of a candidate for spot checks by nervous soldiers."

"I think it might be a *Halachik* (Jewish law) requirement to change your name," suggested Rami Feffer, talking as a lawyer.

"Not necessarily," said Avraham. "I've been thinking about it on the way over here. Taher might be an Arab name, but in simple Hebrew it means to purify."

Baruch removed the pipe from his mouth and cleared his throat: "I think you are all missing the point. The name that must be changed is the family name. Firstly, it is the usual Jewish custom to change the family name of a convert and, secondly, because in Taher's case, it is well known among Arabs, particularly in the Hebron area; I would suggest that he should consider 'Ben Avraham,' a name often taken by converts."

Taher thanked everyone for their advice, he would discuss the whole matter with Tali.

The four participants were meeting as friends, each to gain support from the others. They were all concerned at what they considered to be the erosion of values in Israel's society. The pursuit of wealth at the expense of spiritual enhancement clouded the political judgment of a large section of the community.

Avraham and Baruch had long ago left their more comfortable Jerusalem suburban homes and taken their large families to live in one of the settlements springing up all over the West Bank. Some sixty thousand like-minded Jews had gone to put down roots in these new settlements since the Six Day War. Rami was the odd one out; he had not made this change, for he couldn't conceive of leaving his beloved Jerusalem.

"Well, we have come to discuss the Agreement," Avraham took the lead. "You have all read the clauses as reconstructed by Rami and Taher. We are here to discuss forming a policy regarding the Agreement, to see if we are of one mind. Should we try and retrieve the original? This is the question we are here to decide. I'd like to hear all your views, but first I'll tell you mine."

It was clear that the others were quite happy to hear Avraham's views first, so Avraham continued, "Our interest is to find and destroy the document, for it would be an embarrassment were a future government to decide formally to base its policy on it. I believe that our two lawyers here are more knowledgeable on the legal terminology, but I see recognition of the Agreement in two stages. At the present time, and since the Six Day War when Jerusalem returned to Jewish control, our government has followed a policy identical to the stipulations in the Agreement. In other words, they have accorded the Agreement de facto recognition.

"Despite efforts of right-wing and ultra-orthodox Jewish groups, the Temple Mount has remained solidly in the hands of the Arabs even during the five years of the present Likud right-wing government. Were a government to ratify the old Agreement, the status would change from de facto to de jure. This clearly would be a more serious and possibly irreversible situation.

"And now for my recommendation. First of all, from a practical point of view, the possibility of recovering the Agreement is remote. We know that the Shabak is looking for the Agreement, and we believe that the prime minister is involved in the matter. However, I do believe that if the Agreement is found by them, it might well be destroyed or conveniently lost.

"I would remind you that, to the best of my knowledge, a previous draft agreement in 1950, initialled by Dayan and Shiloah with the Jordanian prime minister and the defense minister, witnessed by King Abdullah, has been conveniently misplaced, nobody knows where it is. It wasn't ratified, but now it has an extra status – lost!

"You all know my views on the present government; it is a great disappointment to us on the right wing. The ministers have had so much opportunity to set things right for generations to come, but they let so many crucial matters slip through their fingers. Moreover, Begin has never really exercised his democratically acquired control. In so many matters, he merely continues old Mapai policies and propagates the practices and expediencies of the previous regime.

"Begin has surrounded himself with advisers, officials retained from the previous administration. These range from the late and celebrated Moshe Dayan, down to civil service veterans in all of the ministries. Precedent seems to be Begin's prime consideration and he will, in my opinion, chose to lose or destroy the 1951 Agreement if he succeeds in retrieving it. Our problem, as I see it, would lie with future left-wing governments, should the Agreement eventually fall into their hands."

Avraham finished. He sat back, searched for a cigarette and looked around to see who wished to speak next.

Baruch took the pipe out of his mouth and cleared his throat. "I agree with your views and your conclusion, which I understand to be that we sit back and let the Shabak find the Agreement. A friend of mine in a senior position at the Office of the Prime Minister agrees with your analysis. I spent many hours with him discussing the Agreement. He hadn't been informed about it at the office, and believes that only one or two people who are actually dealing with it are aware of the Agreement and its contents. This, he considers, strengthens the supposition that if found, the Agreement will be destroyed.

"I have learned to value my friend's opinion; in these circumstances, I would agree that we sit back and await developments. We have enough battles to wage; the expense and dangers involved in searching for the Agreement, in competition with the efficient and well-funded Shabak, are too much for us to promote or undertake."

"There is another angle," said Rami tentatively, "and that is the legal situation. Taher has had the document in his possession for over thirty years. He found it in

Jordan, not in Israel, and I cannot find any Israeli law that covers the right of the authorities to take it from him."

The other three listened attentively. Avraham and Baruch were grinning broadly.

"I know what you are thinking, but we all know that in the real world might is right. We can't argue with the Shabak, it simply doesn't pay. On the other hand, perhaps I should fly a kite and, on behalf of my client, ask the section chief, if he can have his copy back, and what plans there are for the original, if it is found."

"I don't think it is a good idea," replied Baruch, "your course of action would merely keep Taher in Shabak sights, and that cannot be considered desirable from his point of view. My opinion is that we should pretend to back off and reduce our exposure to a minimum."

Avraham and Taher agreed with Baruch's analysis. They all knew that Baruch had clients that had suffered considerably at the hands of the Shabak, that his considerations should be taken seriously.

The meeting broke up with the four participants concurring that no efforts should be made in attempting to find the Agreement. Avraham and Rami left for another meeting in Tel Aviv, while Baruch took Taher back to Jerusalem.

Late that night, when Avraham Nissim returned home, there was a message to phone his friend Ketselle at his office in the Old City or at his home in Bet El, the successful settlement he had established north of Ramallah. It could wait until the morning, thought a tired Avraham, as he prepared for bed.

Ketselle had survived the Yom Kippur War, although his two best friends and many others had not. With the backing of a strong wife and partner, he had embarked on a life devoted to rebuilding Israel and teaching future generations the sources of their Judaism.

He had established a *yishuv* – a new community – in Bet El, where three thousand years earlier, the Patriarch Jacob had dreamed of angels ascending a ladder to heaven. In this new *yishuv*, he had also established a *yeshivah*, a seminary where three hundred boys were schooled in the philosophies of the Talmud and the tenets of the scriptures. Many in Israel believed that Ketselle was the most powerful man in Judea and Samaria, an area attracting tens of thousands of Jewish settlers.

Avraham's day started early. He rose each morning at 5, washed, dressed and spent thirty minutes preparing the *Daf Yomi*, the lesson in Talmud that he gave every morning to a dozen students in the small settlement in which they all lived. At 6 they prayed together. Immediately afterwards he gave the lesson, while they all sipped hot tea or coffee.

Returning home at 7.30, he helped his wife rush their kids through breakfast. He prepared their sandwiches and schoolbooks and accompanied them some hundred and fifty yards to the gate of the settlement. There, they would be picked up by the local school bus, which would take them to a school in another settlement, some six miles and two hills away.

It was 8 am before Avraham was free to dial Ketselle's number. Ketselle asked when they could meet in Jerusalem on an important and confidential matter. "Not for the phone," said Ketselle.

They agreed to meet at the Cafe Atara in the early afternoon.

In the Shabak office in Katamon, the agent monitoring the call took off his head phones, stood up and stretched himself. He withdrew the tape from the machine and went upstairs to consult with the section chief.

Sipping juice, the two friends sat at a table on the pavement outside the Cafe Atara in Ben Yehuda Street. A month earlier a bomb, in the form of dynamite in the tube frame of a bicycle, placed against the popular coffee house had killed two, and injured ten, customers. The shop front had been blown away and considerable wreckage had been caused.

The two looked at the rebuilt premises. Business was running smoothly. All the seats were taken. A few unlucky customers were waiting for tables to be vacated.

"Isn't it amazing that these bomb blasts don't appear to affect business at all," observed Ketselle.

"It's back to business as usual," said Avraham. Two customers rose from a table, and someone waiting in line dived for one of the vacated chairs. "Now, what exciting news have you got for me?"

"Well, as you know, I am preoccupied with building up the yeshivah and settlement at Bet El. However, lately I've also been helping Michael, my brother-in-law, buy up Muslim houses in the Old City, to reclaim them for Jews. This brings me in touch with a wide section of Old City inhabitants."

He sipped his drink and continued: "Yesterday I was approached by an Arab, who claims to have a friend with a copy of an agreement signed many years ago by Moshe Dayan, Ben Gurion and King Abdullah. This agreement, so he tells me, concerns the Old City, and particularly the Temple Mount, which, regretfully, is still in Arab hands."

Avraham moved close to Ketselle in a conspiratorial mode. Quietly, he replied: "How well do you know the Arab? Can you check on him? Has he got a criminal past or is he straight? More to the point, is he really only a third party, or is he himself the principal? Now, Ketselle, what I'm going to tell you is for your ears only; is that understood?"

Ketselle undertook to keep the secret. Avraham looked around quickly to see if anyone else was interested in their conversation. Was he imagining it, or had he detected interest on the face of the customer who had just sat down?

"Not the copy, but the original of the agreement that you are talking about, was stolen in the Bank Hapoalim robbery. We know that the Shabak is looking for it." Avraham looked around at the neighboring table and noted that the single occupant seemed engrossed in eating a slice of apple pie. "My own interest in the agreement is to see it destroyed. If we could buy it cheaply enough, it would only be for the purpose of destroying it."

"I don't know the Arab myself, but I'll check him out quickly enough; then we can meet him."

Ketselle looked at his watch. "I have to run. I've got two Old City houses going through to completion. If you pay for the cold drinks I'll be off."

Avraham sat back smiling as Ketselle ran off. In all the years that they had known each other, he had never seen Ketselle pay a bill, not ever.

Ehud waited until Avraham Nissim left the scene. He rose from the table, paid for his coffee and pie and made his way quickly back to Katamon.

Kobbi arrived from Tel Aviv in record time. He, the section chief and a self-satisfied Ehud were sitting around the desk in the section chief's room. They were listening for the third time to the tape of the conversation recorded by Ehud at the Cafe Atara.

"Well done, Ehud," said Kobbi. "You have a clear tape. And now we have to decide how to proceed, but first I want to put the PM in the picture. In the meantime, let's put Ketselle under surveillance and tap his phones."

The section chief laughed, "You don't know whom you are dealing with. First of all, the guy has a sensational war record and is on close terms with half the top politicians and generals in the country. Secondly, he is brilliant and fearless. Thirdly, he is so secretive and careful that his own left hand never knows what his right hand is up to."

The section chief raised his hand as if to keep Kobbi at bay: "For some time we have tried unsuccessfully to keep tabs on his operations in the Old City. The PM himself asked that we monitor his transactions with Arabs in the Muslim Quarter, considered by a number of people a threat to stability. Frankly, we failed in that task, and eventually Ketselle got political friends to bring pressure on Begin to have us taken off his tail."

The phone rang. Kobbi raised the receiver to hear that the prime minister would see him as soon as Kobbi could get over to his office.

Rising from his chair, Kobbi asked the section chief about the various lists of bank customers that had been collected, "While I'm gone, I want a new and comprehensive list of all churches and other customers that have dealings with the Bank Hapoalim branch. I want a complete list of all church employees over the past five years, especially those that operated the accounts or went to the bank for any reason whatsoever. Liaise with Inspector Haft. Use his computer. We can be relatively certain that at least one of the bank robbers comes from the Old City; it can't be too difficult to find them."

He walked to the door and turned: "And one more thing, get Inspector Haft to run a criminal record crosscheck on all the names from the Old City."

Prime Minister Menahem Begin sat in his office in the Knesset. He received Kobbi alone. He had considered having Peled brought in, but decided first to hear from Kobbi.

Kobbi reported on the meeting that had taken place only hours earlier at the Cafe Atara. The prime minister knew both Ketselle and Avraham Nissim, both of whom he admired, although he was worried about their excessive zeal. "But that's youth," he had once confided to Peled, "if ever they assume real power and responsibility, they will have to compromise."

"Kobbi, first I want to commend you on coming to me at this stage," said the PM. "What I'm weighing up is the possibility of making an arrangement with Avraham and Ketselle, my interest and theirs are identical. And by working with them, we will speed up solving the robbery. However, I want to think it over. Leave your phone numbers with my secretary and I'll get back to you later today."

Begin, always the gentleman, rose and came around his desk. Extending his hand, he repeated his thanks. Kobbi, who had been brought up on a kibbutz, and whose politics were left of center, never failed to be impressed by his ultimate employer.

Arriving back at Katamon, Kobbi found a hive of activity in the operations room. The section chief had arranged to connect the computer via a modem to the computer at the police command center.

The information coming through the computers had been retrieved from a central Old City list, then broken down into separate church lists and other customer lists. Shortly, the section chief would proceed with a process of name elimination. The objective was to leave a limited list of prime suspects, who could then be checked out individually.

Kobbi sat at a table with the section chief. He was fed lists of names by Ehud, who seemed to be in high spirits. Kobbi and the section chief started eliminating names. The four patriarchs, eight archbishops, fourteen bishops, three qualified accountants, eight lawyers and another four senior permanent officials of various churches who were well known and considered clean, were eliminated. Four well-known businessmen who operated sizable accounts at the bank were also set to one side. Ten names remained: drivers, messengers, minor officials.

"Get them checked on the police computer for criminal records. Have the police provide us with the list of names of people who worked for the churches and other institutions during the past five years and are not on the current lists," barked Kobbi. He felt that the net was beginning to close in on the prey.

"We have asked for the additional names, and they should come through the computer within the hour," replied the section chief.

The phone rang and Kobbi reached for the receiver. It was the PM's private secretary: "The prime minister has asked if you can please return to attend a meeting that he will have in thirty minutes with Inspector Haft. An officer from the Mossad is on his way here from Tel Aviv. Mr. Begin apologizes for the inconvenience of bringing you back, but he has only just had a request from the Mossad for the meeting."

As Kobbi replaced the receiver, he heard the section chief talking on the other phone to Inspector Haft. Replacing his receiver, the section chief filled his boss in with the details, "It appears that Haft himself interviewed the girl from the bank, and she sang an interesting song implicating the Vatican. Haft felt that he should bring in the Mossad, who, in turn, felt that they wanted guidelines from the top. Haft phoned to say that a meeting with the PM has been arranged, to take place in thirty minutes. He suggested that I should be there as well."

"Well, my call was from the PM's secretary on the same matter, so we'll go together. Hopefully, when we return, we will have received further information – maybe some tangible results."

Leaving Ehud in charge, they both left for the Knesset.

Israel operates a number of services concerned with the defense of the state. The largest in terms of numbers and exposure to the general public are the Armed Forces, the Police and the Border Police.

Around the world, the Mossad is the best known of Israel's secret services. The Mossad, however, is the smallest force, with some 1200 case officers. It operates strictly outside Israel's territory. Its areas of operation involve espionage and counter-espionage. Dealings are often in twilight areas. Responsibilities include running illegal agents, spies and systems, for the gathering, codification and dissemination of information in enemy or neutral countries around the world. Occasionally Mossad agents get their wires crossed, operating inside friendly countries in a manner that would compromise Israel. The consequences may then be disastrous.

Over the years, the Mossad has earned the admiration and envy of the much larger CIA, the M15 and the KGB. With a slender staff and a considerably smaller budget than the secret services of many other countries, it has a well-earned reputation for excellence. It gets jobs done efficiently, with little cost in human life and money.

The demarcation line between the Mossad and the Shabak is simple and designed to eliminate confusion. The Shabak operates exclusively inside Israel and in the territories – the West Bank and Gaza.

Whenever either agency finds that its lines are getting entangled with or extended to the other agency's territory, a meeting is arranged and a decision taken that settles any possible confusion. The chain of command must be clear at all times; and as both these services are answerable directly to the prime minister, mistakes in the chain of command are rare.

On the matter of the Agreement, the Shabak was represented at meetings at the office of the prime minister by Kobbi, its deputy chief. The Mossad also sent its Deputy Chief to the meeting requested by Police Inspector Haft. The Mossad was very mindful of its image.

Inspector Haft reported on his interrogation of Sari and of the Vatican's interest in the Agreement. The prime minister then asked Kobbi to tell the others about developments in the Old City.

The prime minister noticed Meir Peled taking notes and put a stop to that: "This meeting is off the record and no notes or protocols will be kept," he said. "The Vatican development is interesting but not alarming, if, indeed, it is the Vatican that wants the Agreement. This, of course, has to be thoroughly checked. Its concern can only be negative. It have nothing to gain by this Agreement and its interest lies in its elimination. The conclusive elimination of the Agreement does not worry me, so if it would fall into their hands, it would not be the end of the world. However, I would prefer that it is returned to me, and all three of your agencies must proceed with that in mind."

Menahem Begin sat back in his chair in a pensive mood and none of those present thought that the time had come for questions or comments. Begin scribbled a few notes on a small pad on his desk and addressed the meeting again: "I want the Mossad to check out the Italians and the Vatican connection. Meir, I want you to invite Ketselle over here for a chat as soon as possible, and I want Kobbi present. In the meantime, I want the Shabak and the police to narrow the list of suspects by a continued process of elimination. Finally, I nominate Kobbi as head of the inquiry. He will coordinate with the Inspector and with the Mossad, both of whom will answer to him. Have any of you gentlemen any questions or suggestions?"

He paused, waited for a few seconds and concluded, "Thank you, gentlemen, for your cooperation."

Later that same evening, Kobbi made his way for a third time to see the prime minister. Unlike the previous meetings, this one was called to take place at the prime minister's office just down the road from the Knesset. He was ushered into the room before the other invited guests arrived, as the prime minister wanted to set the ground rules with him. Kobbi was preoccupied with the wretched police computer, which had developed a glitch and required the expertise of technicians. He had not received an indication of how long their work would take.

"My gut feeling is that, with the cooperation of Ketselle, the whole unhappy burglary will be settled with greater speed and discretion, both of which are important," began the PM. "But I do want your views on this... I have considered the matter more fully. I believe that, in reality, the solution sought by Ketselle, the Vatican and ourselves, is identical. The Government of Israel would have no interest in resuscitating a thirty year old Agreement signed by a monarch who died so many years ago. I must make it clear to you that I would not wish to cooperate with the Vatican on this matter. However, I have no problem in dealing with Ketselle and my friends on the right."

Kobbi realized that, at this stage, he must state his own views: "I agree that with Ketselle on our side, things will be quicker and quieter. At this moment we still have a number of suspects. As for the Vatican, I'm sure that our friends at the Mossad will do their job efficiently."

"Call in Ketselle," said the PM.

Ketselle entered in good spirits. He shook the prime minister's outstretched hand with great vigor and then turned and said Shalom to Kobbi, whom he knew from the army. Ketselle was reputed to know everyone worth knowing.

Sitting down opposite the prime minister's desk and displaying a confidence that the meeting had been called purely for his own convenience, Ketselle thanked the PM for calling him and set about explaining what weighed on his mind: "I have a problem with the Ministry of Finance and I need your help." Mr. Begin smiled and gave a good-natured sigh; Ketselle in good form was unstoppable.

"Our friends in the Old City have contracted to buy three important properties next to the Torat Kohanim Yeshivah, and the Ministry of Housing has agreed to help finance the purchase. However, they in turn require Ministry of Finance ratification, as they have already exceeded their overall budget for the year. Mr. Prime Minister, I know you want to help us in our sacred work in the Old City. One phone call from you to your finance minister and these transactions for the repurchases of properties that were once owned by Jews can be completed."

Without pausing for breath, Ketselle continued: "Today's meeting must have been arranged in heaven as you and you alone can help us at Bet El. The yeshivah, thank G-d, has nearly three hundred young boys, wonderful young men, every one of them. They will build up the Land of Israel and continue our own work. However, the financial burden is impossible to live with. With inflation reaching catastrophic proportions, the banks are now charging interest at over 100% per annum. I have been reduced to collecting money to pay the interest charges; the head of our yeshivah claims that I am no longer working for the yeshivah but for the banks. The Ministry of Religious Affairs has been promising us grants for nearly a year, but every time I approach them, they find another excuse to delay the payment. Mr. Prime Minister, the yeshivah needs your help. Please phone the minister and tell him to make the payment."

Ketselle paused for breath and the prime minister grabbed the opportunity, "My dear Ketselle, I did not invite you here in order to help fund your projects, however meritorious they may be. We have other matters to discuss. However, I'll bear your problems in mind." Ketselle, who had no idea why he had been invited, sat back in his chair, straightened the leg that was almost entirely shot off during the Yom Kippur War, the war that had completely changed the direction of his life.

"I understand that you have been offered a copy of an old agreement," said the PM. "It is possible that your source has access to the original, and it is the original which we want to retrieve. We believe that it was recently stolen from a bank. I understand that you and your friends would like this agreement destroyed, and this coincides with my own plans. We would like to cooperate with you to bring the recent bank robbery to a speedy and discreet conclusion." The PM stopped for effect.

"If you cooperate, you and Avraham Nissim will be present, when the agreement is destroyed."

The prime minister was asking for his cooperation. Ketselle was not in a position to deny it. Moreover, he was sure that the PM would be persuaded to place calls to his two ministers.

Ketselle returned with Kobbi to the Shabak operations room, where he was shown a list of four potential suspects. None of them was known to him. "Perhaps," he said, "I have not been dealing with the source but with an intermediary."

"Make contact, insist on negotiating directly with the principal," advised Kobbi. "We will be close by at all times and you will be wired. When you get to the source, we will still be close by and will take over when appropriate. The section chief will fine tune the details."

CHAPTER 35

While the authorities were pursuing their connections in the Old City, Arturo Be'eri received a call from his clerical contact suggesting that he too come to the Old City for a meeting.

After the ritual strong black coffee and marrons glacés, Bishop Vassilius told his Jewish associate that he had not found any current Jerusalem connections to the Agreement. "I was, however, luckier elsewhere," he said. "In Amman, I learned that Jammal had gone to live in Aqaba, some four years after the King's assassination.

"I have an old friend, a Father Anton, who is a priest to the small Catholic community in Aqaba. I phoned him and told him what I was looking for. He suggested that I come down to see him. He refused to discuss the matter on the phone. That is all I have to tell you for the time being. If you want, I can leave for Amman early next week, and proceed from there by plane or taxi to Aqaba."

Bishop Vassilius was entertaining his Jewish guest in his beautiful high-ceilinged room on the first floor of the Patriarchate's offices. The large and ornate French windows were wide open. The two associates sat in carved wooden antique chairs. Arturo Be'eri had the feeling of being a veritable part of the comfort and security of this wonderful, eternal, ancient City.

Outside, the skyline was punctuated by the spires and domes of churches and mosques. How he envied his clerical friend for these beautiful surroundings and atmosphere!

Just across the street, another beautiful building was occupied by the Jerusalem municipality, housing its department for city improvements. Two of the rooms on the second floor were used on an as and when required basis by the Shabak, which had listening posts all over the Old City.

Dating from the episode of Archbishop Capucci, a sophisticated listening device that beamed into the offices of the Patriarchate opposite was located in one of the rooms. While the entrepreneurial Bishop Vassilius entertained Arturo, the device was being activated. As the meeting came to a close, a report was sent to Katamon, for the immediate attention of the section head.

Some days later, Bishop Vassilius crossed the border by way of the Allenby Bridge. Using his diplomatic passport, he had no problems at the border. The entire trip to Amman took him less than an hour and a half. Having ascertained that he had missed the daily flight south, he negotiated a shared taxi ride and left for Aqaba some two hundred miles south.

The King's Highway was a good, straight road, albeit without a divider in the center. The journey was fast and uneventful. At the port city of Aqaba, the Bishop booked into the Gulf Hotel.

The temperature in Aqaba, some ten degrees centigrade higher than in Amman and Jerusalem, demanded a change of habits and tempo. The streets on the way through town towards the sea were deserted. The locals were enjoying a siesta away from the noonday sun. The bishop took a shower and rested before seeing his old friend, whom he had invited to the hotel for 5 pm.

At the appointed hour, Bishop Vassilius waited in an armchair in the lobby. Hoisting up his somewhat portly figure, he embraced his old friend, whom he hadn't seen for some years. After exchanging pleasantries, they withdrew to a quiet corner and sat down to chat with tea and cakes.

"I don't know if you remember," began Father Anton, "but I have a younger brother here in Aqaba. He remembers you from many years ago and sends his regards. My brother, Mario is his name, used to work at the king's winter palace in Aqaba. He was a senior aide and personal secretary until he was fired some years ago."

The local cleric took a bite of cake and sipped some tea.

"He believes that he was fired on the king's orders. I, however, believe that he was removed by his immediate superior, who was jealous of him. In any case, he has gone through a difficult time. For nearly two years he was unemployed, until I arranged an administrative post for him at the Princess Haya el-Hussein Hospital.

"When he left, he was very bitter and his anger was directed at the whole royal household. As I was his nearest friend and relation, and we have always been very close to one another, he confided in me. I'm sure he told me many things that he shouldn't, but I have always been paid to be a good listener." The priest chuckled at his own humor.

"It appears that, shortly before Mario was dismissed, Jammal had phoned and made an appointment to see His Majesty, King Hussein. On the day of his appointment, the king wished to go sailing, so he asked my brother to take his place.

"Jammal was not prepared, however, to talk with my brother. He requested that another appointment be scheduled with the king. He pointed out that he wished to impart something from the late king Abdullah, whom he had served loyally for many years. When the king and his brother, Prince Hassan, returned from sailing, they were informed by my brother of Jammal's request. They instructed Mario to bring him back to the palace.

"Jammal returned and was shown out onto the terrace by my brother, who then remained in the adjoining room to clear some papers. Through the window he saw Jammal take a white envelope from his pocket and hand it to the king, who proceeded to read it, together with his brother, with great interest. They then discussed its contents with Jammal and asked him questions.

"Through an open window, my brother heard snippets of the conversation. The document, it appeared, was an old agreement taken by Jammal from the body of King Abdullah after he was assassinated. Jammal had taken it, to protect it from falling into wrong hands."

"Are you aware of the subject matter of the Agreement?" asked Vassilius.

"I don't know the details, but it concerned Jerusalem."

"Have you any idea where that Agreement is today?"

"No," replied the priest, "but at the time it was stored in His Majesty's private safe. If you want to know more, I think you should speak to Mario. I could phone and ask him to join us. He should be at home just now."

Mario joined them within the half hour.

Vassilius told Mario of the Church's interest in the old Agreement. He also assured him that the terms of the Agreement were in conflict with the interests of the Church.

Mario still harbored resentment towards his former employers. He was eager to assist the bishop from Jerusalem. "I understood at the time that King Hussein intended to leave the Agreement in the safe in Aqaba and not take it to Amman. I cannot tell you if that is still the case, or if it is still in the safe." Mario paused and was clearly trying to think of something. "I know people at the palace; some I consider to be my friends. It is possible that I could induce one of them to help; but for that I would need to pay. Have you got a budget for such expenses?"

"How much money are we talking about and what level of assistance could we have?"

"I think that for $1000 I would be told with a high level of certainty if the Agreement is still in the safe. The safe, at least for as long as I was at the palace, was controlled by a combination lock, the number of which was known only to His Majesty and the Crown Prince."

Bishop Vassilius put his hand through the slit in his long blue robe and withdrew a fine leather wallet from an inside shirt pocket. Opening the wallet, he counted out ten bills, each of $100, and passed them to Mario. Mario noticed that the bishop did not seem to have made much of a dent in his wad of notes. "There will be the same amount for you, if I get the information tonight," said the bishop.

Back in the Old City two days later, Arturo was again sitting in the bishop's magnificent room in its beautiful setting. The monitoring device across the street was working, when Bishop Vassilius reported to Arturo that King Hussein's copy of the Agreement was safe and sound in His Majesty's private safe at the palace in Aqaba.

When the report on the meeting at the Patriarchate was relayed to the operations room at Katamon, both the section chief and Kobbi were with the prime minister drinking a toast.

Chapter **36**

Taher had arranged to meet his friend Avraham Nissim. Together they would proceed by bus to the lecture hall in Bet Hakerem where Avraham was to give his weekly lesson on *Pirkei Avot* – the Ethics of the Fathers.

On the bus Taher recounted the tale of his condolence visit to Tali's father in Ramat Gan, where he was mourning the loss of the Torah scroll that had been destroyed in the synagogue fire. The journey of less than thirty minutes was sufficient for Avraham to get an interesting insight into the lives of Tali's parents.

At the hall, they found a crowd of over sixty young men and women, about three times as many as attended earlier lessons. Avraham's fame as a teacher had spread. Standing before his class, Avraham opened the *Pirkei Avot* at the fourth chapter. "I think you will agree it is fortuitous that we have reached this particular part of the Mishna. Our portion today commences with a statement from the Sage Ben Zoma who says:

> '*Which person is wise?* and he answers: *He who learns from every person!* To illustrate his point, Ben Zoma quotes from the Book of Psalms: *From all my teachers I grew wise.*'

"Our Mishna sage wished to emphasize that those who seek to learn will acquire knowledge from all sources. If you truly value wisdom, you will seek it wherever it can be found. Should a student decline to learn from someone whom he doesn't like or respect, he would be wrongly elevating his own feelings over the pursuit of knowledge."

Avraham closed the Mishna in front of him on the podium.

"I intend to digress and tell you what I myself have just learned on the way here this afternoon from my friend Taher."

One or two of the students turned in their seats to look at Taher. Some of the students taking copious notes wondered if they should take a break and listen, or continue writing.

"Taher told me of his recent visit to a Jew who was sitting *shiva*. He was in mourning, not for the passing of a relation, but for a Torah scroll. The mourner had miraculously survived the Holocaust, having managed to bring to Israel, after a long and tortuous journey, his family's Torah, saved from the fires and horrors of Lodz. After many years in Israel, the scroll was lost in the fire that burned down the synagogue in Ramat Gan last week.

"On entering the room, Taher found the mourner sitting on the floor, unshaven and without leather shoes. He moaned and moaned, repeating a single phrase from the Talmud that he had learned as a child: *'Hacol Talui beMazal afilu Sefer Torah asher BeHechal.'* Neither Taher nor I had ever really understood the meaning of this phrase. What had a Torah in the safety of its ark to do with fate, luck or fortune? The mourner in Ramat Gan had stumbled on the meaning. A brutal clarification had revealed the real significance of this difficult phrase, and Taher conveyed it to me. Now I wish to share it with my class. *'From all my teachers I grew wise.'* And now with your leave I will digress further from the text and tell you a little of my own history." The class sat still. Avraham had his audience captivated, hanging on his every word.

"Here in Israel, I am often referred to as the Sephardi, or the Syrian. When my family lived in Damascus – for three generations – we were always called 'the *Halabim*' the Jews from Aleppo.

"My great-grandfather escaped from riots in Aleppo in the year 1875 and brought his family to Damascus. There he was welcomed by the Jewish community; he made his living working as a scribe.

"To digress even further, I should tell you about Aleppo. As I have already indicated, in Hebrew Aleppo is called *Haleb* which means milk. For it is told that our Patriarch Abraham distributed the milk of his sheep to the poor of Aleppo.

"There has been a Jewish community in Aleppo since Roman times. This community was rich in culture and learning. Its music, prayer, poetry and writings enriched Jewry all over the world. Unfortunately, however, at many points in history there were also pogroms, pain and suffering.

"My great-grandfather was a pious man who wrote the Torah in gratitude for his deliverance from near certain death. The pogrom started when the Jews were accused of killing a young boy missing from his home. He was subsequently found in a nearby village, but not before Jews had been killed and their possessions plundered.

"In Damascus my ancestor gave the Torah scroll to a local synagogue, subject to the proviso that when his offspring would leave for the Holy Land, they would take it with them. In his will, he left the express wish that one day this particular scroll would come to a final resting place here in Jerusalem.

"I came to Israel as a boy, together with my father and five siblings. We did not come by plane on El Al but overland, crossing borders illegally until we connected with a small boat that took us from the coast of Turkey to Haifa. We took few possessions but were privileged to carry with us our family *Sefer Torah*.

"This *Sefer Torah* came to its proper destination, to Jerusalem, just as it was intended to: *Hacol Talui beMazal, afilu Sefer Torah asher BeHechal.* – Everything depends on Fortune, even a Torah scroll that sits in its Ark."

CHAPTER 37

After leaving the meeting with the PM two days earlier, Ketselle hurried back to the Old City. Following Kobbi's instructions, he telephoned his Arab contact and suggested a meeting. The Arab, an agent, not the principal, came to see him at once. While expressing interest in the Agreement, Ketselle said that he first wanted to see a copy of the signatures and the opening paragraphs.

Closely followed by three agents of the Shabak, the Arab left his brief meeting with Ketselle to find his source. It wasn't difficult for the agents to keep tabs on the Arab, who took no precautions. It seemed that he simply didn't conceive of the possibility of being followed. The Arab came out of the Jewish Quarter, then turned left on the ring road that runs just inside the outer wall of the Old City between the Zion Gate and the Dung Gate.

Proceeding down the steep hill, he passed through the Dung Gate, crossed the road and took a narrow path past three small shops and down a very steep incline that cut into the village of Silwan. He then made a sharp right into a lane that serviced a number of houses built under the main road above.

Two agents followed. The third stayed outside on the main road to follow progress from his vantage point above. At the fourth house, the Arab disappeared into a courtyard and was momentarily out of sight of his pursuers. When one of them cautiously entered the deserted courtyard, he saw that the house had two entrances, the one that they had used and a second, at a higher level, that exited directly out onto the road above. This second entrance was now covered by the agent that had remained behind. Both entrances led to a central staircase that reached three apartments in the building.

The Arab had disappeared, leaving no trace.

Working according to standard procedures, one agent stayed outside the courtyard. The other returned to the Dung Gate. From there he proceeded along the road above until he met his colleague, who was keeping watch at the other entrance to the building. They decided that one of them would return to base.

Fortuitously, an empty taxi cruised by. One of the agents hailed it and was whisked back to Katamon. Within minutes of his return, the computer in the operations room was spitting out information on the occupants of the house in Silwan.

Mugrabi was the name common to the house and to the list of former employees of the Armenian Church. It was one of four names that the Shabak wished to crosscheck. Furthermore, the computer confirmed that a man named Mugrabi had recently been released from a term in jail.

One of the main operational differences between the Mossad and the Shabak is in methods of arrest and enforcement. The Shabak will question a suspect in their own facilities, but when it comes to taking a statement that may be used in a court of law, they do so at a police station, at which stage the suspect is advised of his legal rights.

Kobbi decided that, in this case, the arrest would be a joint operation, and he called Inspector Haft to coordinate. There were standard procedures for the arrests of Arabs, especially those with residence status in villages so near to Jerusalem. Kobbi wanted the best results, which included recovery of all stolen property and a lead to other participants in the burglary. Furthermore, he wanted as little fuss as possible.

While arrangements were being coordinated, the second agent phoned from the Dung Gate to say that the man who had led them to Mugrabi was leaving.

"Let him go," instructed Kobbi. "Ketselle knows how to find him, there's no need to detain him at the moment, if at all." Kobbi called Ehud over. "While we are gone, I want you to check on Mugrabi's friends in jail; we are looking for accomplices that know about banks and safes."

Less than an hour later, armed agents and police had quietly surrounded the house in Silwan, without attracting too much attention from neighbors. It was now dark and the village of Silwan seemed to sleep.

Kobbi, the section chief and Inspector Haft proceeded into the courtyard, followed by three armed agents. They quickly took up positions from which they could give their officers some cover. They went into the building from the lower level into the central entrance and looked at the mailboxes. There were just three, all with names in Arabic letters. Kobbi, who knew Arabic fluently, read Mugrabi on box No 2.

The central staircase in the building had steps leading upstairs. Leaving the others, Kobbi silently ran up the steps. Flashing a small pencil torch, he saw the number 2 and the name Mugrabi on the door on the first landing. He motioned with the torch for his colleagues to join him.

Kobbi knocked on the door. It opened so quickly that Mugrabi, who faced them with a puzzled look on his face, must have been standing inside with his hand on the handle. The look quickly changed to alarm, as Mugrabi realized that he was facing three very serious looking Jews. Involuntarily, he backed into a deserted room. His uninvited visitors followed. "I think you can guess who we are and why we are here," said Kobbi. "We are investigating the recent robbery of the Bank Hapoalim Bank in King George Street and believe you can help us."

"I want to see my lawyer. Until I do, I won't say a word," replied Mugrabi.

Kobbi indicated to his two colleagues that they should look around the house; with an air of authority he advised Mugrabi to sit down and listen to what he had to say. Mugrabi sat down.

"I am not from the police but from the Shabak; you may either talk now in the comfort of your home, or come with us to our offices."

"I won't talk without a lawyer and that's final."

Within minutes Mugrabi was sitting in a small closed white van being whisked away to Katamon. Agents were left to check the premises thoroughly; their initial report was that they could find no sign of stolen goods.

While the men of the Shabak and the police were still taking up their positions, Ahmed el-Alamy walked through the Dung Gate. He crossed the road, walked down the incline and began to follow the path to Mugrabi's house. He wished to talk to him about the Agreement.

Growing aware of the force of silent men that were surrounding the house, the quick-witted Ahmed walked straight past the house, as if bent on getting to the church further along the road. Once there, and only when he knew that he couldn't be seen anymore by the men behind him, did he turn around and take a position from which to spy on the activities at Mugrabi's house. A few minutes passed and he saw men emerge from the exit at the higher level. They proceeded straight into a waiting van. He guessed correctly that Mugrabi was a central figure in that shadowy group of men.

Ahmed sat and thought about the size of the force that had surrounded the house. Mugrabi must have been in the big league, possibly the biggest.

"Curse that Armenian dog," mumbled Ahmed, "I should have come earlier in the day. I might not see him again for many years."

A week earlier, Ahmed had been in Amman, crossing the border over the Allenby Bridge. In Amman he mentioned the Agreement to an acquaintance, familiar with the politics within Islam. This acquaintance told him that, years earlier, the Mufti had contacted him from his exile in Egypt, to ask if he knew of this same Agreement. Exhaustive inquiries at the time had drawn a blank.

The following morning, his Amman contact came to see him. "I would urge you to go and talk to the Blind Haji at the Omayyad Mosque in Damascus. He is interested to meet you."

Ahmed had intended to pursue other business matters in Amman and then return to Jerusalem, but was curious to investigate the Syrian connection. There was also, perhaps, a chance to earn a large fee. Accordingly, he crammed into the rest of the day all that he had planned for the next two days. Late in the afternoon, he made his way to the service taxi station on Shabsough Street, where he managed to obtain an uncomfortable middle seat in a three row, eight seat, Peugeot station wagon.

Ahmed would have preferred to take a bus; both the Jordanian Jett Bus and the Syrian Karnak ran twice daily services. Although the buses took about seven hours, some two hours longer than taxis, they were airconditioned and more comfortable. However, both buses were fully booked, so he was relegated to the service taxi where there was always room, because when one taxi was full, another drew up and took its place.

The border crossing at Ramtha Der'a was the smoothest that Ahmed could remember. "It's simply the time of day," said the driver, "during the day it's quite impossible, with the crowds and the traffic; they are getting worse and worse. Another border point must be opened to take off the pressure. For us drivers, it is becoming a nightmare."

Arriving after ten in the evening at the taxi station on Palestine Avenue only two blocks from the Tichrin Stadium, he walked towards the Old City and took a room in one of the cheaper hotels near the Hejas Railway Station on An-Nasr Avenue.

From here he would be able to walk quickly into the Old City for his early morning meeting with the mullah at the mosque.

The day had been a long one, Ahmed was exhausted. The middle seat in the taxi had the effect of doubling wear and tear on the traveller. The cheap commercial hotel didn't offer a bath, but the mattress was reasonably comfortable. The room was shared with two other occupants who both snored terribly. Ahmed was too tired to care.

In the morning he rose early, washed, dressed in clean clothes, and left the hotel. He entered the Old City through the colorful market entrance into the Souk al-Hamidiyyeh. The market was busy with early morning traffic, buyers and tourists.

Progress past the open stalls and shops was slow. It took him ten minutes to reach the far end and emerge through the Temple of Jupiter that dates back to the 3rd century C.E. Draped garishly in numerous cables and lights, the stalls at the foot of the columns sell religious articles and souvenirs. These prepare the visitor emerging from the souk for the great Mosque of Omayyad in front.

Emerging from the Temple of Jupiter, Ahmed stood at the Bab al-Barid, the Western Gate of the mosque. Even Ahmed, a visitor from Jerusalem, whose own el-Aqsa Mosque is considered to be one of the most impressive edifices in the world, always approached this famous Damascus site with great reverence. The sheer size of the mosque was awesome. Despite his many previous visits, the view from the entrance to the mosque took his breath away.

The Mosque of Omayyad and the Temple of Jupiter occupy a site that goes back 3000 years. The original temple on the site was built by the Arameans. The Temple of Jupiter was built much later, in the third century, by the Romans. In the fourth century, the Christians changed the edifice into a massive church, named after John the Baptist. His head is reputed to be buried on the site.

In the seventh century, when the focal point of Islam was moved to Damascus, the site was converted to a gigantic mosque. Al-Walid, the sixth Caliph, decided that the Omayyad Mosque would be the biggest ever built in the world. He employed one thousand stone masons for over ten years on building operations. Most of the structures, however, were destroyed by fire at the end of the last century, after which the interior was largely reconstructed.

Ahmed came as a Muslim, not as a tourist. He entered through the Western Gate and removed his shoes. Following instructions he had received in Amman, he turned to the left and made in the direction of the open courtyard in the northern part. He passed over beautifully smooth marble floors, and proceeded towards the pillars placed on either side of the fountain. He recognized the stern figure of the grey-coated, white-bearded, blind mullah who left the terraced portico some sixty feet away and walked with great dignity towards him.

The great cavernous mosque was almost empty.

There were a few groups of tourists with their guides, but they made small impact in the gigantic edifice. Some tourists were receiving explanations under the Dome of the Eagle on the south side. Another group, probably Christians, were listening with rapt attention to explanations about the Shrine of St. John the Baptist not far from the great Dome. The only other noticeable presence in the mosque, particularly in the open courtyard, were the many pigeons that fluttered in and out, leaving their droppings with little show of respect for the sanctity of the building.

"Allah be praised for bringing us a visitor from *El Kuds*," said the mullah in a strong, stern voice. Pointing to the low benches around the pillar he said, "Please be seated." It was an order, not an invitation.

The mullah sat beside him, smoothed his coat of any possible wrinkles, and sat with his back ramrod straight. He wore a full beard. Dark glasses covered his eyes, blinded following his Hajj, the pilgrimage to Mecca many years earlier. Having beheld the beauty and grandeur of the black stone of Kaaba in Mecca, there was no other thing in the world that the mullah wished to see. His posture, his well-groomed beard, his smart but simple clothes and, above all, his voice, marked a man of great authority – a man to be feared. "Now, Mr. el-Alamy, please be so good as to tell me all you know about the Agreement."

Ahmed had been well briefed by the unfortunate Aboud Mugrabi. He explained in detail about the five clauses, the signatories and the date of the Agreement.

"To recap," said the mullah, "the most important clause refers to the sites on the Temple Mount that are holy to Islam and the trusteeship of these sites in favor of the Hashemites in perpetuity. And in return for that control, the Hashemites walk away from the West Bank and hand sovereignty over Jerusalem to the Zionists."

"That is correct, Holy One," answered Ahmed, "those were the important factors."

"It is indeed fortunate," replied the mullah with force, "that Islam has sincere adherents who will help us in our sacred work. For, together, we will rid this poor world of the infidels and impostors who write agreements with the Zionist devil.

You, Ahmed, are ordered to bring me a copy of this Agreement, in order that I may be privileged to expose it."

"Holy One, permit me to raise a delicate matter. The copy was offered to me by a man not of the faith, an Armenian who has lived in the Old City of Jerusalem for many years. He demanded an enormous fee of $100,000 which is certainly excessive. I can approach him, but I know he will surely continue to demand a considerable sum. How much may I offer him for the Agreement?"

"He will be pleased to take but a quarter of the original amount asked," answered the mullah, with the pure and uncomplicated power of complete understanding. "I have faith that you will find your way to securing the copy that we must have. Bring it to me, and you will be put in funds. For financial details, you can talk with my assistant Hassan. He speaks with my full authority."

Rising from the bench, the blind mullah bowed ever so slightly to Ahmed and with the blessing "Allah be with you on your return to El Kuds," turned, and with great dignity walked on a perfect course towards the point in the portico from which he had emerged. His assistant, who had not been introduced, but who Ahmed understood to be Hassan, nodded without humor, turned and followed the mullah.

Ahmed el-Alamy retraced his steps to the Bab al-Barid, passed through the Temple of Jupiter, and hustled his way through the souk until he emerged from the Old City back onto An-Nasr Avenue, bathed in bright sunlit. It was like emerging from a cave. Ahmed felt exposed. The temperature, he thought, must be five degrees or more higher outside.

Ahmed secured a better window seat in the shared taxi, with a husband in the awful middle seat and his wife next to him on the far side, as Islamic modesty required. The old taxi began its five hour journey back to Amman. Ahmed now had plenty of time to consider the order that he had received from the holy man. For it was certainly an order and one to be taken seriously. Ahmed, who prided himself on being a realist, weighed up the task ahead. He was confident that he would be able to reduce the asking price, but an unaccountable intuition cautioned him that, perhaps, he had manufactured a rod for his own back.

After the arrest of Aboud Mugrabi, Meir Peled arranged a meeting at short notice. At the meeting, a senior prosecutor from the office of the attorney general was briefed by Kobbi and Inspector Haft. "We have arrested one of the burglars, but he remains obstinately silent and insists on seeing his lawyer. I must emphasize that he has offered no denial of being implicated. We have found none of the goods. However, in our experience, it will not take us long to get a full pattern of his life, where he hangs out, and who his friends are. This should lead us to where the goods have been stored. It is only a matter of time, possibly days. Our suspect used to work for the Armenian Church. He regularly visited the bank until five years ago, when he was arrested and imprisoned. He was released only very recently. We are running a check on his jail friends, particularly those released at around the same time.

"I believe, although he hasn't said so, that he wants to do a deal, and wants his lawyer to negotiate the terms. If I'm right, he'll sing like a bird, and we will pick up his friends and retrieve the stolen property. If we don't do a deal and he doesn't break for, say, two days, we might find that his partners and the stolen goods, including the Agreement, will disappear."

Kobbi had been consulting notes on a pad and had covered all relevant points. He now required instructions on how to proceed.

Meir Peled coughed and indicated that he wished to speak, "The PM wanted to be in on this meeting but, unfortunately, he is attending an affair at the American embassy in Tel Aviv. However, he will be briefed fully tonight; at his request, I'm taping this meeting. He has asked that we all voice our own recommendations. I, for one, think that we should make a deal with Mugrabi and his lawyer, if they can prove that they can deliver."

"As we already agreed that a deal would be made for evidence leading to a conviction," said the state attorney, "I would have no problem."

Kobbi looked at Inspector Haft, who nodded. "Haft and I agree that, in the special circumstances, we would advise a deal."

Meir Peled rose from his chair and thanked everyone for coming at such a late hour, "I guess that you, Kobbi, and Inspector Haft want to get back to the case. I am awaiting a call from the PM. As soon as I get his answer, I'll phone you."

"We'll both be at Katamon," said Inspector Haft a little wearily.

That night the deal was struck. Mugrabi sang like a canary. He gave the names of his two partners, both of whom were already shortlisted suspects, based on police computer information. In the middle of the night, Mugrabi took Kobbi and his agents to a room he had rented in the Old City. The Agreement, bonds, share certificates and other documents that he was handling, and had not yet converted into cash, were all handed over to Kobbi and the inspector.

Before morning broke, two agents, with back-up police teams in the Tel Aviv area, picked up two very surprised partners-in-crime. They also recovered a substantial amount of cash and valuables.

The following evening Kobbi, Ketselle, the police inspector and the section chief were invited to the office of the prime minister. When they entered his room, they saw that he was chatting with Meir Peled and Taher, whom the PM had asked to be present. The PM was particularly interested in Taher's history, in the details of his grandmother's lighting candles, and in hearing about the pogrom of 1929, as told to Taher by his late father.

"Your father was a great man," said Menahem Begin, "a friend of our people who helped us in our hour of need. A man of courage, who never sought thanks or recognition."

Drinks were served to all present. *"Le'Haim* – long life, and thanks to all of you for your splendid work," said the PM.

After the others had left, the PM took Ketselle and Taher into his room and closed the door behind him. Taking a match from a packet on his desk in one hand and the Agreement in the other, he set it on fire, placing it in a large metal ash tray. They all watched, transfixed by the flames, until only ashes remained.

As they were shaking hands and preparing to go, Kobbi came back to report on the meeting in the Old City between Arturo and the bishop. Ketselle and Taher were released, Begin sat down to hear the report.

The prime minister listened in silence and then gave his decision: "I don't think that we will want to intervene. However, I'd be interested to know of developments. Make certain that you and the Mossad are totally discreet. Under no circumstances can we be implicated. Do I make myself perfectly clear?"

Book 3

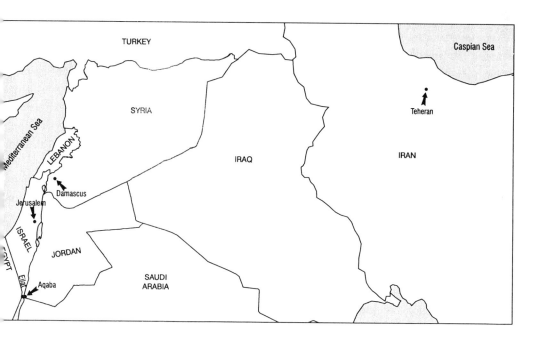

THE LOCALE
Showing the principal places
referred to in the narrative

Chapter 38

The return of the Ayatollah Ruholla Khomeini to Iran on February 1, 1979, after years in exile, marked the greatest cataclysm within Shi'ite Islam since the demise of the Umayyad dynasty in the year 750. That year, the Abbasids transferred the capital of Islam from Mecca to Baghdad, where it remained for 500 years. However, with the great changes in communications during the intervening twelve hundred years, the effect in modern times was infinitely more devastating, its repercussions were more immediately felt throughout the world.

The Ayatollah's return from exile marked a stop to any forms of compromise or religious tolerance. Iran was transformed into a doctrinaire Islamic state.

One million Shi'ite Muslims were on hand to welcome the Ayatollah at the Teheran airport. They shouted Agha Uhmad, *Our Master has returned*. During the triumphant ride from the airport to a nearby site, where the impassive leader was to address his frenzied people, hundreds were crushed to death, trampled on by others, or run over by the wheels of the vehicles carrying the holy man. They died exultant, in the sublime knowledge that they would achieve the ultimate reward in the world to come, as they had verily submitted to His holy will. For Islam means *Submission*, and its literal meaning is the very essence of the Muslim religion.

The Shah of Iran left his country for the last time just two weeks earlier. Thereafter, in short order, magistrates, judges, parliament, police and civil servants were dismissed and quickly replaced by komitehs consisting of groups of young Shi'ite fundamentalists. The leader of each komiteh was a mullah. Within a matter of days, the whole fabric of everyday life changed. Women were obliged to wear the chador, a simple black cloak that hid their face and body. The population had to live their daily lives in accordance with the laws of the Koran.

The penalty for non-compliance was incarceration or death. Religious revolutionary courts worked day and night to expunge the terrifying backlog of heinous crimes against the Koran, the true Prophet Muhammad, and the Ayatollah whose name means "the reflection of G-d". It is estimated that in Teheran alone, within months of Khomeini's return, tens of thousands of infidels and sinners were executed by firing squads, all operating in the name of the faith.

Islam, the youngest of the three great monotheistic religions, was founded at the beginning of the sixth century by the illiterate Prophet Muhammad. The illiteracy must not be considered a disparagement for, indeed, it is as important to Islam as the virginity of Mary to the Christian religion. Both provide the substance to their claim to Divine Revelation. According to Islam, the Koran is written in the finest and most poetic Arabic, in a language so beautiful and comprehensive that only the angel Gabriel could have transmitted its Divine Message in such form to the illiterate Muhammad.

The Arabic language formed a cornerstone of Muhammad's theology. The Prophet intended not to compete with existing monotheistic religions, which clearly influenced him, but to innovate in the Arabic language and provide the masses with a religion whose Koran would be available in their own tongue. When he failed to impress the Jews of Medina and Mecca, Muhammad decided that his doctrine was in fact different from that of the Jews. He embarked on a policy of emphasizing the differences. First, he instituted a change in the direction of prayers-to Mecca instead of to Jerusalem. He then named Friday as the day of assembly but rejected prohibition of work on Fridays, except during mandatory noontime prayers. And then, reflecting changing times, he rejected most of the dietary laws observed by the Jews.

When Muhammad died in 632, he left no clear line of succession. In the absence of a son, his son-in-law Ali, married to his favorite daughter, was proposed by the Shi'ites, adherents of one of five principal branches of Islam. The Shi'ites believed strongly that succesion must remain in the family of the True Prophet. However, the Sunnis were stronger. They believed in selection by consensus and appointed Abu Bakr as Caliph. He lasted but two years. Subsequently, the Sunnis chose Omar (634-644) and Uthman (644-56). It was only at that stage, and after two of the first-nominated caliphs had been murdered by other aspiring Sunnis, that Muhammad's son-in-law Ali was appointed caliph.

Sunnis aim for consensus, expediency and compromise; Shi'ites are more volatile and mystical. Their leaders are considered semi-divine; they require charisma and are held infallible. They are passionate in the practise of their religion and require outward expressions of penitence and mourning. An exception is the case of Friday midday prayers, which are not emphasized to the same extent as with the Sunnis, who see in the mass prayer meeting in the town's central mosque considerable political significance.

Shi'ite Muslims adhere strictly to the law under which a Jew or Christian living in an Islamic State is considered a *protected subject*. These subjects should be prevented from leaving for a non-Islamic State ruled by non-Shi'ites, which Shi'ites consider "enemy territory." Shi'ites derive this from a passage in the Koran: *Fight against those who believe not in Allah, until they pay the tribute readily, being brought low.*

Many Islamic states observe the "Dhimma" Laws which govern the behavior and lives of non-Muslims living among Muslims. These come in various forms in different countries and include: heavy head taxes, residence restrictions, prohibition to hold public office and to work in certain professions. In many Islamic countries the wearing of yellow patches was obligatory for Jews. Moreover, the non-acceptance of Jewish or Christian evidence against a Muslim in a court of law was generally enforced.

Under Islamic law, death is decreed for the murder of a Muslim by a non-Muslim. However, if a Muslim kills a non-Muslim, then only "blood money" would be paid. If, however, the evidence is provided by a Jew or Christian, then even this lesser punishment would be waived.

Shi'ites believe that the Imam, the ultimate living religious authority, is vested with total power. He is the medium, the interpreter of law, the ultimate judge and the unquestioned leader. He is imbibed with prophetic knowledge and carries the Light of Prophecy from one cycle to another. The fourth Caliph, Ali, was the first to attain the status of Imam. From all over the world, Shi'ites make pilgrimages to his tomb.

Nearly all Muslims in Iran are Shi'ites. It is in the context of the above aspirations that one million of them waited in ecstasy outside the airport in February 1979 for the return of their Ayatollah Khomeini. They fully believed he would become their Imam.

In the months that followed his return, every detail of government and administration underwent change. Revolutionary komitehs of fundamentalists were established. Some flourished, some were broken up. Some were expanded and reorganized, until they could adequately assume the cumbersome tasks of administration previously entrusted to men of experience. Mistakes were often made and only sometimes corrected. Mullahs, untrained in most cases for anything other than spiritual guidance, ran the komitehs. Crucial matters of importance were left to the mullahs to decide, but in most cases they were not equipped with the minimum knowledge or experience. In Iran, in the 1980s, the blind were often leading the blind.

Ironically, what kept the Iranians united, was the ten year war against their neighbor Iraq. Mullahs joined the men on the front lines and led the soldiers in the Holy War, giving them religious encouragement to fight the enemy, assuring the poor soldiers that Paradise for those who fell was assured. Many, many fell.

Behind the lines, in the towns and villages from where the hundreds of thousands of weary soldiers came and were replenished, encouragement for the brave and for the families of the martyrs were orchestrated by yet another group of mullahs and their revolutionary komitehs.

At the top of the pyramid stood an elderly and impassioned Ayatollah, the beloved symbol of the nation. His word was law. It brooked no disobedience. And the Ayatollah, a man of granite determination, would not stop the war. Compromise was not known to him. The big powers, neighboring states, honest brokers and even Iraq tried to end this useless and expensive conflict, but the all powerful controller of Iran would not budge.

Indeed, while this conflict continued to rage, Khomeini began to plan the widening of his sphere of influence, well beyond his own country's borders. One interest close to his heart was Mecca and Medina, controlled by his enemies, the Saudi royal family, across the Gulf of Iran. Another interest was Jerusalem, now part of the hated Zionist State of Israel, controlled by imported infidel Jews that had displaced local Palestinian Muslims. He, the Ayatollah, the Imam of Islam, would use the might of Iran to rectify the misdeeds of history. Komitehs were organized to select worthy emissaries to go forth with missionary zeal and prepare territories for future operations and influence. A fertile target was Lebanon, on Israel's northern border, where many thousands of frustrated Palestinian refugees presented excellent territory on which the seeds of revolution could be built.

Emissaries were sent to Syria, which mouthed verbal backing to Iran in its war against Iraq. Syria had long been considered the capital of world terrorism. In Damascus, some of the most sought after terrorists were to be found.

Moreover, in Syria, the Sunni Muslim majority was held in check by the Alawite Muslim minority. These conflicting conditions indicated to the Ayatollah that Syria was an area in which revolutionary Islam must be represented.

More emissaries were sent to Algeria, to Yemen and to Egypt, where they went to gauge the potential for Islamic rebellion and the potential for Islamic statehood.

Others were sent to Jordan, and from there some infiltrated into Israel, sowing bile and discontent inside the occupied territories on the West Bank of the River Jordan, in Gaza and in Jerusalem. But the Ayatollah also wanted to comprehend the potential for converts from

Jordan's Sunni community to Shi'ism. He wanted to strike a blow against the decadent Hashemite monarchy, whom he considered a blot on the name of Islam.

CHAPTER 39

Within two years of the return of the Ayatollah to Iran, the revolutionary komitehs sent twenty four young Shi'ite idealists as emissaries to Jordan; two of them set themselves up as grain and general produce merchants in the sleepy port of Aqaba. The two young men, Hushang and Nader Rezani, were brothers, born to a mixed marriage. Their father was a Persian from Isfahan, their mother a Palestinian Arab from Nablus on the West Bank. From their mother, they had learned to speak Arabic fluently. They came to Aqaba with stars in their eyes, for their love of their leader, the saintly Ayatollah knew no bounds. They were eager to get started on their holy mission.

Hushang and Nader rented a small apartment in downtown Aqaba, not too far from the Fisherman's Wharf where they expected to transact their business. They bought bicycles, paid a bribe to obtain a telephone speedily, and began to advertise their presence. Among their early friends were Nasser and Zayid, the teenage grandsons of the late Jammal, who had recently passed away. Nasser, the older boy, now eighteen, worked with his father and uncle in the family fish business. It was he who first met Hushang, who was interested in trading fish meal. Ziyad, at seventeen, had secured a job in the palace, as a messenger and general trainee. The two boys were at an impressionable age, they relished stories of the great Ayatollah and his heroic return from exile to command the Iranian nation through its historic changes.

Soon the four young men became inseparable, spending many of their evenings and Fridays together. The older Iranian boys were well versed in the Koran and in all matters of theology. For hours they would recount tales of the early Imams, of Imam Ali and his two sons Hassan and Hussein, after whom were named the Jordanian king and crown prince.

The religion of Nasser and Ziyad's own family was Modernist Islam, an updated version of Sunni; this dominated Jordan. It made few demands on them and the youngsters needed a challenge. Hushang and Nader offered them what they were looking for through the medium of a sterner, more emotional Shi'ism.

Nasser had received a rubber dinghy with an outboard motor for his recent birthday. It was designed to sit three, but as the friends were of slight build, all four would take it out into the bay in the warm evenings, and jump from it into the sea, for a swim. One day, as they passed the Royal Palace and approached the Israeli border, Ziyad quipped, "They say that the king built his palace so near to the border with Israel, because he believed that the Israelis would afford him greater protection than he could expect from his own Arabs."

The four laughed at this, and Nader asked Ziyad about the work he did at the palace. "Well, at the moment I'm just a messenger and as I can't drive, I cycle backwards and forwards as instructed by just about anybody. However, I hope that if I keep my nose clean, I will eventually be trained to be an aide to His Majesty when he visits Aqaba."

Nader and Hushang noted the reverence that the young boy obviously felt for Jordanian royalty. "Don't you feel that, in letting Jerusalem be taken by the infidels in the Six Day War, the Hashemites proved that they were traitors to Islam? They certainly gave away our holy places without much of a fight," noted Hushang.

Nasser and Ziyad exchanged smiles, "Our king's grandfather, the late King Abdullah, took care of the holy places. He signed an Agreement with the Israelis that gave the Hashemites control of the Temple Mount for generations to come. And our own grandfather, of blessed memory, who recently passed away, delivered this Agreement to His Majesty King Hussein."

This story was news to the Iranians. Their appetite for more information was truly whetted. After further questioning from Hushang, Ziyad and his older cousin Nasser duly related all that they remembered about the Agreement and the circumstances under which it was returned to the king at the palace in Aqaba. "And where is the Agreement now?" asked a thoughtful Hushang.

"As far as I know, it remains here in Aqaba, in the private safe of the king."

No more was said, but later that evening an agitated Hushang planned with his brother to send a report of this conversation back to the revolutionary komiteh in Teheran which controlled their activities. They also decided to increase their influence over Jammal's grandsons.

The report prepared carefully by Hushang took some months to pass through appropriate channels and be dealt with properly. Iran was in a state of flux, with many basic services in the towns and country villages not functioning.

In the first month after the Ayatollah's return, the secular government fell, and its prime minister fled to France. A new revolutionary government was established by the Ayatollah, controlled by and answerable to him. Komitehs were established, entrusted with cleansing the nation of blasphemous and subversive elements. At the head of their lists of targets were supporters of the Shah, considered to be the devil incarnate. Then came the royalists, members of SAVAK, the Shah's secret police, communists, Zionists, usurers, adulterers, and any other sinners against the teachings of the Holy Koran. To assist these komitehs in enforcing their holy tasks, the new government established Green bands of revolutionary guards. The Green guards made arrests. They carted their poor victims from their warm beds in the middle of the night and incarcerated them in horrendous prisons. There they languished until called to appear before religious revolutionary courts, headed by mullahs and their komitehs of untrained jurists. These zealots dispensed the will of G-d, according to their own interpretations of the Holy Koran.

The revolutionary komiteh headed by Mullah Ali Mashdi centered its activities in downtown Teheran. Its particular targets were the many sinners within Teheran's famous bazaar. Teheran, had mushroomed into a large city, with a population of some four million people.

The nerve center of Iran's business activities was in the bazaar, which acted not merely as an enormous market, where every commodity could be bought, sold or bartered, but where domestic and international transactions were negotiated and financed. Currencies, notes of deposit and loan notes were bargained and settled in the bazaar. In Iran, as elsewhere, at the root of all transactions was money, without which the wheels of trade would not turn. The extension of terms of credit was, of necessity, an everyday factor of business activity. Loans from the bazaaris had been made to the Shah and his enterprises during his time in power, and loans had been extended to the Ayatollah and his institutions, to finance his return to Iran and to bolster his sacred activities.

The Koran specifically forbade Muslims to charge interest on loans. As the bazaaris would not lend money without interest, they were all, in the eyes of the Koran, guilty of usury. On the return of the Ayatollah, banks were prohibited from charging interest to their customers. To prevent business activity from grinding to a halt, the bazaaris were kept busier than ever, for to a large extent they were now forced to replace the banking system.

Mullah Ali Mashdi was considered a cut above the general level of mullahs. First, he was born and raised in Teheran and had been sent at an early age for studies and religious instruction to the Holy City of Mashhad, from where his father's family had originated and from where he derived his family name. Secondly, he had married a sister of a young woman wedded to one of the sons of the Ayatollah. This gave him a direct avenue to the inner halls of power. His star shone brightly in Teheran.

The informers in the bazaar, usually men with a grudge or a financial reason for their unsavory activities, kept the komiteh and Green guards busy. Every day searches would be carried out in the maelstroms of the enormous bazaar to find and bring before the komiteh the sinners committing the heinous iniquity of usury. The mullah and his local bazaar komiteh, would decide if there was enough prima facie evidence to indicate their guilt. If there was, the unlucky transgressors would be sent to the infamous Evin Prison, to await trial before the mullah judges, whose reputation had become terrifying.

The bazaar mullah would then authorize the Green guards to seek out witnesses, who would be required to make their way to the Evin Prison. There, in due course, they would give their evidence, which in many cases would incriminate them too, leading to their own cruel punishment. As a result, the witnesses were often as terrified as the accused.

When the report from Aqaba arrived in Teheran, it was difficult to find Mullah Ali Mashdi to whom it was addressed, as he and his komiteh were moving to new premises in which to work. After gathering dust for some months, the letter was eventually delivered to the mullah's new office close by the bazaar. Here he worked in an apartment owned previously by a Jew, before it had been confiscated by the state.

Prior to the arrival of Mullah Mashdi in the bazaar area, a poorly educated mullah and his komiteh of low-lifes had controlled the area. Their obvious thirst for revenge against the rich bazaaris had become so infamous, that doubts about their activities had permeated higher revolutionary councils. After a short investigation, they had been dispatched to a remote area of Iran for para-military training, where they would cause less harm. Their activities had, however, led to the removal of the Jew and the confiscation of his apartment. This would now be the venue for the new komiteh and Mullah Mashdi's ongoing activities.

The Jew, Isaac Levy, had been employed for many years as the senior bookkeeper of one of the most powerful business houses in the bazaar. Its many interests ranged from a flourishing domestic and export trade in Persian carpets to an equally profitable one in semi-precious stones, a property development and investment department, and a thriving travel agency. Lines of credit to its customers and to the general public were extended as a matter of course. One of these loans had been given to a Muslim businessman who was now in financial difficulties.

Following the return of the Ayatollah, the businessman's lines of bank credits were called in, as the banks were no longer allowed to charge interest on old loans. This merely compounded the borrower's financial difficulties. Isaac Levy's boss, realizing what was happening, applied pressure to reduce his own exposure. The customer chose to forget the many years of business activities, and retaliated by informing the komiteh of the usury which he claimed to be rampant in the bazaar.

Green guards were sent into the bazaar to haul Farzal Bakhtiari, the prominent businessman, before the komiteh. He was an impressive man. Towering over the ill-educated mullah and his henchmen, he threatened them with access to the Imam himself. These threats, however, were commonplace and made little impression on a komiteh drunk with its own newly-found power. Bakhtiari was sent to the Evin Prison to await trial.

The mullah then sent the Green guards back into the depths of the bazaar to find at least one independent witness who, together with the testimony of the accuser, would seal the fate of another fiend and enemy of the revolution. They had no difficulty in finding the employee, Isaac Levy, who was trussed up and sent to the Evin Prison. Levy knew that, under Islamic law, a Jew's evidence could not be taken against a Muslim. Accordingly, he confidently expected to be sent home without causing harm to his boss, for whom he had some affection.

Isaac Levy and his employer, Farzal Bakhtiari, spent the night with over fifty other accused men and their witnesses. They were all crowded within a cold and miserable cell that had been designed to house twelve prisoners. All around were men tormented by the certainty that they would never emerge from the Evin Prison alive. Two stinking pails were used as toilets. They regularly spilled over until they were emptied and replaced by one of the less bestial guards prepared to accept a pishkesh, a bribe. By the time the two were called to appear before the mullah the next day, they both looked totally dishevelled. Gone were any signs of stature as the businessman was led away to account for his deeds.

The prison mullah, surrounded by his komiteh of four fundamentalists, sat around a wooden table in an improvised courtroom. On the table lay a large, open Koran. There were also lists of the accused and the witnesses that were due to appear.

When Bakhtiari was ushered into the room, he saw that his accuser had already given evidence before the mullah. He himself was now interrogated about his religious observance: How often did he go to the mosque to pray, did he prostrate himself five times daily, had he ever eaten pork, had he ever been on a pilgrimage to Mecca. He answered all questions as expected and thanked his lucky stars that he had in fact gone to Mecca the previous year, in conjuction with a business trip to carpet customers in Riyadh. This pilgrimage would undoubtedly stand in his favor.

The mullah then asked about his business practices. Here he was on more difficult ground. He had already decided that he would admit to advancing credit to customers, but deny any third party loans. He also denied that he had ever charged interest on loans.

"But you are accused of just that," said the mullah. "We have a witness who has testified that you lent him money and charged him interest. What do you have to say?"

Farzal Bakhtiari, knowing that he would have to face this charge, had carefully prepared his answer. "No, indeed no, Your Excellency, we extended credit against purchases. We were merely pressing repayments according to our agreement. The accused is in financial difficulties, he is seeking to use this honorable court to help him evade repayment."

The mullah and his komiteh had heard this argument before and, although not versed in business affairs, could appreciate that the court might be used wrongly by a debtor trying to evade repayments. "Have we any other witnesses?" asked the mullah. At this point one of the komiteh referred to the lists in front of him and said, "We have listed an Isaac Levy, but he surely is a Jew, and we will not be able to take his testimony."

"Why not?" asked the mullah. "We are only using his testimony as a professional witness to clarify the situation; we are not setting up his testimony against that of the accused. Bring in the witness, Isaac Levy."

While the guards went back to the cells to bring the witness, the mullah cast his mind back to a lesson at the theological seminary which he had attended for a short period. The subject of the lesson was the punishment of a Jew who had charged an exorbitant price for a currency exchange some centuries earlier in the Islamic state in Egypt. The tale, as he remembered it, had been as follows:

A visiting businessman had gone to a moneychanger to exchange a coin and was charged a rate of 16 pieces of another coin. Subsequently, the visitor had attempted to purchase merchandise but was charged at a rate of 15. He complained to the local Islamic Sharif, who was furious, as he himself had recently instituted a single rate of exchange of 16. The Muslim trader who had short-changed the visitor was arrested and brought before him.

In his defense, the trader had claimed that 16 was an inappropriate price, and he had to charge what all other traders were charging. The ruler was furious and sentenced the trader to death. At this point, the ruler's secretary intervened and confirmed that he knew that the trader was telling the truth, as only the previous day he had been charged a rate of 15 by a Jewish trader in the souk. The ruler ordered the arrest of the Jewish trader, who was brought, terrified, before the ruler, in the presence of the overseas visitor and the Muslim trader. When the Jew confirmed that, indeed, he had charged a rate of 15, the wise Sharif sentenced the Jew to death and released the Muslim trader. Authority had to be applied, the law must be suitably imposed, he had decided. But it was far more expedient to exercise G-d's will on an infidel.

The mullah in the Evin Prison was proud of his knowledge and of his ability to use holy precedent in the administration of justice. Farzal Bakhtiari, the businessman, was released and sent home. Isaac Levy, the Jew, who had only been called as a witness, was sent down the corridor, stood up against a wall and shot.

Green guards were then sent to impound all property owned by the Jew. After his wife and children were ejected from their home (on a day's notice), a large proclamation was pinned to the door of their apartment announcing to the world that the property had been "Confiscated For Crimes Against The Islamic State." The apartment was handed over to the new komiteh and its mullah, Ali Mashdi.

To the more moderate Mullah Mashdi, the report from Aqaba was a welcome relief from the tedious business of assessing the guilt of the sinners in the bazaar. Ali Mashdi was a modest, unpretentious person, who prided himself on going about his work with a sense of dedication and idealism. The young men that he had sent to Jordan were clearly making progress and had come up with something of interest, and possibly of importance. He himself could not be the judge of that, as it was outside his area of competence. That evening, when he had finished the chores of his office, he would walk over to the home of his brother-in-law and show him the report. As he said to the members of his komiteh, "Insh'Alla, with assistance from superiors, a correct interpretation and decison will be made."

Later that evening, his brother-in-law said that he would consult higher authority. The young mullah had the feeling that the matter of how to proceed would be settled at a very high level. Who knows, he thought privately, perhaps the saintly Ayatollah himself would make the decision.

The powers that controlled Iran had other matters on their minds. The war with Iraq was going badly, with enormous military casualties every day. Moreover, Teheran had recently been subjected to Scud missiles that had been accurately aimed. They carried their deadly cargoes right into the homes of the hard pressed Teheranians. On the economic front, matters were going from bad to worse. The war was imposing great financial strain on a country forced to spend ever increasing amounts on military purchases. Oil production had dropped alarmingly as foreign experts and engineers fled the country, leaving chaos behind. Pumps were idle in the oil fields, and the government's attempt to restore oil production and exports back to normal made it a laughing-stock.

Under the circumstances, it was not surprising that the Aqaba report was put on a back burner. Yet it was not forgotten altogether, for, after a period of four months, Mullah Mashdi was summoned to a meeting at the Supreme Revolutionary Komiteh. In his innocence, the young mullah marvelled at the ability of the Supreme Council to weigh all matters in their due time. The meeting was businesslike and to the point. He was commended for having brought the report to their attention and for not trying to deal with it on his own. He was told to select a group of men to go to Jordan to retrieve the Agreement. A budget of up to $100,000 was earmarked for the retrieval, to be spent as he thought fit.

On his way home to his modest apartment, he thanked Allah for giving him the opportunity to participate in meaningful holy projects. He prayed that he would prove worthy of the trust of his superiors. As he approached his home, he remembered the previous bazaar komiteh, whose members were undergoing paramilitary training. Perhaps, he thought, they would be appropriate for a holy mission to Aqaba. He also thought about the question of opening a locked safe and decided that arrangements should be made to teach the secrets of opening safes to two of the members of the mission.

CHAPTER **40**

Following his ordeal at the Evin Prison, Farzal Bakhtiari returned home in a state of near collapse. He stripped off his clothes and soaked in a hot bath to try and rid himself of the dirt and disgust that contaminated him. He folded all his clothes into a bundle, handed them to his old and trusted servant, and sent him off with strict instructions to burn them until nothing remained of his prison garb. "No," he confirmed in reply to the surprised query, "they are not to be cleaned or laundered. They are to be taken into the backyard and burned."

Farzal had always considered himself to be a moderate and fair person. His religious beliefs were modern, far removed from the fundamentalist approach of those now ruling his beautiful and beloved country. Engaging Isaac Levy to work for him so many years ago indicated his open mind. The close working relationship they had enjoyed was based on respect for each other's way of life. How would he now tell Isaac's poor wife what had happened today. How would he explain that Isaac had died as a sacrificial lamb in his place, merely because he was a Jew. The story was so horrendous that, lying in the bath only hours after being a reluctant participant in these awful events, he still could not comprehend what had happened.

Full of remorse, he became aware of noises on the floor below indicating that his wife was returning home; no doubt from a shopping trip, he thought. On being told that the master was soaking in a bath, she stripped off the mandatory chador and ran upstairs to inquire what happy circumstance had sent her husband home so unexpectedly at midday. Bursting into the bathroom, she saw her husband lying quite still in the steaming hot water. He looked pale and peculiarly smaller; somehow, he had shrunk in size and importance since leaving home the previous day. She had no idea where he had been or where he had spent the night. His secretary had phoned her the day before, on her husband's instructions, and reported that he had gone away on business and might stay overnight.

His usual smile at seeing her was gone, quite gone. In its place was a blank and frightened stare. Where had this pillar of strength in the business community and in his own home, been robbed of his dignity and strength. Her first thought was that her husband had suffered a stroke or some other serious illness. Lifting a hand as if to stave off questions, Bakhtiari merely asked his wife to leave him to his thoughts; he promised to talk to her when he had completed his bath. Twenty minutes later he appeared at the drawing room door, wrapped in a silk dressing-gown. She looked up from her household accounts. She was attempting to keep herself busy.

"You are seeing a man who has returned from the dead," he said. "Another man, a good, decent and blameless man, has taken my place. To him I owe my life." Clearly shaken, he sank down on the couch opposite his wife. Immediately, she ordered some sweet tea, which she knew would soothe him. She remained silent, knowing that her husband, whom she loved and respected, would tell her in his own good time. He related to his wife the awful story of the past twenty-four hours, leaving out no relevant part of the sordid events. "And now," said Farzal, "I have to speak to Isaac's poor wife and explain to her what has happened, why this unspeakable regime has thought fit to murder her husband, the father of her little children."

"How old are her children?" asked his wife with sympathy.

"As far as I remember there are four children; the oldest is a boy of possibly eighteen, but there are two who are under the age of ten."

"I will come with you," offered his wife, "you can't do this alone, especially in the state that you are in."

"We have another problem," continued the husband, "the komiteh responsible for this outrage will probably confiscate the late Isaac's possessions; his family will, more than likely, be thrown out into the street."

"Have you thought this one through, are you prepared to find the family alternative accommodation?"

"Absolutely, I thought that they could move in and stay in our annex. Since our children left, it has remained empty. But I don't believe that to be a long-term solution. In view of what is happening to our beloved country, I believe that Jews should leave, go to live in Israel, or some other country where sanity still prevails."

"Darling, I agree with every word, but we must be careful how we speak. Talk of Israel is, in itself, an offence, helping Jews to go there a crime. However, rest assured that you have my full backing for any move you wish to make. We owe this family and brave Isaac Levy your life, and we must do everything we can to help them."

Farzal Bakhtiari worked in his building at the bazaar in a suite of offices at the rear of the ground floor. The front part, opening to the street, was occupied by his flourishing travel agency, one of the largest in Teheran. His other businesses occupied spacious offices on the three floors above.

Some months after his arrest and trial, he opened the door that connected his office suite to the agency and saw at the front desk two faces whose image was imprinted on his brain; they belonged to members of the dreaded komiteh that had sent him to the Evin Prison. Terror stricken, he retreated to his office, his face a chalky white. Sitting down heavily, he called his secretary, who ran quickly to fetch cold water. When he had rested, he looked at his watch to see how much time had elapsed, expecting to be arrested. The minutes ticked by. Nothing sinister approached his sanctum. Heaving himself out of his chair, he walked over to the door and peeked through; the two young men were gone. Feeling immeasurably better, he walked to the counter where they had stood. As casually as he could, he asked the chadored girl sitting there about the two men she had been talking to.

"They were here to book four tickets to Aqaba via Amman. They plan to go in a couple of weeks time. Do you know them?" she asked.

"No, I must have mixed them up with some cousins of mine," he replied, and returned to his office.

Isaac Levy's son David had recently commenced work at the travel agency and was making good progress. A good and diligent fellow like his late father, thought Farzal. Later that day he called him into his office.

"When the others leave this afternoon, I want you to stay behind. I want you to check on the file relating to a booking of four tickets to Amman and Aqaba. Please report to me anything you find out, but do not let anyone know that we are inquiring."

Later that evening, David drove home with his employer in the latter's comfortable Mercedes. He had grown attached to the older man, and the feeling was clearly reciprocated. David mourned the death of his father, who had always been dear to him. The circumstances of the death were incomprehensible and would haunt him for the rest of his life. In the meantime, his boss was trying hard to replace his father, a special bond had been established between their two families. He had obtained all the information that his boss required: "The client is the revolutionary komiteh. It is purchasing four tickets in the names of its members. It appears that through our agency, two other members were sent to Aqaba some months ago. The new purchases must be connected, as they are all in the same file."

"David, I must tell you something, as it may be important for the future. That particular komiteh and its members were those who sent your late father and me to the Evin Prison. We are not in a position to take vengeance on them and, in any case, they were doing their horrible job as they were trained to do. However, we should keep an eye on them, and try to understand what they may be up to. I am sure that they are planning nothing good. Perhaps when they come next time, you should engage them in conversation and try to learn why they are going to Jordan."

A week later the two revolutionaries returned for their tickets.

"A thousand apologies," said David, who was now dealing with the file. "A mistake has been made, and it is necessary to reissue the tickets. Would you care to wait and have some tea?" Coldly efficient, and without any outward signs of emotion, David showed the two young men into an office in the rear. Sitting down with them while they sipped piping hot sweet tea, he asked them casually what they would be doing in Jordan.

"We are being sent to locate an old agreement relating to Jerusalem," replied the younger one importantly, "and that is all I am allowed to tell you, except that the Ayatollah himself has approved of our plans." The other looked at his younger colleague in mild rebuke for talking too much, but he too glowed in the importance of the mission.

Alone later that night in the comfort of his book-lined study, Farzal thought about the young revolutionaries' plans. Years earlier, he had invested in a number of business projects in which the Shah and his large family had interests. Israeli companies had operated extensively in Iran, especially in the construction of roads, bridges and housing estates. The Hilton Hotel, the largest hotel in Teheran, had been built by Solel Boneh, the Israeli construction company.

During those years, some of these projects had brought Farzal into the company of Israeli Mossad agents, who operated freely in Iran, hand-in-glove with the SAVAK. With some of these Israeli agents, Farzal had become friendly. Of course, to admit these things today would put him in immediate danger of arrest. The pro-Israel stand of the Shah, who had visited Israel, was well known. He had often publicly proclaimed his admiration for the new state and had collaborated openly with its service agencies. Today, there was a new regime. Israel was now a taboo subject, and Zionism, or support of it, a crime.

The subject of Jerusalem was highly emotive, the planned trip to Jordan by four revolutionary thugs might well be of interest to his old friends at the Mossad. The question was how to transmit the information. Gone were the days when citizens of each country could dial one another directly. The prisons were allegedly full of people whose only sin was contact with the outside world.

David and his mother had been receptive to the idea of emigration. Israel was attractive to them, as they had relatives there who had left Iran years earlier. However, there were difficulties. Exit visas from Iran were granted only to businessmen and government officials, who had to show good cause for going. A few old people had managed to obtain one-way exit visas, but they had been the exception. The only effective way out of the country for most Iranians, especially Jews, was illegally over the Pakistan or Turkish borders. These trips were costly and hazardous, with long stretches of the journey on mules or by foot. Farzal couldn't see matters improving for many years. He had decided to talk again with David and his mother and had invited them to dinner the following evening. If they agreed to move, then David could be a courier to his friend Colonel Lior of the Mossad.

Bearing in mind weather conditions and other considerations, he had decided to recommend that they take the shorter route via Turkey. There, the Israeli authorities were well established, and their representatives would await them at the border. The disadvantage was the danger of taking a route that would run parallel with the border of Iraq. This border represented an active war zone. This element and Farzal's proposals to counter potential dangers, would be discussed with the Levys over dinner.

In the pursuit of his assignment, Mullah Ali Mashdi decided to visit the Evin Prison. On arrival, he was shown deferentially to the room of Mullah Sayeed, whose responsibilities covered prison administration. This, Ali quickly learned, included details and conditions of incarceration, and arrangements in connection with executions. "I am terribly understaffed," complained the prison mullah, "and hopelessly overworked. We receive prisoners of all types from bazaari dogs to proud air force officers, from communist agitators to scoundrels that worked for the SAVAK. Each and every one demands preferential treatment and some, with their inflated egos, demand the conditions of a five star hotel." He looked at the younger Mullah Mashdi to see if he was conjuring up any sympathy, but saw only an impassive and unimaginative looking cleric sitting opposite him.

"Another problem is that we have to care for witnesses and accused men. Because of chronic lack of space, we are forced to keep them all together. The prison is run at four to five times capacity, with up to fifty men sharing a cell designed for ten or twelve."

The older mullah was happy that someone was coming to share his burdens. He had heard rumors that this young mullah was well-connected. He hoped to get some encouraging signs of sympathy for all his toil under such difficult conditions.

"We are living through very difficult times," replied Mullah Ali Mashdi at last. "And we all have to continue to toil for the sake of Allah and his Prophet. Each one of us must make his own contribution. For, Allah be praised, we are all participating in a most holy enterprise under the leadership of the Imam, our revered Ayatollah."

The prison mullah was impressed by the reverence the younger man displayed. In prison life he did not often have access to such refinement, for he mixed with the dogs of the bazaar and their ilk.

"Now in what way can I help you?" he asked.

"I have been commissioned to look for the services of a safe-cracker to help me in my sacred work," said Mullah Mashdi with conviction. "I thought that in such a large prison you would have some inmates following that profession."

"Well, I'm sure that in the old days, before the return of our revered Imam, may his name always be blessed, we had safe-crackers, burglars, rapists and murderers. However, when the doors to the prison were broken down in February last year, those that weren't killed in the rush were all released. Since then the prison incarcerates exclusively those who committed crimes against Islam. And with most of our inmates receiving the ultimate punishment, we probably have the greatest turnover of convicts in any prison in the world."

"So you haven't got any safe-crackers that can assist me?" asked Mashdi in disbelief. He rose from his seat. The older mullah rose to accompany his young guest. "Leave it to me for a day or two, I'll put out some feelers amongst our SAVAK inmates and ask the mullahs in some of the other prisons," he promised.

The two walked out into the corridor. A dishevelled middle-aged prisoner was being frog-marched by two guards, who were having difficulty keeping the wretched man on his feet. The Mullah Mashdi looked at the man carefully. From his clothes, the cut of his hair, and the set of his jaw, he judged him to have previously enjoyed a certain aristocratic bearing. This had almost disappeared. The prisoner's eyes were red and bleary, his soiled trousers reeked. His tie was loose, stained with vomit. His hair was a mess. He looked both tormented and demented, as one facing imminent and inexplicable death.

The soldiers and their prisoner turned left into a square of some size and stopped. The prisoner was placed against a stone pillar, to which he was secured with a rope. The jailers stood back. Two marksmen with rifles came forward from an adjoining room. One guard wearily raised his arm. The two marksmen fired. The unfortunate prisoner, a wreck of a man, who had already been robbed of his dignity, slumped forward against the rope that had secured his frame.

Mullah Mashdi left the prison gate and breathed fresh air into his lungs, trying to blot out the sights, smells and sounds of the awful prison that functioned in the name of Allah and the holy revolution.

The following morning, Mullah Mashdi received a phone call from his colleague at the prison: "Despite my busy schedule and my enormous workload, I found time to secure for you the services of the expert that you require. His name is Sayeed Bakr, and he will arrive in Teheran this afternoon. May we both be blessed with the ability to contribute further to our holy revolution! Allah Akbar!"

When two of the young men had received training for some days, Sayeed Bakr suggested that they be allowed to pick a real target and test their skills. The mullah had developed a loathing for Bakr and thought that he should certainly be a candidate for an extended jail sentence. He was scandalized by the thought that the young revolutionaries in his charge would be encouraged to practice their foul training on the safes of unsuspecting local citizenry. But the other members of his komiteh convinced him that it was vital for the students to train in what they termed "live time" conditions.

"What will happen if they are caught red-handed?" asked the mullah; but he already knew that he had lost the argument. One of the boys had just returned from the travel agency where he had collected the four tickets to Aqaba. He had noticed that the tickets were kept in an old and very heavy-looking safe at the rear of the office. "Let us tackle the safe at the travel agency. Although I don't expect that they have a night guard, they are probably connected to burglar alarms, possibly direct to the police. We will break in, cut the alarms and crack the safe open. You will explain our deeds to the owners when they come to work. Needless to say, everything in the safe will be returned to them untouched."

The mullah, who had been reared with a degree of finesse unshared by any of the others, was not happy with the proposal. However, it was warmly approved by all the others. Finding himself to be the minority opinion, he agreed to the proposal, subject to being present from the moment of entry onto the premises, until the arrival in the morning of the owner of the business. Arrangements were made for the break-in to be held at 5 am, in order that they would not have to wait too long for the owner to show up.

The burglary went off without a hitch, alarms were cut, and the connection to the police dismantled. The safe, which had both a combination and a manual key lock, was opened in expert fashion, causing limited damage. The contents of the safe, tickets, credit service dockets and hotel vouchers, were stacked neatly on a table, behind which sat the mullah, who presided over the entire proceedings.

When Farzal Bakhtiari arrived to open the building at a few minutes after seven, as he did each day, he was received by a full komiteh, complete with mullah, an expert safe-cracker and two student mercenaries. The last had been part of the komiteh that had sent him and his late friend Isaac Levy to the Evin Prison. The mullah sat behind his desk and patiently explained that it had been necessary to test the skills of two students. It was obvious from the rather stupid grins on the faces of two of the young men, who were the students in safe-breaking. Mullah Mashdi assured the businessman that nothing had been taken. He handed him all of the contents of the safe and promised to fix the damage that had been caused.

Handing him a piece of paper on which he had written his name and the address of the komiteh, which Farzal immediately recognized as Isaac Levy's old home, he said, "Without knowing it, you have been of enormous help and for that, in the name of the Islamic Revolution I thank you." It was obvious to Farzal that the students that were to travel to Aqaba were expected to crack a safe. This information must be added to any message that he might send to the Mossad.

That night at dinner, his wife served fish horisht to their guests, in deference to the Jewish dietary laws. Farzal recounted the bizarre tale of what he had encountered at his office that morning. David, who had been at the office, had already heard the story.

The ability to break into a safe was clearly important to the trainee mercenaries. This must relate to their search in Jordan for the old Agreement about Jerusalem. The information was emphasized by Farzal to his employee. David would have to pass it to Colonel Lior. "And now I think it is time to make detailed plans," said the host. "I have thought long and weighed the pros and cons for an escape via Turkey through Pakistan. In favor of Pakistan is the absence of any war zone between us. Moreover, it is an easier passage over the borders. Against Pakistan is the enormous distance, both from Teheran to the border, and then onwards from Pakistan to Israel. Another problem is that Pakistan does not have diplomatic relations with Israel. The journey's continuation will be more difficult without Israeli emissaries, who are not allowed to set foot in that country."

Farzal looked at the Levys, who would have to make the decision themselves. He could see that they were carefully weighing the alternatives. "Turkey, on the other hand, has three advantages," he continued. "First, it is much nearer to Teheran. Secondly, from Turkey onwards it will be easy, as you will be met by Israelis who will look after you. Thirdly, Turkey is as near as can be; a direct route from here to Israel, the journey time will be cut to a fraction of the alternative Pakistan route."

"What will we do if the Israelis are not waiting for us?" asked Mrs. Levy.

"I am assured that they will. Don't ask me where I get my information, but believe it or not, to this day still the Israelis have contacts in this country, and they have proved their efficiency in oiling the wheels of the Turkish route. Furthermore, if, Allah forbid, they are not there, then you will have funds and will merely travel by taxi to the Israeli consulate in Istanbul."

Mrs. Levy looked at her son for encouragement as she wished to broach the difficult subject of money. "I have only very limited funds. As you know my husband worked all his life for a salary and...."

Farzal, his face flushed, held up his hand to cut her off, "You will have no money problems. Over the years, with your late husband's help and encouragement, I was able to send money overseas. My wife and I have decided that a third of that nestegg is put aside for your family."

As Mrs. Levy prepared to protest this generosity, Farzal again held up his hand. "We are paying only a small part of our debt. We know that our efforts are wholly inadequate. We can never fully repay our debt to Isaac Levy. You will be taking cash with you. We will sew hundred dollar bills into your clothes and into the clothes of all the children. You will also have cash with you to pay expenses such as bribes or travel charges, if required. When you arrive in Israel, there will be funds waiting for you at a bank in Tel Aviv, enough to buy an apartment and get you started in your new life."

Farzal helped himself to more horisht; everyone ate in silence for a few minutes. Wiping his mouth with a napkin, he sat back in his chair. "My opinion is that the Turkish route is the better one. The major problem is that, if you were to travel directly in the direction of Turkey, you would be going parallel to, and not very far from, the border with Iraq, which today is a war zone. Frankly, that would be risky, the danger not coming from the Iraqis, but rather from our own army checkposts and police controls in that vicinity. I've given a lot of thought to this and have formed the following plan."

Farzal leaned forward to emphasize details of his plan: "We will all leave here in our Volkswagen Transporter. We shall carry the maximum baggage that would be prudent for you to take, which, I'm afraid, will be no more than one case per person. Travelling towards the Russian border in a north-westerly direction, we will make for our vacation house this side of Astera, near the far end of the Caspian Sea. This journey covers some 450 kilometers, partly over rough roads. We will also have to buy fuel, passing through local villages where peasants might sometimes be hostile. When we reach our vacation house, we will rest up and allow ourselves to be seen in the vicinity for a few days. This is not the straightest route to Turkey but it will keep us at maximum distance from the Iraqi front, and away from Iranian army and police controls.

"When we have ascertained that our departure from Teheran has not made waves, and when we have made contact and arranged a rendezvous in Turkey, we will continue travelling, this time in a westerly direction. We will pass by Tabriz on its northern side, and then make for the northern tip of the Sea of Urmiya. From there to the Turkish border is a trouble free one hundred kilometers. A guide will then take you over the border, where you will be met by an Israeli. By that time, my wife and I will be on our way back to our house at the Caspian Sea, where we will stay for a genuine vacation."

The Levy family had already given much thought to the trip to Israel and knew of the dangers that would be encountered. The mountain passes into Turkey were hazardous. There were no border guards or customs as the area was high, cold and totally barren, without towns or even villages nearby. They would have to travel on donkeys for the better part of a whole day. With the younger children, this part would be the most difficult.

They also knew that the first couple of hundred kilometers inside Turkey would be no picnic, as all of Turkey's eastern reaches were hilly and snow-covered. Until they reached the town of Erzurus, some 170 kilometers from the border, they would be travelling rough, no matter which Israeli met them at the border. Yet on balance, the Levys preferred the shorter Turkish route. Moreover, the comfort of travelling with such close friends for so much of the way was a deciding factor. The vacation house at the Caspian Sea seemed a real godsend.

CHAPTER 41

The journey was no more and no less hazardous than expected.

The drive to the Caspian Sea was completed in a single, long day. Leaving Teheran early on a wet February morning, they made a good start before passing through a checkpost between Reshet and Mianeh. Their papers were in order, their claim to be travelling to the Caspian Sea, was accepted. From there onwards, the trip was slowed by heavy rains on bad roads that had fallen into disrepair.

The two families stayed at the vacation house for three days. Farzal took care of the Transporter and, despite the general scarcity of gasoline, managed to have it refuelled. He also disappeared into town by himself on a few occasions. After one of these trips, he returned with the good news that he had made contact and arranged a rendezvous. He never let anyone know who his contact was or how he had reached him.

On the third day, the first day free of rain, the two families left Astara. They set off in the Transporter as if making a sightseeing trip to the lake of Urmiyah. However, they took care to keep further north, not wanting to be stopped at any checkposts waiting on the approaches to Tabriz. The going was not easy. As they ascended the snow-covered high mountain ranges that separate Tabriz from the smaller town of Choy, they looked down into the valley below for a pass that would connect them to a point west of where they would be met by their guide. They also required a place to rest up overnight, although, they had made provision to sleep in the Transporter, if necessary.

They emerged from the mountains nearer to Choy than they had planned and soon found a small and pleasant tavern. The tavern was set next to a fast-running river that was fed in the winter months by water pouring down from the massive snow-covered mountain ranges above them. The air was clear and cold. The rustic scenery, far from any signs of industrialization, was magnificent. Before turning in for the night, they ate the food that they had brought with them, augmented by lots of hot sweet tea. They even went for an invigorating walk along the river bank, lightly covered with snow. They were training for the walks ahead, joked Mrs. Levy.

Next day they found their guide waiting at the rendezvous further along the valley. They were only an hour from the Turkish border. Farzal took the guide to one side and paid him. He confirmed that he was to take the Levys through the border to a rendezvous. There, they would be met by a man who would hand the guide $500 in addition to the amount that Farzal had just given him.

The Levy children had adopted Farzal and his kind wife as their uncle and aunt. The farewells were tearful. Moreover, the time had come for Mrs. Levy to accept the mantle of responsibility for her family. Having lived in a chauvinistic society, this was a new experience fo her.

After Isaac's death, Farzal had temporarily substituted for her husband, protecting her from decision-making and managing the family. Farzal assured his dear friends that this was merely au revoir, not goodby. He promised that when matters improved in Iran, he would come to visit them. Their relationship would not be terminated. He had given a confidential letter to David to take to Colonel Lior and now asked David to check again that it was secreted in a safe place.

With the children and Mrs. Bakhtiari crying, the Levy family joined their guide in his battered, old jeep covered by flimsy canvas flaps. They transferred their luggage of five medium-sized suitcases to a platform at the rear, and tried not to turn back to see the Transporter disappear behind them.

The guide, pleasant, wiry, of middle age, explained to David that he made these trips regularly. He drove east, crossing the valley on pot-marked roads, that in many places had no remaining hint of asphalt. He explained that, in the later winter months of March and sometimes April, the valley, which was situated at an altitude of 1700 meters, would be ice-bound and filled with snow driven down from the mountains, whose peaks in the area reached between 4000 and 5000 meters. When the roads cleared in the summer, the asphalt would be destroyed. The government, which needed its money for its ongoing war with Iraq, had allowed the situation to deteriorate.

With the exception of a small hilly area, they could have stayed in the valley all the way to Van Lake in Turkey, some hundred kilometers over the border. However, the valley border point, being relatively clear of snow, was sometimes patrolled by the Turks and, to a lesser degree, by the Iranians. To avoid getting caught, it would be necessary to leave the valley, climbing to a safe pass almost 1000 meters higher up. For this, they would leave the jeep and transfer to mountain donkeys. If everything went well, they would have to spend no more than six to ten hours on the donkeys.

The donkeys were waiting. The ride was uneventful, though extremely cold and uncomfortable. First they traversed the pass, then dropped down the far side and back into the valley. At some point, they did not know exactly where, they left Iranian territory and entered Turkey. Over the border, they pressed on another ten kilometers, until they reached the rendezvous. Altogether, they had spent ten hours on the donkeys. At the destination, Zvika Harnoy, the Israeli agent, was waiting for them, standing beside a battered large Ford, with a trunk large enough to take all their bags.

When Zvika saw that Mrs. Levy was about to pay the guide herself, he warned her off in Hebrew. It was essential, for the sake of future refugees, that the guide believe that the source of his payment was the Israeli at the rendezvous. That would ensure that the rendezvous would always be kept. Mrs. Levy was surprised that Farzal had not alerted her this. She was pleased that her Hebrew, learned years earlier at school in Teheran, was still adequate. They bade farewell to the guide. Zvika, a young man in his late twenties, was born in Israel of Turkish parents. He spoke Turkish fluently, and knew the country, "We must be careful. We should not speak Hebrew loudly or call attention to ourselves. It is not that the Turks in this area are anti-Semitic, they just don't like foreigners or things out of the ordinary.

"The route is long. We have to make for Antalya on the Mediterranean. The distance by road is over 1200 kilometers. Moreover, we will have to make many detours to avoid high mountains and keep to roads that are passable. If we are lucky, we will make a ship that leaves Antalya in three days' time. By the way, if you look behind you at the far range of mountains on the skyline, you'll see Ararat, where Noah's ark is supposed to be. The peak is over 5000 meters high."

The old Ford served them faithfully. Mrs. Levy sat in front with Zvika, practicing her rusty Hebrew. David sat with his three siblings in the rear seats. The journey was tiring but uneventful. They arrived at Antalya with time to spare.

Next morning they proceeded to the port, where Zvika was received by local officials like an old friend. He processed the Levys through border and customs controls, using temporary Israeli travel documents. These were not quite passports, but something close, bearing photos of the travellers and official-looking Israeli consulate stamps. Similar documents had clearly been used before. Officials were happy enough to stamp them and pass the passengers through to the ship.

Once on board, Zvika bade hasty goodbys and left them, assuring them that they would be met in Haifa by representatives of the Jewish Agency. Zvika explained that another family was waiting for him at the rendezvous, and he was forced to hurry back to the Iranian border.

The ship, full of returning Israeli tourists, had a festive air, with music, colored flags, a small heated swimming pool, and plenty of good food served buffet style. Pulling away from the coast line a few minutes after noon, David and his mother stood on the deck and waved to the small town of Antalya that symbolized to both of them the gateway to freedom. The younger children, without cares, had already found some friendly Israeli children to play with. For them, their new life had already begun.

The sight of Israel's approaching coastline early the following day, evoked an emotional response in his mother that David did not know she was capable of. She stood watching the town of Haifa and the Carmel Mountain range behind it, tears uncontrollably coursing down her face. At first she tried to dab the tears with a handkerchief, but she soon gave up trying to stem the flow and fully vented her pent-up emotions.

Immigration was in three lines, returning Israelis, foreign tourists and immigrants. The Levy family, being the sole immigrants, had a line all to themselves. They were processed quickly with the aid of the waiting Jewish Agency representative, just as Zvika had promised. Within ninety minutes of landing, they were led out of the terminal to a Transporter just like Farzal's in Iran. Soon they were on the open coast road as they sped towards an absorption hostel near Tel Aviv where they would live for their first six months in Israel.

That night, while his mother and the other children were making themselves comfortable in a furnished three room flat in an absorption center, David went to find a public phone. Finding Colonel Lior's home number without too much difficulty, he dialled his contact: "I have just arrived from Iran together with my family. I've brought you a letter from Farzal Bakhtiari. I promised to give it to you personally."

The colonel and his wife lived some twenty kilometers outside of Tel Aviv in a new suburban community. That evening they intended to drive to the Tel Aviv area to visit some friends. Lior promised that they would come and see the newly-arrived immigrants on their way in. Though emotionally exhausted, Mrs. Levy patiently dressed herself. After putting the younger children to bed, she went down to the lounge area on the ground floor that was common to all the immigrants in the building. There, she and her son awaited their guests.

The Liors never did get to their friends that evening. Bringing a home-made cake and flowers to welcome the new arrivals, they sat down with the Levys. They listened with rapt attention to an account of general developments in Teheran, where they had spent three years. They were eager to hear firsthand evidence of the social and political changes.

Slowly the shy immigrants began to relate their own horrifying story and explain their close connection with the non-Jewish Bakhtiaris. Mrs. Lior dissolved into tears when told of how Isaac Levy had never returned from giving evidence at the Evin Prison. She excused herself and went to the ladies' room where she wept uncontrollably.

David steered the discussion to business. He told Colonel Lior that he had two practical matters to discuss with him. The first was money, and he understood that one of two letters that he had brought with him would enable Lior to transfer funds to the Levys from Bakhtiari's account. Lior nodded and confirmed that he had control over some Bakhtiari funds. "The second matter is much more complicated and refers to the developing interest of Iranian Muslim revolutionaries in an old agreement concerning Jerusalem." He saw that Lior was confused. "I suggest that you read the letters, then I'll answer any questions that you may have."

On their way home that night, the Liors sat in the car, each deeply wrapped in thoughts. Hers were of the terrible injustice in Iran, and the burden on poor Mrs. Levy to bring up a family by herself without a husband. Mr. Lior –for he had long stopped using a military rank – thought about Farzal's letter regarding Jordan. By the time he pulled into the parking lot in front of the duplex house that he had recently built, Lior had persuaded himself that Farzal's story was probably of no importance and had been influenced by the involvement of members of the same komiteh that had caused his family so much grief. Nevertheless, he would run a check; his only question was – through what channels?

Lior had been an army man for over thirty years, the latter period of which he had served in intelligence. This had led to his being *volunteered* for an overseas posting to Iran, where he had been employed by the Israeli embassy as an advisor on anti-terrorist activities. As his work was closely connected to that of the SAVAK, no amount of explaining would persuade nationals of his host country that he wasn't recruited from the Mossad, whose activities in Iran were well-known. So far as his Iranian hosts were concerned, he was a colonel in the Mossad.

On his return to Israel, he had opted for early retirement, joining an international import-export business as a consultant on armaments, on which subject he had some expertise. Some interesting connections in Iran were put to profitable use, for during its war with Iraq, the Iranians were prepared to deal with the devil himself, and buy tanks, artillery and spare parts from the Israelis. He knew that Kobbi, his neighbor and tennis partner, had a high position in the Shabak. Although Lior realized that the Mossad was possibly the more appropriate agency, he decided to sound Kobbi out, weather permitting, after their tennis game the following morning.

It was dry in the morning and, after the game, he asked his friend if he knew anything about an old agreement about Jerusalem. Kobbi was dumbfounded for, as far as he knew, there had been no leaks from his office. "What have you on your mind?" asked Kobbi guardedly.

"Well it might be of no importance, but last night I received a letter from a non-Jewish friend in Teheran. In it he refers to plans to send revolutionaries to Aqaba to look for an old agreement regarding Jerusalem. Furthermore, he knows that mercenaries have been trained to break open safes."

"I think that I should take a look at the letter," said Kobbi. "If it is convenient, I'll pop by your home after breakfast."

Later the two friends rode to Tel Aviv together. While Lior drove, Kobbi read the letter carefully and then requesteded, "Now, please explain exactly how you received it." Lior told of his meeting with the Iranian immigrants and of his good impression of young David Levy.

"I'd like to see him, possibly today, if it could be arranged. Where did you say he was staying?"

Later that day, a car was sent to take David to Kobbi at his office in Hadar Dafna, a northern area of Tel Aviv. David, whose English was better than his Hebrew, chose that language to relate his account. ".... and so in less than a week from now, the four revolutionaries will leave to join their friends in Aqaba. They are flying to Amman first but will immediately change planes. As far as I know, their only mission is to retrieve the Agreement."

Thanking the young man for his help, Kobbi arranged for David to be returned to the absorption center, with the promise that they would keep in touch. He gave

David a warm letter of introduction to a bank where he could open an account and deposit the funds that Lior would be transferring.

CHAPTER 42

Standing in front of the border control desk at Ben Gurion Airport, Arturo Be'eri handed over his passport, ticket, receipted travel tax voucher and a form signed by the Israeli army allowing him, a man of military age, to travel overseas. The Agreement had been retrieved and the burglars arrested; any new efforts must be directed at Aqaba. For that, he would need assistance from his friends in Rome.

The policewoman took the documents and punched Arturo's name and passport number into a computer. A pulsating light appeared on the console in front of her. This indicated that, while this person's departure would be recorded by one of the special services, there was no reason to detain him. She entered details of Arturo's planned destination as she had been taught. Taking the passport in one hand, she stamped the exit authorization on it and passed it back. "Next, please," she called.

Four hours later, in Rome, Arturo took a taxi and drove straight from La Vinci Airport to the bank. He was followed by an agent of the Mossad. The purpose of his visit was to get further instructions. It was one thing to chase an agreement stolen from a bank in Israel but another to plan a heist of an agreement deposited in the private safe of a king. During his forty-eight hours in Rome, he met twice with Monsignor Angelo. Both meetings were held over meals at restaurants, as the cleric was not keen to be seen at the Vatican with his visitor from Israel. The Mossad agent monitored both encounters.

Arturo left Rome with renegotiated terms. The new arrangement was to his liking. Out-of-pocket expenses and the cost of operatives would be paid by his Italian banker. For himself, he would receive a fee of $500,000 net of all expenses – if he would deliver the original Agreement. In addition, the Italians would send him three first-class operatives to Aqaba. One of these would be an expert safe-cracker.

The plan, codenamed "Abdul," would become operative within a week, when the three Italians would fly to Aqaba, ostensibly for a vacation in the winter sun.

There Arturo would meet them. He was furnished with a new Italian passport, issued in the name Arturo Bernard Barry.

The plan called for him to fly to Amman from Cyprus. There, he would rent a car for a leisurely drive down to the Red Sea resort, where he would meet his colleagues and assume control of operations. The Italians would stay at the Holiday Inn Hotel, a short stroll away from the palace.

Meir Peled had been entrusted by the prime minister to monitor developments. Kobbi had already warned the PM that both Iranian fundamentalists and the Italian Mafia would try to steal King Hussein's copy of the Agreement from the palace safe in Aqaba.

Menahem Begin had toyed with the idea of finding a way to warn the Jordanian monarch but had decided not to do so. He and his cabinet were preoccupied with the worsening situation in Lebanon and with the recently reported massacre by Syrian President Assad's troops in the town of Hama. 25,000 people were said to have been killed, entire districts levelled to the ground.

Anticipating an Israeli push into Lebanon, the world press and the Knesset's left-wingers were giving the government a hard time. There were suggestions that Menahem Begin was losing control, led by the nose by his defense minister, the charismatic and domineering General Arik Sharon.

An early probe was launched by the Israel Defense Forces, intended to clear a security belt on the Lebanese side of the border, creating a demilitarized zone for the protection of pressuring Israel's northern settlements from continued Katiusha attacks. However, General Sharon was pressuring Begin to drive the troops deep enough into Lebanon to encompass Beirut. For his part, Menahem Begin had never been reconciled to the daily atrocities against Lebanese minorities, exposed to the unrestrained wrath of stronger groups. Largely unprotected, these minorities were subjected to extreme forms of violence.

Drawing on history, Begin drew a comparison between the demographic and political changes in Palestine during the nineteenth century and those in Lebanon a century later. During the second half of the nineteenth century, Jewish immigration into Palestine had produced a Jewish majority in Jerusalem. In the face of those changes, the Christian and Muslim world had joined in denying the Jews their fair share of political control. A century later, widespread demographic changes were taking place in Lebanon. The Maronites, a sect splintered off from mainstream Catholicism, no longer maintained their traditional majority. They grew terrified of the consequences of ceding political control to the swelling ranks of militant Islam. This defiance of majority rule so infuriated the Muslims that they resorted to armed conflict.

Decades earlier, throughout the period of the British Mandate, the High Commissioner would never sanction a Jewish mayor in Jerusalem. He appointed mayors only from the ranks of the minority Muslims. Now, in Lebanon, the tables were turned, and the majority Muslims were unable to gain their rightful political voice, as the constitution guaranteed political supremacy to the Maronites. Civil war had erupted in 1958. No fewer than twenty-eight ethnic groups were at each others' throats within Lebanon, which had not known quiet and peace for nearly a quarter of a century.

Against the background of developments in Lebanon and Syria, Begin delegated responsibility for matters of lesser importance. Handing over the case of the old Agreement to Meir Peled, he advised him to adhere to the following approach: "The best scenario would be for the Jordanian copy to fall into our hands and be destroyed. However, I'm not prepared to send a mission of burglars and safe-crackers into Aqaba for an operation against King Hussein. If Hussein is going to lose his copy to others, then the Italians would be preferable to the Iranians. The Mossad may keep an eye on matters only as an observer, and only on the strictest understanding that their activities are never to be seen or reported on. If their operations are ever exposed, I will have the heads of those responsible."

"One other thing," said the PM as an afterthought, "When all our other matters are settled and we return to more normal conditions, please arrange for the Levys to come and see me. I'd like to welcome them to Israel."

The meeting called by Meir Peled in his room at the Prime Minister's Office, was attended by a senior Mossad officer and by Kobbi. Peled reviewed the information that had been received regarding the travel plans of the Italians and the Iranians. Peled then informed his guests exactly how the prime minister saw the situation.

Finally, he explained that the PM had expressed the wish that Kobbi should continue to be in overall charge at operational level.

The three participants agreed to adopt the Italians' code name of Abdul for the operation and confirmed that Kobbi would work within the prime minister's guidelines. Kobbi would liaise with Meir Peled and the Mossad as he felt appropriate.

On the way down, the Mossad agent told Kobbi of his recent visit to a factory which was developing a long-distance low-light TV video camera, "The reason I mention it is that they showed me a film taken in Eilat of a maneuver involving vessels and inflatable craft, three kilometers out at sea. It was really very impressive. Images operating at great distances, in almost total darkness, are seen clearly. I think you should check it out."

Kobbi jotted down the name of the company. "Be sure to ask for Benzi," the agent continued, "He is the only one there that understands the potential. Oh, by the way, we ran a check on him, and he's reliable."

Soon after returning to Tel Aviv, Kobbi had Benzi on the phone.

"If you come up on the early flight to Mahanaim from the Sde Dov Airport in Tel Aviv, you will arrive at about 7 am. I'll wait for you at the airport, and we will be at the plant before the workers arrive."

"And how will I get back?" asked Kobbi.

"That's problematical. From Mahanaim, we only have one flight out every day, and that's at 5 pm."

Next, Kobbi phoned Seffi Jacobs, the section head in Eilat, whom he knew from his reserve duty in the army. "Seffi, Shalom! I need a map showing the border area with Aqaba, with as much detail as you have of the other side. I'm particularly interested in the details of Hussein's palace and the surrounding area. I also want you to select a building on our side of the border from which we would be able to spy on the palace. Finally, I want you to get me a room in a hotel nearby from tomorrow night. As I am up north, I still have to find a way of getting to you, first thing tomorrow morning."

"Come from Haifa. They have an early afternoon flight via Jerusalem," suggested the section chief.

At 6 am the next morning, Kobbi boarded the tiny sixteen-seat plane to Mahanaim. The flight was fully booked and Kobbi used connections to have one of the passengers bumped off to make room for him. His secretary arranged a seat from Haifa to Eilat.

Military experts had analyzed the Yom Kippur War. The early Syrian push over the Golan was the subject of many hours of consideration by strategists and politicians. One of the areas of defense, thought to be particularly weak, was night vision. It was recognized that, in this field, the Syrians had a significant advantage.

There are three types of night vision. Following the Yom Kippur war, and in line with a policy of strategic independence from outside sources of supply, the Israelis decided to become expert on all of them as quickly as possible. The three technologies were incompatible with each other.

Thermal technology is the formation of an image using the relative heat in a number of objects and the transliteration of the information into a composite picture. All images, a tank, a wall, a person, etc., radiate different degrees of heat, The advantages of thermal imaging are that one can see a picture through heavy rain or fog. It can also form images of subjects behind a brick wall.

The second and best-known system of night vision is based on infra-red technology. Infra-red systems direct a beam which causes magnification. The problems with infra-red, as the Syrians found out, is that when used by tanks or infantry, the source of the beams is detectable by the enemy.

The third system, called SLS, is a passive system, based on the multiplication of rays of light; for example, the stars or a quarter moon. The system operates on the notion that there is no such thing as total darkness, even the smallest rays of light can, when magnified seventy thousand times, produce a clear picture. The magnification, conducted in a vacuum tube with the aid of an optic fiber, demands the highest degree of exactitude in manufacture. There are only a handful of companies around the world that are capable of producing such tubes.

The plant in the north, which Kobbi went to visit, specializes in SLS tubes. They are fitted to gun and tank sites. The factory also produces a range of sophisticated products using tubes in goggles, helmets and tank periscopes. But the glory of the plant is its low light video TV system which can be operated by remote control. A camera in a pilotless spotter plane, or at a border between two countries, sends back a clear picture to be seen on a TV monitor. The filmed picture can be stored and kept for future reference.

On arrival, Kobbi was taken speedily around the installation and given the mandatory tour of the tube manufacturing procedure. A large part of the assembly work was completed in clean-room conditions. The slightest speck of dust would spoil the product and render it useless.

By 8.30 am Kobbi was sitting in what would be considered by most laymen to be a completely dark room. Put in charge of the dimmer switch, which controlled the amount of light that the single bulb in the room could emit, Kobbi was made to feel part of the experiment. Opposite was a camera which projected on to a white wall. Kobbi turned the knob, reducing light until the room was so dark that he could not see where Benzi was sitting. Benzi switched on the camera. On the far wall, Kobbi saw a picture of himself sitting with the switch in his hands. The effect was impressive.

Benzi took pride in the project. He explained how further picture enhancement, using laser technology, could magnify or zoom into specific areas. Objects within a larger picture could be detailed. To explain this further, he took his visitor into an adjoining room that contained a video camera and TV screen. "What you are about to see is an exercise by soldiers who were being dropped from a troop carrier into small rubber dinghies some three miles out at sea. The only light was provided by stars and a quarter moon."

He flicked the switch on the video; a great expanse of sea appeared with a tiny ship far in the distance. The zoom control was then put into effect. The ship loomed larger until its image occupied most of the screen. The ripples of the waves against it were clearly seen. Kobbi could make out images of men dropping over the edge of the ship. "Now look and see what we can do with our image intensifier," said an excited Benzi. He flicked a switch on a small console and turned a knob which operated a digitalized control. A beam appeared; he could direct it around the screen, using one of the controls on the console. The beam high-lighted any specified area. When the beam centered on the area of the rubber dinghies, Kobbi could make out the numbers on the side of a small boat, even the identification tabs worn by the soldiers – three miles out at sea and in the dead of night!

Benzi was getting all worked up, as if he were seeing these results for the first time. Kobbi was equally impressed. "Give me examples of some other applications," he said.

"Last night we took a small portable TV monitor and camera up to the Golan Heights where there was almost no light. We were demonstrating the TV for representatives of an overseas port authority that is trying to combat illegal drug trafficking. We set up the equipment and zoomed in on an area in a valley, one and a half kilometers away. In the valley there is an old fashioned telephone pole. On the pole we had marked a small **x**, carved into the wood. We first took a general picture, then operated the zoom. With the image intensifier, we looked for the cross, which we found in less than one minute. It was cool; just beautiful.

"Now imagine that we want to keep constant tabs on that area, on that pole and on that cross. We could leave the camera suitably camouflaged, and activate the zoom and intensifier by remote control, say, in this room. From a distance, and in comfort, we would be able to watch what was happening on our TV monitor. Furthermore, we would be undetectable.

"Now take it one step further: We could have one man in this room keeping an eye on ten situations over a vast area. He could keep track either by looking at a bank of TV monitors or, alternatively, one screen with different channels, which he would change from time to time. Using our equipment, one operator would be able to monitor an entire border, running hundreds of miles."

Kobbi chose his words carefully: "I came today because I have a particular house that I wish to keep under surveillance from a distance of some 500 – 600 meters, without being detected. If I need your help, would you come down to Eilat and help set up the operation? If it works successfully, I think your company would benefit."

"No problem at all. I'll come down on the first plane, just tell me when." Suddenly remembering, Benzi continued, "But next week I have to go on reserve duty for twenty one days."

"Send my office the details and I'll arrange for your reserve duty to be postponed." Looking at his watch, Kobbi continued, "I need to get to Haifa to catch a 1 pm plane to Eilat, what's the best way to get there?"

"No problem, I have to visit some engineers at Rafael, with whom we are working on a laser range-finder device. Let me clear my desk, I'll get you there with time to spare for your plane."

Kobbi caught his plane and arrived in Eilat at 2.30, where he was met by the section chief, "I'm not sure exactly what you are looking for, but I have some alternatives. We can drive via the office, where I have large-scale blowups of the area. We pride ourselves on knowing quite a lot about what goes on on the other side of the border."

"Not half as much as we'll get to know if we get Benzi's cameras properly going," thought Kobbi.

The Eilat Shabak office was smaller than its offices in Tel Aviv or Jerusalem. It controlled a lesser area, with fewer operatives. On the walls of Seffi's room were some impressive blowups of territory on both sides of the border.

Kobbi, whose knowledge of Eilat was no greater than that of an interested tourist, asked for guidance. Seffi picked out the Eilat hotel section inside the bay area, not far from the airport and the lagoon which was being extended. The hotel nearest the border was the old Queen of Sheba which had been leased to Club Med. Seffi pointed out a cluster of hotels over the border on the Bay of Aqaba. Adjoining them, and in the direction of the border with Israel, were six large villas, each surrounded by parkland, grass verges and many transplanted palm trees.

"What are those buildings?" asked Kobbi, pointing to the rather grand cluster.

"Those are royal palaces. Six altogether, one for each prince, emir or what have you," replied Seffi. "The one nearest to the border is used by King Hussein."

"And how far is it, say, from the Sheba to King Hussein's palace?"

"I'd estimate about 700 meters, possibly more; but we can get an exact distance calculated pretty easily."

"O.K. I suggest that we go and have a look at the area; I take it we'll have no difficulty getting on the roofs."

"No, I don't think so, it's a bit of a village over here, and I know someone in nearly every building."

The Sheba was clearly the best bet; it wasn't perfect and its roof was an awful mess, dotted with solar water heating equipment and airconditioning units. However, it afforded a view of the palace. Kobbi was sure that this view would be immeasurably enhanced by Benzi and his equipment.

The hotel was full of noisy Club Med diving enthusiasts. Kobbi decided to stay elsewhere. He checked in at a hotel nearby, rented a small car and phoned his office to make arrangements for Benzi to be released from the army and flown down two days later. He had two to three days before the Iranians and Italians were due to arrive, time to set up the operation. He still wanted to check out all the facilities of Eilat. When Seffi visited him later, Kobbi decided to engage his services for a thorough tour of Eilat.

"What do people come here for?" he asked.

"Well, most come for winter sun," answered Seffi. "Every year more hotel rooms are built, and every year they are kept occupied, especially in the winter months. We have direct charter flights from Scandinavia, Germany, France and England.

Then there are tourists that keep returning, even in the summer when the temperatures settle around 40c. It isn't humid here, and the stark mountains in the background and the cobalt sea have their attractions. All the indications are that Eilat will double in size over the next ten years. Personally, my passion is deep-sea diving. There's no better place, now that we've returned the Sinai."

"Tell me more about diving," said Kobbi, "I admit to being uninformed about these things."

Seffi just loved to talk about his favorite hobby. He gave a full account of a diver's activities, including details of the equipment he used.

"If you wanted to swim at night over to the Jordanian side of the border and land near King Hussein's palace, without being seen on arrival, would you use a wet suit and oxygen tanks?" asked Kobbi of a somewhat surprised section chief.

"No, I very much doubt I would chose that route; I think I would simply swim in from a dinghy, which would wait to take me back."

Seffi didn't ask any more questions. When Kobbi is ready, he thought, he'll tell me his plans. In fact he didn't have long to wait, for later, over a dinner of Chinese food, Kobbi brought the local section chief fully into the picture.

"Does that mean that we have a mandate to take unilateral action, or are we restricted to the role of observers?" asked Seffi.

"It means that we have to take great care," replied Kobbi carefully. "Now let us plan our immediate objectives. Benzi will turn up in two days' time with his equipment; I want to be ready for him, so please arrange for the Sheba roof to be given over to us, and find an operative to prepare it, so that we don't waste time when Benzi arrives. Do you have an agent with a technical background who will understand the technolgy and the equipment? Ideally, I want Benzi to set up the equipment, explain exactly how it works and what problems we might anticipate, and then leave us. I do not want Benzi to know exactly what we are looking for, is that understood? Finally, I want you to think over all that I've told you about the Iranians, the Italians and their objectives. You know this area, if you have any ideas, let me have them as soon as possible."

Chapter 43

While Kobbi was orchestrating preparations in Eilat, Arturo Be'eri left Israel on a short flight to Cyprus. There he changed planes and, using his new Italian passport, continued to Amman.

Procedures at the airport in Jordan were archaic. The line in front of immigration was long, passengers advanced at a snail's pace. Arturo stood impatiently, he counted twelve people in front of him. Calculating two minutes for each, he figured a wait of under half an hour. He was off by fifty percent, nearly fifty minutes passed before he approached the immigration window.

Through the window, he handed his new and clean passport to one of three officials sitting at a table. The first merely handed the passport to the second. The second looked at all the pages without showing any signs of comprehending what he had seen. He opened it flat and passed it to the third, indicating the details on the first page. He also explained to the last official in line that the name was Meester Martin.

Arturo, who at first couldn't understand what they meant, looked at the passport in the hands of the third official and saw that his first two names, Arturo Martin were written on one line, and his surname, Barry, underneath on a second line. The three officials knew little English and were convinced that he was Signor, or Mr. Martin. The third official, laboriously in longhand, entered details from the passport into a ledger. He used Arabic numerals. After looking through the pages again to make sure that all matters had been covered, he searched on his desk for a visa stamp, as if this were the first time that day that he had been required to stamp a passport.

"These guys are a hundred years behind the rest of the world," thought Arturo.

Leaving customs, he approached a Hertz outlet and hired a two year old Chevrolet for a week. He paid a cash deposit of $200 and signed an American Express voucher as security. He then badgered the three Hertz employees into giving him all the facts and details they knew about Petra, the Rom Valley and Jerash. He took all the tourist literature that they could find on those historical sites.

The Hertz employees asked if he would be proceeding to Aqaba, only an hour's drive from the Valley Rom. To this query, Arturo replied loud and clear that he wasn't an American tourist looking for winter sunshine, but a traveller from Italy, a country rich in archeology, art and culture. He had come to see the beautiful historical sites of Jordan. This, he told anyone interested in listening, was the only point of his visit.

In fact, he had decided to stay quietly at the Gulf Hotel in Aqaba, a distance of one kilometer away from the royal palace and the nearby Holiday Inn, where he had booked rooms for the three Italians.

He had prudently decided to distance himself from his colleagues.

Armed with visible camera equipment and holding road maps in his hand, Arturo emerged from the airport building dressed in jeans, tan leather boots, a loud checked shirt, and a large white straw hat on his head. With detailed explanations as to how to enter the King's Highway to the south, he started on his holiday. There were few people at the airport who didn't notice the flamboyant Italian tourist, many wished him a pleasant vacation in Jordan.

Two hours out of Amman, he turned left off the highway in the direction of Petra, which was well signposted. Thirty minutes later, he rolled into the sleepy village, continuing straight through it, until he came to the Forum Hotel built next to the entrance of the historic site. It was getting dark, so there would be no sightseeing today. He parked the car and booked into the hotel, taking a room for two nights.

The following morning, when he entered the gates to the red sandstone park, the first thing that struck him were the hundreds of beautiful Arabian horses. Never averse to a horseback ride, he followed the example of most of the other guests. Engaging a horse and guide, he began a thrilling ride. After fifteen minutes on sandy paths between magnificent rock formations, he emerged into an opening opposite the famous Treasury Building, probably the most photographed in Jordan.

The imposing facade, complete with neolithic columns, arches and detailed stone embossings, was built into the red sandstone two thousand years ago by the Nabateans. Travelling many miles north from an area to the east of the Red Sea, these nomads had conquered the Edomites who lived in the region. Here the Nabateans left their lasting impression.

Suddenly, drenched in the morning sun as he emerged from between the canyons that soared above him, Arturo stopped in his tracks. The majesty of the scene was overwhelming. He jumped down from his horse and proceeded to photograph the famous building from all angles. Arturo then secured the services of guides and vendors to snap photos of himself, with the building and the rock formations behind him.

After loud haggling over prices, he bought some ancient coins of dubious provenance, a decorative curved silver Beduin dagger, a bottle of multi-colored local sands depicting a desert scene, and a couple of small square boxes made from camels' hooves. The negotiations, replete with wild gesticulations, attracted a large crowd of onlookers and rival vendors, who smiled kindly at the colorful Italian tourist.

Arturo remounted his horse after a brief visit to the single large room behind the facade of the Treasury Building. He was about to give the nod to his guide to proceed, when he spotted two tall, charismatic Beduin soldiers of the Jordan Legion. They looked magnificent in their army uniforms, complete with gold and red epaulets and ceremonial daggers.

Down off his horse he jumped and ran to the soldiers, bent on yet another photography session. The soldiers shared no common language with Arturo; nevertheless, they realized his objective and were quite happy to cooperate. A large crowd of onlookers quickly formed, creating a bottleneck for others wishing to continue out of the square and into the passes. But the tourists and their guides were all in holiday spirits. They were happy to put up with the small inconvenience caused by the Italian wishing to get himself photographed in a number of poses with the two handsome Beduins, against the dramatic backdrop of the Treasury Building.

Arturo spent another three hours riding around the canyons and having himself photographed amidst breathtaking scenery. Using his zoom lens, he and his guide were photographed by a Beduin vendor while they stood in the middle reaches of the Roman amphitheater. Later on, at the entrance to the ancient and imposing Law Court, which is built above two layers of arches hewn in the rock, he once again organized complicated zoom photography of himself.

From the Law Courts he rode for one kilometer along the Roman highway, known as the Cardo. Roman pillars stood on either side. He proceeded past beautifully reconstructed Roman archways until he reached the museum. There, he again dismounted, ate salad sandwiches and drank strong black Beduin coffee in the pleasant and clean restaurant, set under the shade of willow trees and overhanging rocks.

That night, after a long bath and a rest from his strenuous excursion, Arturo and his guide partook of a simple dinner at the hotel. Wine and beer were not served in the dining room in deference to Islamic prohibition. He questioned his guide about Jerash and Rom Valley, and invited the views of passing waiters and guests sitting at nearby tables, who had already visited those places. By the end of the evening, there were few people at the hotel who did not know all of Arturo's touring plans.

The following morning, Arturo made an early start, paying his five dinar entrance fee at the window next to the gate. It was well before 8 am. Riding quickly down to the Treasury, he proceeded straight through the canyon pass in the direction of the amphitheater. There he took a left turn, following a trail that soared up into the hills to the Mountain of the Sacrifices. A short pause among the mountain goats enabled Arturo to enjoy the panoramic views from the crest.

Proceeding carefully, he then followed a little-used trail that wound down the far range of the mountains to a point from which he could connect back to the Cardo.

During this part of the trek, Arturo had an opportunity to see the primitive conditions of the local Beduins, who still dwelt in caves cut into the back of the mountain range, just as they had done for two thousand years. Incongruously, womenfolk were hanging out washing to dry, on lines that ran right to their cave entrance. In stark contrast, Arabic music blared out loudly from transistor radios placed at their sides. To complete the contrast, parked some hundred yards lower down was a brightly colored Japanese pick-up truck.

At the approaches to the Cardo, Arturo mingled with the tourists. Following his practice of the previous day, he again made his presence felt, attracting attention to the red bandanna that now adorned his white hat.

By ten in the morning he felt that enough people could testify to his having spent the day in Petra. Riding back up to the entrance gate, he paid off his guide and returned to the hotel. Within an hour, he was speeding away from Petra in a southerly direction. Contrary to his well-publicized intentions, Arturo did not take the exit from the King's Highway towards Valley Rom but drove hard down to Aqaba, where he checked into the Gulf Hotel in time for a late lunch. Before sitting down in the dining room, he phoned Mario Belucci at the Princess Haya el-Hussein Hospital and made a date for later in the day.

CHAPTER 44

Newspapers had reported that three men had been caught and charged with the theft at the Bank Hapoalim: two of them – Jews from the Tel Aviv area, and the third an Arab from Jerusalem. Ahmed el-Alamy very much wanted to speak with Aboud Mugrabi, but realized that any direct approach to the latter might put himself under suspicion.

When Ahmed thought that the dust had settled, he ventured into the village of Silwan. Walking purposefully to the local grocery, he busied himself looking at the various products on the shelves while waiting for the shop's other customers to depart. He then approached the store owner, whom he knew from regular Friday prayers at the mosque. "*Kif halak*, Abu Dis."

"*Ahlan we Sahalan,*" answered the shopkeeper. "What brings you to our area?"

"I would like to talk to Aboud Mugrabi's wife; would it be possible to meet her here in your store?" asked Ahmed.

The shopkeeper looked inquisitively at his visitor, wondering what business Ahmed had with Aboud Mugrabi, whom he had always considered a mysterious character. "I understand that you don't wish to go to her house. Your caution is prudent, as Shabak eyes might still be watching for contacts. The wife comes here at least once every day. I suggest that when she comes later today, I'll arrange a time for tomorrow. When would it be convenient?"

The next day Ahmed returned, exiting the Old City through the Dung Gate and crossing the road into the narrow lanes of Silwan. A curious Mrs. Mugrabi was waiting at 11 am, the appointed time. "Your husband was discussing a deal with me before he was arrested," he said to the calm-looking wife. "Do you see him, and are you able to act as a go-between?"

"Yes, I see him every day and take food to him at the lockup in the Russian Compound, where they will keep him until the trial. There is no problem in talking to him, if you come along with me on one of my visits, you will be able to talk with him yourself."

Ahmed considered this information, but decided to decline the invitation. Someone might see him and take note of his visit. "No, I don't feel like visiting the Russian Compound," he replied firmly. "It gives me the creeps. Please tell him that I have found a buyer who offers $10,000 for a copy. If he can lay his hands on the copy from his present position, I will give you the money."

"Copy of what?" asked Mrs. Mugrabi.

"Just tell him the copy; he will know exactly what I am talking about."

"I will take him his lunch in an hour; if you wish, we can meet here this afternoon at 4 pm."

"That would be agreeable," said Ahmed. "Please send him my regards and good wishes."

That evening, a copy of the Agreement was given to Ahmed, who paid $10,000 to Mrs. Mugrabi. The wily Aboud had made a number of copies, which he had left at various addresses in the Old City. He assured his wife during her visit that the Shabak had not even asked him if he had made copies and were only interested in retrieving the original. Mrs. Mugrabi's attitude was cold and pragmatic. Her husband was incarcerated and, although optimistic that he would be released, she did not know exactly when that would be. In the meantime, Mrs. Mugrabi had to run the home, feed and clothe the children; the money would be useful.

Ahmed el-Alamy hoped that he would have no further call to do business with the Mugrabis. He took the envelope containing the copy of the Agreement and, taking a circuitous route through the Zion Gate, walked back to the Old City. He turned his back on Silwan, an area he intended to avoid.

Two days later, he again sat on the bench in the courtyard of the famous and ancient Damascus Mosque, where he handed over the copy of the thirty year old Agreement to the blind mullah. He did not tell him from whom he had received the copy, and decided not to bore the worthy cleric with unnecessary details concerning his contact's inconvenient incarceration. The full price that had been authorized on his previous visit was handed over to him.

When Ahmed left the mosque, the mullah and Hassan retired to a small office concealed in the portico. Here, Hassan was asked to read the Agreement to the sightless clergyman for a second time. When the latter was quite sure that the entire contents had been committed to his memory, he gave instructions to his assistant, "Get a message to Yasser Arafat that he must come and see me as soon as possible."

Yasser Arafat was in Beirut when he received the message from Damascus. He had never liked the blind mullah from the Omayyad Mosque, but knew that he had a substantial following. Many of his followers revered him as the holiest man of their generation, on a par with the Ayatollah in Teheran.

Arafat would have been happy if both these meddlesome clerics were to disappear, leaving him and his PLO Council to run things his way, without religious interference. It also rankled him that these clerics sat in their mosques and demanded, as of right, that he, the Chairman of the PLO, the president of the Palestinian people, should leave everything and come to see them at their whim. It was demeaning; one day he would put a stop to this nonsense, but for the time being, he had to obey.

The following week he had planned a reconciliation meeting with King Hussein in Jordan, the first in twelve years. Deciding to fly first to Damascus, he called in his assistant to make the arrangements: "Arrange for a meeting with President Assad in Damascus next Tuesday." That, he figured, would serve two purposes. First, it would put Hussein on his guard and reduce the importance of the Jordanian visit, and second, it would show the meddlesome mullah that he had not come to Damascus specially to see him.

Nonetheless, by the time he approached the Omayyad Mosque a week later, his curiosity had been aroused, as he realized that there must be a good reason for the summons. The wily mullah must have something important, at least in the cleric's views. Most probably, he thought, the wily mullah wanted to implicate him in the recent massacre at Hama, in which many thousands of Sunni Muslims had been slaughtered by President Assad's own Alawite Muslims.

As a sign of respect for Arafat's official position as head of the PLO, the Muslim clergyman waited for his important guest at the Western Gate. On a personal level, he had little respect for the unshaven Fatah leader. On the other hand, he respected Arafat's many achievements and his tireless efforts on behalf of the Palestinians. As he reminded his assistant Hassan, "There are certainly no other Palestinian leaders that would have accomplished so much."

After embracing each other at the entrance, as custom required, the cleric told the PLO Chairman that he wished to discuss a matter with him alone. The two men walked to the benches in the courtyard. Sitting down with his guest, the mullah told him of the old Agreement that had come into his hands. Using his phenomenal memory he recounted all five clauses.

Arafat marvelled at the performance. "I have heard of the Agreement, O Holy one," said the Chairman respectfully, "but have never before heard details of the clauses. In fact, we have heard about the Agreement on different occasions during the past thirty years." Arafat sighed in contemplation of the passing years. "For, indeed, several decades have elapsed since that scoundrel British puppet king had the temerity to make an agreement with the Zionist dogs. However, despite much effort, we were never able to obtain a copy. May I offer you my congratulations and my personal thanks for your own successful efforts."

Taking a copy, one of many that Hassan had made, and passing it to the Chairman, the blind mullah asked simply, "Now that I have produced the Agreement, what may I expect you to do with it?"

Not for a minute had the canny Yasser Arafat considered that this blind cleric might be altruistic. Arafat was sure that he would demand his pound of flesh, "I will take the matter up with King Hussein, whom I will be seeing tomorrow in Amman. I will let him know that the Palestinian people will not stomach either the form, or the substance of the Agreement."

The mullah considered the reply, the latter part of which he hadn't exactly understood. He put it down to phraseology used by the modern generation of jet-setting politicians. "You must insist that Jordan rescind the Agreement and confirm that all the clauses are null and void. It must be made clear, unequivocally, that the Palestinians have sole rights to the whole of Palestine, with Jerusalem as their capital. Finally, the Hashemites must agree formally that they have no claims in respect of the Mosque and Islamic holy places on the Temple Mount."

The cleric sat ramrod straight, with his back not touching the pillar behind him. His facial muscles had not moved during his little speech, and this stance reminded Yasser Arafat of the late Mufti of Jerusalem. Arafat realized he was being given an order; not an opinion, or a consideration, or a piece of advice, but an order.

Unlike with the kings, princes, emirs, politicians and international statesmen with whom he chewed chaff every day, Arafat knew that it would be useless here to apply his usual charm and bluff. He had always been successful elsewhere, but recognized the unbending rigidity of the mullah sitting next to him. The Chairman would have to rely on his own insincerity. "I can assure you, Holy One, that our thoughts on this matter are not merely similar, but identical. You have performed a holy service to Islam; it is now my job, a duty of my office, to force the Jordanian monarch to come to terms with our just demands."

The blind mullah turned to another pressing matter: "And now Mr. Chairman, I cannot allow this opportunity to pass without discussing with you the awful tragedy at Hama. There are reports that between 15,000 and 25,000 Sunni Muslims have been killed. This is a holocaust. I need to know if you are willing to take a stand on this matter and make representations to President Assad. For, in the name of Allah, his behavior and the murderous inclinations of his brother Rifaat must stop."

"Revered Holy One," replied Arafat, "like you and every decent Muslim, I grieve for the sons of Mohammed whose blood was so cruelly spilled at Hama. However, I am a poor chairman of a poor Palestinian people that lives in exile from its own country. Here, in Damascus, I am but a guest in a neighboring country, and your president, despite his faults, extends to me his gracious hospitality. Moreover, he supports our cause and even allows the use of his soil to train our freedom fighters for their holy battle against Zionism. My single cause is the return of Palestine to its people, and I regret with all my heart that I am obliged to restrict my activities to furthering that one aim. I dare not risk taking up other causes, no matter how just they may be, as they may endanger the success of my sacred mission, my life's purpose.

"President Assad rules this great Syrian nation from a small power base. As you well know, he is an Alawite Muslim, a minority that numbers only ten percent of the country, dwarfed by the more powerful Sunni Muslims. Accordingly, he feels insecure. His Mukhabarat secret agents warn him of plots centred in Hama that would lead to bloody revolution, Assad and his brother feel forced to take preemptive steps. In these circumstances, my involvement would be considered undesirable interference in Syria's internal problems. It would undoubtedly come to haunt me and endanger my efforts on behalf of the Palestinians, who are the only people I represent.

"Holy One, I stand for a people that suffers great indignity, I know about suffering. My heart goes out to all those martyrs that were butchered at Hama, and to you and other Sunni Muslims who are themselves bleeding with grief. But,

I repeat, my hands are tied; any representations by me would be counter-productive."

Several days later, returning to Beirut, Chairman Arafat received messages from three separate sources that the mullah in Damascus was awaiting a report on his meeting with King Hussein. Noting with concern the diversity of the sources, he realized that the mullah intended to exert considerable pressure.

As usual, Arafat was besieged by many other problems and would have been happy to leave the question of the Temple Mount aside indefinitely. Arafat's visit to Jordan had been his first since Black September, twelve years earlier. Considerable diplomatic efforts had been made by intermediaries before a reconciliation with King Hussein had been effected and an invitation to Amman received. He couldn't see any reason to cause unnecessary problems to the Hashemite king at this stage.

Arafat viewed his own role as that of a chief executive, galvanizing regional and world support for the huge revival of Palestinian aspirations. He had to concentrate on the larger picture, the defeat of the Zionist state and the return of Palestine to the Palestinians. Quibbling at this stage over which religious mullah would control the Islamic Holy places was academic. Exerting his energies on such matters would not be fruitful.

On the other hand, the more militant branches of the PLO and other terrorist organizations were centered in Damascus. Damascus had always been happy to sponsor terrorism. Among the well-known terrorists that resided in the Syrian capital under the patronage of the powerful Syrian president was Arafat's archrival Dr. George Habash. This difficult man maintained his own splinter organization of hard-line terrorists, the Popular Front for the Liberation of Palestine (PFLP). Sometimes they operated within the umbrella PLO, but more often than not, independently.

Over the years, there had never been mutual love or respect between Arafat and the mullah. While visiting the mosque, Arafat had wondered why the religious leader had not approached Dr. Habash. Or perhaps he had?

Arafat devoted some thought to the question of to how to deal with the mullah. The pressure now awaiting him was an added factor. He would send an emissary with a message detailing the progress that he had made. There would be nothing in writing. He would gain time.

The Chairman detailed his assistant to contact the mullah and arrange a meeting with him. "Try and postpone it for as long as possible," he ordered.

While Arafat was en route to Beirut, a meeting on the subject of the Agreement was in fact already taking place at the Omayyad Mosque between the blind mullah and a senior lieutenant of Dr. Habash.

The mullah opened the private meeting by expressing his concern for Dr. Habash, who was ill and unable to attend meetings. "I am well aware that Habash is not a devoted Muslim, and more is the pity. I pray to Allah that He will look kindly in the direction of our sick friend, for he is a true son of the Palestinian people, whose sincerity in the battle against the Zionist dogs is beyond doubt."

Without any show of irritation at dealing with an underling, the mullah informed his guest of his recent meeting with Yasser Arafat and of the contents of the Agreement signed so many years earlier. Exercising his amazing memory, he again reviewed all the clauses in the Agreement, and allowed his guest to take notes. He did not offer to show his visitor the Agreement itself, as he wanted to limit the number of copies in circulation.

"I don't expect good news from Arafat, not now and not ever," he said without any particular signs of annoyance. "As for his meeting yesterday in Amman, from what I have heard from sources at the palace, he didn't bother to raise the matter – despite his specific promises to me. He has his own agenda and his own priorities. What I now wish to ascertain is where Dr. Habash stands on this matter, which I am sure you will understand is of utmost importance to me."

Answering carefully, the Habash official, himself a ranking member of the PFLP, made the following observations: "We are a non-religious group whose interests in many matters coincide with your own. We certainly want Jerusalem taken entirely out of the hands of the Zionist dogs and handed over to the Palestinian people, to be the capital of Palestine. If only for pragmatic reasons, control over the Temple Mount must be returned to the Palestinians and to no other party, certainly not the Hashemites sitting on the other side of the Jordan River. The administration will obviously be entrusted to Palestinian Muslims. More than this I will not say without discussing the matter with Dr. Habash; and then I will have another meeting with Your Excellency."

Standing up to indicate that the meeting was drawing to a close, the mullah took the arm of his guest and began to walk towards the Western Gate, "Please give my best wishes to Dr. Habash, may Allah spare him suffering. Tell him that, perhaps, he should consider raising the question of the Agreement at a PLO Meeting, where he should insist on a direct reply from the Chairman."

The blind mullah stopped and seemed to look directly into the eyes of his guest, as if through his darkened glasses he had suddenly regained his sight. "If the proper pressure is not brought to bear, Arafat will avoid his responsibilities in this matter. I want an answer on this from Dr. Habash."

The guest withdrew and walked away from the mosque. When the mullah had "looked" at his eyes and squeezed his arm, ever so slightly, the visitor had felt as if a cold shaft of steel had entered his spine. He had clearly been given an order from a formidable man, a man he would not wish to cross.

CHAPTER 45

Arturo had wasted little time since coming to Aqaba. He wished to come to a working understanding with Mario, who had arrived promptly for the 4 pm meeting at his hotel. Coming immediately to the point, Arturo Be'eri advised the local man, "The Vatican believes that the terms of the Agreement signed many years ago by the late King Abdullah are prejudicial to the interests of the Catholic Church. Although the Agreement was never ratified by the Jordanian and Israeli parliaments, its continued existence and place of custody pose a potential threat. The Church would like to see this threat eliminated."

Mario seemed ill at ease, restlessly looking round the lobby area as if afraid he was being watched. "Perhaps we should take a drive or a walk; it might be better if we talk outside," said Mario.

Arturo was now dressed in conservative clothes, not wishing to draw attention to himself. They left by the front entrance and walked to Mario's small Fiat. Mario drove slowly round the bay in the direction of the port but took a left that ran up into the foothills of the mountain range dominating the gulf. On an almost deserted stretch of road, he pulled to a stop on a spur that projected onto a lovely view of the Bay of Aqaba not far below.

"My friend at the palace," began Mario when he had switched off the engine, "was recently asked by the king to make copies of the Agreement. The copying machine was cold and not adjusted, and the first copy that he took had blackened edges. My friend kept this first copy and would be happy to sell it. He is thinking of a figure of $2,500." Mario paused to see how the proposition would appeal to Arturo. He had reasoned that if Bishop Vassilius had a large wad of notes, then the financier – for that had been his impression of Arturo's role – would have a far larger one.

"To tell you the truth," said Arturo, "I don't really want copies; I would, however, pay much more if I could get the original."

Mario's feelings for the palace were less than warm. However, participating in the unlawful removal of an historic document that His Majesty thought necessary to keep in his private safe was a difficult proposition. He needed to think it over. Stalling for time he replied, "I can't see how the original could be taken out of the safe, unless the king himself decides to have another look at it. By the way, His Majesty is coming down to Aqaba either today or tomorrow."

Arturo was shocked at this unexpected information and sat back in his seat to consider its immediate implications, "How long will he stay here?"

"I don't know; I imagine that he is coming for just a few days. However, I should have more details soon. When he comes, the palace is put on what is called an operational footing. The staff is increased. More importantly, the guard is totally changed."

"How strong will the guard be?" asked Arturo.

"The king's own Beduin Palace Guard is ten strong. When he is not in residence, a caretaker force of four regular soldiers from the local barracks takes over and operates on a shift basis, with two on duty at any one time."

"That doesn't sound very much, considering the size of the palace and the access in front and at the rear."

"Well, they are equipped with walkie-talkies and are connected to a larger force that is permanently quartered in the late King Abdullah's palace just three buildings down the road."

"How about us driving down and taking a look at the palaces," suggested Arturo.

"We can get near enough driving on the corniche until a point past the hotels, but cars are not encouraged to drive into the slip road that houses the palaces. License numbers of all cars are recorded. The driver's papers are usually scrutinized by policemen, who are nearly always to be found in the vicinity."

Mario turned the switch and the Fiat sprang to life. They drove towards the palace, driving on the Corniche Bay Road. Passing the Old Fort and the adjoining Visitors Center, they continued to skirt round the bay between the town and the sea. Passing the Gulf Hotel on the right and the Ayla excavations just opposite, they swept on towards a separate hotel area with a cluster of four hotels. In quick succession, they rolled by the Aquamarine, the Aqaba Hotel and the Holiday Inn and then turned left off the road into the park of the Coral Beach Hotel.

Leaving the Fiat in the car park, they emerged onto the road and turned left. Within a few yards they came to the slip road that led to the six royal winter houses or palaces. They had no problems walking into the slip road, nor were they stopped by any guards as they walked along the leafy and attractive setting. The villas were set back from the road, and the areas surrounding them and down to the road were covered with cultivated green grass and tall and graceful palm trees.

Coming from a background of intrigue and subterfuge, Arturo wondered if their progress along the road was being monitored. He had brought his camera with him and, once again playing the tourist, he took as many pictures as he could without appearing overly inquisitive.

As they approached the final and most impressive house on the road, Mario observed, "It looks to me as if final preparations for His Majesty's visit are still being made. I am not sure if he is already in residence. I guess he's only coming later tonight or in the morning."

At that moment, a gate at the side of the house swung open and an official but unostentatious Mercedes emerged and turned left towards them. As it drove past, the young man in the passenger seat waved at Mario, who involuntarily waved back.

"That's young Zayid; he's a nice boy," said Mario quietly, and then as the connection dawned on him, he continued, "he is the grandson of Jammal who used to work for King Abdullah and who brought the Agreement to His Majesty."

They didn't linger too long, and after taking some photographs of the royal palace, which any tourist would reasonably do, they retraced their steps to the car.

"Mario," began Arturo, "I'm told that you have very good connections." He paused, but Mario did not react, so he continued: "Would you be able to secure the services of a fast boat and a reliable skipper who would take me, say, three miles out into the bay for a rendezvous with another boat? He would have to be totally discreet and trustworthy."

Mario did not appear very surprised. He had already been propositioned to heist a document that was kept in his monarch's safe, so a boat ride to a rendezvous was something he could certainly cope with, "I think I know someone whom you can trust. If we go now, we should find him with the fishermen."

Arturo prided himself on sizing up people on first meeting. He decided that the boatman, a young man of about twenty five, would do almost anything if the price was right. "I need to go out and meet another boat about three miles out at sea at a place near the hotel at Taba. I plan to make the trip on a number of occasions and want to agree a price per trip."

"Will you be bringing anything back with you or transferring anything to the other boat?" asked the skipper knowingly.

"There will be no drugs, if that's what you mean. However, we might be taking some other packages back with us."

"And whom will we be meeting?" asked the skipper.

"That's none of your business; you will be paid to take me, return me and keep your mouth shut."

"Under those circumstances, I would want $500 per trip."

"I'll pay you $200 and that's plenty," answered Arturo. They settled for $300, and Arturo said that he was interested in going out that evening to test the route. They arranged to meet at 7 pm, some sixty minutes after nightfall.

That day Benzi set up the equipment on the roof at the Sheba. "I can run a cable into a room on the floor underneath and, instead of sitting on the roof, you could watch everything in comfort."

"No, I think we'll be happy on the roof," Kobbi answered. "It will give us a feeling of reality. Possibly we'll notice other things with the naked eye that might help us."

The camera had been set on a sophisticated tripod, which enabled it to be handled manually or be engaged in fixed grooves, one of which was set to cover the palace. By dusk, Benzi's work was completed. He had covered every eventuality of potential operating problems with Pinni, an operative selected because of his technical knowhow.

After dark, Kobbi, Seffi the section chief, Benzi and Pinni the operator took turns in selecting alternative areas to view. Using the rangefinder and focus, they would then improve the picture until it could be seen perfectly through a green haze. The palace was asleep. With the exception of a couple of guards walking around with a gun in one hand and a walkie-talkie in the other, there was little of interest to look at.

Benzi wanted to show off the capability of his equipment. He focused on the marina, still a hive of activity, with boats returning from fishing or cruising. Benzi had clearly developed a knack at finding obscure objects and zooming the camera on them; when he took the swivel handle of the tripod, the camera came to life.

"Look," he called to Kobbi, "there's a fast boat edging its way out to sea. I wonder where it is off to?" While Benzi looked through the viewfinder of the camera, Kobbi and the others followed the progress of the small boat on the monitor.

"I know that boat," said Seffi. "Let's use the image intensifier; if it's the guy I think it is, he's probably up to no good. Last year we were sure he was involved in shipping drugs, but we could never nail him. If we would only have had the use of this equipment!"

They followed the progress of the small but powerful boat all the way out to sea. It was being driven relatively slowly, not wishing to draw attention. Out in the middle of the gulf, about midway between the Israeli and Jordanian coasts, the boat stopped. The engines were cut.

Moving the camera in a small arch, Benzi picked up another boat. It was far closer to the Jordanian part of the gulf and was making out to sea. Using the zoom, he could make out two figures inside the second boat. Although there was some distance between the boats, all the watchers agreed with Kobbi when he asked if it wasn't probable that the two boats were planning to meet.

The camera continued to monitor their progress. Every few minutes Benzi would move the camera back to the first boat to ensure that it hadn't moved. It became more and more obvious that the boats intended to rendezvous.

"Well," said Seffi to Benzi. "We are certainly proving one good purpose for your equipment. Have you, in fact, sold any video cameras to the coast guard?"

"We are trying our best. Everyone showers compliments and enthusiasm when we give them a demonstration; however, between enthusiasm and actual orders..." Benzi shrugged in a gesture to show how difficult life was.

Kobbi had other things on his mind. He asked Benzi to use every technique to get the best picture of the people in the boats.

"I think that the first boat is a little far out." Benzi replied, "I doubt if I would be able to recognize a particular face. We might get a better fix on the second boat, let's see what we can do."

First using the zoom, Benzi soon had the boat filling the frame of the monitor with a clear picture of two men inside. Taking control of the image intensifier, he framed each figure separately until the faces were recognizable.

"I think that one of those characters is our friend Arturo. Seffi," instructed Kobbi, "phone through to your office and have them bring over a picture of Arturo."

By the time the picture arrived, about ten minutes had elapsed, and the second boat had proceeded too far for them to identify the images. Looking at Arturo's photo a little later, however, all four viewers were sure that it had been he.

By now it was certain that the second boat was proceeding on course to a rendezvous with the first. Within minutes, it pulled alongside. The three participants in this silent play all seemed to know one another; at least that was the impression from such a distance. After handshakes and some talking, the lone skipper of the first boat reached for a small box which he passed to one of his visitors, who bent down and stowed it out of view in his own boat."

"Well, well, well," said Kobbi "I wonder what's in that box."

"How big do you think the box is?" Seffi asked Benzi.

"I would think that it's big enough for some light guns – and maybe an Uzi," he replied shrewdly.

The engine of the first boat had come to life, and the two boats parted company to return to their home ports. Within just a few minutes, some distance had developed between them. They did not want to appear to be connected. Kobbi gave Benzi and Pinni instructions to tail both boats and, motioning with his hand, took Seffi over to the far end of the roof for a quiet chat. "We have to decide what to do. We can await the skipper of the Israeli boat and frighten him into telling us what he is up to. Alternatively, we could just keep an eye on him. However, if this is a once only trip, we will miss out. What do you think?"

Seffi thought for just a moment before replying: "I want to get a good look at the Israeli; if it is the guy I think it is, he would sell his own mother, and in that case perhaps we should go and see him. He won't mess with me, and I'm sure he will cooperate."

"Its a risk, nevertheless," said Kobbi. "If he warns Arturo, our little game is up."

"Not necessarily," argued Seffi, "it would merely put them on notice that we have sophisticated methods of monitoring them. They wouldn't call it all off and would probably proceed nonetheless. And after all, from your point of view, you'd rather that the Agreement fell into his hands than the Iranians'."

After a few minutes of thought, Kobbi reached his decision: "I think that you should pick him up when he lands. Frighten him without telling him all of what we know. Look for the box, tell him that you know it was on board when he left Eilat. Ask him what he did with it. Let us see how loudly he sings."

They returned to the monitor to see the Israeli boat getting back into a range suitable for the image intensifier. As soon as the equipment focused, Seffi cried, "That's the guy all right, no doubt about it. I'll go down to the marina and prepare a welcome home for him." Seffi left to find two agents to accompany him.

In the meantime, Kobbi followed the progress of both boats and watched while the Jordanian boat berthed among the Aqaba fishing vessels. The box was taken out of the boat and up onto the quay, where it was put into the trunk of a waiting Chevrolet. The video equipment couldn't quite get the license number from the plates, but the video screen showed Arturo's happy and satisfied face as he handed over some bills before driving away.

When the powerful boat slid quietly into its berth in the Eilat marina, the skipper jumped off onto the quay and pulled the rope tight around the metal ring rising from its concrete bed. He secured two other ropes to ensure that the boat wouldn't bang against its neighbors. Straightening up, he slapped his back pocket, where he had put the $500 that he had received from Arturo, and sauntered along the jetty towards the pub. Leaning on the bar, he called for a beer, then turned to face Seffi who was standing next to him on his right. Seffi told the barman, "Make it three."

To his left, he saw another agent. It wasn't a chance meeting. "What the hell do you two goons want?" he asked angrily, "can't a guy have a quiet beer by himself?"

"I am interested to know what you have been doing out at sea so late, whom you have been seeing, and what you have been up to," said Seffi, sipping his Maccabi beer.

"There's no law against a boat ride at night; and I've been keeping my nose clean. You can search my boat if you like and even take your dogs on it, they won't smell anything."

"Who's talking of drugs – perhaps you have been gunrunning?"

The skipper turned a chalky white. Seffi had touched a nerve.

"Let's finish our drinks and come back to our place for a chat," said Seffi. The skipper knew he had no alternative.

Kobbi was waiting at the Shabak offices when Seffi brought in the skipper. He had decided not to be directly involved in the questioning. The Mossad had phoned through with two pieces of information. The first was that the Iranians, four of them, had arrived in Amman en route for Aqaba. The second was that three Italians were booked on an Alitalia night flight from Rome to Amman from where they would continue on an internal flight to Aqaba.

Seffi took his visitor into an interview room, released the other agent, and offered the skipper a seat and a cigarette. Both were accepted. "We want to know what you did with the wooden crate that was aboard on your outward trip and didn't come back with you."

The skipper, not the most brilliant of men, was now very scared. Was there room for a deal that would get him off the hook? "What's in it for me if I come clean and help you?"

"Well, it depends on whether we think we can trust you. As it stands, selling guns to Aqaba would probably get you five years."

The skipper reeled as if he'd been punched in the stomach.

Seffi left the room and went to talk with Kobbi. "I have no doubt that he will cooperate fully; perhaps you should come and tell him exactly what you want."

Kobi returned with Seffi. The skipper looked awful. He clearly wished to offer his services.

"Why don't you tell us all about your relationship with Arturo," suggested Kobbi, who had not been introduced.

"I met him in Tel Aviv a week ago. We were introduced by a mutual friend. He said that he needed a fast boat in Eilat to rendezvous with another boat. After we had agreed on a fee of $500, he gave me a crate to take to Eilat. I was told to take care of it until Arturo would contact me."

"Are there more meetings scheduled?" asked Kobbi

"We plan to meet again in three days' at the same time. If he doesn't show up, then I have to try the following day and then again the following day until we meet."

"Have you any idea what he is doing or planning to do in Aqaba?" asked Kobbi.

"No idea at all; you must believe me," answered the skipper.

"Do you know what was in the crate?"

"I have a good idea; I didn't look, but judging from the weight, I'd guess they were guns of one sort or another."

"We might be able to come to an arrangement with you. It depends on our believing that you will be reliable," said Kobbi cautiously. "We would want you to continue to take the boat out to meet him. Whatever he pays you, you may keep. However, you must never say or hint that we know about him. If you warn him off, we'll deal with you properly, you'd better believe it."

"I'll do whatever you want, I swear I'll not let you down," whined the skipper.

"How well do you know the Jordanian skipper?" asked Kobbi.

"I have done things with him before," replied the skipper simply.

"Well, I think we will just have to trust each other," said Kobbi. "We will probably see you for another chat before your next trip. By the way, are you expected to take anything else to him?"

"Not that I know of. But someone he knows might contact me; if so, what do I do?"

"You play along and keep us fully informed."

After he had gone, Kobbi said to Seffi, "It appears that after the heist, Arturo wants to leave the scene of the crime via Israel. It's his best route. My guess is that the Italians will return to Rome via Amman, and Arturo will come to Israel with or without the Agreement."

"One question that, perhaps, we should consider," said Seffi, "is whether we can use our skipper to warn Arturo about the Iranians."

"That would be dangerous, we will just have to hope that he takes care of the Iranians on his own," he replied.

CHAPTER 46

Lounging comfortably on a deck chair aboard the royal yacht in the Gulf of Aqaba, His Majesty, King Hussein, had an opportunity to reflect on problems of state without the continual interference of couriers, phone calls, politicians and petitioners. In the background, the Jordanian coast with the impressive dark red and copper mountains soon merged with the territory of Saudi Arabia. That oil rich and powerful desert kingdom had years ago gobbled up the Emirate of Hedjas, which had been ruled by King Hussein's great-grandfather of the same name. In its time, the Emirate had stretched along this same Red Sea with its *Tihama*, the barren coastal plain and mountainous fertile oasis behind. His Majesty liked to think that the judicious Hashemite rule of his Kingdom of Jordan had redressed, in some measure, the shabby history of the region.

Lying in the sun, with a sea breeze on his face, King Hussein pondered his own recent meeting with Yasser Arafat, the Chairman of the PLO, that scruffy, unshaven political maverick who always expected to be received like royalty. Arafat, who not so long ago had been the secret boss of an underground movement, had undoubtedly emerged as one of the strong men of the region. To many he was a brilliant coordinator with long term political understanding, for he had managed to turn his terrorist group into a political and organisational force.

The chairman had come to Amman with his usual begging bowl. His list of petitions included a demand that more Palestinians be enabled to leave the camps and take up residence in Amman and other large cities. On this matter His Majesty had taken a tough line. Both he and Arafat knew full well the danger posed by demographic changes to law and order within his kingdom.

The next matter was the perennial plea for His Majesty to intercede with the Gulf States to get them to honor their financial pledges and fill up the empty coffers of the PLO. Although he had answered with encouragement, he did not think that it was in the present interests of the kingdom to advocate the PLO cause.

The next point on the PLO agenda was Arafat's intention to visit the United Nations. He wanted to hear if His Majesty supported such a visit and if so, would he use his good connections to get him a welcome from the US government. Such a visit was premature, the US didn't recognize the PLO as anything other than an unloved and undesirable terrorist organization, a position which His Majesty entirely understood.

It was the matter that had not been raised, which occupied His Majesty's mind as he sat enjoying the March sun. He had the distinct impression that Arafat was preparing to bring up for discussion the Agreement that King Abdullah had signed so many years ago. His Majesty knew that Arafat couldn't have seen his own copy and found it hard to believe that, after all these years, the Israeli copy might have turned up in the wrong hands. So what on earth was the sly fox driving at? He made a mental note to discuss the matter with his brother on the latter's return to Amman. Perhaps the crown prince would be able to throw some light on what Arafat had been hinting at. The Agreement was under lock and key in the safe in Aqaba. All was as it should be.

However, notwithstanding the beautiful weather and the calm sea, he found it difficult to unwind from the worries of state and the problems of the region. His thoughts were soon dwelling on the recent Syrian massacre at Hama.

A foreign journalist had tried to draw a comparison between the 1970 Jordanian battles with its belligerent Palestinian refugees and the recent merciless killing by the ruling Alawite Muslims of their numerically superior Sunni brothers in Hama, a fairly large Syrian town. During the many years of his rule, King Hussein had developed a detached pragmatism to cope with the hotheadedness usually associated with the Arabs. This comparison, however, had angered him immensely. How could anyone compare his own benevolent rule with the cruel display of power exercised by the dreaded butcher of Damascus? In the certain knowledge that dwelling on this subject further would ruin his brief vacation, His Majesty forced himself to think of other matters.

After Mario had introduced Arturo to the skipper of the boat, he decided to return to his office at the hospital. As he approached his car, he saw Zayid's older cousin, Nasser, who worked with the fishermen at the docks. Nasser came across to say hello, and the two lingered to talk. Mario had always liked the two boys and their parents. "How is Zayid doing at the palace?" Mario asked.

A cloud passed over Nasser's pleasant face. "To tell you the truth I don't know, and I seem to be losing the close contact that I always had with my cousin," Nasser replied. "Let's sit in the car for a few minutes and I'll tell you about it."

Sitting in the car, they rolled down the windows to increase the supply of fresh air. Nasser recounted the story about his new Iranian friends who had recently come to live and do business in Aqaba "They are both Shi'ite fundamentalists. I think they were probably sent here to look for converts. At first they divided their time with both of us, but lately they have been concentrating their attentions on Zayid, and I sense that he feels greatly pressured.

"It all started innocuously enough when, during a discussion about the monarchy and Zayid's job at the palace, Zayid recounted how our late grandfather had brought an old agreement from King Abdullah, for whom he had worked, and delivered it to King Hussein. The agreement discussed the holy places of Islam in Jerusalem, control of which would remain with the Hashemite dynasty."

"Yes," interjected Mario, "I remember well, as I was the official delegated by His Majesty to receive Jammal when he first came to the palace."

"Well," continued Nasser, "I understand that these Iranians desperately want to get the Agreement by fair means or foul and are pressuring poor Zayid to help them. Zayid is very young, and he finds his loyalties divided between his king and the Iranians, whose branch of Islam he frankly finds appealing. As far as I can understand, the Iranians say that Hussein and his wishy-washy form of religion cannot be trusted to keep such an Agreement. In the long term, they believe, he'll compromise with the Americans and the Zionists."

"But surely Zayid would't have access to the Agreement."

"That's correct, but he has friends on the palace staff that might, for a fee, assist him. Alternatively, and this is what is really worrying me, these Iranians might employ force."

"How could two Iranians possibly take on the Palace Guard," laughed Mario.

"I understand that more Iranians are coming to help them. From what I understand, they are due to arrive tomorrow."

"My advice to you is that you should talk to your uncle, Zayid's father," said Mario thoughtfully. "You must prevent Zayid's being further involved with these guys. In fact, the sooner they are run out of town the better."

After a couple of minutes of thought, Nasser replied. "I have a problem. Zayid might be young, but I feel obliged to give him some freedom. Frankly, both of us see the benefits of Shi'ism, which is idealistic and committed. The Sunnis around here just pay lip service. The young Iranians might be too pushy on this particular matter, but their ideals on the broader aspects of religion are attractive."

"Would you mind if I have the Iranians watched?" asked Mario.

"I would not want to get them into trouble," answered Nasser. "But I'll keep you in mind, and if things get out of hand I'll contact you."

When Nasser left the car, it took considerable effort for Mario to ignite and drive away; he just didn't know what direction to take.

Later that evening, the boat returned on low throttle to its berth amid the fishing vessels in Aqaba. Assisted by the skipper, Arturo disembarked and carried a wooden crate to the trunk of his car. He was annoyed to see Mario waiting in the shadows. He did not wish Mario to know the details of his planning. Mario seemed agitated and insisted that they talk. Parked some distance from the boats, the two sat in the Chevrolet, and Mario quickly told him of his meeting with Nasser.

"So you don't know where these Iranians hang out?" asked Arturo.

"No, but I've been thinking; there are a number of possibilities. The first is that when they landed in Amman they must have registered an address, and it won't be difficult to get the information. Another is that they have not yet arrived, so we might pick up them up at the airport and follow them. Still another possibility is that we can follow Zayid, and he will surely lead us to them."

"Yes, I imagine it won't take us long to find them. Tomorrow morning some of my colleagues will get here, but they will make their own way from the airport to the Holiday Inn where they will be staying. I suggest that you try and locate the Iranians, while I organize my associates. We can meet at lunchtime tomorrow, at the Holiday Inn.

"Vincente Freiz will be staying in a suite on the ground floor; it has a door opening onto a patio leading to the gardens at the rear. That suite will be our control center. In any case, our plans will probably be frozen until His Majesty leaves Aqaba, as I don't fancy taking on ten of his elite palace guards. Let's meet at the control room, in suite number 10, tomorrow at 1 pm."

The three Italians and the four Iranians all arrived in Aqaba the following day. Mario remained agitated the whole night. He parked his car in the car park of the Holiday Inn at a little before 10 am and decided to keep an eye on the slip road leading to the palace. His hopes of catching Zayid paid off. Shortly after 11 am, he caught sight of him outside the Coral Beach, walking along towards him, deep in conversation with a young man.

Zayid had some time ago confided in his Iranian friend that he had a colleague at the palace who could get at the Agreement for a fee. The man he had in mind had worked at the palace for over twenty years. Recently Zayid had learned that this trusted servant had considerable problems at home, caused by a son who had become involved in drugs and gambling, both illegal and very expensive. The boy had incurred large debts, had used up all his family's savings and put them into further debt in their useless effort to straighten him out.

Zayid knew that a sizable bribe would secure the services of his co-worker. He had not confided in the Iranians all of what he knew of his colleague's problems. He was still afraid to do so. Today, Hushang, his Iranian friend, was trying to pressure him in a final effort before reinforcements arrived from Iran. The implication was that if he didn't produce the Agreement peacefully, force might have to be employed.

Zayid was truly torn. He was being drawn more and more towards fundamentalist Shi'ism. Like most converts, he wanted to prove his zeal. On the other hand, he had a long-ingrained loyalty to king and country. He was being asked to reverse his own family's history of allegiance to the Crown. If he complied, he would be reneging on the fealty and friendship of his grandfather to the late king and the Hashemite royal family. For he would participate in stealing the very Agreement that his grandfather had carefully guarded for so many years.

Lately Zayid had not been sleeping well. During the days he had been tired and listless. He had developed bags under his eyes and an unhappy, dishevelled appearance.

Today, more than on any previous occasion, Hushang was merciless in his pressure. He pointed out that the royal visit might make it easier to get the Agreement, as His Majesty would probably need access to his safe, and an opportunity would then present itself to take out the document, "Think about it. If we are lucky, he might not miss the Agreement for months."

Mario hid in the entrance to the car park and watched the two pace backward and forward in conversation.

The Iranian might also have worried about the clear picture he and Zayid made to inquisitive eyes. He suddenly looked at his watch and terminated the discussion. Saying goodby, he turned on his heel, leaving a dejected looking young Jordanian, as he walked back towards the palace.

The Iranian strode past the driveway in which Mario had taken refuge. Mario waited a couple of minutes and followed him.

The walk was short. Mario trailed Hushang along the Corniche until he came to the Ayla excavations, a location about half way to the down-town area. There the Iranian took a right on a narrow lane leading towards the Fisherman's Wharf. He arrived at a house near the wharf, and let himself in without turning round once to see if he was being followed. Mario had found the base from which the Iranians operated.

At lunchtime, Mario knocked on the door to the suite known as the control room. He was welcomed by a swarthy-looking Italian, who spoke good Arabic with a French accent. "*Salam Aleikum Mario, Kif Halak*, my name is Vincente Freiz." Vincente knew all about Mario.

"Probably learnt Arabic in the back streets of Algiers," thought Mario, as he followed him into the lounge area, where Arturo was sipping a cold drink and munching salted peanuts.

"Let's talk before the others arrive," said Arturo who was sitting quietly on the patio. "I have told Vincente all that I know. The others will do as they are told, and it's not necessary to tell them too much."

"I have already offered my view," said Vincente in French-accented English. "Although we are equipped to take the Agreement by force, and believe me that we can – if we can get the papers by, how do you say – an accommodation – then it is preferable. No blood, no noise and no wrath of heaven upon us all."

Mario thought back to the heavy-looking wooden box that had been taken from the boat and deposited in the trunk of Arturo's car. He had no doubt as to what that box contained.

"From our point of view, the best result would be achieved if the Iranians get the document through their friend within the palace, and then we take it from the Iranians," said Arturo. "Have you got any more news on the Iranians?"

"Yes, I think that I have located their base," replied Mario and told them about his spying on Zayid and then following the Iranian.

"Good work," said Arturo, "A light lunch and we can take a walk and look."

The other two Italians joined them, and a light snack was ordered from room service. They ate on the patio, against the panoramic view of the bay.

After lunch, equipped with cameras, the group of tourists led by Mario walked down to the Fisherman's Wharf, noting on the way the house used by the Iranians. Arturo delegated two of the Italians, the ones that Mario had decided to call "the goons," to stay in the area and keep an eye on the house. Arturo, Mario and Vincente returned to the hotel.

Addressing Mario, Arturo suggested, "I think that you should go and visit Zayid's brother again and see if you can get some more information. What I have in mind is the name of the colleague at the palace who might be willing to help Zayid to take the Agreement from the safe."

The Italians, Mario and Arturo, lunching on the patio, were unaware of the high-powered binoculars trained on them from the roof of Hotel Sheba in Eilat.

"Take an exact fix and let's focus the telescope," said Kobbi, who had decided that the roof could be put to use during daylight hours, and not only at night.

"It's a shame that we can't hear what they are discussing," said Kobbi as if talking to himself.

The telescope couldn't pick up the Italian tourists leaving the hotel by the front entrance, which was obscured. The Israelis' field of view was restricted to the back terrace.

Later that night, Seffi took a boat trip with his cooperative skipper. Aware of the instructions given to Kobbi from the highest possible source, he had thought it better not to inform the others of his plans.

The boat left the marina and sailed to a point as near as possible to Seffi's objective. The skipper cut the engine, releasing an anchor at a point some three hundred yards from the Holiday Inn. They had entered Jordanian waters, and yet nobody seemed interested in their presence. From experience, Seffi knew that they would not be bothered.

While the skipper prepared fishing lines, Seffi changed into a wet suit and flippers. A knife was attached to his lower calf, and he wore a mask and snorkel, when he silently dropped over the side of the boat that faced the open sea. Skirting the boat, he checked his bearings and swam towards the shore with only the snorkel visible above the water line. As he swam, he wondered whether he was under surveillance from the Sheba roof in Eilat.

Seffi landed on the deserted pebble beach about one hundred yards from the hotel in the direction of the Fisherman's Wharf, almost at the exact point he had targeted. He quietly stowed his flippers, mask and snorkel under the low sea wall, carefully noting the exact location. Hoisting himself over the wall, he strode confidently along the sea walk above towards the hotel, like any tourist returning from a night swim in the warm Red Sea.

The rear entrance of the hotel was open. He counted out the rooms and patios from the end of the building, in order to correctly identify the suite used by the Italians. There was no sign of life from the patio or from the room behind, both of which were in darkness.

Reaching the patio, he leisurely let himself in through the small gate. He turned to look back at the sea as if admiring its beauty. Showing every sign of appreciating the lovely night, he lingered slowly, just in case he was being watched. Without any excessive movement, he reached down and undid zip fasteners on his wet suit. There were two waterproof bags inside. He sat down as if enjoying the night air.

Opening the pouches, he withdrew a small cell-operated microphone and transmitter. When it was assembled to his total satisfaction, he rose from his chair. Stretching leisurely, he approached the door to the suite. It was locked with an old-fashioned English Yale lock.

Removing from his pouches a small, strong, flexible piece of plastic resembling a credit card, he inserted it between the door and the jamb. One quick wrist movement and the door swung open. Anyone watching from a distance would have sworn that he had taken his key from his wet suit pocket and inserted it in the key hole.

His practiced eye told him exactly where to place the listening device between window and curtain, on the inside of the curtain rail. The whole job took less than two minutes. Leaving the room, he stepped out onto the patio and silently closed the door behind him.

With an exaggerated pretence of looking for his snorkel, first on the patio and then in the garden, Seffi resignedly left the gate and returned to the beach to search for his lost equipment. As he started to walk along the sea, he heard a group of tourists coming towards him, talking loudly in Italian which he didn't understand.

"Do you speak English?" he asked as he passed, "I've lost my snorkel, perhaps you have seen it?"

Vincente translated for his two friends. The three had a good laugh at the unfortunate tourist looking for his lost equipment at night.

On his return to Eilat, Seffi went straight to the Sheba and up to the roof. Connecting a high powered radio to an electric lead, he swivelled the dials until once again he heard the same Italian voices. Next day, he would arrange to bring an Italian-speaking agent up to the roof. Pinni was the only other agent still up there, and he was preparing to shut down for the night. "I think that the Italians might have had an uninvited guest in the form of a man in a wet suit," he reported to his superior.

"Just forget it and don't record anything in your report," replied Seffi.

The two agents exchanged good night wishes and parted.

Chapter **47**

Soon after the arrest of the bank robbers and his formal acceptance of the religious responsibilities of Judaism, Taher changed his surname to Ben Avraham. A short while later, he and Tali were married inside the walls of the Old City in a modest ceremony at the exquisite Sephardi synagogue named after the ancient sage, Yohanan Ben Zakkai. Tali's son David, now twelve years old, became reconciled to the match and came to the wedding. He had initially voiced objections, but time heals, and he had learned to respect Taher as a good and honest man intent on giving his mother a better life.

Second weddings are more often than not small and unostentatious; Tali's to Taher, was no exception. When she first heard Tali's intentions, her mother had also registered her unhappiness at Tali's decision to marry a man of Arab background. On this matter she received no support from her husband, who since his days of mourning the loss of his old Torah scroll, had embarked on a new life of positive thinking, of looking for the good, rather than the bad, in all around him. By the time of the wedding, Tali's parents were supportive and ready to play their part.

Partners and employees at the law office where Tali worked all came to participate in Tali's simcha – her time of joy. They exhibited no signs of curiosity; nor were they uncomfortable or inquisitive, for they had all grown to know and like the quiet and friendly Taher, who regularly visited their offices.

Apart from her family, close friends and co-workers, the guests were drawn from among those attending Taher's Jewish studies classes and from among the settlers with whom he had struck up friendships. Avraham Nissim and all his family came, and Avraham assisted in the ceremony.

While the men escorted the groom to his place under the *chupah*, singing and dancing as they made their way to the central part of the synagogue, the women fussed over the bride in a separate room. Following tradition, the couple had not set eyes on one another for seven days before the ceremony.

From her throne-like chair, covered beautifully in flowers, Tali then rose and was led to the entrance of the synagogue. From there, escorted by her parents, she walked towards her betrothed. The same males that had previously sung and danced around Taher now turned their attentions to the bride. Raising their voices in a united *Ketzad merakdim lifne hakalah* – How do we dance before the bride – in a trice they turned the solemn walk into an ecstatic dance of song and joy, with the objective of joining the couple in a marriage of happiness and rejoicing.

There were two guests at the wedding that were not family, colleagues, study partners or settlers. Meir Peled and Kobbi had agreed to come incognito. Apart from Ketselle and Avraham Nissim, who knew them, they were assumed by others to be grey members of officialdom. Taher had promised not to advertise their line of work. Prime Minister Begin considered coming himself, if only for a short while. However, his wife, Aliza, was ill, and he wished to spend as much time as he could at her side.

The actual ceremony took little more than ten minutes. Addressing the bride and groom under the *chupah*, the canopy held on poles under which the couple were united in marriage, Avraham spoke to them, reminding them of their duties to one another, their duties to their people, and to the Land of Israel.

After Avraham's moving little speech, the couple left for *yichud*, a short period by themselves, in the privacy of a locked room. In the interim, the guests helped themselves to light snacks and drinks in an anteroom. And it was during this time that a discussion or argument developed which was to dominate the rest of the evening.

The origins of the argument were a casual introduction of Kobbi to one of the more militant settlers from Mount Hebron. The settler gained the impression that Kobbi's political leanings were to the left and that he didn't sympathise with the views of settlers on the West Bank. Why he gained this impression remained a mystery, for Kobbi was always discretion itself. Within seconds, Kobbi found himself defending the position of a political centrist, living in the comfort and security of a commuter community near the fleshpots of Tel Aviv.

As the argument developed, the voice of Moshe Beker the settler, rose to a higher pitch. A crowd gathered around and Avraham, who was scared that perhaps Kobbi's identity had been discovered, ran over to take control. "Maybe," Kobbi was saying, "it is time we gave peace a chance. If the price we have to pay is territorial compromise, so be it. Surely it would be worth giving back parts of the West Bank in exchange for a real peace treaty and a normalization of relations with our neighbors."

Moshe Beker grew red in the face and looked as if he were about to have a fit. Avraham assumed charge of the situation. "We do not believe that we are entitled to trade land that was given us by Divine decree. In the Torah, we are commanded *vehitnahaltem ba* – to settle the land. We have no room for compromise. To quote David Ben Gurion, Israel's visionary first prime minister and a noted secularist, who stated at the Zionist Congress in Zurich in 1937: *No Zionist can forego the smallest part of Eretz Israel.* What has happened to this vision among the ranks of his own Labor Party today? Why do all his old friends forget the words of their mentor? Why do they now all seek compromise?"

Kobbi countered in measured tones, "I think you know that I sympathize with the ideals of the Labor Party; it was clever of you to quote Ben Gurion to me. Allow me to answer you in your own currency. *Pikuach nefesh* – safeguarding life – is the most sacred of commandments, one that takes preference over all other commandments. Shabbat, Yom Kippur, food regulations – all are set aside, if there is danger to life. Should not retaining the Land likewise be set aside if it threatens danger to life – i.e., war? On this matter a leading British rabbi recently stated that we must opt for territorial compromise in the quest for peace. He was even prepared for a Palestinian flag to fly over part of Jerusalem!"

Recalling this statement sent a quiver of annoyance among the settlers. It took Avraham some minutes to calm his friends. "We are here for a wedding, to rejoice and make merry with our bride and groom. I will tolerate no fighting. Discussion yes – but only if we can keep it at a reasonable level."

When order was restored, Avraham asked his friends to be patient, so that he could argue their case. As none of the settlers could compete with Avraham's knowledge and debating skill, he was given the floor. "First I compliment you on quoting the notion of *pikuach nefesh*. However, I hope to show you that it is a non-starter. And in doing so, I will deal with the unfortunate remarks of the publicity-seeking rabbi in London, a man who chooses to live comfortably, well away from our scene.

"In the same year that Ben Gurion made the remark which I have already quoted, the Council of Torah Sages, here in the Land of Israel, made a similar statement. They resolved that: *"The borders of our Holy Land have been fixed by Him who has set down the possession of lands in His Holy Torah. They are fixed for everlasting*

generations. Accordingly, it is impossible for the Jewish People, for its part, to make
any compromise in any manner whatsoever on these borders."

"Now I would like to remind you," continued Avraham, "that these rabbis lived
in Eretz Israel of 1937. They had no state, no autonomy, no control, – nothing. In
the background was rising turmoil in Europe. In the Middle East, an awakening
militancy among the Arabs. Arab riots against Jews in Jerusalem were on such a
scale that the mufti had been expelled by the British High Commissioner. And here
were these rabbis saying NO to the concept of partition, NO to compromise. Now,
compare for a moment that brave stand, and set it against your suggestion of today.

"So much for the polemics," continued Avraham, raising both his arms in an
attempt to keep order. "You have mentioned *pikuach nefesh*. I will attempt to answer
that red herring. I will answer it in two parts.

"First, there are rabbis that prefer to put the onus of decision on military experts.
That is to say, if the generals were to warn that holding on to the lands would lead
to a war in which Israel's chances would be dangerously low, then the government
might consider withdrawing. However, the situation is quite the reverse. Most
military experts argue that the real danger would lie in withdrawing from territories
which they regard as having major strategic importance. In other words, for the sake
of *pikuach nefesh* the territories and settlements must be kept! If the border is
brought nearer to the heart of Jewish settlement, then the *halacha* – Jewish law –
forbids the return of those territories.

"Let me give you a second answer, and this I do in the name of the late Rabbi
Ehrenberg, of blessed memory, who first advanced it. Although *pikuach nefesh*
overrides other *mitzvot*, it is not relevant in relation to the question of war. The Torah
itself permits the waging of war in certain circumstances. All wars involve
casualties, therefore the danger to life – *pikuach nefesh* – in the case of war is clearly
disregarded. Torah sages have no right to stand in the gates and cry out in the name
of the Torah that we must give back part of the territories owing to the danger of
war."

It was at this stage that the bride and groom returned to their guests, who were
then invited to adjourn to the dining room. The beautiful Ben Zakkai Synagogue is
one of a complex of three renovated buildings, all of historic interest. The synagogue
lies below the level of the road in the Jewish Quarter of the Old City; it is approached
down a steep staircase that leads into a stone-covered courtyard. Along one side of
the courtyard is the synagogue, and opposite, a reception room and kitchen. To this

suite on the other side of the courtyard the guests moved for the wedding dinner. It was served buffet style.

Avraham and his wife made up a table with Ketselle and his wife; they were joined by Meir Peled and Kobbi. When they had all brought their plates, heaped with food, to the table, the debate continued. It was now Kobbi's turn to come back to the topic. "The differences between us can be summed up in just three words: pragmatism versus mysticism. It is my belief that the silent majority is in favor of the former, and the noisy minority represents the latter."

Avraham cleared his throat as if he wanted to answer, but Kobbi held up his hands to indicate that he hadn't finished. "Let me clarify what I mean by pragmatism," he continued.

"1. The Jewish population in Judea and Samaria is hopelessly dwarfed by the Arab population.

"2. The annual increase in the Arab population, due to a higher birthrate, outpaces Jewish augmentation, despite the swelling of our ranks with new arrivals.

"3. The cost of safeguarding the settlers and policing the areas is enormous and a burden the state cannot afford.

"4. Almost the entire international community is pressuring us to give back these territories, since they consider them acquired by conquest.

"5. By keeping the West Bank, we run the risk that, with the passage of time, say twenty or thirty years, the Arabs will outnumber the Jews in Greater Israel. This would lead to apartheid."

Avraham sipped some white wine from his glass, sat back in his chair and prepared to answer Kobbi, a man he had grown to respect and whose integrity was beyond doubt.

Meir Peled, in the meantime, scribbled down some points of his own, "Please let me just add a word or two to Kobbi's list. The pressure for us to return territories is applied not only by international politicians. Many Jewish communities and their spiritual leaders support compromise."

Avraham looked at his friends. He knew that their arguments were offered in good faith. In the politics of Israel, it was difficult to change the views of grown men, especially on this emotive subject. Men and women were leaving other tables to join in dancing with the bride and groom. Two circles had formed; men danced with the groom, while the women danced with the bride. Avraham's table was the only one at which all guests remained seated when he began to reply: "Let me deal, first, with Kobbi's pragmatism, and then I will address the views of pressure groups from overseas.

"Pragmatically, I suggest that to give up the territories would be to invite war – and a threatened onslaught on the remaining, truncated Israel, which would be extremely vulnerable. This pragmatic view holds that a hostile Arab state ten miles from Tel Aviv would be dangerous beyond words. Would you be comfortable in your home near Tel Aviv with the PLO in your backyard? And do you honestly believe that this new emerging state will remain disarmed and militarily neutralized?

"Allow me to remind you of what the PLO stands for. I will quote you from just three of the articles in its Charter:

"Article 15. The liberation of Palestine aims at the elimination of Zionism from Palestine.

"Article 20. Claims of historical or religious ties of Jews with Palestine are incompatible with the facts of history.

"Article 21. The Palestinian people reject all solutions which are substitutes for the total liberation of Palestine.

"What you are advocating is that Israel must be influenced by demographic problems on the West Bank and accommodate itself to the prevailing mood of the world. Let me remind you that, eighty years ago, many Jewish leaders were prepared to entertain the notion of setting up a Jewish state in Uganda – thousands of miles from our heritage and our birthright. However, there was vigorous opposition by the noisy minority of that time!

"When the second partition issue was raised following Arab riots in 1936-1939, it was the same leadership that adopted the path of pragmatism. In that case, they may have had far more moral right; the persecution of German Jewry was at its height, the shadows of impending war were lengthening across Europe. There was a sense of desperation in Jewish circles – to accept something we did not have – a territory in which we would be free to decide on Jewish immigration, without outside limitations.

"In 1957, after the Suez Campaign, American Secretary of State John Foster Dulles forced Israel to withdraw from the Sinai. Ben Gurion, well aware of the dangers, struggled to extract the best possible promises and guarantees. As we know, when the hour of trial came, these were found to be of no value at all. Ultimately, the Six Day War eventuated as a result of the withdrawal from Sinai and Gaza in 1957.

"Now, regarding today's wild-eyed mystics. Would you give the same objective description to the founders of the state? Would it be applicable, for example, to Herzl, who envisioned (correctly, as it turned out) the establishment of a Jewish State within 50 years, and taught "if you will it, it is no dream." And what of the founders of early settlements, Hanita, Deganya and Nahalal, the Negev settlers and the Jezreel Valley farmers? I cannot understand why all of those good people were regarded as patriots and idealists, while we, who continue the same process today, should be perceived as wild-eyed mystics. At a time when old idealism has given way to materialism, is it not refreshing to find a revival of the pioneering spirit – a return to planting and building – even at personal cost and sacrifice?"

Avraham talked smoothly, quietly and without having to grope for a suitable phrase. He easily held the attention of all those at the table. Even Ketselle, an incorrigible talker, held his tongue.

"The crux of our argument is the source of our rights to this land. Those of us with a religious outlook see the whole of Greater Israel as the rightful historic patrimony of the Jewish People. Abraham, Isaac, Jacob, were Divinely promised this land for their descendants.

"Abraham, our first Patriarch, acquired the cave of Machpela in the ancient town of Hebron. He paid the full asking price in silver pieces. From then on it was precisely this area that was first settled by the Patriarchs. And it was to the towns of Hebron and Shechem that the Book of Genesis refers, when it states: "Unto thee will I give it, and unto thy seed." Much later, at the commencement of the first Jewish Commonwealth, when the monarchy was established, it was Hebron that was the first seat of government of the nation. King David ruled from Hebron for seven years before he established Jerusalem as the capital of all Israel.

"So much for Hebron, which is in Judea. Now I will conclude with an account of Samaria. The ancient city of Samaria was built by Omri, King of Israel, in the 8th Century B.C.E. He gained his throne by a coup d'état and is described as wicked and sinful. Sages in the Talmud ask why this evil man was able to establish a dynasty that was to rule three generations, while good kings were often not succeeded by their sons. And the answer they give is, because Omri added and settled a large city within the Land of Israel!"

"And that brings me to the pacifists, and particularly those who offer their advice from London, New York and other faraway places. Please allow me to give you a small lesson from history, for after all, I am a teacher. Two thousand five hundred years ago, the Jews of Jerusalem were led out of their beloved city and taken into bondage. The pain and anguish that accompanied them was too great to describe. Poets mourned the tears of the Jews as they wept by the waters of Babylon.

"However, sorrows that seemed quite unbearable at first grew with time to be more lightly borne. The first generation of exiles sat and wept, but their children made hay. They took their parents' harps and had them retuned. The Jews in Babylon learned to face their life in captivity and to make the best of it. Many felt that they were truer patriots in exile than they had been for generations in the Land of Israel. Jeremiah and Ezekiel, the prophets of the time, were listened to, as never before. The Law of Moses was read and the Psalms were sung in poor but crowded places of worship. These synagogues were filled with more devout worshippers than had ever assembled in the marbled courts of the Temple in Jerusalem.

"And then the anticlimax. For when Cyrus, the Persian ruler, gave his permission, there was no eager rush to leave the fleshpots of Babylon to return home. For many, Babylon was now the country of their children. This proved more powerful than that the Land of Israel was the land of their fathers. Forty-two thousand Jews returned. The others remained. They sent good wishes, advice and supplies.

"Those Jews that returned from exile found a desolate city, with its walls pulled down and the Temple in ruins. The ruins were cleared, walls were erected, and the foundation stones of the new Temple were laid. This hard work was undertaken, not by the Jews that remained in Babylon, but by the Jews who came back to the Land of Israel; back to Jerusalem, the very cradle of Judaism. In relative terms, the advice and, even the gifts, sent by the Jews in Babylon mattered very little.

"Now let us return to the present. Surely the Jews in London, Paris and New York can be compared to those Jews of Babylon. Their sympathies might well be genuine, but is not their commitment of little real substance? A Zionist is not a Jew who gives money to a second Jew to finance a third Jew to go and live in Israel. A Zionist is one who leaves Babylon, or the modern fleshpots of New York, and returns home to the land of his fathers.

"So, Meir, in reply to your own question regarding overseas Jewish pressure groups, we settlers believe that it is our job to settle and rebuild the land. We intend to have large families and thus repopulate the region with our own internal immigration. We are prepared to accept offers of help from our overseas brethren, but do not pay too much attention to their counsel. And as for their pious protests about Jewish concepts of peace and compromise, well they are out of line – as were their forefathers in Babylon, two thousand five hundred years ago."

Avraham took another long drink and rested a minute before continuing: "We have come to dance at Taher's and Tali's wedding, and it would be unfair to allow this argument to monopolize the evening. I'll rest my case, at least for tonight.

However, before anyone could rise from the table to join in the merriment, Ketselle indicated that he too wished to contribute to the discussion.

"I would like to dwell on the world's reaction to our existence. The world did not participate in building Jerusalem and its surroundings. We do it ourselves, for we see it to be our sacred duty, and it is therefore our joy. The world did not build Jerusalem, they did not live in it. They did not defend it when others came to destroy it.

"When Jerusalem was ruled by the tyrant Herod, it was inhabited by the famed Hillel and other Jewish sages who concerned themselves with studying scriptures and writing the Mishna and the Talmud. During this difficult but productive period of our history, New York, London, and Paris were but swamps and scrubland.

"Twice or more the Jews were driven out of Jerusalem, taken into bondage by invading armies. Leaving their beloved city, they swore never to forget her, for before doing so *they would see their tongues cleave to their palates and their right arms wither.*"

Turning to face Meir, he continued: "Let me turn from external international pressures to differences here at home. You are a secularist and must note the differences between our religious wedding ceremonies, and secular weddings. Does it not strike you as a remarkable indication of our strength of purpose that at each of our weddings we conclude our ceremonies with a defiant chant of this dramatic oath from Psalm 137 – *if I forget thee, O Jerusalem, let my right hand forget its cunning, let my tongue cleave to its palate, if I do not remember thee, if I do not raise Jerusalem above my foremost joy.*

"Inquisitions, pogroms, blood libels, expulsions and anti-Semitism never broke our spirit or resolve to return to Jerusalem. Thrice each day we pray, *Gather us up from the four corners of the world, bring us standing upright to our Land, return us in Mercy to Jerusalem, Thy City.*

"And then horror of all horrors – and in our own times – the unimaginable Holocaust. Can we believe today that, just thirty five years ago, genteel Germans, lovers of Kant and Goethe, Beethoven and Strauss, created and operated a mass system of extermination? And as Germans do all other things, they completed their tasks with great efficiency, killing six million Jews, wiping out half our people.

"Where were the world's great advisers, where were the statesmen, the humanitarians, the philosophers and the politicians? How did they sit back and see the systematic killing of helpless men, women and children in the gas ovens of Auschwitz, Dachau, Bergen Belsen!

"Almost immediately after the Holocaust, the State of Israel was born. The Jordanians controlled the Old City of Jerusalem, but a United Nations resolution sought to ensure that Jews from adjoining Israel would be given access to our holy places, to the Western Wall and to the ancient burial sites on the Mount of Olives. But the Jordanians did not play according to the rules. They sacked, plundered and destroyed no fewer than thirty-seven Jerusalem synagogues. They desecrated the Jewish cemeteries, broke up tombstones and distributed them for building blocks for roads, army camps, latrines and hotels.

"Where were the world's humanitarians, the statesmen! Where were the politicians of the world when Jordan raped our Jewish soul! Where were they when, earlier, the Arab Legion put a siege around our holy city and starved our citizens to death!

"Statesmen, humanitarians, philosophers and politicians now come to counsel us. They speak of *just compromises*. They talk of progress and a new beginning. It is incumbent on us Jews, so they tell us, to show a good example. They quote from our own Jewish sources that we must be a *light unto the nations of the world*.

"Their real purpose is to wrest control of Jerusalem from our Jewish hands. For the first time in thousands of years, all citizens have equal rights and there is religious freedom for all. They come now, when Jerusalem is united, united under Jewish rule.

"I am a Jew descended from Polish immigrants, some of the very few fortunate ones that escaped before that country's three million Jews were butchered. I was a young Jewish soldier privileged to defend our young state at the historic time of the reunification of Jerusalem. I tell these advisers, these counsellors, these politicians and humanitarians, Go home! Leave us alone! We Jews will do what we know is right. We are better qualified than they are to know right from wrong! Jerusalem is under our control and it will stay that way!"

With the noise of singing and dancing enveloping them, this small group of friends was not experiencing the kind of hush that might have accompanied the drama and pathos at the climax of the debate. Ketselle had talked passionately. He was no orator or even debater. He talked from the heart and echoed the yearnings of his people over thousands of years.

As Ketselle completed his say, the dancing reached a new high pitch. The tune, sung loudly by all the participants, was borrowed from Lubavitch hassidim. The words, *ufaratzta, yama vekedma, tzaphona venegba*, were particularly apt. Their meaning – *and you shall go up to the east and to the west, to the north, and to the south* – was a challenge thrown down to expand our teaching of Torah, expand our boundaries in all directions.

Avraham Nissim rose from the table. With one strong arm, he swept Kobbi along with him; with the other, he enveloped Meir Peled. Together the three men joined the dancing, swinging round the room with abandon. The argument was now placed behind them. Their single purpose was to enjoy the wedding feast of their friends and bring joy to the bride and groom.

CHAPTER 48

The two brothers, Hushang and Nader, took a bus to the small Aqaba Airport to meet their new associates, none of whom they knew. It wasn't difficult for them to recognize their four compatriots among the other passengers flying down from Amman. The four young men travelled light, each carrying just one medium-sized item of luggage. For all four, this was their first journey beyond the borders of Iran; they glowed with the excitement of their first mission. As there was not enough room for six in a single taxi, Hushang decided that they would travel by bus to the town center.

The arrival of the six Iranians at the brothers' small house was duly noted by the three Italians who had been detailed to keep watch. The Italians then walked along the sea front, back to their hotel, to report on the arrivals. They approached the hotel through the garden at the back. Vincente received his friends in the lobby. He heard their report, bade them good night, and returned to his own room. From there, he placed a phone call to Arturo at the Gulf Hotel and gave him the news.

The Iranian newcomers were quite fresh and rested. They had spent a day in Amman and slept long and comfortably in hotel beds, a change from what they were accustomed to in Iran.

Instead of turning in, the six Iranians sat down to discuss their mission. The newcomers wanted a briefing from Hushang and Nader. Hushang duly told them all he knew. He discussed his relationship with Zayid and explained that, in his view, Zayid was close to a breakdown. He doubted if he would be able to force the young man to deliver the Agreement. At this point Nader, who rarely talked while in the presence of his older brother, had an interesting idea: "Why don't we ask Zayid to disclose the identity of his colleague, the one who might actually deliver? Then we should encourage Zayid to take a few days off and return to the palace only after we have received the Agreement."

"That's a terrific idea," said one of the new Iranians, "then he will remain in the clear. He will establish an alibi."

"I like the idea," said Hushang, "because we will be able to maintain our connections with him, which I think are strong and will be fruitful for the long term. I'll phone him early in the morning, before he goes to work, and arrange to see him."

The next morning Mario went down to Fisherman's Wharf and looked for Nasser. He found him tinkering with his motorbike. Nasser seemed pleased to see Mario, one of the few people he had been able to confide in about his brother's problems.

"Frankly, the story that you told me about the Iranians worried me so much, I couldn't sleep," Mario said. "We have to get Zayid away from those thugs before disaster befalls him."

"I agree with you," replied Nasser. "The question is how to do it without compromising his religious zeal."

Mario had thought about which of Zayid's colleagues would be prepared to help and had narrowed down the possibilities to a single senior employee who, he had heard, had befriended Zayid when he had first come to work at the palace. He had heard rumors about his son being in financial troubles, and that strengthened his assumption. Deciding to fly a kite he suggested, "Why don't you arrange for Zayid to go on vacation, perhaps visit a relative or go out with the fishing vessels for a couple of days. During that time, perhaps, things will come to a head, especially if we can arrange for the Iranians to be introduced directly to Zayid's friend at the palace, the one who wants to help. Would I be correct in assuming that it is Ismael?"

Mario had sounded so genuinely interested to help his brother, that the question did not raise any suspicion. "Yes, it is Ismael. He's got his own problems, poor guy. How will we introduce him to the Iranians?"

"Well, you know all the parties. Why don't you merely introduce the Iranians to Ismael and, at the same time, tell them to leave Zayid out of it?"

"I won't pretend that I haven't thought about it. The problem is that it makes me an accomplice, and frankly, I don't want the slightest involvement."

"What if you went to see your Iranian friends," persisted Mario, "and simply told them that, if they would contact Ismael and leave your brother alone, they might obtain what they are looking for. At the same time, make it clear that you don't want to know any details; nor do you want to know what it is they are looking for."

Nasser checked his watch, "I have to go and do some work, I'll think about what you said; in any case, two or three days on the boats would be a good thing for Zayid. And thanks very much for your concern, I really appreciate it."

Mario, while genuinely concerned for Zayid had, of course, been thinking about his own role, too. He had lived all his life in Aqaba and had nowhere else to go. Furthermore, although Aqaba seemed to be a sleepy port town, the police and security forces could play quite rough. To remain in town and be a fugitive from the law was not appealing. If he himself took a role in introducing Ismael to either the Iranians or the Italians, it would spell disaster if found out. In his experience, these kinds of plots were always revealed.

He was already worried about being seen in the company of the Italians. A hotel waiter, a reception clerk, or any number of other people could link him, a local man, with these foreigners who would surely disappear into thin air as soon as their mission was completed. This would leave him to explain his relationship. Mario had not exaggerated when he told Nasser that he hadn't been sleeping at night. He promised himself that, in future, he would be far more circumspect and would not be seen again with Arturo or the Italians.

After leaving Nasser, he went to a public phone and placed a call to Arturo at the Gulf Hotel, trying to disguise his voice from the operator. Arturo was not to be found, so he contacted the control room at the Holiday Inn. Vincente got on the line and demonstrated that he had no difficulty in recognizing the disguised voice when he shouted to Arturo, "Lift the extension on the patio, and speak to Mario."

"Come over and join us for some lunch," said Arturo into the mouthpiece.

"No, thank you," said Mario with resolve, "but I do want to see you and I have interesting news. I know the name of a man who will help. I am scared to come to the hotel and want to see you elsewhere. May I suggest a rendezvous where we stopped on your first day, overlooking the port."

"Fine," said Arturo with understanding, "I'll come directly over, arrivederci."

"I am leaving to see Mario," explained Arturo to his cohorts, "he says he knows who will help us, but he's scared to come to the hotel; maybe he's right to take precautions."

Listening to this exchange on the roof of the Sheba over the border in Israel, Seffi and Kobbi exchanged glances and smiled.

Mario hoped that Arturo would come alone, as he wanted to negotiate terms to cover all his work and connections. Seeing the blue Chevrolet approach with the single figure of Arturo inside, he felt relieved. He left his own, less comfortable car and joined Arturo when the Chevrolet pulled to a stop.

An honest approach was the best approach, Mario decided.

"There are four matters I wish to discuss with you," began Mario, who had spent a sleepless night preparing himself. "The first is the issue of my own security. Although I'm happy to assist you, I'm also painfully aware that when the Agreement is safely in your hands, you will leave Aqaba. I, on the other hand, will have to remain here. I'm sure you will appreciate my concern. I don't want to be left holding the baby. Consequently, from now on, I want to limit the contact between us.

"The second matter is the manner in which you will achieve your objective. You can either negotiate or use force. I want your word that you will use force only if all attempts to negotiate fail.

"The third is the question of my remuneration. If you get the Agreement, I want $100,000 – over and above any fees that you may pay to any other party.

"The fourth point will be of most interest to you. I think I can introduce you to someone, an employee at the palace, who will be able to deliver the Agreement. But, for reasons of my own security, you'll have to negotiate your own terms with him. I won't want him to know that I am in any way involved."

Mario sat back in the comfortable front seat and tried to look less strained than he felt. As a courtier at the palace, and later in his administrative position at the hospital, he had been trained to listen, not to make speeches. Framing his thoughts carefully had been quite an effort. Now, as he began to relax again, he thought that his careful preparation had paid off.

Arturo anticipated a successful conclusion to his mission. He seemed not to notice the man's tension, and was impressed by the other man's ingenuity. He agreed that negotiation was the best way to proceed. As for the fees, he had hoped to settle for a total price of $100,000, i.e., including third party payments. He believed he would still be able to bargain with Mario – after all, this was the Middle East. He might use the possibility of violence as a card in negotiating Mario's final price. Arturo appreciated the validity of the latter's concern to ensure his secure future within his community, free from harassment by the authorities. "Such security," thought Arturo, "must also have its price."

Ten minutes of haggling was enough for Arturo to persuade the local man that he would have to reduce his demands. The two settled on $60,000, of which $10,000 would be paid immediately. From years of experience, Arturo knew that an immediate cash payment often clinched a heavily discounted price. Arturo pulled out a wad of used one hundred dollar bills from his inside pocket and paid Mario his first installment.

The unexpected one hundred well-thumbed bills that Mario found in his hand increased his tension, as he worried where to secrete his windfall. He wore no jacket and carried no case. If he stuffed the cash into his shirt pockets, it would be clearly visible.Eventually he divided the notes into three parts. One he stuffed uncomfortably into his back trouser pocket and then, from his awkward position in the car seat, attempted unsuccessfully to button it. To his chagrin, he found that the wad of money left insufficient room for the button to be engaged. The other two small parcels he put into his two trouser side pockets; each left a bulge which immediately made him feel self-conscious.

On balance, with cash in his pocket, Mario felt happier. "Now for the introduction," he said. "You must phone Ismael at the number that I have written down on this paper. Tell him his cousin Yacoub suggested that you contact him. Arrange to meet him in a quiet place. It is vital you keep him out of trouble. Don't play with him. Tell him what you want and negotiate a price. I assure you that he is in urgent need of money."

"What if he checks with his cousin?" asked Arturo.

"Yacoub is in the army and can't be contacted. You've nothing to worry about. Also, in future please use my code name – Abdul – when you call me, or refer to me in any way. Tell your friends as well."

Later that evening and after a short phone call, Ismael met with Arturo on the dark sea walk that separates the row of hotels from the sea wall. The negligible public lighting eliminated the danger of their being exposed. Pretending to take a stroll, the two men paced back and forth and negotiated terms. Ismael would receive $50,000 in exchange for the Agreement. Arturo agreed to pay him ten percent as a down payment. Ismael explained that he would remove the Agreement from His Majesty's safe when next asked to open it. He was sure that he would be given the opportunity within the next couple of days, during the royal visit. Arturo promised that the Agreement would be immediately removed from Jordan. Those that acquired it would tell no one. Ismael realized that he had no choice but to take Arturo's word.

Besides, Arturo assured him that it would not be in anyone's interest to advertise that the Agreement had been taken.

"How quickly will it be noticed that the document is missing?" asked Arturo.

"The more time we have, the more difficult it will be to trace us," Ismael replied. But he couldn't give any guarantees. He didn't ask, nor was he told where the document was going. "Maybe we should place a very good copy in the safe. This might stall anyone looking for the original," suggested Arturo.

"Yes, that sounds a good idea," replied Ismael thoughtfully, as he recalled the copy already in his possession. "I will take care to place a good copy in the safe. Anyone finding it might suppose that the original was sent to Amman."

Parting company for the present, they agreed to meet at the same place on the sea walk each night at 7 pm.

Arturo hurried back to his control room in the Holiday Inn, where he reported on his negotiations to his Italian friends. Ismael hurried in the opposite direction, to keep his appointment with the Iranians at Fisherman's Wharf. The cash deposit in his pocket failed to alleviate feelings of guilt at his traitorous actions.

Zayid had been showing signs of strain and, before leaving the palace, Ismael had given him permission to take two or three days off. Under normal conditions, when His Majesty was in residence, such lenience would have been unheard of. But Zayid looked as if he was about to crack, and Ismael decided he would be less of a menace away from his job. He and the other members of the staff would cover for him. Zayid had then told Ismael that some Iranians in town might be prepared to pay for a copy of the Agreement – the same copy that Mario had tried, unsuccessfully, to peddle to Arturo for $2,500. Zayid had given Ismael Hushang's name, address and phone number.

Ismael had deduced, correctly, that Mario's connection was Arturo. He had now dealt with Arturo on the original Agreement. That left another buyer in the market interested in a copy. Ismael needed money. He was desperate to settle his son's financial problems before they dragged the entire family into disgrace. It was this fear that, after so many years of devoted service, had forced him to turn his back on his beloved royal family.

Flushed with the comfort of $5000 padding his inside pocket, Ismael proceeded to his second meeting with a feeling of high expectations, but his confidence was short-lived. He was ushered into a cramped room. No windows. Dim light. Across from him sat an entire komiteh. Six scowling faces.

Ismael's initial instinct was to find an excuse and turn tail. But he remembered that Zayid had made the introduction, and he trusted Zayid. Besides, he was confident that he had a marketable asset in his possession.

"In a safe place," he began, responding to a curt inquiry from one of the faces opposite him, "I have placed a signed copy of an agreement between King Abdullah and the Israeli government leaders, Ben Gurion and Moshe Dayan. It was signed in 1951, just weeks before King Abdullah was assassinated."

"Abdullah was a traitor to the Arab cause," said one of the Iranians vehemently. "He deserved to die."

For a moment, Ismael was scared for his own safety. What would these fanatics think of him, his modern values, and his love for the royals!

"Can we see the copy?" asked another Iranian.

"I can tell you about its contents. If we agree on a price, I will arrange for it to be transferred to you against payment."

"That's a good idea," said Hushang, as though trying to calm him down. "Why don't you give us the contents?"

It suddenly occurred to Ismael that the Iranians were bent on purchasing an agreement they knew nothing about. He decided to whet their appetite. "The Agreement has five clauses," he explained. "They cover an arrangement, whereby Jordan will relinquish administrative control of the West Bank and sovereignty over Jerusalem to the Israelis. In return, the Hashemite dynasty will retain control over the Islamic holy places on the Temple Mount. Furthermore, Jordan will retain the right to nominate the mufti."

The komiteh members were impressed! Again they were amazed at the wisdom of the mentor in Teheran who had sent them on this mission.

Hushang's budget was far more modest than that of the Italian customers. "You have been sent to us by our good friend Zayid," said Hushang, smoothly. "Zayid's loyalty and his good intentions are unquestioned. Nevertheless, I am sure you will appreciate that I simply cannot pay for a copy of the document until I have discussed the matter with my komiteh."

What they had on the table, at that moment, was the opportunity to buy a copy of the Agreement in its entirety. Personally, Hushang was inclined to secure the offer now, while they had the opportunity. They could try and acquire the original at a later date. But he must guide his komiteh. Insha'ala, they would reach the correct decision.

"How much are you asking for this copy?" asked Hushang.

Here, once again, Ismael felt at home. "It will cost you $10,000," he answered.

"We will have to discuss the matter and reach a decision. As you can see, this apartment is too small for comfort, so I must ask you to leave. Would you return in, say 30 minutes?"

For the second time that day, Ismael paced up and down the sea walk. When he reached the Holiday Inn, he happened to see Arturo and some other men talking animatedly on the patio but, not wishing to be seen, he kept in the shadows and retraced his steps. Walking down to the wharf, he watched the fishermen clean their nets and prepare their boats and equipment for the next day's excursion. There was a pleasant breeze and the air smelled sweet. Keeping one eye on his watch, he ensured that exactly thirty minutes later, he presented himself again at the apartment of his Iranian clients.

The moment he entered the room, Ismael knew that he had a sale. He was sure that they had decided to take the copy, but felt they would haggle over the price.

"My komiteh thinks the price too high for a copy," began Hushang.

"It's a case of supply and demand," replied Ismael.

"True... everything has a price, and if the price is right we would be interested."

Ismael stood his ground and didn't answer. The komiteh members were losing ground. "We can offer you $4,000," Hushang offered the local man, but he was clearly not convinced.

Ismael smelled victory. "I'm sorry," he said, "the price is fixed. This is the only existing copy of the Agreement. I am told it would fetch more than I'm asking merely as a collector's item."

Nader now came to his brother's assistance. "Well," he said, with a sudden burst of camaraderie, "I'm sure we can all compromise a little."

"No, I'm afraid not. I contacted you at Ziyad's request because he thought you would be interested. I myself had thought of offering it to other contacts." These last few words were uttered with a touch of emotion, as if Ismael really felt that he was honor-bound to offer it elsewhere, and was only talking to the komiteh because of the special introduction.

"Please don't misunderstand us. We are glad that you came to us. Zayid told us only good things about you – and we don't think you should endanger yourself by offering such a sensitive item elsewhere." Nader was pleased with the way he had phrased his reply. "But a gesture from you on the price would be appreciated."

The six komiteh members were on foreign turf. The Jordanian had beaten them at their own game. He simply wouldn't reduce the price. Hushang and Nader arranged to meet Ismael within the hour in the lobby of the Coral Sea Hotel and make the exchange. Ismael left the building, wondering what he would do for the next hour, for the copy that he was about to deliver had been in his jacket pocket all along.

His Majesty had two major speeches to make on his return to Amman. He rose early, in order to spend a couple of quiet hours at his desk before starting his day. He would review his final drafts, have Ismael fax them back to his secretary – and then he would be free to get out on his boat. The large French doors to his office were open. The sea and the weather were at their best. "No doubt about it," he thought, "March is by far the best month for sailing in the Red Sea."

Ismael knocked quietly at the door.

"Coming to pay his morning respects," thought King Hussein.

"Good morning, Your Majesty, is there anything I can do for you?" He uses the same phrase every morning, thought His Majesty,

"Yes, come through with me to the inner office and help me look for some papers in the safe." Hussein pushed his swivel chair away from his desk and led the way to the anteroom where the fax, the teleprinter and the safe were kept. Spinning the combination lock back and forth to the programmed number 12.07.51, which was the date of the assassination of the king's grandfather, he opened the safe and stood back. Ismael stood aside, at a respectful distance.

"I'd like you to find the speech that I made at the university a couple of months ago. Also, while you're looking, try to find copies of the speeches I made in 1970, after the struggles with the Palestinians. I'm going out on the boat again, but I'll return in the early afternoon, as I need to fly back to Amman later today."

Accordingly, Ismael selected various papers from the neat pile in the safe. His hand was shaking when he lifted out the original signed Agreement. With a feeling of self disgust, he secreted it into the inside pocket of his jacket. The copies of the speeches he took into the next room, obediently laying them on the desk.

"What a reliable man," thought Hussein, as he turned and left the room.

Chapter 49

A t seven that evening, Arturo walked along the sea walk. He didn't wait long
before Ismael came striding jauntily toward him from the direction of
Fisherman's Wharf. They met like old acquaintances, wishing each other a good
evening. They even exchanged niceties regarding the fine weather and the mildness
of the sea. Slowly, they started back in the direction of the hotels.

"I should be able to deliver the Agreement later tonight – possibly, within about
an hour or so," said Ismael guardedly. "Will you have the money ready?"

Arturo was thrilled. A perfectly executed mission, he thought. No noise, no
bullets, no commotion and – before long – not even a trace of negotiations. "Do you
see the Holiday Inn over there?" he replied. "If you count the second patio on the
ground floor from the far side of the building, you will see three guys playing cards."

"Yes, I see them," said Ismael.

"At 9 p.m., come to that patio from this direction. The garden door will be open,
I'll be there with the money. You'll be able to count the money, if you want to. It
will be yours, when you hand over the Agreement."

Two hours later Ismael returned, accompanied by his son Tawfiq, a swarthy
looking fellow with a barrel chest and prominent muscles. Such an enormous
amount of money made Ismael quite breathless – Tawfiq made him feel secure. As
they approached the patio from the direction of the beach, they saw Arturo and
Vincente sitting with their legs up against the railing, chatting and drinking from
liquor glasses. The other Italians, whom Ismael had caught sight of the previous
evening, were nowhere to be seen. Deeming it unnecessary for them to witness the
exchange, Arturo had sent them to keep an eye on the Iranians.

As promised, the money was all there, secure in the inevitable black leather
briefcase. So far things were proceding as though according to some pre-designed
movie plot. "The case gets thrown in as a bonus," laughed Arturo. Ismael, never

proud where money was concerned, looked over the stacked bundles. He picked out several individual notes at random and checked them carefully.

"Believe me," laughed Arturo again, "if I wanted to pass you duds, you'd never recognize them, but I promise you – they're genuine. They come from a most kosher source." Again Arturo laughed at his own joke. Vincente laughed with him. "Now, how about showing us the Agreement?"

In his excitement at seeing so much cash in such a confined space, Ismael had quite forgotten that he had his own papers to deliver. "Of course, of course, no problem," he mumbled and groped in his pocket, where the Agreement had been since morning. Withdrawing it carefully, he passed it over to its new owners.

Now they are not joking. Arturo, every muscle of face and body tight with concentration, is poring over the paper, studying it word for word. His strong-armed support is reading with him, checking, perhaps, what Arturo might have missed. Ismael has not expected this. He thinks, maybe the Agreement isn't all it's cracked up to be? Maybe it will fall short of their expectation and the deal will be over?.... What, in fact, are they looking for? Damn it! I told them what it was about! Arturo reads clear through to the three famous signatures at the end of the document. He raises his head slowly – and beams. "This," says Arturo, "is the real thing."

From their perch on the rooftop in Eilat, the Israelis listen to the exchange. Arturo, they believe, is due to return to Israel by boat the following night. They will wait until then. "If he decides to take the Agreement himself to Italy from Jordan," said Kobbi, "or, alternatively, if he sends the Agreement with the Italians, then the entire thing will be a matter for the Mossad."

Kobbi turned to Seffi and Pinni and continued confidently: "My bet is that he will bring the Agreement with him by boat. It will be in our hands tomorrow night."

That evening Mario called Arturo. He arranged to meet him at 8 the following morning on the lonely stretch of road overlooking the port. Meanwhile, Arturo and Vincente made plans to withdraw from Aqaba the following day. Vincente and the others would book out of the hotel immediately after Arturo returned from his meeting with Mario. They would drive Arturo's rented Chevrolet back to Amman, making sure to stop at Valley Rom on the way, and they would drive past Amman to the famous Roman remains at the Jerash archeological site. At both tourist centers, they would make sure to be noticed taking photos, and generally enjoying the sites, but they would be careful not to visit Petra where the blue Chevrolet might be remembered.

The Italians would return the car to Hertz at Amman airport, claiming that they were settling Arturo's bill for him, so that he wouldn't miss his plane.

"What will you do with the box of weapons?" asked Vincente.

"Perhaps I'll leave them with Mario. I certainly won't carry them back to Israel."

Everything was going according to plan. The Agreement had not been missed at the palace. For their part, the Iranians had no reason to suspect that it had been sold to another party. Zayid was out at sea with his fishermen, and His Majesty was due to return to Amman.

Mario received the balance of his money in the morning. He also agreed to do Arturo a great favor by taking delivery of the crate of guns. Mario knew that, if caught with such weapons, he would be badly compromised, but he had heard that the Iranians were looking to buy guns. If he played his cards right, he could earn another commission.

Early in the morning, the Holiday Inn suite, with its useful patio and its Israeli listening device, had been vacated. The three Italians in the Hertz Chevrolet were on their way north. Arturo returned to the Gulf Hotel from his meeting with Mario. He arranged a late checkout for 6.30 that evening. For the rest of the day, he would enjoy being a tourist and benefit from the glorious winter sun of the Red Sea.

He enjoyed his day on the beach; he even managed to pick up a really nice tan. On a stroll round the bay, he visited the fourteenth century Arab Fort, one of the few tourist sites in Aqaba. Later, as the sun sank like a ball of fire into the sea, Arturo paid his bill, walked from the hotel across the Corniche and past the Ayla excavations towards the wharf.

On his way, he passed the house of the Iranians. Two of them were lifting his wooden box from the trunk of a taxi and carrying it into the house. "Clever bastard, that Mario," he thought. Not missing a beat, he simply walked on towards the wharf. There, just as he had arranged, he found the boat and skipper waiting.

Whistling a romantic Italian ballad, Arturo swung aboard. All he had with him was a small bag with a few bare essentials. The Agreement was in his inside jacket pocket, and his remaining cash was secured in moneybags around his waist.

In Israel he would hand the Agreement over to one of the Angelo brothers who would come from Rome especially to take delivery. "The beauty of this operation," he purred to himself between the stanzas of his ballad, "is that no one will know about it for months – perhaps even longer." Stretching out to the full length of his stout body, a cigarillo between his fingers, he thought: "A neat, clean and quiet job, well done. No fuss, no publicity."

Arturo was not the only witness to see the wooden crate being taken from the car into the house occupied by the Iranians. A policeman had been stationed for some hours across the street, at a window of his sister's apartment.

On their flight from Amman, the four Iranians had been required to fill out the usual papers. As it happened, the airport official that processed the papers had an antipathy for this scary new breed of Shi'ites. Pictures of them in threatening poses and mob scenes were frequently exhibited on TV. He considered it his patriotic duty to alert the authorities to their whereabouts. Consequently, he informed the Aqaba Police of their arrival, and suggested that their activities be monitored. Corporal Ahmed Bey was detailed to investigate.

Corporal Bey had heard from his brother-in-law of the two Iranians bent on converting Jordanians into Shi'ite fundamentalists, and he shared his brother-in-law's disgust at their activities. He had advised his relative to inform him if things got out of hand.

That afternoon his sister had phoned, saying that the two Iranians across the road had more company. Their number had swollen to six. Corporal Bey picked himself up from his desk at the police station and repositioned himself, again, in his sister's apartment. From this excellent look-out, he noted the activities across the road. Various Iranians were coming and going, but there was no sign of unlawful activities – until dusk. During the day, however, he was aware that two other unknown men were also seemingly keeping an eye on the Iranians' home. Corporal Bey could not guess what their interest might be.

At a little after 6 pm, a taxi drew up beneath his window. Two Iranians emerged from the taxi and, together with the driver, went around to the rear. The driver opened the trunk, and one of the passengers then paid the taxi fare. Two Iranians lifted out what seemed to be an extremely heavy wooden crate, walked to the house opposite, and disappeared. Many years of police experience, together, no doubt, with a measure of biased intuition, led to one conclusion: The crate held weapons. But the corporal was a desk man, armed action and heroics were not his scene. He decided to return to base and report to his superior officer.

The officer, in turn, needed some persuading. "After all," he reasoned "the crate could just as easily be carrying a hundred Korans."

"Let's go and demand to see the contents," said the corporal. "If you're right, we'll sleep all the better tonight; if my intuition is correct, we'll put them behind bars."

Following the September 1970 riots, the officer in question had been awarded a medal for bravery and dedication. But he was also a realist. He knew that his local police force was ill equippped to engage a group of armed Islamic fundamentalists in close combat. "Get me the major on duty at the army barracks," he called to his desk sergeant. "We're going to need some backup."

Shortly before midnight twenty armed men, comprised equally of police and militia, surrounded the house of the Iranians. The soldiers came equipped with automatic rifles, the police with small revolvers. The neighborhood was asleep. The Iranian apartment was the only one with signs of life. Only two hours earlier, the Iranians had opened the crate and distributed the Israeli-made weapons.

The officer kicked the bottom of the door with his foot. "You're surrounded by armed soldiers," he cried, the text straight out of a movie. "I know that there are six of you inside, and I want you to come out, one at a time, with your hands on your heads."

As he spoke, all six men were sitting on cushions on the floor. Each one was holding a lethal weapon in his hands. Panic! An argument ensued in furious, rapid Farsi, most of the men, at least initially, trying to keep their voices down. Then the first broke from the circle, screaming, "It's the infidels, the scum of mankind," and ran to the closed window. "We should never have made a deal with an unbeliever," rasped another in a hoarse whisper, and rose from his position, ready for battle. "The Catholic dog has betrayed us, may Allah curse him."

Hushang tried desperately to take control. By now, all the men were cursing at the top of their voices. He needed quiet. He needed to concentrate. His first inclination was to negotiate, but how could he do so without a mandate.

Four of the men were glued to the window frames, cursing and jostling for the most exposed position. None of them paid him any heed. When he distributed the weapons, he had been alarmed by the almost joyous reaction of the four newcomers. For himself, Hushang had objected to the acquisition of the arms but had been overruled. He had agreed to buy them only under pressure from his superiors in Teheran.

Until that evening, Hushang's apartment had been home to religious projects. He and his colleagues had spread the word of the holy Imam. Now, it was being violated by the weapons they had taken into their possession. Hushang was overwhelmed with a feeling of déja vu: he had been here before. He saw chaos spreading around him. He sensed an awful, cataclysmic finality.

But – the finality brought about while fighting the infidel brings eternal glory. To a Muslim, it represents the ultimate achievement, the finest hour, the high peak of true belief, the zenith of life. Now he wasn't so sure, he smelt fear around him – and uncertainty. Worse, these fears were emanating from his own heart and mind.

The two youngest men, no more than boys, had been the first to reach the windows. They clearly had no hesitations. Their faith was intact. One of them threw the window open and pointed his automatic weapon into the street.

The soldier positioned in the darkened room on the other side of the street had been instructed not to fire until either ordered to do so, or fired upon. But he had one wild Iranian perfectly framed in his sights, and he prayed for the opportunity. As for his target, at that moment he recognized only the call to eternal glory.

Hushang's worst fears were metamorphosing into absurd reality: a slow record on a fast track. His man – no more than eighteen years old – was uncontrollable. He fired wildly, indiscriminately, onto the deserted street below. And the marksman opposite had received the answer to his prayer. Pressing the trigger, he downed his first victim.

All hell broke loose. Four of the Iranians opened fire at once, blind and deaf to Hushang's protests. Two men barraged the door with bullets, aiming at the policeman on the other side, while the others fired wildly through the windows. The solitary Jordanian marksman across the road calmly realigned his sites and picked off his second victim.

Hushang was screaming to his men to cease firing. He pleaded with the boy nearest the light switch to turn it off. He screamed for the madmen to get away from the window, to crouch down – at least to move their bodies away from the light. It didn't help, all were in some sort of unmilitary ecstasy. For a second, Hushang was riveted with fear. How can he control his men? If they're killed, we will all have failed. How will the Islamic revolution and the holy Imam – may his name be blessed – benefit from such failure? Is such a failure rewarded in heaven? Hushang couldn't think. His head ached. "I'm coming out! I'm unarmed!" he shouted, and ran for the door.

There is a police officer lying, face down, in a pool of his own blood. Two soldiers are pointing their rifles at the door.

"It's a trap," screams one of them. Both open fire. Hushang crumples to the ground. His body writhes for a moment atop the dead body of the Jordanian police officer, and falls still. "My G-d," cries the marksman. "He was speaking the bloody truth," says his partner.

An ear-piercing wail fills the air. Nader leaps like a wounded leopard from his perch, to catch his falling brother. Too late. The Jordanians on the landing opposite see his gun. "Get the bastard!" They blow a hole through Nader's head.

Bullets fill the open doorway, aimed by the two Iranians still in the apartment. Both Jordanian marksmen are killed instantly. For a split second, the two soldiers of Islam fill the open door frame, thirsty for further revenge. They in turn, are shot by Jordanian soldiers.

Aqaba can go back to sleep.

Chapter 50

The Israeli boat with Yitsik, its skipper, was waiting for Arturo at the rendezvous. Arturo Be'eri paid off Mustafa, the Jordanian skipper, telling him to return to Aqaba and keep quiet. Peeved, the skipper responded, "It is not in my interest to advertise my activities."

In Eilat, Kobbi and Seffi had told the Israeli skipper that Arturo would probably wish to return with him this time to Israel. "Don't foul up," they had warned. "We want Arturo in one piece, and we don't want him suspecting anything."

Consequently, Yitsik brought the boat in as carefully as possible. Arturo was impressed by the skill of his navigation, sure that they wouldn't be noticed as they glided silently into the marina. But Yitsik had worries of his own. On the one hand he was on the look-out for a reception committee, on the other, he was worried that Arturo might cut up rough when he realized what was in store. But he couldn't see anyone waiting.

They drew alongside the wharf. Yitsik jumped ashore, caught the rope that Arturo threw him, and quickly secured the boat. Still no sign of anyone. Leaning over, Yitsik extended his hand and Arturo, bag in hand, jumped on to the concrete. The two men walked together along the wharf toward the single exit some hundred yards away. "What about my pay," asked Yitsik, "and when will you want to go out again?"

"Of course," said Arturo, stopping to take some bills from his trouser pocket. "Here – $300 should make you happy."

Yitsik forced a grin and pocketed the money.

"But this is probably our last trip, at least until I come down to Eilat again," commented Arturo and slapped the skipper on the back good-naturedly. "For the time being, my business is finished."

Still no one came toward them.

Emerging from the marina, Arturo asked if the skipper knew of a hotel that wouldn't be too crowded, for it was too late to catch a plane to Tel Aviv. The skipper was just about to reply, when three men appeared from the shadows. Two of them grasped Arturo firmly by the arms, the third said, "You won't be requiring a hotel Mr. Be'eri. We will be looking after you."

When Kobbi returned to Jerusalem, he contacted Meir Peled, "Our mission was successful," he said simply.

"Good," said Peled, "The PM will be only too happy to take a break from his Lebanese worries. Let me get back to you."

Peled returned to Kobbi within the hour. The prime minister would be in the Knesset most of the day. Kobbi should join him for dinner in Jerusalem, 7 p.m. in the members' dining room.

There were four people at the table: the prime minister, Kobbi, Meir Peled and Taher. Begin was charming and hospitable, playing the Polish gentleman just as he liked to do. He asked about Taher's conversion, his wedding, and his future plans. After a few minutes, he turned and thanked Kobbi for the effort and the many hours he had devoted to the matter in hand. He even thanked Meir Peled for his discreet management and competent coordination. "Well," said the prime minister, as he finally sat back and beamed at them, "how about showing us the results?"

Kobbi took the Agreement from a small black attache case and placed it on the table. Begin picked it up, sat back in his chair and looked it over carefully, reading each and every clause with the thoroughness demanded by his legal training. After scrutinizing the signatures, he said, "I bet that Moshe Dayan – may his memory be blessed – kept King Abdullah's pen."

The members' dining room was crowded. Some people were waiting for tables to be cleared, others sat down on any available seat. Everywhere, talk centered on the latest political scandal, or the intrigues being hatched or nurtured. As usual, idle gossip – under the guise of politics – was the predominant preoccupation.

Noise level was high, decorum low. Members were often paged and seen scurrying to the telephones. Others were wandering from table to table, tapping people on their shoulders, exchanging jokes, gossip and fascinating titbits.

Younger members used the dining room as a pretext to see and be seen. Political secretaries, lobbyists and newspaper correspondents used it as their quasi-headquarters, canvassing their way through the dinner hour, haggling from table to table.

Then there were the "party princes" and their entourages. Yitzhak Rabin, the former prime minister, Arik Sharon, the controversial defense minister, Abba Eban and his brother-in-law, Haim Herzog – both still at the peak of their political expectations. And David Levy, always aspiring to greater things. They were all there, surrounded by their retinues. Each follower trying to hitch his or her wagon to a star. All were there that day, eating, drinking, and discussing the burning issues of the moment in the members' dining room.

Small surprise then that little notice was taken of the prime minister and his table of insignificant guests, eating quietly at the back of the room. At the best of times, Begin wasn't interested in food. He ate his simple meal quickly and without ceremony. Following the example of their host, the guests also ordered plain food. Every now and then, an aide came across the room to hand a slip of paper, or deliver a whispered message, to the prime minister.

During the meal, Begin revealed some of his personal feelings regarding the Temple Mount. Talking directly to Taher, he referred to a subject that had clearly caused him some pain. "In 1977, when I formed the first Likud government, I invited the late Moshe Dayan to leave the opposition and become foreign minister. It was considered a controversial move on my part, and both Dayan and I made certain demands. But we shared a mutual goal: We both wanted to bring peace to the region, and we both wanted to talk with the Egyptians. Three months after the elections, I went to Rumania for a meeting with President Ceauçescu. Ceauçescu was on good terms with President Sadat, so I asked him to offer an Israeli withdrawal from Sinai in return for a full peace treaty with Egypt.

"Unfortunately Sadat didn't believe the offer. He was sure that Ceauçescu had his wires crossed. In any event, we were obliged to try another avenue. In mid-September, Dayan travelled incognito to Morocco. There he met with the Egyptian deputy prime minister, Hasan Tohami. Dayan repeated the offer. This time Sadat believed it. Ultimately, the credit for the peace treaty and the Camp David Accords goes to our efficient teamwork.

"But, as I said before, Dayan made demands. He was never a pushover. When he joined my government, he insisted that I honor all decisions made by him in previous administrations. The decisions that I found most difficult to accept were those which involved the Temple Mount.

"There are certain decisions – momentous ones – that fall to politicians just once in a lifetime, if at all. The issue of the Old City was of that nature. As minister of defense during the Six Day War, the critical issue of whether or not to take control of the Temple Mount fell to Moshe Dayan. It was his call. Levi Eshkol, the prime minister at that time, felt that it was politically expedient to leave this decision to his minister of defense.

"Think back, for a moment, to the Six Day War: General Motta Gur is an ambitious soldier. His greatest ambition is to recapture the Old City. His dreams are realized. Leaving blown-out Jordanian tanks lining the narrow streets of the Old City behind him, the general forges doggedly on, in the direction of the Golden Dome. With coordinated troop movements and barrages of artillery and aerial support, two battalions of our finest men converge on the ultimate prize. History is on their side; they are unstoppable. As they drive, march – or crawl – in the direction of Har Habayit, the Temple Mount, all the men are aware that Jerusalem is being liberated, that history is being made.

"No politician, writer or man of words can adequately describe the exhaustion and exultation that the Israeli fighting forces felt during those moments. For at one and the same moment they were forging history, and realizing the dream of every Jew around the world. At the head of his army, General Motta Gur was the man most blessed by fate. He was the man lucky enough to lead his army through the Gates.

"Imagine the scene: The smoke of burning tanks, the noise, stench and fear of warfare, artillery blasting all around, soldiers lying dead and wounded in the blood-stained streets. Imagine the wonder, the exultation of our men as they see and touch, for the first time, the ancient stones of the Old City. Imagine the dust mingling with the smoke, the blood and the tears of this day; tears accumulated through two thousand years of history. And at the front, the first Jew to reach and stand before the Lions' Gate is Motta Gur, a modern Jewish warrior.

"Motta Gur is the first Jew on the Temple Mount. *Har Habayit Beyadenu* he shouts – The Temple Mount is in our hands – *Har Habayit Beyadenu*, he repeats time and time again. Flanked by his men, all drunk with joy, he runs past the Golden Dome and across the broad plaza. Behind him tanks, half-tracks and hundreds of exhilarated Jewish soldiers converge onto the scene in a mad rush to participate in the remaking of history. Within minutes, the State of Israel hears the news. Moments later, the people of Israel know. And now – the world knows – *Har Habayit Beyadenu; Har Habayit Beyadenu!*"

Menahem Begin sits back in his chair and sips cold water from his glass. The emotional tale has exhausted him. Silence greets his story, as his guests wait to see how their prime minister will continue. Begin clears his throat. "Within seconds, Dayan hears the news. He learns that Levi Eshkol has left a meeting in Tel Aviv, returning by car to Jerusalem to join his soldiers on the Temple Mount. Dayan is ambitious, eager to keep center stage. He is well aware of the significance of the occasion, and of Motta's historic cry: *Har Habayit Beyadenu.* He takes a helicopter to Jerusalem and arrives ahead of his prime minister.

"And then the anticlimax. The war is over. Arrangements are made to incorporate the Old City, its inhabitants and its different religions into normal civilian life. The ancient stone walls, the rooftops with their domed ceilings, the narrow, winding paths of the souk must now form part of a single, unified city under Israeli rule.

"The future of Jerusalem is entrusted to the hero of the Six Day War, Israel's minister of defense, General Moshe Dayan. And what does he do? He passes the keys of the Temple Mount to the Muslims. *Keheref ayin Har Habayit kvar lo beyadenu* – in the blink of an eyelid the Temple Mount is no longer in our hands!"

Begin sighs. He looks tired and old. He turns to his guests, each one in turn. "Without consulting anyone, Dayan hands control of the Temple Mount to the Wakf. I cannot applaud that decision."

Again Begin sat back, as if pondering over the terrible reversal for the first time. "My government was formed ten years later, and then, because of my agreement with Dayan, I was unable to do anything about the Jerusalem issue.

"As I grow older, I realize that I've made, or accepted after the fact, numerous decisions that I am no longer happy with. What is more, many of my friends share my doubts. Of all the issues that I have had to deal with, the issue of the Temple Mount is the most painful.

"Dayan was blessed with an opportunity that comes only once in a hundred lifetimes. He threw that opportunity away. His critical decision regarding the Temple Mount will be remembered by future generations, history will not forgive him for failing his people. As for me, well I will probably be judged by association." Begin sat sadly in his chair. He was such a little man. Everyone around him seemed so much larger, so much more robust. The meal was over. Begin rose from the table apologizing stiffly that duty called. A veil descended, separating the prime minister from those around him. A certain formality, even a coldness, had come between them.

"It must indeed be lonely at the top," murmured Taher to himself. Once more Begin warned his guests that the issue of the Agreement must remain confidential; then, with a curt, formal nod, he left them for his office, to fulfill his obligations.

As the prime minister entered his office, his secretary greeted him: "Monsignor Angelo and the Apostolic Delegate have just arrived at the Polombo Gate and are being processed."

Without hesitation, Begin replied: "Only the Monsignor has been invited. Tell them to keep the other cleric at the gate and escort the Monsignor up to my office, alone." Begin had specifically indicated that he would meet only with the Monsignor, and he was in no frame of mind to allow the Vatican to dictate the rules to him here in Israel. "Let the other man cool his heels at the gate," he told his secretary.

A little later, Monsignor Angelo, red in the face and perspiring profusely, was shown into the prime minister's office. Two days in Jerusalem awaiting news of Arturo Be'eri had made him extremely uneasy: First, Arturo had disappeared; then, out of the blue, he received an invitation to meet with the prime minister. But he had not planned any formal interviews for this visit. The Monsignor had realized that there might be a connection between this meeting, the Agreement, and his missing associate.

Since childhood, anxiety had often placed the Monsignor in embarrassing predicaments. These last few days had been no exception. The cleric was suffering from a severe attack of diarrhea. He knew that the invitation was restricted to himself, but he had brought the resident Apostolic Delegate with him to help him, so to speak, in his hour of need. They were greeted at the gate by a cordial official. At first it seemed as if the extra guest would pose no problem, but just as they were about to walk up the wind-battered path towards the Knesset building, the guard received a call and told the colleague to wait at the gate.

He went alone, angry with himself that he had agreed at all to come to this meeting. Suddenly he was assailed by a violent call of nature, and was obliged to rush, in an undignified manner, up the unfriendly path. At the entrance to the Knesset, he was again greeted by a smiling official but, as he was now in great discomfort, he brushed the man aside, rushed past the uniformed men standing guard at the entrance, and made a mad dash for the toilets. By this time he was in a state of near collapse. He stayed in the bathroom long enough to regain a measure of his usual composure, but was still far from confident and quite unable to stop the perspiration that was pouring down his neck as he proceeded, again in the company of the official, to the prime minister's office.

Unaware of the Monsignor's physical distress, the prime minister received his guest civilly, but with little signs of warmth. Rising from behind his desk, he led his visitor to a nest of comfortable chairs grouped around a glass table. The two men sat down. No drinks were offered. Mr. Begin cleared his throat. "There are two matters that I wish to discuss with you."

No niceties, no introductions. Mr. Begin was getting straight to the point. With rising concern, the Monsignor realized that the two had not even shaken hands.

"First, I must inform you that a certain Arturo Be'eri, whom I understand you have come to meet here in Jerusalem, is in custody. I believe you know that he recently entered Israel unlawfully from Jordan."

An ominous rumbling emanated from the Monsignor's stomach. He said nothing.

"I believe you are also aware," continued the prime minister, "that Mr. Be'eri was in the improper possession of an old agreement. It is fortunate that you did not take possession of this document yourself, as it would, in my opinion, have greatly compromised the position of the Church."

Mr. Begin cleared his throat, "However, we might be able to put an end to this matter without bringing it to public attention."

The tight ball in the pit of Monsigneur's stomach relaxed. "I believe," continued Begin, "that the removal of the Agreement from its previous hiding place has significantly improved the interests of the Vatican. I also believe that, in this particular matter, the interests of the Vatican and those of the State of Israel are similar."

The prime minister gave his visitor no pause, no opportunity to reply or to comment. Instead, he immediately launched into a separate issue. "I understand, Monsignor Angelo, that at the Vatican you keep a brief on the affairs between Israel and Lebanon, in which case you will be aware of the acute situation developing on our border. I am not referring to the constant barrage of Katyusha fire from southern Lebanon on our northern towns and villages. That is our affair. I refer to the deteriorating plight of the Christian communities in Lebanon, in particular to the continued bloodletting among the Maronites."

Begin paused. The Monsignor kept his peace.

"The Maronites are affiliated with the Vatican," added the prime minister, somewhat gratuitously, then continued: "I'm sure the Vatican knows that we maintain close ties with several Maronite families in Lebanon, and that these families are begging us to protect their communities from increasing factional violence. The region is dominated for the most part by Islam. Here, both the Christians and the Jews are minorities. The Muslims are flexing their muscles in their attempt to realize political – we might say, Koranic control. You must appreciate that if we politicians fail to take care of immediate problems, there will be no future for us in this region."

The prime minister cleared his throat, "Consequently, Israel is contemplating taking unilateral steps to protect the Christians in Lebanon, steps which will not be universally popular."

Begin paused and looked steadily into the eyes of his visitor. "In the past, the Vatican has never come to our defense or expressed sympathy with our goals. I, myself, have never concealed my disappointment that the Vatican has withheld de jure recognition from the State of Israel. It goes without saying that I disapprove of the Vatican's dogma that the Holy City of Jerusalem be rebuilt only by Catholics. Apart from causing a rift with the Jews of this region, it was that dogma which, a hundred years ago, led the Turks, and subsequently the Europeans, to establish a status quo in this area at your expense.

"Nevertheless, at this particular point in history, we share the concerns of the Catholic Church for its people in Lebanon. On this matter at least, we share common interests."

The prime minister looked steadily, perhaps even coldly, into the eyes of his guest. "I hope the Vatican will support us in our efforts. It would be beneficial if we could improve the relationship between Christians and Jews in this region."

For the first time Begin smiled. "Of course," he said with a shrug, "we would also like to forget your unfortunate involvement with Mr. Be'eri."

Mr. Begin stood up. The audience was over. "What an amazing little man," thought Monsignor Angelo, whose stomach problems had now disappeared, "blunt almost to the point of rudeness, honest to the point of arrogance." Then, as the two men reached the door, Begin turned to his guest with a hint of genuine charm and a real twinkle in his eye. "It seems," he said "that the old Agreement regarding the Temple Mount and the assistance that we plan to extend to the Christians in Lebanon are connected after all."

✧ ✧ ✧

EPILOGUE

In June 1982 Israel invaded Lebanon.

In 1985, Azziz Shehadeh, the noted West Bank lawyer and proponent of civil rights, was assassinated outside his home in Ramallah. The murder was never solved and the assassins never caught. His funeral was attended by leading Arabs, Palestinians and Israeli politicians.

At the general elections in 1992, Yitzhak Rabin unseated the Likud Government. The government formed by Rabin maintained a bare parliamentary majority, in coalition with communists and the minority Arab parties. Nonetheless, Rabin reached out in a dramatic effort to bring peace to the region. Despite years of mutual hatred, he recognized the PLO and, after secret negotiations conducted in Norway by his tireless foreign minister Shimon Peres, agreed the terms of a peace treaty in September 1993. In return for normalization of relations, Israel gave the Palestinians "autonomy" over Jericho and Gaza. Israel promised further autonomy areas on the West Bank, to follow in phases.

As for Jerusalem, it was mentioned in only two instances. Palestinians living there would be able to participate in the Palestinian election process. However, discussions about the status of Jerusalem were to be postponed until negotiations on a permanent settlement would take place.

PLO leader Yasser Arafat claims repeatedly that his objective is a Palestinian state, with Jerusalem as its capital. He pledged to revoke those sections of the PLO Charter that call for the destruction of the State of Israel and for the return of Jews to their countries of origin. Israel agreed to release many thousands of Palestinian prisoners. For their statesmanship, Messrs. Arafat, Rabin and Peres were jointly awarded the Nobel Peace Prize in November 1994.

In December 1993, the Vatican decided to join in the peace process. In a "Fundamental Agreement," Israel undertook to honor the "status quo," while undertaking to protect and respect Catholic sacred places. In 1994, after years of secret negotiations, Jordan decided to participate formally in meetings with the Israelis. In June 1994, U.S. Secretary of State Christopher, Prime Minister Rabin and King Hussein opened a new border crossing point between the two countries, joining Eilat to Aqaba. This was the first formal recognition of, and normalization between, the neighboring states. Four months later, US President Clinton flew with a huge entourage to the same border crossing, where a thirty-point peace treaty between the two countries was signed.

The second article of this treaty calls for the mutual recognition of each country's territorial sovereignty and political independence.

In possible contradiction to the terms of Article 2, the ninth article concerns the freedom of religious access to holy places in each other's territories. In it, Israel *honors the historic role of the Hashemite Kingdom in respect of the places holy to Islam in Jerusalem* The section continues with a promise that in agreeing permanent arrangements, Israel will grant *high priority to Jordan's historical role in respect of these places.*

The publication of the terms of the peace treaty aroused the anger of right-wing Jews and Palestinians. Claiming that ultimately Jerusalem would be their capital, the Palestinians would not tolerate remote control from the Hashemites on the other side of the Jordan. The wounds of 1951 were reopening.

During the week preceding the signing of the 1994 Israel-Jordan peace agreement, the Mufti of Jerusalem passed away. The agreement and its ninth article were put to an immediate test. Within days, Jordan announced the appointment of a successor to the mufti, who is described as the ultimate arbiter of Islamic law. Hours later, Yasser Arafat announced his own, rival appointment. Both new muftis reported for work on the Temple Mount and were granted offices by the Wakf.

18.10.1994. The Jewish Organization of the Temple Faithful, which for years had been denied access to the Temple Mount by successive Israeli governments, released a statement. It castigates the Rabin government for signing an agreement with the Hashemite king. It decries the signatories, who will never be forgiven for their shameful act of placing sovereignty of our most holy places into the hands of our enemies of yesterday and of tomorrow.

18.10.1994. The Jerusalem police decided to increase its presence in the Old City in the light of fighting between the Coptic and Ethiopian Churches in relation to their respective standing at the Church of the Holy Sepulchre. The canons of this Church are drawn from the Greek Orthodox, Armenian, Coptic, Syrian, Ethiopian and Roman Catholic Churches. The Israelis decided to use force, if and when necessary, to enforce the century old status quo.

In explaining to the Jordan Parliament the significance and advantages of the peace accord, King Hussein emphasized the continuing role that Jordan will exercise *over Jerusalem and its holy places*. Following the signing of the peace treaty with the PLO, the Israelis began to release Palestinian prisoners. Many of these had been convicted of murdering harmless Israeli citizens. Within months of their release, some had to be taken back into custody following further crimes. Others have been rewarded by membership in the para-military Palestinian police force, where they have been given back their arms.

Some of these arms have since passed to terrorists on the political right of the PLO, to members of the Hamas and Jihad movements, who have used them against Israeli citizens and soldiers. More than one hundred unarmed Israeli citizens were murdered within twelve months of the peace agreement with the PLO.

While the Rabin administration was busily releasing Palestinians from jails, the authorities were incarcerating Jewish activists. During the period of the signing of the peace treaties, a number of right-wing Jewish activists were rounded up and placed under administrative detention. They and their lawyers were not advised of the nature of charges or suspicions against them. They had no access to files presented by the Shabak to the courts that were asked to approve their continued incarceration. After periods of six or nine months, these activists were released, but some were handed new administrative orders, signed by local military governors, severely restricting their movements.

In October 1994, during his visit to the Middle East, President Clinton paid a visit to President Hafez Assad in Syria, a state high on the American list of countries supporting terrorism. The visit was intended to pressure Syria towards a comprehensive peace agreement.

18.10.1994. The leading Israeli morning newspaper *Ha'aretz* reported that the Israel-Jordan draft agreement of 24th February 1950, initialled by Moshe Dayan and Reuven Shiloah on behalf of Israel, and by the prime minister and defense minister of Jordan and witnessed by King Abdullah, was missing from the Israel National Archives.

16.7.1995. Following a long illness bravely born, General Motta Gur, Israel's deputy defense minister, died. In a moving tribute before his cabinet, Prime Minister Rabin reviewed his comrade's career. Above all, Rabin said, Gur will be remembered for his command of the paratroops that regained Jerusalem during the Six Day War. Rabin concluded with an interesting misquote: "And we will all remember his historic call, '*Hakotel Beyadenu* – The Western Wall is in our hands'." On later occasions Rabin corrected himself and quoted General Gur correctly: "*Har Habayit Beyadenu!* The Temple Mount is in our hands!".

4.11.1995. At a Peace Now rally in Tel Aviv, Prime Minister Rabin was shot dead by a Jewish right-wing assassin.